Bolan judged the distance, aimed the LAW and fired

The rocket sped through the open air and hit the tarmac, exploding with a crack and burst of fire that sent asphalt debris flying in all directions.

The An-26 swerved off the strip and rumbled into the grass. Bolan retreated to avoid the aircraft, watching it bounce along the uneven surface.

There was nothing more that he could do except hope that the roughness of the terrain would collapse the landing gear before the plane became airborne. The props whined, and the aircraft scratched and clawed its way off the ground. It increased its speed as soon as its wheels were up, then weaved into a long turn and headed south.

"Striker? We lost them. They escaped on foot into the grass. We'll have to pursue them the same way."

Bolan said nothing, watching the An-26 fade to a dot.

"Sarge, you there?"

"I'm here. I don't want to go after Troschenkova on foot. He can live to fight another day. I've got other priorities."

The transport plane disappeared into the overcast sky.

DON PENDLETON's
MACK BOLAN®
HIGH AGGRESSION

A GOLD EAGLE BOOK FROM
WORLDWIDE®

TORONTO • NEW YORK • LONDON
AMSTERDAM • PARIS • SYDNEY • HAMBURG
STOCKHOLM • ATHENS • TOKYO • MILAN
MADRID • WARSAW • BUDAPEST • AUCKLAND

First edition June 1997

ISBN 0-373-61454-3

Special thanks and acknowledgment to
Tim Somheil for his contribution to this work.

HIGH AGGRESSION

Printed in U.S.A.

Now to what higher object, to what greater character, can any mortal aspire than to…procure redress of wrongs, to assert and maintain liberty and virtue, to discourage and abolish tyranny and vice?

—John Adams
1735-1826

My personal quarrel is with truly evil men who have no regard for the sanctity of human life, who yearn to place the necks of good people beneath their bootheels. My aim is to cast off that yoke of oppression and to crush the tyrants.

—Mack Bolan

CHAPTER ONE

Kazakhstan

The sun baked the tall dead grass. The heat radiated from the parched earth, forging the narrow trail of dirt into a twin set of rock-hard tire paths.

Tuleutai Sarsenov had lived in the region all his life, had always been at home in its arid reaches. But now it had turned against him. The land had betrayed him, had become his enemy.

He gripped the muzzle of the AK-47, his eyes darting among the brown grass and stark, low shrubs and trees, wondering how a man could hide so well in such sparse vegetation, wondering who would be the next to die.

One of the water buffalo snorted, and the animals came to a sudden halt as the right wheel of the cart wedged into a chasm of dried mud. The driver jumped down, his face livid, shouting obscenities and attacking the beasts with his switch. The water buffalo rolled their eyes and howled in pain, straining at their ropes.

"Get it free! Get it free right now!" Sarsenov shouted, waving his rifle at the four guards taking up the rear. They shouldered their guns and ran to the cart, adding their muscle to the beasts' efforts, while one of them chopped at the earth around the wheels. They were all looking over their shoulders as they struggled fever-ishly, Sarsenov and the two front guards keeping an eye on the desert. The driver kicked at the flank of the nearer animal and thrashed at its rear end, his stick drawing blood. But the pain worked. The creature gave a desperate lunge, and the cart wheel pulled out of the dirt.

The four rear guards were on their feet instantly, bringing their AK-47s into firing position, pointing them into the desert, scanning the sea of grass. None of them found a target or spotted the ghost that had been haunting them for the past twenty-four hours.

The driver leaped into the cart and slashed the water buffalo again. The exhausted beasts staggered forward, followed by the fear-crazed guards.

They were almost exactly at the halfway point, and their numbers were reduced by exactly half.

They had yet to glimpse the desert phantom that was killing them off one by one.

The sunlight glared into Sarsenov's eyes when he looked behind him, and he knew by its angle it was late afternoon. Night would be upon them all too soon.

The previous night, after darkness closed in, they had lost four men, three slaughtered by different means. One of them had simply disappeared into the darkness. Sarsenov had no doubts that the man was dead, nourishing the carrion feeders with the others.

Sarsenov watched the shadows preceding him lengthen, and the virtually imperceptible cooling of the wasteland added to the gloom of the dying day.

He turned back and, for the hundredth time that day, counted the rear guard. There were still four of them. They were staring about crazily, the hours of tension and fear maddening them, thrashing at the weeds that reached out and brushed against their legs. The cart driver's eyes were white and haggard, and he closed them to rub them hard with his thumb and fingers. Sarsenov saw the hemp noose float from the desert and settle on the driver's shoulders, but it happened so quietly that he wasn't certain at first that it was really happening. He blinked hard and saw the noose tighten violently and he shouted.

The driver managed only a small, fitful croak before his breath was cut raggedly short and his eyes flung open. He grabbed at his throat and ascended from his perch on the wagon like a supernatural creature taking flight. With his feet kicking and arms swinging, he slammed into the earth, wriggling like a wounded spider on the end of his web. Grabbing at the rope, he managed to release some of the tension for a moment and croaked, then slithered into the grass and disappeared.

"Kill it! Shoot it!" he screamed, then his AK-47 was rattling in his hands, sending a deadly hail of rounds into the wasteland. The others joined in, until the desert turned to a din of firing weapons and the air was filled with brown confetti. The firing seemed to go on for minutes, but Sarsenov knew it was just thirty or forty seconds, then all the magazines were used up.

A trimmed blade of a grass fluttered into his face and fell away. The desert was again abysmally silent.

"We have to get out of here," one of the guards muttered.

"Go get him," Sarsenov said, struggling with the terror in his voice. "You take over driving."

"We have to get out of here!" the guard repeated. "We're all going to be killed. Let's leave the wagon and get out!"

"There is no way we are going to abandon the shipment—"

"He's right," another guard agreed. "If we leave the drugs, we can make a run for it. Whoever it is can't attack if we're on the run."

"What do you think will happen to us if we get to the landing site without the shipment? You think it will be a better fate than that?" Sarsenov waved his hand at the driver's empty seat. "You think you'll survive? That shipment is worth more than every man here will make in a lifetime."

"Then we won't go back to the airfield! We can make it to Pavlodar or Semey! They'll never find us!"

"We are going to the airfield and we are taking the shipment with us," Sarsenov said quietly. He changed the magazine in his AK-47 as he spoke, then leveled the rifle at the guards, sweeping the muzzle across them. "If any of you disagree with this course of action, step forward now and you won't have to worry about falling victim to the desert killer."

The silence became lethal. Sarsenov knew that he was outgunned. If a serious mutiny was imminent he didn't stand a chance against the remaining guards. If they shot him, he was dead. If the desert killer struck him, he was dead. And if he made it to their airfield without the shipment, he was dead.

Not much of a choice.

But if he made it to the airfield with the shipment, he was a wealthy man, by the standards of a Kazakh villager.

The guard took the post on the cart, switched the water buffalo and the great beasts lumbered forward.

The guards paced along with them.

No one bothered to retrieve the corpse from the grass.

The guard in the seat let the beasts find the trail on their own. He was too busy watching the wasteland for signs of another silent noose descending as if from heaven.

Sarsenov watched the dim shadows become darker and searched for a camping place, struggling to develop a guard system that would negate the possibility of another disastrous night. But he wasn't a skilled strategist. His father had been killed in the civil wars five years earlier. Unable to deal with the responsibilities of caring for a crippled mother and a blind sister, he had abandoned them and the family farm two years earlier and found a livelihood among the drug traders of the desert. It was a dangerous life, and he found himself time and again at the wrong end of a gun, but he was determined and ruthless, and made a name for himself as a vicious fighter.

But he had never faced an enemy like this.

The other men had started referring to the enemy as a phantom because they had never seen him—not a glimpse of the shadows he cast. No human could time and again come into their midst, perpetrate such violence and leave again. So it had to be a supernatural entity, they said.

Sarsenov argued that their enemy was indeed a man—or several men, more likely—and they were reacting to his modus operandi just as he wished them to, with superstitious fear. He wanted their drugs, and he was simply going to keep killing them until they became so afraid they ran away.

But Sarsenov's words failed when every fresh corpse multiplied their fear. Now, when they referred to the phantom of the wasteland, Sarsenov didn't argue the point. He was beginning to think of the enemy in those terms himself.

With a raised hand he brought the party to a halt as their trail opened into a rock face, twenty feet tall, jagged and sloping to create a slight overhang.

"We'll overnight here," he said. "We can back up to the rock and keep an eye on the desert. Even the phantom won't be able to get at us here. Unless he oozes straight through the rock."

"What is that?" one of the guards asked, gesturing with his gun to the rock face.

Sarsenov saw what he was indicating, but couldn't make it out, either. He approached the wall carefully. There was no evidence of a trap. The ground was bare, but freshly cut shards of stone were lying at the base of the barrier.

He heard a strange swishing sound and looked directly into the sky. A massive chunk of rock was dropping toward him. He didn't have time to dodge out of the way as it fell on him like a meteor. Sarsenov thought he saw something on the cliff above him, a silhouette in the dimming light. He knew he was seeing the elusive phantom, but it was no supernatural thing; it was just a man. He released his AK-47, but even before it touched the ground the hundred pounds of solid stone crushed his head and bore him to the earth like a mouse under a huge foot.

IN A JUNGLE not so far away, not so many years ago, they had called it psywar, short for "psychological warfare." It involved tricks and tactics designed to confuse, frustrate and frighten one's enemies, forcing them to make mistakes, get desperate, get scared.

Mack Bolan didn't care if he was taking advantage

of the uneducated and superstitious minds of the locals. He was using tactics that worked. He was one man against what had begun as a small army of sixteen soldiers who toted automatic weapons. He was armed with a large fighting knife and a single 9 mm handgun.

They were murderers, dealers in death, shipping a massive load of opium through the deserts of the former Kazakh Soviet Socialist Republic. It was the size of shipment that would have made nationwide news if seized in any large city in North America. Its value on the streets was high enough to make everybody in the supply chain wealthy. It was enough to ruin a thousand lives.

Outmanned and outgunned, Bolan nevertheless was determined to keep the shipment from reaching potential users. He wasn't sure how, at the outset, he would manage it, nor how he was going to get close enough, time and time again, to a team of sixteen soldiers without getting riddled with AK fire. But the moment a contact had informed him about what was in the cart, his determination became absolute. He would stop that opium shipment at all costs.

A day after the mission began, the psywar was proceeding nicely. Half his enemies were dead and those who remained were afraid and discussing their options, including abandoning their shipment. The Executioner knew they were as afraid of the owners of the shipment as they were of him. He had to tip the scales.

His black clothing making him invisible in the shadows of the desert dusk, he watched the remaining men hoist the body of their leader and fling it into the weeds. Then they set up camp.

Bolan was impressed by their practicality. The site was the best possible spot for an overnight stay, with the rock formation providing excellent protection. He had anticipated they would be too afraid of the spot after the death of their leader, who had remained a cohesive influence throughout the journey. But they brought the cart close to the cliff, triangulated three large fires around it and sat to watch the dark wasteland.

The big American waited for the men to exhaust their wood supply. The dry branches would burn fast, so they had two or three hours at best.

Again the men surprised him. They realized their dilemma an hour into night and allowed two of the fires to burn out while huddling around the central blaze. They pulled the water buffalo in closer and quickly unhitched the wagon so the rear end of it faced them, allowing them to keep an eye on the opium bags piled inside.

Bolan wasn't dissuaded by the glimmer of combat sense demonstrated by the death dealers. They were still sitting there, with the darkness of the midnight desert virtually suffocating them. By morning, he swore silently, their numbers would be halved again.

THE MEN INCHED BACK into the comforting overhang of the rock, staring at the fire but watching the blackness beyond it, waiting for death to emerge in an as-yet-unknown form. The nearly full moon was behind the cliff. There was only the ceaseless low murmur of breeze and the growing tension.

The hours passed, and the fuel for the fire grew more scarce. The men knew they would be out of dry wood well before first light, knew they should use the light of the fire to find more. But the darkness was too ominous.

Yet the waiting was agony.

A few of the most exhausted men slumped into a comatose sleep. They were scarcely less prepared than the others when the attack finally came.

THE BREEZE BECAME a steady wind, and deadly dust rose. Carried from dried-up rivers to the south, the dust was toxic with pesticides and natural salts the dead river had collected over the decades. With more-immediate dangers to consider, the men didn't think to tie rags over their faces.

One of the men crawled to the fire and poked it, edging one of the logs into the blaze and eliciting a fresh yellow tongue of flame. The others watched him stiffen and fall down, his face in the fire. His hair leaped to life with a sudden blaze.

Bolan emerged from the underbrush into the sparseness of the clearing as the men stumbled to their feet, shouting in alarm. But the fire was fading fast, and the light didn't reach him. A black figure standing in blackness, he was invisible. But he saw them, shadows moving on pale rock. He targeted the shadows and fired the suppressed Beretta 93-R and one of the silhouettes collapsed. The men never heard the subsonic rounds over their own terror, and it took them a full three seconds to realize more death had come into their midst.

The Executioner ran and dived as the gunmen panicked and began to strafe the night with their AK-47s. He was counting on them not to know how close their attacker actually was, and the rounds flew into the desert above his head.

He had just three rounds left in the Beretta, and four gunners to take out.

The road to this point had been a hard one. The Executioner had been out of contact with civilization longer than planned, and his resources had run thin.

But he was an expert at making do, and he wasn't worried by the prospect of depleting his ammunition. He rolled onto his stomach and crawled on his elbows in the direction of the wall as the survivors transferred their attention to the point where he had been lying, still firing high, proving they had no idea as to his proximity.

He reached the wall as the last of the survivors drained his magazine and listened to them scrambling for replacements, biding his time during those precious seconds.

Bolan inched into the even deeper blackness of the rock overhang, ten paces from his nearest adversary.

They all waited; the desert was pregnant with the expectation of more death.

Something in the desert, a bug, a rat or a touch of a breeze, moved. The nearest man triggered his Kalashnikov, and a volley of 7.62 mm rounds rocketed into the night.

Bolan reacted instantly, firing the Beretta once under the cover of the noise, and saw the gunner spin and drop, cutting off his autofire. He fired a second round into the next man, who was turning toward his collapsing comrade. The 9 mm round took him in the chest and dropped him at the feet of his two surviving comrades.

Bolan inched forward and grabbed at the closer Kalashnikov. One of the men finally spotted him. The big American couldn't make out the enemy's features, but he recognized reaction in the man's demeanor.

The enemy gunner saw a body moving among the dead and guessed it wasn't one of his companions. He gave a shout and whipped his AK-47 into firing position.

The Executioner triggered the last bullet in the Beretta 93-R. The retort of the suppressed round came a fraction of a second before the first round from the AK, and it took the gunman in the hand, crashing into his ribs and sending him staggering into the open. His companion twisted in his direction and spotted the figure lying among the dead men, a living shadow that was bringing a pilfered weapon into target acquisition. With a cry of alarm the last enemy threw himself backward, but the AK-47 rattled briefly in the big American's hands and drilled three rounds through the drug smuggler's heart and lungs. He fell on his back in the dirt and rolled from side to side, triggering a torrent of rounds into the sky before relaxing in death and dropping the gun.

Bolan sprang to his feet and jumped behind the wagon, grabbing at the dead man's autorifle and taking aim at the wounded man writhing on the ground a half dozen paces away, watching him just long enough to determine the man wasn't capable of defending himself. He approached the man and kicked away his dropped weapon.

The soldier grabbed the gunman's shirt collar and wrenched it apart, which caused the material to tear at the wound. Dragging the shirt down to the man's abdomen, Bolan then rolled him on his face in the dirt, wrenching the shirt over the shattered hand and eliciting a scream of pain. With a quick twist he rolled the shirt into a semblance of a rope and knotted the gunman's wrists.

Bolan pushed the burning corpse out of the fire with the toe of his boot and made a quick check of the other corpses to confirm their deaths. But there was only one survivor of the sixteen men who had started the trip just a day and a half earlier.

"Speak English?" the Executioner demanded.

The wounded man rolled his eyes as he was turned on his back again. He wore a look of numb terror and overwhelming pain. Bolan knew he might not have long to get what he needed.

"Speak English?" he repeated.

The man nodded.

"Who are you?"

The question seem to bring the man back from some brink. His eyes focused on the soldier.

"I am Kuanysh Sultanov."

"What organization are you with? Who's in charge? Where were you taking the drugs?"

"We are guards for a man in this area named Suley-menov. He works for a man who is named Troschen-kova."

"Where is Troschenkova?"

Sultanov shook his head slightly. "I do not know. I have never seen him. He's in Russia. But he is the one we send our shipments to."

"How do they get to Russia?"

The drug guard looked into the desert canopy, where there was nothing but mottled blackness. "A plane. One more day west."

"A town?"

"Yes."

"What's its name?"

"Akshetau." He raised his head with tremendous difficulty. "I will guide you if you let me live."

Bolan nodded. "You've got a deal." But he knew better. Because of his wounds, Kuanysh Sultanov wouldn't survive to see the sun.

CHAPTER TWO

Akshetau was a tiny outpost in the desert, the earth a solid cracked sheet, the nearby stream laden with sediment. The only reason for the village's existence was a stretch of land smoothed enough to allow the landing of certain aircraft.

Bolan sat in a bush on a hill and watched the village activity through field glasses. He had been at this post for long hours—and he was growing impatient with the inactivity. But his plan depended on a specific series of events, and rash action would change how events unfolded.

He had spread the opium in the desert and was confident that the morning breeze had picked up most of it. It might poison the grasslands of the nearby desert and stunt the growth of a few bushes, but it wouldn't ruin any human lives.

Scavenging among the dead men's weaponry turned up a decent-looking AK-47, and he pocketed every round and extra magazine he could locate. He felt better being armed with the autorifle, although he would have preferred being able to use the 93-R.

He placed Kuanysh Sultanov's corpse in the wagon and drove it through the desert. Pulling a nearly empty cart and being well rested, the water buffalo made good time, arriving at the village midmorning.

Bolan stopped about half a mile from the village and removed the tethers from the beasts, allowing them to wander off as he set fire to the wagon. The smoke attracted attention in a matter of minutes.

Several well-armed Kazakh appeared, and Bolan watched as they poked around in the remains of the cart and examined the charred corpse of Sultanov. It didn't take them long to organize a search party, which headed into the desert, back along the route Bolan had taken. The Executioner sat in the bush on the hill and waited.

He was sure a large building on the far side of the village was a hangar. It had brick walls, and the roof— a crude wooden frame covered with old thatch—was low at the rear and angled to a height of almost twenty feet at the front. The guards posted around it convinced him the plane or perhaps more opium was inside, preparing to go on its enigmatic journey.

Bolan pondered the possibilities as he watched. Who was Troschenkova? How had he managed to set up operations in this remote corner of the world? Where was it he landed his drug shipments, and where precisely did the opium end up?

Not that it mattered, really. A city was more or less a city, whether it was in Kazakhstan or in the midwestern U.S. And a shipment of opium had pretty much the same effect—wasted lives, ruined dreams, death.

Bolan wanted to find out more about Troschenkova, who he was, where he based his organization, maybe figure out a way of shutting down his operation at the highest levels, rather than here, in the desert, at the bottom.

To do so he had to get to Troschenkova's headquarters, and inside that hangar was transportation that would take him there.

The party that had started to backtrail him into the desert had been gone five hours when Bolan started to move again. He figured the search party would be back in another hour if they moved fast. He went to ground and began a slow circle of the village.

The villagers were used to the presence of the guards and went about their evening routine as if the armed men weren't in their midst.

Bolan watched water being brought from the stream in pots. Front-yard fires were lit, and soon he smelled the aroma of roasting meats and boiling broth. He ignored it, focusing his senses on the hard trail he had chosen, making his way through the underbrush within view of the village but not so close as to be visible to the villagers. It took him thirty minutes to make it to the point in the desert closest to the hangar.

Five yards stretched between the desert bush and the back wall of the building, the open ground covered only with tufts of trampled grass. A single guard sat against the back wall with an AK-47 across his crossed legs.

Bolan watched him for another twenty minutes. The guard dozed, but periodically his head would snap up and he would look around with blinking eyes.

The soldier waited. Sooner or later would come the distraction he needed to get to the building without raising alarm. When it came, he would be ready. There was a shout from the village, and the guard got to his feet. The villagers and guards were moving to the desert's edge, where the search party was now emerging. The sleepy sentry went with them, eager for news.

Before the man even disappeared from sight, Bolan stepped into the open area and sprinted to the hangar, flattening against the windowless back wall. He stood still, listening, then grabbed at the thatch above his head and hauled on it, pulling enough out of the way to allow him a perch on top of the brick wall to cut into the roof with his combat knife. The desiccated branches came away easily, giving him a view of the hangar interior.

He stood almost directly above the tail of an Antonov Colt, a Russian-built biplane. The decades-old design was a favorite of the Russians, and they built thousands of the aircraft. This one had seen better days.

Bolan saw that the plane was configured to carry cargo, but its cargo doors were closed. No guards were in sight. Everybody was probably out greeting the returned search party. The soldier knew that if he was going to get into the plane unnoticed, he had one chance, and that chance was now.

He wrenched aside a section of crackling thatch and slid through, resting his body weight briefly on the rear of the plane while he performed quick repairs on the thatch. He didn't have time to do a perfect job, but the roof was tattered, and maybe no one would notice. He stepped off the rear of the aircraft and landed on the packed dry earth in a squat, eyes roaming under the fuselage of the aircraft for the feet of an as-yet-unseen guard. There was no one; he was in the hangar alone.

But not for long. The villagers would be back in less than a minute. Bolan jumped up the steps onto the crate that served as a loading platform into the Colt and opened the door, stepping boldly inside and sweeping the interior with the AK-47.

No one was inside. The aircraft contained four metal seats and a cargo area, which was stacked with canvas-wrapped bales. The Executioner shut the door behind him and headed to the rear, where he made quick work of examining the layout of the bales. They were tied into place with plenty of rope and twine. He drew his knife and slashed at the twine quickly, maneuvered the last stack of bales away from the wall, then wedged himself behind it and dragged the stack back into position as best he could.

The aircraft door opened, and footsteps told Bolan a single man had entered the plane and opened the cockpit door.

"This is Hastur, calling for the Czar," the man said, then paused. "Relay this message—the second of two shipments has been stolen. Half the guard is missing, and the other half is killed. I'm awaiting instructions."

There was another long period of silence, then Bolan heard someone else enter the airplane, but this one closed the cockpit door when he entered. There was more discussion over the radio, but the big American couldn't make it out.

Troschenkova, wherever he was, was getting some bad news. Half his guards had hijacked a valuable drug shipment from another half of his guards and disappeared into the desert with it. That interpretation was fine with the Executioner. It would have them concentrating their efforts in the wrong direction.

The cockpit door opened again and the men emerged, speaking rapidly in their native tongue. The engines started. The pilot had to have received orders to proceed with his flight despite the fact that he was missing part of his shipment.

The doors opened and closed a few more times, and Bolan couldn't tell who, besides the pilot, was still on board. Then the plane began to move gradually out of the hangar and proceeded slowly to the end of the long earthen runway.

The twin Shvetsov engines whined louder, and the plane began to move, shuddering over the uneven surface. Then the aircraft become airborne.

Bolan shifted into a more comfortable position and wondered how long he would be stuck here.

BOLAN INCHED out of his hiding place an hour after takeoff. Careful listening had revealed no sounds of passengers in the cargo section of the craft—not that he would have been able to hear the breathing of a single passenger over the throbbing engines.

But when he peered over the tops of the canvas bales, he found the steel seats empty. He forced the bales aside and stepped into the open compartment, searching for anyone who might have been crouched on the floor, however unlikely the possibility, then forced the bale back into position and stood hidden behind it, considering his options.

There would be no more than three people in the cockpit, though two was more likely. He could deal with two or three men, especially since his adversaries had no indication he was there.

All he had to do was wait.

In another forty minutes things fell into place. The door to the cockpit opened, and he heard voices again, speaking what Bolan assumed was Kazakh.

The cockpit door closed, and the conversation stopped. He heard the door to the lavatory next to the cockpit get pulled open and shut again.

He finally emerged from behind the bales of opium and approached the lavatory. When the door swung open, the copilot was still zipping his trousers and saw only Bolan's feet and legs. He looked up sharply and never uttered the words forming on his lips. The butt of the AK-47 slammed into his head with a crack that sent him flying into the plane's fuselage and left him slumped on the floor like a broken doll.

Bolan cut some twine from the opium bales to tie the copilot's wrists together and secure them to a ceiling girder, where he dangled like a stuck pig being drained of blood.

The big American stepped to the cockpit door and opened it quickly. Inside the small cockpit was a single pilot. He strode up behind the pilot and snatched the Browning Hi-Power from his shoulder holster, then nudged him with the muzzle of the AK-47. The pilot shouted in Kazakh.

"Speak English," Bolan said.

"Who are you?" the pilot demanded.

"That doesn't matter. Where are we headed?"

The pilot was trying to crane his neck to get a look at Bolan, who jabbed him in the temple with the muzzle of the AK-47. "Keep your eyes on the road and tell me where we're going."

The pilot said nothing.

"I'll be forced to do to you what I did to your copilot."

"Russia."

"Is that where Troschenkova's base is?"

"Who?" the pilot asked clumsily.

"If we're going all the way into Russia, it's going to be a long flight, and my patience is already very thin. I've got the skills to fly this plane on my own if I'm forced to."

"I'll answer your questions! Don't shoot me!"

"I'm waiting."

"Yes, we are headed to one of Troschenkova's bases. He's got a spot outside Bisk where he makes a camp.

He's paid off the local provincial heads, so he can do as he pleases.''

"Why there?"

"I suppose just because it is in his territory. He controls the drug trade for hundreds of miles, all the way to the Volga."

"That's where he's sending the opium?"

"I am just the pilot. I fly it in and out. He does not tell me."

Bolan took the extra seat, situated behind the empty copilot's seat, and laid the AK-47 on his lap without removing his hands from it. "Maybe he'll tell *me*."

The pilot glanced back long enough to see the business end of the autorifle aimed squarely at him. "You still want to fly to Troschenkova?"

"That's why I hitched the ride in the first place."

The pilot shrugged and turned back to the cloudy afternoon sky and muttered something under his breath.

"I'll need the coordinates of our destination," he said, grabbing the radio microphone.

IVAN TROSCHENKOVA opened the door to the trailer. "Liposk!"

Three men gathered in a huddle around a burning barrel reacted to the anger in his voice, and one of them came to the trailer at a trot, clanging up the aluminum stairs and catching the door before it slammed shut behind his boss, who slumped at the desk in the makeshift office in the semitrailer.

The air inside was toasty warm. Andrei Liposk appreciated it, but knew he wasn't being invited in for a friendly chat.

"Yes, boss?"

"I need you in Kazakhstan, Andrei."

"Problem with the shipment?"

"The problem is that there is only half a shipment. The other half disappeared en route to Akshetau. I've just been informed by our controller in Bisk."

"That's a lot of money."

Troschenkova lit an expensive Turkish cigarette with his gold-plated lighter and closed it with a metallic ring. Liposk had seen this act performed a hundred times for the benefit of others. Now it was a habit; Troschenkova knew he didn't need to impress Liposk. They had worked together for fifteen years, since the days Troschenkova sold marijuana on the streets of Troitsk and Liposk took care of policing his dealers.

"What's the situation?"

Troschenkova sucked on the cigarette and exhaled, filling the room with the odor of tobacco and cloves. "The wagon was left outside of the village this morning, burning. There was a dead man in it—one of our men—but no sign of the shipment. A group of our guys traced the trail into the desert and found half the men murdered. The other half are missing. There is no sign of my shipment. You figure it out."

Liposk sat in the chair in front of the desk, frowning.

"What's the problem?"

"I don't get it," Liposk said.

"What's not to get? The guards stole my opium and went to sell it somewhere else."

Liposk nodded. "But the wagon? That's what I don't get. I mean, if half the guards killed the other half and only one guy got away, he would have made a run for it and left the wagon behind. He wouldn't and couldn't have eluded the other half of the guard in the wagon. They'd have caught up to him in minutes."

"I guess you're right," Troschenkova said, leaning forward. "But I don't see what difference it makes."

Liposk considered it a minute. "It's fishy. Somebody brought the wagon to the village specifically to burn it and attract some kind of attention."

"Try to figure it out when you're there. I'm going to have you go in and find my shipment—and get it back. And take care of whoever took it. The Colt will be arriving in several hours, and I'm having it turn around and go right back. You'll be on it."

"You sure that's a good idea?"

Troschenkova stabbed out the butt. "Why would I think it is a bad idea?"

"Because our plane is coming in from Novosibirsk within eighteen hours, as well."

"I'm not worried about that," Troschenkova said.

"You should be. It'll be carrying a U.S.-made piece of equipment and a U.S. citizen. The Americans are going to come looking for it."

"Not very soon they're not."

"In addition there are several parties interested in that equipment, parties that might not be willing to stand by and watch it go to someone else simply because they were outbid for it."

"You think the Chinese are going to come here looking for it?"

Liposk shrugged. "I wouldn't put it past them if they know where we are—and I see no reason they wouldn't know where we are."

Troschenkova tapped the desk. "You suggest what?"

"That I stay on here. I'm your best man when it comes to organizing the troops. I think you ought to have this place on full alert until the U.S. equipment comes in and gets out, and I'm the man to do it. You know that.''

"You're also my man when it comes to solving problems. That's why you're needed in Kazakhstan.''

"Look at it this way, Ivan. The deal for the U.S. equipment is obviously your top priority. Delay the Colt until tomorrow morning. I'll organize the guard for the staging of the U.S. equipment. Once it is safely gone, I go to Kazakhstan in the Colt.''

Troschenkova nodded. "Yes. Do that. I don't think you're correct about the Chinese, and I don't expect the U.S. to respond for days. But it's worth letting the trail get a little cold in Kazakhstan for a little peace of mind in case I am incorrect.''

THE PILOT HUNG UP the mike. "Okay,'' he stated. "I'm cleared to land.''

Bolan was peering at the oncoming swatch of brown in the northern Russian landscape. There was a single strip of runway but no buildings. Large trucks waited a hundred yards to the east of the runway, and a single tanker truck stood nearby, ready to refuel the aircraft.

"Take it down,'' he ordered. "If I see anything suspicious, I'll shoot you in the head and finish landing. Do you understand?''

The pilot had been unable to relax during his hours under the gun, and as the tension grew he had began to tremble. He nodded and began to ease the plane onto the runway as Bolan watched for any sign of alarm around the trucks. Men were gathered near the vehicles, but their demeanor didn't suggest imminent attack. Still, an armed force might be hiding anywhere, alerted by some code word the pilot had given and ready to storm the plane the moment it rolled to a stop.

"What's your normal procedure upon landing?"

"I park it next to the fuel truck," the pilot said.

"Not this time. Take it to the far end of the runway and bring it to a halt."

"Then what?"

"I'll let you know."

The Colt bounced on the runway with chirping tires, and the pilot slowed it quickly. Bolan braced himself in his seat in case the pilot tried any quick moves that could throw him off balance, but soon they were rolling at just a few miles per hour.

The soldier got to his feet and looked out one of the high side windows. The airfield was empty of armed men, and there was no sign of an attack force lying in wait in the grassy field to the sides or at the end of the runway.

"All right, when you reach the end of the runway, start to make the turn into the dirt, then put on the brakes. Bring it to a stop pointing in a northeast direction. Understand?"

"What then?" the pilot asked.

"Do you understand?" Bolan demanded.

"Yes!" The pilot was almost weeping, sure that when the plane came to a stop, his usefulness would cease and he would be shot.

Bolan kept an eye on him, knowing he was at the breaking point and might make a desperate move at any moment. But his good sense held, and he did as Bolan instructed. The Colt came to a sudden halt halfway through its turn and about as far as it could get from the station of men and trucks.

"Now what?"

"Get up." Bolan jumped to his feet and backed out of the cockpit. The bound man was conscious and glared at him hatefully. Bolan unsheathed his knife, and the copilot's hatred transformed into terror.

"Nyet!"

Bolan severed the twine from the ceiling girder with a quick slash, and the copilot collapsed to the floor. The Executioner waved the front end of the AK-47 at the fallen man.

"Help him up and get out of this plane. You have thirty seconds."

The soldier withdrew his last remaining high-explosive grenade.

"There are still hundreds of gallons of fuel in this plane!" the pilot shouted.

"Then you'd better get moving."

The pilot scrambled for the door and seized the release lever. As the doorway unfolded into steps, he grabbed at the fallen copilot.

Bolan waited as they stumbled to the earth and began to run away from the aircraft, then he returned to the cockpit. He slammed the butt of the AK-47 into the pilot's window again and again, finally cracking it, then used the metal of the stock to clean out the remaining shards of glass.

He moved back into the main cabin and checked out the door. The pilot and copilot had reached a distance of two hundred yards and were yelling in the direction of the trucks. Bolan saw men looking at them curiously, a few starting to move toward them.

He sent the HE flying into the rear of the Colt and scrambled into the cockpit, ejecting himself through the open window and hanging on to the nose of the plane for a fraction of a second before he dropped to the earth and twisted into a judo fall. He leaped into a crouch and sprinted away from the aircraft through the waist-high grass, chancing only a single look back to ensure he was keeping the wheels of the plane between himself and the spectators.

He heard the crack of the grenade and flung himself into the grass. The Colt belched smoke, and a huge tongue of flame erupted from its belly. Then the fuel ignited, and the back end jumped off the tarmac as if kicked by a giant foot. The blast rolled across Bolan, and the ground shuddered under him. He covered his head a moment later when metal debris rained to the ground around him.

When the force of the blast had dissipated, he glanced back, satisfied to see the collapsed, flaming hulk of the Colt serving as a wall that completely blocked him from the truck and the men. He jumped to his feet and made his way deeper into the Russian grasslands.

TROSCHENKOVA RACED out of the semitrailer, feeling the bitter wind cutting into his torso through his thin shirt, then almost feeling the searing blast of heat from the burning hulk of the transport plane.

Liposk ran to the gathering crowd and pushed his way into the middle. One of the men was cutting twine from the wrists of the copilot, and his limp hands looked white and dead. The pilot was talking excitedly, sounding almost hysterical.

"What happened?" Troschenkova demanded, the men melting away to let him through. "Explain this to me."

The copilot was barely staying on his feet, and a section of his head was a mass of dried blood and hair. The pilot didn't interrupt his maniacal flow of words but turned to address Troschenkova.

"Slow down," Liposk said quietly. "Calm down and explain what happened."

The pilot stopped talking midword and breathed deeply a few times, looking at the ground. Then he began to speak again, his narrative less incoherent, and he described being hijacked not long after they left Akshetau. A man who stowed away on board had immobilized the copilot and used a gun on the pilot.

"So why did the plane explode?" Troschenkova demanded.

"He did it!" the pilot replied. "He had a grenade, and he told us we had thirty seconds to run away. I told him there was fuel still in the plane, but he blew it up anyway. He blew himself, too!"

Troschenkova approached the pilot, grasped his shoulder and slammed his fist into his gut. The airman's breath exploded out of him, and he doubled over, staggering back three paces before curling into a fetal ball on the ground.

Liposk didn't move or say a word, but when Troschenkova held his hand out, he knew better than to protest and silently handed him his Makarov handgun. The drug czar snatched it and pointed it at the fallen pilot. "You think I'm an imbecile? You think I'm some sort of moron?"

The pilot stared into the mouth of death for the second time that day. "What do you mean?"

"You expect me to believe that bullshit! Why would a man blow himself up?"

"Maybe he didn't mean to. Maybe he meant to run away himself, but something happened and he didn't make it. Why would I lie?"

"To cover the fact that you and your friends in Ka-

zakhstan took all my opium and are marketing it your-
selves. Why else?''

The pilot broke down, sobbing, his nerves shattered.
''No, no, no. That's not what happened. We had the
opium on the plane—the half that made it to Akshetau,
I swear.'' He squeezed his eyes shut tight and laid his
head on the ground.

Troschenkova held the gun on him for another five
seconds, then turned it on the copilot, who was being
supported by two other men, eyes glassy and unfo-
cused.

''Bring him into my office. Bring them both. As soon
as that wreck starts to cool down, I want it searched for
evidence of my opium and for the body of this alleged
hijacker. You,'' he said, glancing at the pilot again,
''had better hope we find some cooked bones.''

LIPOSK DIDN'T NEED a doctor's report to tell him that
the copilot's hand would have to be amputated. He had
also been convinced of the pilot's sincerity. These men
had been hired for their flying skills, and they didn't
have the staunch fighting will that the other men in the
compound were hired for. It was very doubtful, in his
mind, that they had engineered events to fit their
story.

But he didn't express his opinion. Not yet. When
Troschenkova was in this state, he valued others' opin-
ions only when they confirmed his own, and right now
the man was still half-convinced that the pilots were
accomplices to whoever it was who had stolen and/or
burned his precious opium. Eventually, maybe, he
would begin entertaining other possibilities, and then
Liposk would offer his own point of view.

Right now Liposk had more-immediate concerns.

THE SOLDIER CROUCHED in the grass and watched the vehicles start up and crawl across the compound to the wreckage of the plane, leaving the remaining semitrailers in virtual darkness with a skeletal guard.

He had spent nearly two hours making a wide circle of the compound and now approached it from the east, avoiding the single gravel road that led to it and staying hidden in the grass and behind the occasional tree.

There were four semi trucks, serving as what was essentially a mobile military base. Two of the trailers had been transformed into mobile bunkhouses. One was a mess, and he had witnessed the men going to dinner in shifts. The other seemed to be a command post of sorts, and only two men had access to it. One of them might be the leader, Troschenkova.

When the crew was heavily involved in the search of the wreck, he made his silent approach. A single man stood guard outside the command trailer, with another at each of the bunkhouses. All three were armed with AK-47s and all were more interested in the distant search than their watch. Bolan crept farther to the south and approached, keeping the command trailer between himself and the central area of the compound. He watched for signs of movement in a slatted window in the trailer, where the yellow glow of a light was occasionally crossed with shadow from its occupants.

He could have made a bolder entrance and started to reduce the numbers of the compound staff by wiping out the guards, but first he wanted more information. He wanted to be sure he had the man in charge, so that when he did bring this operation to a grinding halt it would be for maximum effect.

The electricity in the trailer was supplied by a generator, the power running to the command post through a large cable. Rungs were bolted into the side of the trailer to facilitate quick connection and disconnection. Bolan grabbed on to one, and, stepping up with one foot, slowly transferred his weight. He felt the trailer shift only very slightly under his weight, then, slothlike, he ascended one rung after another.

CHAPTER THREE

The need for manpower to search the smoking Colt had thrown a kink into Liposk's deployment strategy. On the other hand, there was no longer a need to use men to guard the opium. Ten men had gone to work on the aircraft wreckage just after midnight, parking trucks and military-style jeeps around the smoldering hulk to illuminate it as best they could. By 3:00 a.m. nothing had been found in the rubble, not a scrap of baling twine or a blackened lump of powder. If the opium had been on board, it was utterly incinerated.

"Considering the heat of the fire," Liposk reported to his boss, "I simply can't tell you one way or another if it was there or not."

"The body?"

"No. Not yet." He shrugged.

"What?"

"Two thoughts. One, if the guy was holding on to the grenade when it went off, there might be nothing left of him to find. Two, he could have escaped through a window on the opposite side of the plane."

"Liposk, none of the windows are big enough for a man to fit through," Troschenkova growled.

"They are in the cockpit. He might have broken it

out and jumped for it. If so, he could still be hiding in the vicinity."

That got Troschenkova's attention, but he said nothing. A stiff wind rushed against the side of the trailer, and it creaked and moved.

"Any other time I would start a search. But not now," Liposk said. "Not with the American and her equipment on the way."

"Right. That's our first priority now. We'll pick up the pieces of this mess tomorrow morning, *after* the THADSAC has come and gone."

"The only thing that worries me is that if there was a hijacker and he did escape into the fields, what's to stop him from raising some hell when the general's plane arrives?"

Troschenkova pointed at Liposk with his Turkish cigarette. "You are."

BOLAN LAY FLAT on the roof of the trailer next to the exhaust hood. The conversation was obviously finished, and he could feel the movement of one of the men inside. He used the movement to disguise his own and slithered to the edge of the roof as the door below opened. A man stepped out and walked away, the moonlight bringing him only briefly into profile. Bolan filed that silhouette in his mental file. No names had been mentioned; all he could gather about the men was that one was clearly subordinate to the other. That didn't mean for certain that the man in charge was Troschenkova.

What was more intriguing was the subject of the conversation. What was THADSAC? Where was it coming from, and where was it going to? Who was "the general'' and why was a general involved with a Russian crime organization? And who was ''the American''?

Dawn would tell all.

THE SOLDIER COULD MOVE quickly when called upon to do so, and he could move with extreme care and patience other times.

It was the dead of the night, and even during this warm season the Russian grasslands grew dank and chill. Bolan ignored it. Nights in the cold jungle a lifetime ago had taught him to disregard petty discomforts.

He extracted a multipurpose tool from his pack and went to work on the corroded bolts securing the vent hood. The stainless-steel pliers, as strong as they were, were ripped to shreds, but after a long hour of work, the fourth bolt began to turn and grind in its socket. Bolan twisted it free slowly, feeling the sound travel through the steel roof of the trailer.

The two inhabitants had left hours earlier, but the guard detail had been increased. A man stood at the front door of the trailer, just a few feet away, and other guards were patrolling the camp's perimeter, on full alert. There would be no dozing at the post this night.

When the last bolt was extracted, the soldier rose onto his knees and scanned for the patrols, waiting for a single sentry to finish his beat across the open compound and disappear behind the mess trailer. Then Bolan stood for the first time in hours, stretched briefly to relieve the cramps in his arms and legs and crouched to embrace the vent hood. The hood was flimsy aluminum on a steel base, and it flexed with a creak as he lifted it. Bolan froze, adjusted his grip and lifted again, moving the curved hood off the roof opening.

He stepped into the opening, holding on to the roof

and lowering himself carefully inside. He hung for a moment in the blackness of the office, listening for sounds of alarm, then dropped the last eight inches to the carpeted office floor.

The soldier moved without hesitation to the desk, pulling open the drawers and finding only scraps of paper and a bottle of vodka. The desktop had a small, battery-operated clock, a phone and a cheap plastic radio. A handgun was taped under the surface of the desk. None of it was of any value to Bolan.

The probe need not be a total waste of effort. He lifted the receiver on the telephone and got a dial tone. Troschenkova had to have his own cellular link into the Russian telephone system.

Whether he would be able to get into the United States was another matter. He dialed into a Munich exchange operated by Stony Man Farm. The line rang and was answered by the automated system, but a sudden surge of static cut it off before Bolan could get any further. Two more attempts were no more successful.

Bolan wasn't about to give up. The computer aces at Stony Man Farm, under the direction of Aaron Kurtzman, had gone to extreme lengths to enable secure communications by their agents from any point, however remote.

He dialed a number in Moscow and accessed a silent line. Another dialer might have thought the link was dead again, but he knew better.

"Striker," he said in a clear, quiet tone, then rattled off a string of eighteen numbers.

In an apartment in Moscow a laptop computer was listening. The voice-recognition system digitized the voice, discovered the code matched a code in its memory and allowed the transmission to continue. It opened a voice link on the Internet, coding the message it delivered across Europe to a phone-system satellite uplink. The transmission was sent to another small personal computer, which was sitting on-line in a small office in Cortland, New York. When the message was received, it was forwarded through the U.S.-based computer to another one on a separate open channel, then shuttled throughout Internet service provided by mainframe computers in San Diego and Urbana, Illinois, and finally to a powerful computer sitting on-line in Pittsburgh. There a second, much more sophisticated voice-analysis system analyzed the transmission.

The voice coming over the line was compared to a digital portrait of Mack Bolan's voice stored in its memory, compensating for the degradation in the signal, and a match was achieved. The Pittsburgh computer allowed the transmission to continue.

The process lasted less than four seconds while Bolan was sitting in the dark office in Russia listening to silence.

More gateways opened, and the signal again crisscrossed North America before landing in a scrambler-server in Washington, D.C., where it was spun out into a well-lit, heavily air-conditioned computer room of the most secret paramilitary intelligence operation in the world.

"Striker!"

Bolan had no time for pleasant conversation.

"My condition is yellow, Bear," Bolan said softly and succinctly.

AARON KURTZMAN'S FACE became stone cold with seriousness, his hand jabbing at a button that instantly increased the volume of the call and screened out interference. "We got your shortwave message via Helsinki. What's your situation?"

"No time to go into it. I'm sitting on the West Siberian Plain right now. I'm short on hardware, I need some Intel and I may need a ride out of here soon."

"Help's on the way to the coordinates provided in your last message—about one hundred miles south of Bisk."

"I'm sitting on a small airfield, which may or may not be surrounded by a compound of semitrailers when my ride arrives."

"You've got a tracer?"

"Yeah."

"That'll let us pinpoint you. Activate it. We'll be there before the battery dies, I'll guarantee you that. What's the deal up there, anyway?"

"You tell me. Who or what is THADSAC?"

Kurtzman thought hard and fast. "Sorry, Striker, I'm drawing a blank."

"I started out on the trail of some heavy drug trade perpetrated by a Russian crime boss named Troschenkova. I'm standing in his office right now. But they've got something called THADSAC coming in tomorrow and are selling it to the highest bidder. My impression was the device carried military implications for several nations. It has something to do with an American female."

"Can you hold on while I search?"

"Maybe."

Kurtzman's fingers flew over the keyboard, initiating a multidatabase inquiry. Depending on the obscurity of the reference, the search could take a nanosecond.

The computer monitor instantly scrolled the results of an exact match.

"I'm getting this from a Department of Defense computer system, Striker. It's Tibet Highorbit Aggression Defensive Satellite Control. THADS is a spy satellite that has been in geosynchronous orbit over Tibet for about nine months. Of course, it's watching half the globe from that viewpoint, but the intention is to keep an eye on Chinese activity in Tibet. This thing doesn't even have a secrecy priority. The point is for the Chinese to know they're being watched and that way dissuade overtly aggressive activity against the Tibetans."

"So it's U.S.?"

"Yeah. Well, not anymore." Kurtzman clicked the mouse and scrolled down the screen. "This is getting very interesting. The U.S. is donating a THADSAC unit—a computer that interacts with THADS—to the Russians. They get access to a nifty satellite, and we get the security of knowing that there is one more international set of eyes watching Tibet. It arrived in the city of Novosibirsk with an American control expert who's going to train the Russians to use it."

"I've got a bad feeling about this," Bolan said.

"So do I," Kurtzman agreed. "I'll let the Department of Defense know right away, but it's the Russians who'll have to react."

"If it's not too late already. Troschenkova expected the THADSAC here in a few hours. It has either already been hijacked, or the deed is going down as we speak."

Novosibirsk

THE FLIGHT WAS MISERABLE and endless. As bad as the flight was, the hotel was worse. She'd been promised a room at the nicest hotel in Novosibirsk, and for all she knew, she got it. But it was a pit by Western standards.

The mattress was old and dank, the carpet ancient and the water highly questionable.

Elise Lim hadn't looked forward to this trip, but had never dreamed it could be this bad. What had begun as an adventure had deteriorated rapidly into one long exercise in misery. She'd been gone less than forty-eight hours, and all she could think about now was getting back to the U.S.

She thought the very least this dump of a hotel could provide her was a decent cup of coffee. She had no idea what composed the black sludge they had presented to her in the restaurant that morning. She had almost spit out the sip she had taken.

"Not hungry?" Dmitri Strashnov was standing next to the table, looking with mock disapproval at her scarcely touched breakfast.

"No," she answered shortly. On top of everything else, she was burdened with this Strashnov. He was one of her "bodyguards" during her stay in Russia. He was some sort of Russian Federation secret-service agent, which meant he was ex-KGB—one of those old-guard types who was really angry about losing his special privileges with the fall of communism.

He had leered at her as if she were fresh meat the first time they met, and every time they met thereafter. Worse, he treated her like a mindless bimbo who might actually react positively to his inane patter. Maybe it was because she was of Chinese ancestry. Maybe it was because she was an American. Probably it was simply because she was female.

She slid to the end of the booth.

"We don't have to get going just yet," Strashnov said quickly. "Why don't we sit and talk and I'll have some coffee?"

"They don't have coffee."

"What's in the pot?" Strashnov asked.

"Good question." She grabbed her coat and stood. Strashnov didn't move, so they ended up facing each other with less than two inches of empty space between them. She almost choked on his breath.

"Are you going to get out of my way?"

"In a minute."

"If you don't stop staring at my breasts and get out of my way, I'm going kick your balls up into your throat. Then I'll start screaming rape and have you arrested. Then I'll report you to your superiors."

Strashnov was infinitely amused, but he stepped back and she stomped past him. She heard him following her and knew he was staring at her rear end now. She dragged on her long coat.

"You won't need that, Miss Lim," he said. "It is a nice day. Very warm."

"I'll wear it anyway."

The old Mercedes was waiting at the front of the hotel, engine running, Sergei Platovsek leaning against the door reading a morning paper. He was surprised to see them. He had obviously been told they would be a while. But he rushed to open the door for Lim when she appeared.

"Good morning, Miss Lim," he said, his English requiring a little effort.

Now, this man was another story. Strashnov's partner was a younger agent, probably just out of his twenties. He had the rugged, almost haggard good looks that she had come to regard as distinctly Eastern European. His hair was short, straw colored, and his eyes were the dark color of a green olive. He'd treated her with nothing but respect—which she appreciated in light of his older partner's behavior—but was obvious intensely attracted to her, a feeling she reciprocated.

As they drove out of the city, with Platovsek at the wheel, she made a point of sitting behind the passenger seat so Strashnov had to turn all the way around to see her, an effort for a man with his abundance of girth.

Ignoring Strashnov's attempts at amusing patter, she watched the depressing landscape of the ugly city crawl past. Three more days of training, and then she could get out.

They reached the air-force outpost, and Lim found herself the center of attention. There had to be twenty armed guards on the scene, all watching her as though she were the most unusual creature they had ever seen. It was likely they had never seen a female Chinese-American satellite expert before.

The four young men whom she was assigned to instruct in the workings of the THADSAC linkage were better, probably because they were motivated to learn their jobs as thoroughly as possible in the three days they had and were too distracted to be impolite. She shook hands with them briefly and got to work.

The THADSAC unit was in place and still wrapped, as she had left it the previous night. She carefully began to unwrap the control unit, briefly summarizing its various components as she did so. Lim had accompanied it all the way to the building and made sure she had the hardware she needed to hook up the device.

It didn't require all that much. THADSAC was essentially a glorified personal computer, although its programming was pretty well dedicated to a single task. The processor was unbelievably fast, but with the computer industry essentially doubling processor speed every year and a half, Lim knew the average home computer would be approaching these speeds before she was in her forties.

What made the THADSAC unique was its dedicated capability to interact with THADS, which made it very special indeed.

THADS had been put into orbit by a space shuttle with little fanfare and little international notice, although the U.S. hadn't gone out of its way to keep it a secret. It was rocketed into geostationary orbit, and now sat looking down on a very special part of planet Earth.

The United States had presented virtually unlimited access to THADS as a goodwill gesture to the Russian government. Again the gesture hadn't been widely publicized. But the Chinese knew about it.

THADS orbited at an altitude of 193 miles directly over Tibet, and its one and only purpose was to watch the activity that occurred in that part of the world. With state-of-the-art thermal and infrared detection capability, it could keep a very close watch indeed.

With the Americans watching, the Chinese would be reluctant to make further overt military strikes in the battered province, no matter how aggressive Tibetan revolutionaries became.

With the Russians watching, they would be even more reluctant.

Elise Lim was all for the idea, but she favored the act of giving the THADSAC to the Russians because of an even more subtle effect she hoped it would have.

She knew well enough that no nation—not the United States, and not Russia—was innocent of atrocity and oppression of its people in some form or another. And she was a firm believer that technology such as THADS, which made it impossible for the Chinese to make overt aggressive moves in Tibet undetected, would help prevent such acts from occurring. If Russia was one of the watchers, she reasoned, maybe it would instill an attitude of peacekeeper, thus making Russia itself less likely to commit this kind of blatant aggression.

Another benefit arose from giving the Russians full access to THADS: they would know firsthand the extent of information that would be available from satellites that would be looking at other parts of the world.

"All right, let's get this sucker hooked up," she said.

The trainees looked at one another in bewilderment.

Strashnov, who was watching from a chair by the door, laughed out loud. "They do not understand your use of the word 'sucker,'" he said.

Lim smiled at her trainees as she began unwrapping the rubber ties from the primary satellite-communications unit and said, "Forget it."

Her smile was infectious. They smiled back.

Strashnov leaped out of his chair at the sound of gunfire coming from outside, and loped across the room in two long strides, shouting, "Get down! Everyone!"

Lim looked around wildly and felt Strashnov's meaty hand grab her by the shoulder and force her to the floor, where she landed on all fours.

"Get down!" he repeated.

"What's going on?"

There was another rattle of gunfire, this time closer, and Lim realized there was frank terror on the faces of the trainees, who crouched beside her.

A narrow, high window shattered, and she instinctively covered her face to avoid flying glass, then heard gunfire cutting into the wall on the far side of the room.

Strashnov had withdrawn a hefty black handgun and glanced out the broken window briefly, then withdrew.

"Damn!" He shouted rapidly in Russian, then the

two guards in the room flanked the door and Platovsek moved to Lim, gesturing for her to stay down.

"What's going on?"

"I am not sure, miss," he said calmly.

"Strashnov!" she demanded. "What's going on?"

"We're under attack—what do you think!"

"You must have twenty guards out there!"

Strashnov glanced out the window again. "Not anymore."

Lim's heart grew cold. "What does he mean by that?"

"They're dead," Platovsek said.

"Shit."

There was a shout in Russian outside the door, and the trainees and Platovsek exchanged worried looks.

Strashnov joined them. "All right, we're going to have to try and make a run for it out the back."

"What?" Lim asked. "Don't they have this building surrounded?"

"Yes, but there is no other option."

"Can't you call for backup? You know, reinforcements?"

"There isn't time. The nearest base that could provide military assistance is a half an hour away."

"We can hold out until then."

"We aren't going to hold out another two minutes!" Strashnov declared. "If we're going to live through this, we have to make a break for it and we have to do it now."

"It's suicide, Dmitri," Platovsek said. "They have thirty men out there, maybe more, and you know what they want."

"What? What do they want?" Lim demanded.

"You," Strashnov replied.

"Why me?"

"Because you can operate that." He waved his gun at the THADS control unit. "They want that, too."

"Who are these guys? Why do they want the satellite?"

There were more shouts from outside the building. One of the guards at the door peered out the window and recoiled in time to avoid another volley of automatic gunfire that ripped into the ceiling.

"They want our surrender," Platovsek said.

"That's what they want, and that's what will save us." Strashnov paced to the THADSAC. He shouted in Russian, and another voice replied outside the building.

"He's threatening to destroy the control unit," Platovsek said. "You can't do that, Dmitri."

"What good'll it do?" Lim asked.

"It's what they want. If I destroy it, they'll have no reason to continue the attack at the risk of their own lives."

"Do it!" Lim said.

"You can't!" Platovsek declared.

"Why not! It's just a box! I'll get you another one!"

"They'll court-martial you, Dmitri!"

"Let them. At least we'll all be alive," Strashnov said.

"I'm going to destroy the THADSAC and send the pieces out the window!" he shouted to the attackers.

"Don't, Dmitri," Platovsek said, this time less desperately, with a hint of threat in his voice.

Lim looked at the young agent as if seeing him for the first time. "Shoot it, Strashnov."

Strashnov raised his gun.

Platovsek turned his 9 mm on his comrade without hesitation and triggered the weapon one time. Strashnov

grunted and staggered away from the THADSAC, looking at his partner in dismay, only to witness the gun fire
again. The bullet struck inches above the first impact,
directly in the heart, and he crumpled. Platovsek turned
on the guards at the door and shot them both.

Lim's shock lasted just long enough for the impact
of Strashnov's corpse to shake the floor under her. Then
she launched herself onto Platovsek's back, sending him
lurching forward, but he twisted smartly, brought the
handgun out before him and stood his ground. Lim
froze in a crouch.

"You're in on this," Lim accused him.

Platovsek said nothing.

"You bastard."

He gestured briefly with the handgun and she obeyed,
moving out of his way. The Russian fired the weapon
repeatedly into the three cowering trainees.

Platovsek walked to the door and opened it, nudging
one of the fallen guards out of the way, and waved to
the figures outside, speaking briefly. A stream of armed
men entered the building.

Four of them placed themselves around Elise Lim
and kept her covered with their AK-74 autorifles. Others
made for the THADSAC unit and began rewrapping it
in its packaging.

The Russian agent gave brief orders to the packers,
then turned to Lim. Somewhere he had procured a pair
of manacles on a chain, and he tossed them, the muzzle
of his handgun never wavering from her, as if the four
rifles weren't enough to keep her at bay.

The manacles rattled at her feet.

"Who do you work for?" she demanded.

"Put them on, please."

"The Communists?"

Platovsek shook his head, his lips moving in the faintest impression of a smile. The courtesy of the capable but somewhat shy man she had come to know since her arrival the previous day had completely vanished. It had all been an act.

"The Communists are gone. Russia is a capitalist state now," he said.

"So who do you work for? The Chechens? The Chinese?"

"The highest bidder," Platovsek replied.

HANDS MANACLED in front of her, Lim was led out of the building and she gasped at what she saw. Men were sprawled everywhere, crumpled and bloodied, weapons lying beside them. She realized with a shock that she was the only survivor.

"I don't understand this," she said to Platovsek. "Who would want access to THADS? It's intended to be a tool to prevent violence."

"There are many groups interested in the satellite. You'll be introduced to the buyer eventually."

"Who? Tell me who!"

Platovsek ignored her, looking into the sky behind the building. Lim followed his gaze to a helicopter heading rapidly in their direction at a tree-skimming altitude. Within a minute it descended and the side door rolled open, the rotor noise barely winding down.

"Let's get out of here quickly—but carefully," Platovsek said pointedly to the six men who were carrying the wrapped, boxy THADSAC like pallbearers.

The unit was placed carefully inside the helicopter, then maneuvered to a wall and strapped in place. Platovsek ordered Lim inside and sat her on one of the bench seats, belting her in tightly. He withdrew a length of nylon rope, which he tied to the chain of her manacles and hooked into the floor, shortening it enough that she was forced to lean forward slightly. The last thing Platovsek withdrew was a black scarf.

Somehow, after all the terror she had just witnessed, the thought of being blindfolded was the final straw.

"No blindfold," she said.

"Sorry, Miss Lim."

"Please! No blindfold!"

He placed it around her head, and she was surrounded by darkness. She exhaled long and low, trying not to scream in panic, simultaneously feeling utterly defeated. She heard the shouts as the men cleared the scene of the attack, heading for the vehicles they had arrived in. The helicopter turbine increased its revs, and the rotor noise became thunderous.

CHAPTER FOUR

A distinctive thrum of a dual turbine helicopter rolled over the broad grasslands of northeastern Russia. Bolan curled around the exhaust chimney on the roof of the command trailer, doing his best to remain unseen. The Eurocopter BK-117 approached from the north and swung out of its way to pass over the aircraft wreckage, blackened and cold. Then it crossed to the middle of the field between the runway and the trailer camp and descended rapidly before slowing for a gentle touchdown. The wide door swung open, and a tall man jumped out, autorifle at the ready.

The trailer door slammed, and the commander and his assistant headed to the field. The helicopter was standing by, engines still at high revs as if it were ready to leap into the sky. The pair from the command trailer waved, and the figure with the autorifle responded. Even from a distance of fifty yards, Bolan saw the gunner relax visibly as he recognized the men from the camp. The Executioner guessed he hadn't known about the destruction of the Colt transport aircraft and was concerned about what it implied until he saw the people he expected to meet. The figure ducked into the Eurocopter briefly, and the rotor revs instantly dropped.

The three men met in the airfield and spoke, then two

turned and walked back to the trailer, stopping abruptly. For a moment Bolan wondered if he had been spotted, but they turned back to the Eurocopter, where their companion was shouting and pointing at another aircraft approaching in the distance.

Maybe it was the attack they had discussed and feared.

But there was no alarm exhibited by any of them, and the four-engined prop plane, much like the crashed aircraft in size and configuration, descended onto the airfield. It was an Antonov An-26, a Russian military transport plane, painted flat gray, without markings. It taxied to a halt well before it reached the wreckage, spun 180 degrees and came back along the airstrip, halted and killed all four engines.

One of the men turned and gave quick hand signals to the guards in the compound, and they began to spread out, deploying about the perimeter of the camp. The Executioner noted the features of the man who gave the silent order, knowing he was the subordinate, the man named Liposk, which meant the other man was the guy in charge, Troschenkova. The instinct that told him to camp out on the roof of the trailer was dead-on. The well-spaced guard detail now blanketing the compound and the airfield would have allowed him no room for maneuvering inside the camp if he were in hiding in the grasslands.

Not that his current vantage point was proving efficacious. All the activity was occurring in the airfield. He could only hope Troschenkova would choose to conduct business in his office.

Even from that distance, Bolan observed that the man emerging from the aircraft wore the uniform of a Chinese army official.

CAPTAIN JINGSHENG reached the bottom of the stairs and crossed to the Russians, who didn't move to greet him. He halted a few paces from them and leaned into a handshake that was perfunctory and insincere at best. "Mr. Troschenkova," he said.

The Russian's face was blank. "This way," he said, and walked to the trailers.

A quick perusal showed Jingsheng that a noose of armed men surrounded the airfield.

"Will your men begin loading the THADSAC?" Jingsheng asked without moving a step.

"After we contend with the bureaucracy."

Jingsheng almost asked out loud if this was a trap, then decided that if it was, he'd already walked into it. He turned to the aircraft and signaled to a man standing at the top of the steps. His copilot quickly grabbed a suitcase from the cabin and walked down the steps.

The captain barely nodded in his direction. "Lieutenant Li," he said.

The Russians didn't even acknowledge the copilot's presence. The five of them strode across the scraggly grass to the compound of trailers, the lieutenant bringing up the rear with the heavy case, very aware of the circle of guards moving in behind him.

TWO OF THE GUARDS entered the cabin with the five men and stood at the door. Jingsheng glanced at them as he sat in the chair before Troschenkova's desk. There was just the one chair; the other Russians took up position behind him while his copilot stood stupidly in the middle of the room, unable to decide what to do.

"We've had another bid," Troschenkova said, settling back casually in his seat.

Jingsheng nodded briefly, as if coming to an understanding. "Our earnest payment provided that no other bids would be considered."

Troschenkova nodded. "It did. I stand by that, Captain. We did not accept the other bid."

The captain had no confidence in the integrity of this Russian hoodlum. He was tempted to say so, but he understood when to keep his mouth shut. He was sure, however, that if the other bid wasn't considered, then it was because it didn't exceed the sum in the suitcase. "Why tell me about it, then, Mr. Troschenkova?"

"Because the bid came from my PRC contact."

Jingsheng's face registered no emotion.

"I'm not sure what General Zheng is up to, Captain. I don't care. But I know he is working well outside the limits of his authority. I know for certain that the Chinese army command has no knowledge that he is the man behind this transaction."

"Of course they don't. This is a top secret operation. Orders are coming directly out of Beijing...."

"Bullshit."

Jingsheng didn't respond. He sat where he was, feet flat on the floor, hands on his knees, and was as stoic as a statue while Troschenkova took out a mahogany-colored cigarette. He withdrew a battered but expensive-looking gold lighter from his shirt pocket and snapped it, lighting the smoke and popping the lighter back in his pocket, all the while staring directly at the Chinese pilot.

The captain knew he was supposed to be insulted by the display. It was a flashy, arrogant little bit of play-acting staged for his benefit, yet so transparent as to be a blatant put-down. Troschenkova was essentially telling him he was wealthy and powerful, so powerful he could make a fool of himself in front of hired Chinese military lackeys.

"Are you going to tell me who General Zheng is working for?" Troschenkova said.

"Who else besides the People's Republic?"

"Maybe he's become sympathetic to the Tibetan cause."

Jingsheng smiled sardonically. "I can tell you without hesitation that the general has no sympathy for the Tibetans."

"Then he's working for himself."

The pilot's smile grew stale. "Maybe he is. So what? You said you did not care."

"I don't give a damn what his intentions are with the THADSAC. What I care about is that for all practical purposes he lied to me. He insinuated he was working for the PRC. Now I find out he's playing some lone-wolf sort of game. Maybe you should think about how the PRC reacted to the fact that they've been outbid for the THADSAC."

Jingsheng did think about it. "I suppose they were not happy to hear it," he offered.

"You're right they're not happy. They're pissed as hell, and the only person they have to be pissed at is me."

"You haven't betrayed our confidence—"

"No, I haven't. But in my opinion Zheng betrayed me. He lied to me, and as a result he puts me at risk. Because I have no doubts the Chinese are going to be all over me. In fact, I'm going to have to abandon this airfield, at least for the foreseeable future. You know how much it's going to cost me to set up a new shipping station?"

"I would have thought you knew there are risks involved in playing games like this, Mr. Troschenkova."

Troschenkova stood and leaned forward on the desktop. "Don't patronize me. I know the game better than you ever will. I grew up on the streets of Troitsk. It's the coldest place in the world, and I run it now. You know what that makes me? One tough bastard! You know what that makes you? Nothing! And you're going to be dead if I hear another word come out of your mouth without a tone of respect!"

Jingsheng was silent, his expression rigid, eyes cold.

Troschenkova tossed his cigarette to the floor and ground it under his toe.

"With all due respect, Mr. Troschenkova, are you going to honor the agreement you made with General Zheng?" Jingsheng asked.

"Yeah, but the price has gone up fifty percent."

"We have only brought the agreed-upon amount with us."

"You can bring the rest later. You've got seventy-two hours."

"And until then you'll keep the THADSAC?"

Troschenkova seemed to be considering that, then shook his head. "No. It's too dangerous. You take it with you, just as we agreed. I have better insurance than the THADSAC. I have information that would be of great interest to the PRC. You understand, Captain? If I don't get the extra cash that is owed to me within seventy-two hours of right now—" he made a point of staring at his watch "—then I make a phone call to my PRC contact and I tell them who my buyers were. Got it?"

"Our agreement specifically calls for anonymity!"

"That's the old deal. Zheng nullified it when he lied

to me. This is the new deal. I'm specifying terms. You don't want to take it, you tell me now and I'll call the PRC anyway—they want the THADSAC pretty badly. So you tell me right now, Captain, do we have a deal or not? You have five seconds to decide.''

Jingsheng stalled, then nodded. "We agree to your new terms."

Troschenkova instantly gestured at Platovsek. "Start the transfer." He gestured at the copilot, who was standing awkwardly with the suitcase at his feet. "Put that on the desk."

He gestured at Liposk. "Count it. Let's get this over with and get out of here."

MACK BOLAN WAS ONE of the most knowledgeable paramilitary strategists on the planet, but he couldn't come up with a plan that offered even a marginal probability of success.

There were six or eight Chinese soldiers on the plane and maybe twenty Russians surrounding the airfield. The guards were armed with Kalashnikovs—mostly AK-47s, though some carried the newer AK-74s. The Chinese, when they showed themselves off at the top of the ramp of the aircraft, carried Type 56s.

The unobstructed gunfire of twenty-five or thirty assault rifles was tough to strategize around. No matter how many times he worked it in his mind, the hypothetical attack scenarios always ended with him riddled with 7.62 mm and 5.56 mm rounds.

It was three hours since he'd hung up the phone with Aaron Kurtzman, crawled back on the roof and replaced the exhaust hood. The conversation in the trailer below convinced him that the Russians hadn't been able to protect the THADSAC and its controller from hijacking.

That meant the THADSAC was in the Eurocopter on the airfield. The female operator, the conversation below also led him to believe, was there, too.

The soldier had rarely felt so helpless, and it wasn't a feeling he enjoyed.

He crept back to the vent.

The room below was more or less silent. Then the voice he had come to recognize as Liposk's said, "It's all here."

"That much money in U.S. dollars was extremely difficult to come up with, Mr. Troschenkova," the pilot said. "Coming up with half that much again in U.S. dollars might be impossible, especially in just three days...."

"Make it possible," Troschenkova said.

"What if we paid you in French francs?"

"No way. I don't have access to expertise for verifying their authenticity. I don't even know what a French franc looks like."

"Then what about rubles?"

"Don't insult me."

Bolan heard a distant hum and drew his head from under the vent overhang. He scanned the sky and spotted a tiny dot in the distance.

The Executioner was wearing the headset walkie-talkie around his neck for hours, already tuned to the agreed-on frequency. He dragged it onto his head and cupped the mike to his mouth. "G-Force, tell me that's you."

A familiar voice rang through the tiny headphones instantly. "I'm here, Sarge, and look what I've got!"

"You've got good timing, for one." Bolan squinted in the dim light of the overcast morning. The dot had become a chopper, a big one, with a familiar silhouette.

"Didn't catch that. I assume you aren't able to speak up."

"Affirmative."

"What we've got here is a Russian air force Mil-24 Hind attack helicopter. The Russians are feeling a little sheepish about their failure to protect the THADSAC and were quick to volunteer some hardware, although I don't think they believe our Intel is any good. Anyway, the disadvantage is that I'm not at the helm. We've got a crew of Russians at the controls."

"Tell them to watch out. There's a couple of dozen AKs on the ground and maybe some more serious hardware," Bolan replied.

There was a moment of silence. "I think I got that—lots of AKs and you don't know what else. We spotted yet?"

Bolan had just witnessed the first signs of alarm on the field. "Affirmative."

"We're coming in."

The Hind's distant aspect altered slightly, and the sound of the mounting revs reached Bolan a moment later.

"What's your position?" Jack Grimaldi, ace Stony Man pilot, asked urgently.

"See the trailer nearest the airfield?"

"You're in it?"

"I'm on it."

"Let me know when you change positions."

"The control unit's in the Eurocopter, and maybe a hostage, too."

"Got it."

Bolan felt like a grenade ready to explode if only its pin would be released, but he was trapped. Any move that drew the attention of the occupants of the trailer would see him gunned down by more men than he could count. He had to wait for them to be distracted.

There was a sound from inside, and the door burst open. Bolan crawled on his elbows across the top of the trailer and saw the men streaming out of the trailer and circling immediately to the airfield side, while the guards stationed throughout the compound headed in the direction of the field.

Bolan didn't have to wait any longer. The instant the last man disappeared from view, he slipped over the edge and plummeted to the earth, landing in a crouch with his stolen AK-47 in his hands. He had only two extra magazines; that many rounds would last mere seconds if autofired. The Executioner was determined to make them count.

Another Russian burst out of the trailer that served as a barracks and instantly recognized Bolan as a stranger, bringing his AK-47 into firing position on the run. The Executioner triggered his AK-47, and a burst slammed into the gunner's chest. The guard started to shout, then his body shut down and he collapsed to the ground.

At virtually the same instant, the gunfire began on the airfield. Bolan edged around the trailer, where he witnessed the Russians and Chinese standing their ground together, firing their weapons futilely at the fast-moving gunship. The Russian air-force Hind swept over the end of the airfield, and a pair of front-mounted 7.62 mm machine guns swerved in their sockets and spit out a stream of rounds, making a deadly pass along the guard contingent standing its ground at the south end of the airfield. The first few gunners threw their auto-rifles into the air as if in celebration of death and crumpled, while the last few men dropped to the ground and tried to scramble for safety, but were unable to elude the stream of fire.

Bolan stepped out from behind the trailer long enough to zero in on the group of Russians and Chinese running from the scene of battle. He aimed for the man in the middle, Troschenkova, and adjusted his aim at the last millisecond as one of the nearby gunners spotted him and shouted. The big American fired into the guard before he could bring his AK-47 into play and took out his neighbor, who was twisting into firing position. By then Troschenkova and the Chinese pilots were diving for cover.

The Executioner aimed and fired at the fleeing Russian crime boss as he and his enforcer ran behind one of three automobiles parked on the field. There was a flurry of sudden blood, but Bolan knew he'd scored only a marginal hit on the boss's enforcer.

"BASTARD!" Liposk grabbed at his triceps as his back slammed against the door of the car and he slumped to the ground. Blood streamed between his fingers.

"Who is that? Who the hell is that?" Troschenkova demanded, peering through the car windows. There was another stutter of gunfire, and the windows shattered, sending Troschenkova to the dirt with his hands over his eyes.

"It's our hijacker. He called in reinforcements," Liposk said.

"How could he have done that?" Troschenkova demanded. "There's nothing for miles in any direction. Where could he have found communications?"

Liposk ground his teeth as the pain from his arm increased. "It doesn't matter how. What matters is what we're going to do about it."

The Chinese pilots had flattened on the ground when the firing started and were huddled in the grass five yards away. Troschenkova's Russian gunmen were moving in on the newcomer, spreading out between the cars and the aircraft. A pair of gunners opened fire on the trailer, unloading full magazines in a flurry of fire that raised a deafening thunder as the rounds rattled against the trailer panels. The pilots took the opportunity to scramble for better cover and began to crawl across the grass toward Troschenkova and Liposk.

Bolan returned fire in controlled bursts, and the two gunners stiffened one after the other, falling on their faces in the grass. Almost without pause the Executioner turned on the pilots, loosing a burst in their direction as their movements became even more frantic.

The copilot, Li, jumped forward and rolled to a stop in front of the Russians, but the pilot shouted, his voice high-pitched with sudden pain.

"I'm hit—help me," Jingsheng said, reaching out across the dry grass. Li stared at him openmouthed with horror.

"Help me!"

There was another burst of gunfire, and two more rounds pulped the pilot's other leg. "Help me!" he screamed, clawing at the ground in a vain attempt to drag his body out of the line of fire.

Liposk glared at the frozen copilot and crawled forward on his knees, keeping low. He offered his good arm to the pilot, who grabbed it like a drowning man. The Russian pulled the pilot behind the protection of the car, but not before another round chopped into his foot.

The pilot shouted again and lay on his back, eyes wild with pain.

Liposk spotted a guard crouching in the nearby Eurocopter, firing single rounds at the trailer and the enemy gunman.

"Is there more than one?" he shouted.

The guard shook his head.

"You and you," Liposk shouted to two men crouching nearby, "circle around. If it is just one man, there is no way he can protect himself against attacks from two directions."

The gunners got to their feet and bolted across the open ground to put the trailer between themselves and the attacker. Only one of them made it. His companion was drilled in the temple and fell to the ground in a heap.

"You!" Liposk shouted to another gunman stationed behind the fuel truck. "You go with him."

The man stood up hesitantly, then raced into the open as the guard in the Eurocopter opened fire on the enemy gunner's position. But after firing just four rounds, his AK-47 abruptly quit on him, the magazine empty. Before he could pull back, the enemy returned fire, sweeping the side of the aircraft and cutting into the exposed arm and upper torso of the guard.

BOLAN DELIBERATELY KEPT the fire low to minimize risk to the hostage he assumed was inside the Eurocopter, so he was uncertain as to the usefulness of his fire. But he saw his AK-47 rounds take the guard in the exposed arm and upper torso, and the man collapsed in the opening to the helicopter's interior. The soldier twisted and fired as he aimed, 7.62 mm rounds cutting into the running gunman just before he disappeared behind the far end of the trailer. But Bolan felt good about that one, too—that guard was out of the picture.

But there was still the first gunman, alive and kicking and coming around the back. And even the Executioner couldn't effectively guard himself from attack from both directions.

He cupped the tiny mike to his mouth. "G-Force, come in."

GRIMALDI PRESSED the headphone to his head. "Yeah, Sarge. We took out a whole bunch of bad guys along the south perimeter. We're circling around for a sweep from the east."

"That's me against the southern end of the trailer. I've got a man coming around the rear, and I can't afford to take my attention from the front."

"Slow down!" Grimaldi shouted to the pilot. The young Russian braked the Hind as they sped over the grassland at less than thirty feet altitude, and the compound of trailers swept under them like landscape rolling under a car on the freeway.

"There!" Grimaldi shouted, and the explanation was enough for the pilot, who rapidly decelerated the aircraft while the Stony Man flyboy yanked on the grip of the machine-gun controls.

The gunman stalking along the back of the trailer froze and stared up at the attack helicopter materializing in the sky above him like a thundering dragon.

The twin guns mounted underneath the body of the fearsome gunship swung and blossomed with fire, sending a torrent of 7.62 mm rounds into the trailer, the dry ground and the gunman, who slammed into the trailer and collapsed.

"Rear assault neutralized," Grimaldi said.

BOLAN WAS GLAD to hear it but didn't respond. Stepping forward, he fired at a group of four Russians attempting to make an approach across the grasslands. Knowing he was down to a handful of rounds, he fired the AK-47 dry, then retreated behind the end of the trailer and quickly inserted a fresh clip into his weapon.

"He's out of ammo—get him." The orders were coming from behind the car. That was Liposk, the head enforcer, keeping his men moving. Bolan waited another moment, estimating the moment at which the offensive foursome would be best exposed, then fired around the corner, finding them just where he wanted them. Two of the hardmen collapsed to the ground, blood spurting from a dozen lethal wounds. The other two had no real options. To get to cover behind the Eurocopter would require them to leap their fallen comrades and sprint five yards to safety. Behind them it was ten yards back to the cover of a fuel truck.

Each made a different decision. Bolan fired at the first man as he jumped over his fallen comrades, and he collapsed on top of the bodies. The final survivor of the foursome turned his head to the sky as the roaring Hind gunship appeared above him, machine guns aiming in his direction, and was almost surprised when he felt the killing rounds crash instead into his shoulder and back.

"Target that helicopter!" Liposk shouted in Russian across the airfield, then repeated himself in English for the Chinese.

The Russian gunmen found the helicopter a much more palatable target than risking themselves trying to get at the lone gunman who was wreaking havoc. Twenty Kalashnikovs were aimed into the sky. The Hind gunship spun 180 degrees, and the machine-gun fire from its belly swept over the guards, scoring on at least one of them. The others saw it coming and dived for cover wherever they could find it.

The Hind's belly and armored flanks were peppered with rounds without affecting its operation. The helicopter roared and swept across the field to the west.

Troschenkova ducked closer to the ground as more glass exploded out of the car and rattled onto his forehead. He touched a small but bloody cut on his brow and turned to Liposk.

"Take care of that bastard."

"Right," Liposk said, holding firmly on to his wounded arm and fighting a brief wave of dizziness. "Move in," he shouted across the airfield. "I want everyone moving in, *now!*"

"How many men have we lost?" Troschenkova demanded.

"I don't know."

"Don't you think you ought to consider it?" Troschenkova said acidly.

"We're going against one guy—we've got more than enough men to take him down."

"One man and one attack helicopter."

A quick glance showed the Hind sweeping in a wide circle and coming back at the Russians as they moved themselves into the open to attack the lone gunman.

"I'll deal with that, too," Liposk said.

"Get around the Eurocopter!" he shouted to his men. "The Hind won't risk harming the hostage."

"THEY'RE HEADING to the helicopter," Bolan said into his throat mike. "The control unit is in there, and I'm pretty sure the hostage is, too."

He didn't bother to listen to Grimaldi's response, twisting himself around the corner and triggering a full-auto stream of rounds into the line of Russian gunners heading for the chopper. He watched three of them crash to the ground before his second magazine cycled dry, then he fell back behind his cover and listened to rounds rattling against the metal. As he changed the mag, he heard the 7.62 mm machine gun firing from the belly of the Hind. Risking a glance out into the battlefield, he saw Grimaldi tearing mercilessly into the gunners who were still in the open. But when the enemy guns came into close vicinity of the Eurocopter, they had reached safe haven. Grimaldi knew there was an innocent human being on board that chopper.

"Get that gunner!" Bolan heard the shouted order and saw Liposk's fist gesturing over the top of the car. The hardmen behind the Eurocopter trained their auto-rifles on the Executioner's corner of the trailer, and the rattle of rounds hitting the metal became a thunderous torrent.

Bolan retreated around the back end of the trailer, briefly considering moving inside. He discarded the idea; the trailer would become a death trap if the door was blocked by Troschenkova's troops. He moved around to the other end of the trailer and found himself alone. Troschenkova, Liposk and the Chinese pilots were protected from his angle by one of the other vehicles, but making a run for a better position would expose him to the gunmen now clustering around the Eurocopter.

The aircraft was awash in activity, and one of the gunmen emerged from inside with a long sack of army green canvas. He shouted at his companions, who loosed another barrage at the corner where Bolan had been, and under cover the gunmen sped across the open to the car where the crime bosses were pinned down.

The Hind had drifted across the field to escape the autofire and was spiraling. It accelerated and descended, buzzing in the direction of the parked An-26 transport.

"We're going after the other aircraft, Striker," Grimaldi said in his earphones.

That was the moment Bolan recognized the markings stenciled on the canvas sack. "Pull up! Pull up now!" he shouted into his throat mike.

"You ever fire a bazooka before?" Liposk asked the Russian gunman.

"No."

"Well, I can't do it, so you have fifteen seconds to learn how. Open that sack and take out one of the tubes."

The hardman unzipped the canvas and snatched quickly at the first of the three short fiberglass tubes inside.

"Pull out those pins," he ordered. The gunman yanked the pins and dropped them. "Now grasp it there and there and pull."

The gunman grabbed at the base of the tube and struggled.

"Not there! There!" Liposk shouted.

The gunman got it right and gave a hard pull, and the stubby tube telescoped to a length of three feet. Sights and firing levers at the top of the unit unfolded.

"Now target that helicopter and fire," Liposk said, pointing to the firing mechanism with his one functional hand.

The helicopter slowed prior to reaching the An-26.

"They've got LAWs. Get out of range."

"You've don't need to tell me twice," Grimaldi said, and Bolan heard him shouting to the helicopter pilot.

There was a flash, and the Executioner saw the rocket fire. It was badly aimed, fired by a beginner, and shot into the air like an errant firework, rocketing high above the Eurocopter and out into the airfield nearly fifty yards from the Hind gunship. It hit the ground with a blast of fire.

The Hind pilot had spotted the rocket and veered away from it.

The Light Antitank Weapon was a portable, disposable bazooka designed for land-based craft. Bolan didn't have any doubts that it would be able to down the Hind just as easily as it would stop a tank. Any further offensive efforts by the gunship would be suicide.

"WHERE IS HE?" Liposk demanded.

"Can't see him—we may have tagged him," one of his gunmen replied.

Liposk peered at the corner where the intruder had been. Indeed, except for the distant hum of the Hind helicopter, the battle zone had become amazingly quiet. He sprinted into the open and made it to the Eurocopter in seconds, gripping his wounded arm.

"Okay, we have to move fast. You four—" he gestured by nodding his head "—get inside and get the THADSAC. Transport it to the plane. You three keep an eye on our attacker. Fire if you see him. I want him dead, got it?"

The Hind was buzzing back and forth at the perimeter of the airfield, the tall grasses flattening beneath it. The helicopter resembled an angry, black hornet on the opposite side of the glass, trying to figure out how to get inside and sting somebody.

The hardman at the car was standing his ground, holding a second rocket at the ready and exuding more confidence now. The bazooka was a relatively easy weapon to fire. Liposk knew his aim would be better on his second attempt. Troschenkova was standing behind the bazooka gunner, angry and a little nervous.

The four hardmen emerged with the THADSAC in its wooden crate, hung on poles for easy transport.

"Tell the Chinese to come get their pilots," he said. "We're not carrying them back to their plane for them."

The four men started to make their way quickly across the open ground, heading for the An-26. The Chinese were peeking out of the open doorway. At least two of their number were sprawled and unmoving on the ground.

He didn't give a damn about dead Chinese.

"Start the cars and prepare to get out of here," Liposk said to his subordinates.

"What about the sniper?" Troschenkova called out.

"I say we cut our losses and get out," Liposk said.

"Look what he cost me!"

"And I bet he'll cost us a lot more if we go hunting for him. Let's cut our losses and leave."

While Troschenkova stood there thinking about it, Liposk sent the drivers out to collect the working vehicles.

Then he said, "Bring out the girl."

BOLAN FOUND HIMSELF on top of the trailer again, but this time it was a vantage point instead of a trap. He

crawled across quickly and looked down on the battlefield.

Two Chinese gunners had hoisted the wounded captain, who was shouting in pain as they struggled to carry
him to the aircraft. Troschenkova was getting into one
of the automobiles—a silver Mercedes—while the man
with the bazooka paced beside it, effectively keeping
the Hind at bay.

Bolan could see that Liposk held a 9 mm handgun at
the base of the skull of a dark-haired young woman.
She was of Asian ancestry, but she was obviously the
American hostage. Her hands were chained, and her
mouth was covered in silver tape, her blindfold dragged
down around her neck so she could see to walk. Even
from a distance Bolan saw anger flashing in her eyes.
She wasn't taking imprisonment well, but she didn't
have the defeated look of a victim. Rather, she wore
the vicious countenance of a caged cat.

She was flanked by two gunmen, and Liposk followed close behind her, keeping her covered as they
moved in the direction of the An-26. Liposk wanted
whoever was watching to know he wouldn't hesitate to
put a bullet in the young woman's brain. Beyond them
the engines of the transport plane chugged to life.

Bolan propped himself on his elbows and aimed the
AK-47 as if it were a sniper's rifle.

"G-Force?"

"I hope you've got some idea how to get us in on
the action without getting a bazooka up our collective
ass," Grimaldi replied.

"Be ready."

"We're ready already."

The Executioner fired a burst from the AK-47, and
the LAW flew out of the gunner's hands, hitting the

ground and rolling, while the gunner hit the earth and twitched.

"Come on in," Bolan said.

Through an open window of the Mercedes, a hand emerged with a large gun. Bolan fired at the hand before it could get off a shot, and a spray of blood misted the air. The gun fell out of the window, and the hand disappeared.

Liposk and the two guards twisted Lim so that she faced the trailer.

"That's the American hostage there on the field," Bolan said.

"We won't risk her," Grimaldi replied.

The vehicles were moving away from the field, but Liposk stood still, keeping the young woman between himself and Bolan.

The big American was visible now, but he didn't move, either. He didn't want to further provoke Liposk. There was no way he could tag the Russian without risking the young woman, not with the hardware he had.

The young woman was looking at Bolan, and the soldier saw a change in her emotions. She looked at him with hope.

Liposk muttered. As if doing a strange dance, the four of them walked backward to the base of the stairs that led into the transport plane.

One step at a time Liposk and the woman ascended the stairs. Almost shyly the Chinese peeked out of the door and grabbed the woman when she was within arm's reach.

"The hostage is in the transport plane," Bolan said. "The cars are fair game."

Liposk raced down the stairs and dived into the Mercedes as it slowed. The wheels spun, throwing up grass and soil as it tore away from the An-26. The engines on the plane reached high revs, and the doors slammed shut.

Bolan ejected himself from the roof of the trailer and hit the ground.

"Go after the Russians," Bolan shouted into the headset.

"What about the plane?"

"There's nothing you can do there. Any attacks on the plane will risk the hostage."

"So what are you going to do?"

"Try to keep it from leaving the ground."

Above him the Hind tilted and sped toward the convoy of vehicles, racing away from the airfield.

THE VEHICLES HAD SPREAD out and headed in two different directions as soon as they crossed the airfield to a dirt road. The Hind swung out as it swooped in a long arc that took it to the north along the trail of one of the vehicles.

"We don't care about these two," Grimaldi said to the Russian pilot. "Go after the other two."

The pilot dragged the helicopter into a U-turn. Seconds later they were heading back to the south, and the gunship's speed steadily increased. Stripped, the craft was capable of reaching almost 210 miles per hour. Loaded down, it could still outhaul virtually any land-based vehicle that existed.

"There's the one we want," Grimaldi said, gripping the controls for the articulated machine guns. "Get behind that Mercedes."

The Russian nodded and descended. The Stony Man flyboy was chafing at his impotence. The man at the controls was a fine pilot, but Grimaldi had the experience of air battles of all kinds, in all types of aircraft. He knew his battle instincts would serve them better behind the controls.

That was a pointless train of thought, and he discarded it. "Lower," he said.

The Hind skimmed the asphalt, and Grimaldi triggered the machine guns, firing a steady stream of 7.62 mm rounds into the trunk and rear tires. The rubber disintegrated, but the glass held. The car swerved out of control and raised a cloud of dust as it spun sideways, twisting to a halt in the road.

A quarter mile ahead, the first car, a boxy European Ford station wagon, braked to a halt and made a quick U-turn into the grass, accelerating toward the stalled Mercedes.

"Get that station wagon in my sights," Grimaldi shouted.

"Affirmative," the Russian said, mouth twisting in a grimace as if he were enjoying himself.

The Hind swung like a pendulum to the left to clear the Mercedes, then swung level again directly on the road and careered at the station wagon as if the vehicles were playing an unlikely game of chicken. Grimaldi laid on the 7.62 mm machine guns, and the road was ripped up by the stream of rounds that chomped into the dirt and chewed at the station wagon, drilling into the body panels, shattering the windshield and punching into the bodies of the driver and front-seat passenger. The Hind tilted and cleared the car with five feet to spare. The station wagon roared off the road and hit an embankment, then erupted into the air. It crashed to the ground and stopped moving.

"Give me that Mercedes!"

"Yes, sir," the pilot replied, yanking the Hind into

a tight one-eighty, just in time to see the three or four figures from the car diving into the tall grass.

"Shit!" Grimaldi. "Get over them! Let's see if we can flush them out."

BOLAN SNATCHED the canvas bag and the fallen LAW and sped across the airfield as the transport plane reached the south end of the runway, twisted in a high-speed turn and increased speed for takeoff. He dropped the bag and put the first LAW to his shoulder.

The four prop engines reached high revs. Bolan ignored it. He judged the distance, aimed the LAW at the open runway and fired. He watched the rocket speed through the open air and hit the open tarmac, exploding with a crack and burst of fire that sent asphalt debris flying in all directions. Bolan grabbed the last LAW from the sack. He extracted the pins, expanded the olive fiberglass tube and mounted the throwaway rocket launcher on his shoulder. His first aim was good, and as he looked down the fold-up sights, his best hope was to duplicate it with just a few yards' variance. The LAW flew away from his shoulder and hit the ground, blasting another huge pothole into the runway.

The An-26 swerved off the strip like a motorist trying to avoid a collision and rumbled into the grass, feeding more fuel to the engines. Bolan retreated to avoid the aircraft and watched it bounce in the long grass.

There was nothing more he could do except hope that the rough terrain would collapse the landing gear before the aircraft became airborne. The props whined against the cool air of the Russian grasslands, and the transport aircraft clawed and scratched its way off the ground. It increased its speed as soon as the wheels were up and it caught a second wind, speeding into the sky, weaving into a long turn and heading due south.

"Striker? We lost them. The prime targets, I mean. They escaped on foot into the grass. We'll have to go after them the same way."

Bolan said nothing, watching the An-26 fade to a dot.

"Sarge, you there?"

"I'm here. No, I don't want to go after Troschenkova on foot. He can live to fight another day. I've got other priorities."

The transport plane disappeared into the overcast sky.

CHAPTER FIVE

Xing Jifu clicked the button on his walkie-talkie. "The Russian war bird is on its way back."

"The American is looking for survivors," Kang Xiong said over the radio. "It doesn't look like he is finding any. Whoever he is, he's vicious."

"You sure he's American?"

"I'm sure."

Jifu sank into the grass. He was in green camouflage and had used olive green tape to cover the suit with tufts of grass. When he crouched, he became virtually invisible. The Hind sped overhead, off to his right by a hundred feet, and never suspected he was there. When it was well ahead of him, he turned toward the compound.

Xiong was similarly outfitted, and in the overcast morning there was no sunlight to flash off the lenses of his field glasses. He watched the American carefully, curious. The man wasn't CIA. Xiong had seen CIA agents in action. They lacked the mercilessness of this warrior. He had to be special forces of some kind, maybe a secret wild card, the kind of man no government knew about or admitted to, the kind of ruthless killer used when standard intelligence channels had been exhausted.

Xiong wouldn't want to meet him in battle. Not after what he'd just witnessed. The American had more or less taken on the Russians single-handedly. The gunship was less effective than that one man alone.

Xiong's gut became cold when the American stopped and turned in his direction, frowning, scanning the grassy field that stretched away from the compound for miles. The Chinese agent didn't move, other than to lower his glasses. He even held his breath, although from two hundred yards it was impossible the American agent could detect his breathing.

But it was impossible the agent could know Xiong was there at all. He'd made no noise, no movement, and he was camouflaged perfectly. Yet something was telling the American he was being watched.

The American continued to stare at the field as the Hind descended into the nearby tarmac. Then, reluctantly, he jogged to the Russian gunship and stepped into the rear troop compartment.

Xiong remained motionless until the Hind was a half mile from the compound.

He turned the walkie-talkie back on.

"Xiong, where have you been? I've been trying to raise you for five minutes."

"I almost got spotted."

"Almost?"

"The American left in the Hind."

"Good. Start setting up the dish. We must report without delay."

DIALING THE UPLINK, Jifu was in touch with his Beijing contacts within moments. The line was answered by a woman he had never met. In fact he didn't know the identity of any of his contacts. He only knew they were in Beijing because of a passing mention by his direct supervisor, who had ordered Jifu and Xiong on this mission.

"Operator Six," she said as if she were answering the line at an office.

"Corona Two here." He recited a string of code words for her benefit.

Operator Six didn't respond, but the clicks on the line told Jifu he was going through a series of new connections.

"Corona One," said the deep, gravelly voice of an older man.

"Corona Two reporting."

"Go ahead."

"Hardware and human were transported to an unmarked plane that left this spot twelve minutes ago. There were unexpected arrivals."

"Explain."

"The Americans got here. One American, anyway. He had the support of the Russians, who sent in an attack helicopter. The transfer of the hardware was only possible because the American was unwilling to risk the hostage."

"But the customers did get away?"

"Yes. The American tried to stop them and nearly succeeded. But the plane took off from here. Are we tracking it?"

"Is the Hind following the plane?"

"No."

There was silence. Then the deep voice said, "There was absolutely no designation on the aircraft?"

"No. But the crew was in Chinese military uniforms."

More silence.

"Sir?"

"Make your way back to the pickup point. You'll give a full debriefing to your commander, then forget this mission ever occurred. Understand?"

"Yes, sir."

THE GENERAL disconnected the line and redialed at once. "Shansan here," he said. "Are we tracking that plane?"

"Yes, general," the commander replied. "It's running along the border, but it's making a point of staying inside Kazakh airspace."

"Any evidence the Kazakhs are paying attention to it?"

"No, sir."

"You'll soon be in contact with Major Jang, air command in Urumchi. You will cooperate with him fully, and you will give his orders top priority. Understand?"

"Yes, sir."

General Shansan disconnected and dialed quickly.

"Jang here."

"Are your men ready to fly?" Shansan asked. He didn't need to identify himself.

"Yes, General."

"These are your orders, Major. Listen carefully."

"Yes, sir."

"If and when that plane enters our airspace, I want it shot down at once. There is to be no radio contact with this aircraft. I don't want there to be the slightest risk of scaring it back into foreign airspace if we get it in our sights. Is that understood?"

"Yes, sir."

"I want updates on the half hour."

"Yes, sir." The major seemed about to ask for further information.

"This is need-to-know, Major. Choose your questions carefully."

"Yes, General. I'll talk to you in half an hour."

"STRIKER?"

Bolan's eyes snapped open, although Jack Grimaldi's voice exhibited no urgency, and he entered the cockpit, taking the copilot's seat.

Grimaldi was back in his element—at the controls of a Lockheed C-130 Hercules.

Upon being contacted by Bolan the previous day, when he was still en route to the Siberian plain, Grimaldi had been rushed overseas on the Concorde, then flown into Germany, where he had picked up the C-130. After the clean getaway by the Chinese in the An-26, Grimaldi and Bolan were returned by the Russians to the C-130 and began pursuit.

The C-130 was traveling at a high altitude, but through a sparse cloud covering several thousand feet below, Bolan saw mountainous terrain.

"Where are we?"

"Pakistan. But if I was to swerve a mile to the left, we'd be in China. Our friends in the An-26 have been hugging the border the whole time."

"The Chinese still in the vicinity?"

"Oh, yeah. They're taking shifts, but they've kept at least a couple of fighters on the trail nonstop."

"Any news from Stony?"

"Not yet, but I was about to get Aaron on the horn. That's why I woke you. I'm going to need to arrange for a quick refueling. There's an airfield in eastern

Tadzhikistan that's ideal, and the Russians are running it. It won't take us far out of our way.''

Bolan nodded. "What's the risk of loosing the An-26?"

Grimaldi shrugged. "Good if they decide to land anytime soon. But if they stay in the air, we'll be able to catch up to them again just like we did over Russia. But it can't be helped. We're low on fuel. We've got to stop somewhere, and soon our options will decrease rapidly.''

"Agreed." Bolan thumbed the mike. Grimaldi was already dialed into the satellite uplink with Stony Man Farm, which was, in turn, linked to a U.S. Air Force tracking system—though the U.S. Air Force wasn't aware of it. The USAF system was keeping them locked on to the errant An-26 aircraft.

Bolan asked the tracking operator at the Farm for a transfer and found himself speaking to Hal Brognola moments later.

"Striker, sometimes when we don't hear from you for weeks at a time, I find myself wondering if you haven't bought it in some godforsaken corner of the globe. Good to hear from you.''

The Justice Department issued Hal Brognola's paychecks, but he got his orders from one man—the President of the United States. The big Fed was director of the Stony Man Farm Sensitive Operations Group, based in a top secret locale in Virginia. The Farm served as control center for the SOG's worldwide operations, which included U.S.-based and international teams of agents. Those teams, and the Farm itself, were masterminded by Mack Bolan, and at one point he had more or less worked as an employee of the Farm.

Things had changed. Bolan kept the Farm at arm's

length. It carried on effectively without him most of the time, but when a crisis situation called for his direct involvement and leadership—and Brognola asked him—he didn't hesitate to become a member of the team again.

But there were also times when Bolan became the lone wolf, on the prowl by himself, beyond the reach of whatever law existed in any part of the world. At those times he addressed his personal quarrels with those truly evil men who had no regard for the sanctity of innocent human life. Years ago his primary objective was the destruction of U.S. organized-crime families. Later he targeted the rogue elements of the KGB.

In the post-cold war world, with the influence of the Mafia diminished, Bolan expanded his scope: drug dealers, slavers, killers, exploiters of the innocent, Russian mobsters.

The Executioner had learned not to discriminate.

And sometimes his personal undertakings and the goals of the Farm achieved an unexpected synchronicity.

"We're going to be needing to make a fuel stop in Tadzhikistan. It's going to have to be quick. Our cargo won't clear customs, so we'll need to get in and out without many questions."

Grimaldi had taken the C-130 out of Alaska well stocked with hardware. Getting into Russia after a quick polar flight hadn't been a problem. The Russians were embarrassed by their loss of the U.S. government's gift and were willing to bend over backward. The Tadzhikistan-based Russian military should be just as cooperative, in theory. Bolan knew the chain of command in the Russian military was not always so dependable.

"That shouldn't be a problem," Brognola said, but

even from twelve thousand miles away, his sarcasm was evident. "Let me see if I can pull it off."

Within minutes Grimaldi was receiving coordinates for a mountainous airfield, and the C-130 descended onto a short, rocky runway. It was met by a fuel truck, was refueled in silence by a single Russian mechanic and was waved off.

"We're good to go," Grimaldi said when they were airborne again. "We can follow him all the way into the Bay of Bengal if we need to. Which we won't. No matter what kind of auxiliary tanks they've rigged up on that thing, he can't have that many more miles left in him."

Following instructions forwarded by Stony Man, Grimaldi increased speed to catch up to within several miles of the renegade An-26 aircraft, which was veering east over Pakistan, then reduced speed to once again pace it. Bolan watched the mountains beneath the aircraft grow higher, as if trying to reach up to it and claw at its belly.

The radioman at the Farm read off a list of coordinates.

"Our pilot has changed his tack," Grimaldi said. "He's just crossed the border into Chinese-controlled Indian airspace. He's heading due east."

"There's only one place he can go from there," Bolan said.

It was late in the afternoon of a long day when the An-26 reduced altitude and entered the cloud-strewed mountain landscape of Tibet.

"THAT'S POLITICALLY sensitive territory. The last thing we need is to further anger the Indian government by shooting down aircraft there," Major Jang protested.

Shansan considered this carefully for a long moment. "What's his heading?"

"Due east. He's moving into our Tibetan province, without a doubt. Let's wait and grab him there—in fact let's follow him home."

"That would be good intelligence to have," the general agreed. "All right, tell your men to keep their distance. But if that plane makes any directional changes that will take it out of our airspace, they have permission to down it, whether they're in politically sensitive territory or not."

"OUR CHINESE FRIENDS?"

"They're still up there. They seemed to get excited when we moved into Chinese airspace, but they've calmed down again," Grimaldi said.

"They're going to try to follow the An-26 home," Bolan told him. "They want to know who it is that's trying to get control of THADS. I'd like to know that myself."

"Has to be Tibetan rebels," Grimaldi said.

"They haven't proved to be well funded in the past. Whoever's in the An-26 was able to outbid the People's Republic for the hardware. If they're Tibetan rebels, they've got new backing."

"You sound doubtful," Grimaldi said. "Who else could it be?"

"I have no idea. What are we going to do if the Chinese finish off the An-26 and then decide to come after us? We're not exactly legal, either."

"With this piece of work? I can do a good job of hiding in those peaks." Grimaldi grimaced as if he would welcome the opportunity.

"Can the An-26?"

"If the pilot's got the nerve, who knows?"

The man at the control room at Stony Man spoke briefly in their headphones. The An-26 was changing coordinates.

"He must have the nerve," Grimaldi said, "he's heading into the cloud cover."

A moment later they heard the strident rush of a pair of Nanchang Q-5 air-to-air attack fighters rocketing toward the Himalayan mountaintops.

"I'VE LOST HIM," the radar man said. "He's trying to lose himself in the peaks."

Major Jang grabbed the mike. "Tell me you've still got him," he said to the fighter pilots.

"We've still got him on radar, Control."

"Stay close!"

"We're doing it, Control, but he's moving too slow for us to pace him."

"You stay on him! Stagger if you have to. Is he showing any signs of coming down?"

"No. There's no place for him to land out here, Control."

"There has to be or he wouldn't be there."

"I've lost him. He's gone from my radar."

The Nanchang Q-5 pointed up and roared into the sky, banking and turning back the way it had come before sweeping into a dive.

"I have visual sighting," the pilot announced. "Wait—that is our second plane, the C-130."

"I need a fix on the An-26," the major said over the radio.

"No visual. No radar. He is making good use of the cloud cover."

"I've got him," the other fighter pilot radioed. "Check out your two o'clock. I lost him again."

"You lost him?" Jang shouted over the radio.

"I passed him right up, Major," the other fighter pilot said matter-of-factly. "He is crawling around down there."

"I've got visual!" the fighter pilot said. He watched the An-26 appear out of a bank of clouds on a sweeping, high-altitude snow plain. At the east end of the plain a pair of peaks jutted up like two angry fingers. "He is going to crash!"

The An-26 seemed to be making a suicide run for the two peaks—its wingspan couldn't possibly clear the gap. It had just seconds to spare. It banked without warning and slid between the columns of frozen rock.

"He made it through!"

"I'm circling back," the other fighter pilot said.

The first pilot scanned the valley that had appeared beyond the twin peaks and watched the An-26 swim in and out of the clinging ground-level cloud cover like a dolphin appearing and vanishing playfully in a white-capped ocean. Brave or foolish, immensely skilled or vastly overconfident, the pilot in the small plane was taking his chances trying to navigate the valley and lurking among the hidden peaks of the Himalayas. A fresh, billowing cloud engulfed it again and it was gone.

Pilot One slowed as best he could, feeling the Nan-chang resist the strolling pace. It was an aircraft intended for high-speed maneuverability. Pilot One squinted into the clouds, which thickened and blazed white, washing out his vision temporarily. Squeezing his eyes shut, he radioed the other pilot.

"Position?"

"I'm behind you."

"I've lost him. He's got to come out somewhere," Pilot One said. In fact, he was thinking, he should have emerged already. So where was he? "Tell me when you spot him. I'm coming back around." Pilot One fed fuel to the thrusters, and the Nanchang streaked out of the valley. He pulled the fighter in a miles-wide U-turn that sent it back over the valley, over his partner below. By the time he had turned around again, the other Nanchang was pulling up from the snowy valley as it ended against a solid wall of mountain that streaked up another several thousand feet.

"I didn't see it come out," Pilot Two radioed.

"Radar?"

"Nothing."

Pilot One's monitors showed him nothing, either, and he felt the now-distinctive sluggish behavior of the Nanchang's low-speed operation. He swore silently as his eyes blurred against the fields of snow and shifting cloud cover. He found himself arriving again at the end of the valley and pulled up to put a broad margin of empty space between himself and the mountain wall.

"Nothing."

"Think it went down in the clouds?"

"Maybe." Pilot One was thinking about the sudden banking that had managed to carry the An-26 through the twin peaks. What if the pilot had made the move with more desperation than was apparent and had lost control afterward? It hadn't appeared so in the few seconds the plane was visible after the maneuver and before it became swallowed up in the clouds. What if there was an errant piece of geography jutting up from the valley floor in the midst of those clouds, a claw that had grabbed the An-26 out of the air?

Pilot One's gut told him no. But the fact was the An-

26 was gone. "Base, the target disappeared, presumed down."

"No, we just got the target on radar," Jang exhorted.

Even as he received the message, Pilot One's own radar gave an impertinent beep, and nearly at the edge of his display he spotted the green dot that marked the plane.

"I've got it," Pilot Two radioed. "Where is he?"

"He slipped by us," Pilot One muttered through gritted teeth.

"Repeat," somebody demanded.

"He knows what he's doing. He's mapped his route." The green dot was gone again. "He's not leading us on any wild-goose chase. He knows where he's going better than we do. He's got radar-safe corridors routed."

"How we going to find him, then?" Pilot Two demanded.

"We'll need help, Control."

"That's a negative," Jang declared.

Pilot One stared at his radio for a moment, then felt foolish for doing so and redirected his partner toward the last known heading of the An-26.

"I'm thirty seconds behind you," he told Pilot Two. "What are you getting?"

"Nothing. More cloud cover. I'm following his probable exit course."

"Are you men using your eyes out there?" Jang demanded.

"Affirmative. I'm coming over the last radar location now. The cover is too thick. I see nothing. Nothing on radar. I'm taking a different route. This pilot could be headed in any of five or six directions from where we saw him last."

A moment later he pulled up again. "Nothing, Control."

"Keep at it!"

"We're not giving up. I suggest you send up reconnaissance planes."

"I said negative," Jang answered.

"Even if we spot him again, we'll never be able to get a fix long enough to bring this guy down. Not unless he strays into the open. And he's designed his route so that doesn't happen."

"Keep looking!"

"We're still looking."

"Take the first shot you get."

"Zheng here."

"This is General Shansan in Beijing, General."

"Yes, General?"

"I'm speaking to you strictly under terms of Secrecy Protocol One." Shansan then rattled off a series of code words, but Zheng was too distracted to catch them all. He wasn't too distracted, however, to provide the formulaic response required, and hoped his grin wasn't showing in his voice.

"We've got a serious issue here, General," Shansan said, "one I need your immediate cooperation with."

"Yes, sir."

"We've got a plane over the Himalayas about two hundred miles from your location. It's coming in from Russia—"

"From Russia?"

"Yes. We've tracked it all the way through Kazakh airspace, and it entered our airspace just twenty minutes ago. We've got a couple of fighters up there trying to track it, and they can't do it. The bird we're after keeps hiding in the clouds and eluding our radar. We need to get that bird and take it down.''

''May I ask why, General?''

''No. I'm in no position to give you that security clearance. I'm putting my rank at risk by getting you involved at all. Frankly we can't get at this bird, and we can't waste the time needed to get the necessary aircraft to the scene quickly enough. You've got aircraft in the area that can find this thing and sit on top of it no matter what kind of maneuvers it makes. I need you to get those planes in the air now and take it down.''

''I'm on it, General. Patch your coordinates to my men while I get the necessary support in the air.''

Shansan grunted affirmatively. ''Zheng, I will tell you this much—this is a matter of grave security risk to our Tibetan territory. So you want to do a good job for the sake of your current position.''

Zheng said nothing for a moment, pretending to be weighing the seriousness of the enigmatic words, but he was grinning like a fool and was glad there was nobody around to see it.

''I understand, General Shansan.''

''WHERE'VE THEY ALL gone? This is damn strange.''

Bolan agreed. He scanned the vast, inhospitable landscape of the upper Himalayas out the window as he searched frequencies on the radio. So far he was coming up with nothing. The airwaves were silent. It was as if the pursuit had just given up.

''Maybe they decided the THADSAC isn't worth the trouble.''

''That doesn't seem too likely,'' Bolan replied, staring into the sky. The Nanchangs had played their leap-frogging game for a hundred miles in an attempt to stay on top of the An-26, ignoring the other aircraft. They had ascended and roared away north, leaving the two prop planes alone over the wasteland.

That was when the An-26 began serious efforts to shake Grimaldi and Bolan from its tail.

"They left us to keep an eye on it," Bolan said suddenly. "They couldn't do it in the fighters. So they're allowing us to do it until they can send something back that is capable of tracking it long enough to knock it out of the sky."

Grimaldi looked at him. "They're going to kill that American satellite operator, and we're going to point them to the target."

"Yeah."

"Shit." Grimaldi ascended suddenly, pulling the C-130 out of the bank of clouds that still bore the disturbance of the An-26's passage.

"We've got to somehow keep watch for the aircraft they're sending to knock out the An-26 but stay far enough away from the An-26 so we don't betray its position," Bolan said.

"Not to mention keeping from getting shot down ourselves," Grimaldi added.

The pilot allowed the C-130 to float above the level of the highest peaks, maintaining the approximate pace of the An-26, and they scoured the clouds and valleys for signs of it, simultaneously keeping an eye out for the first sign of the attack craft they knew was coming.

"Three o'clock," Bolan said when he spotted a small Chinese army prop plane, smaller than the An-26.

"They're scouting," Grimaldi stated. "That thing can't be armed. What the hell?"

Below them they briefly spotted the An-26, ducking out of the clouds like a goldfish coming up for a quick glimpse of the world outside its bowl, then settling back into the shallows of the clouds, still visible as a gray shadow moving through the mist. The newcomer responded—it banked left and right and left, signaling to the An-26 that it had been spotted.

The Chinese army plane was in league with the An-26.

"There's something here I'm not getting," Grimaldi said.

Bolan nodded. "You're not the only one."

"If the Chinese army knows about the An-26, why were the Nanchangs after it?"

"I have a feeling not everybody in the Chinese government is on the same wavelength in terms of the THADSAC," Bolan said. "If the An-26 was on a sanctioned PRC effort, they'd never have gone to the trouble of circling half the country before coming home. I think somebody in the Chinese army—or somebody with access to Chinese army aircraft—is at work here."

"Tibetans?"

"That's the most likely possibility, but I don't believe it."

"Tibetan rebels would stand to gain the most from the THADSAC. And I've heard some of those rebels have the potential to be as violent as any rebel force anywhere in the world, despite their Buddhist backgrounds."

"Agreed. But it's hard to see them getting control of Chinese army hardware, especially a plane. The Chinese would track them down as soon as they tried to take off or land it. Besides, the occupants of the An-26 were all Chinese. They didn't strike me as people compassionate enough to be sympathizers with the Tibetan-independence cause."

"What are we left with?"

Bolan's mouth was a hard line. "Somebody in the army of the People's Republic acting independently."

"Why?"

"Good question."

"SIGHTINGS, GENERAL?"

"Negative, General Shansan," Zheng said. "Are you sure the last known coordinates were correct?"

"Yes!"

"I've got ten reconnaissance aircraft flying as we speak, General. It's hard to believe we could be missing them."

Shansan uttered an expletive and disconnected.

Another message was being directed to Zheng on a secured channel, and he grabbed it.

"As sure as the sun is in the sky," said a calm voice almost in a whisper.

Zheng smiled. He didn't answer. The An-26 was still flying, still on course. If it was on schedule, then it would reach him soon.

"More than one light in the sky."

His smile faded. There was another craft in the vicinity of the An-26.

He grabbed the mike. "Who?"

"Unmarked."

Zheng frowned. Someone had to have picked up the trail of the An-26 within recent hours. It was highly improbable that the plane could have been followed all the way from Russia. Wasn't it?

He wouldn't put it past the Americans. Who knew what kind of stealth eyes they had looking down on this corner of the world. Who knew what secret resources they had tucked away.

He hesitated for all of a second before he said, "Take it down."

THE SMALL PROP PLANE gave a burst of speed and banked through a hard turn.

"She's coming up behind us," Bolan said, watching it through the side window until it disappeared, but not before he noticed the distinctive sharp silhouettes of guns mounted under its nose, out of the way of its dual wing-mounted engines. "And she's armed."

"Great. We're not," Grimaldi said, taking their craft into a dive.

"Let's get on top of the An-26."

"That's my immediate plan. We'll have to watch for the PRCAF—and get ready to bail."

"Right."

They heard the distant thrum of the twin-engined plane as it went into a dive behind them, and seconds later the rattle of machine-gun fire reached them. Grimaldi made a sudden move, and their plane went at right angles to the earth, falling like a rock and spinning lazily. The sound of the machine-gun fire turned off, and a moment later the thrum of the Chinese army plane dissipated.

Bolan ignored the sight of the white frozen planet hurtling at them and scanned the sky for the army plane. He managed to glimpse it heading off after the An-26.

Grimaldi massaged the plane out of its dive with at least two thousand feet to spare and headed back into the sky as Bolan assessed their relative position. "She headed off at about seven o'clock," he said.

The Stony Man pilot nodded and pulled the prop plane around until its attacker was in the windshield again, now a dot miles ahead. Almost instantly it twisted on its side, curved and headed back at them.

"He wants to play chicken," Grimaldi said.

"He doesn't have to," Bolan reminded him grimly. "He can knock us out of the sky before we reach him."

The prop plane aimed directly at them and began to fire from a thousand yards, like a World War I biplane reborn, tiny jets of orange fire appearing from the improbably mounted machine guns.

"Hold on," Grimaldi said, and dodged to the left, sending the plane hurtling out of the path of the bullets, seemingly out of control. Bolan felt more than heard the distinctive thunk of rounds slamming into the fuselage.

"Shit!" Grimaldi exploded. The earth swept at them again, and he played with the controls, pulling them level a hundred feet above the ground cloud cover and lifting them up again. "Damn," he muttered.

"He tag something vital?"

Grimaldi nodded. "The flaps are sluggish. I think we've got a leak in the hydraulics system, and this baby isn't built with a redundant hydraulic system like a 747."

The pilot leveled the craft again and was taking it in a long, slow turn to point it back in the direction of the action. The reconnaissance plane had also turned back, hoping they had decided to go home. The An-26 swam in the top of the clouds another quarter mile ahead, low enough to confuse radar without risking disaster every step of the way.

The C-130's Allison engines hummed along in perfect harmony, but Bolan could tell the aircraft was damaged. Grimaldi was repeatedly manipulating the wing-flap controls, sending the C-130 higher and lower in hundred-foot increments, each time more sluggishly.

"What'll we do?"

"We get out of here and find a nice wide stretch of perfectly flat rock or highway to land on," Grimaldi said, then cocked his head. "What's that?"

THE TWO NANCHANGS ripped over the mountaintops with mere yards between their wingtips and steered directly at the C-130, which was wavering like a drunk. It didn't even seem to make an effort to avoid the fighter planes, which left a wake of disturbed air in its flight path and caused it to wobble uncertainly. Then another prop plane appeared in the sky nearby.

"Aircraft number two, identify yourself!" Pilot One demanded.

"THE FIGHTERS ARE BACK—hide!" the pilot barked into the radio, then swapped frequencies in time to hear the Nanchang pilot demand identification.

The pilot spit out a series of ID numbers. "We're out of Tenzing Base."

"Why aren't you carrying any markings?" one of the Nanchang pilots asked.

The pilot began to sweat, feeling the Nanchangs slow and hover high into the air behind him. Every second they stayed in the vicinity, there was a chance they would spot the An-26 below. Any course change on his part now would add to their suspicion of him. If they checked out his numbers, they'd know something was wrong.

"We just finished major repairs," he explained briefly. "Zheng was putting all eyes into the sky."

"Is the An-26 in the area?"

"Negative. We're watching for it. We're also keeping an eye on the C-130 back there."

"Who is in there?"

"You tell me," the pilot said. "We're going to force him down as soon as we're in range of an airfield and take the occupants into custody."

He heard the Nanchangs climb above him and saw them streaking though the atmosphere another half mile above. "Let us know the second you spot the An-26."

"Will do."

"DID YOU SEE THAT?" the other fighter pilot asked.

Pilot One had seen it for a fraction of a second—a third radar blip. It was gone again.

"Affirmative! Reconnaissance vessel, are you sure you do not see the An-26 down there? We just caught something on radar briefly."

"Negative. It looks empty down here. You sure you are not reading that C-130?"

"No. This was something else. Better get out of the way. We're going down for a look."

"I've got orders to stay on that C-130."

"Move, pilot, or we'll take you down, too."

Steering the Nanchang fighters into a horseshoe, they streaked back in the direction they had come, then entered a well-controlled twist that brought them hurtling to the mountaintops. Pilot One could see the reconnaissance plane banking out of their path as hard as it was able.

"Fire if you see that An-26. Do not wait for my orders!" he reminded the other pilot as he scanned the clouds and rock.

There was a flash of gray, and the elusive little aircraft was suddenly just ahead of him, climbing out of a small valley to cover a hillock of rock that separated it from another cloud bank.

"Fire," Pilot One ordered harshly, and thumbed the button that sent a rocket flashing from under his wingtip. The projectile raced through the atmosphere in the general direction of the An-26. Pilot One pulled up, leaving it behind him a half second before the rocket would find its target.

"Firing!" Pilot Two shouted.

Pilot One heard a second explosion a moment later, then the other fighter jet was at his side, heading back into the sky.

"What happened?"

"Unknown! My weapons tracking is worthless down there! I targeted your explosion—I never even saw the An-26. It may have been completely destroyed."

"Let's go in again."

"Roger."

Pilot One steered his fighter back and down, this time with a better idea of the An-26's flight path.

"Be ready," he said.

"Ready."

An aircraft was down there, wobbling in the sky like a dying seagull.

"That's the C-130," Pilot One announced.

"I'd like to send a rocket right up that bastard's tail," Pilot Two said.

"You and me both. Stay sharp for the An-26!"

Pilot One flew over the rocky high point, which showed the scars of the dual rocket explosions. In the settling rubble of rock and snow it was virtually impossible to tell if a small aircraft had gone up in the explosions.

He crossed over the snowy dunes beyond, eyes

peeled for further signs of the prop plane until a mountainside loomed ahead of him. "Pull up, pull up," he reminded his partner, and pulled back on his own controls, bringing his fighter an extra five hundred feet higher and allowing the mountain to pass underneath them.

"Let's go in one more time," Pilot One ordered.

He was getting weary of flying in loops, but again led them in a long circuit that took them over the firing point and across the landscape beyond. There was nothing to see except the crippled C-130, which was hugging the rock faces.

"Come in, Control," he radioed.

"Go."

"The An-26 is down. Location is unclear, but she's definitely not flying anymore."

"Hold on."

The radio operator came back on to say, "Come home."

"Roger. We're out of here. Come in, Tenzing reconnaissance aircraft."

"I have you, fighter pilot."

"I don't think your friends in the C-130 are going to make it. They may have gone down already."

"Roger that, fighter pilot."

"SHANSAN HERE," Zheng heard over the secure line. "Our fighters found and knocked out the target on their own. I guess we didn't need your help, after all, General."

Zheng froze. He didn't speak and he didn't move.

"I'm sorry to waste your time and resources," Shansan added. Then he said, "Are you there, General?"

Zheng recovered. "Glad to be of assistance, General Shansan."

"I guess one of your reconnaissance aircraft is still on the trail of the C-130, but they aren't sure how much longer it can stay in the air. If you bring in anyone alive, let me know at once."

"Yes, General Shansan."

"Shansan out."

"Zheng out."

General Zheng stood like a statue in the radio room of his official base in Tenzing. The room was heated, but he could feel the cold of the concrete floor through his dress boots.

"Radio Z for you, sir," one of the operators said.

Zheng raised his phone to indicate they should switch the channel to his radio. Here it came, confirmation of his worst fears.

"Radio Z here."

"Zheng here."

"Bad news, General..."

CHAPTER SIX

"We've got to get into the valley between those ridges."

Grimaldi rubbed his hand over his sweaty forehead, wiped his hand on his chest and gripped the controls again. "If we go in, I'm not sure we'll come out."

"We've got to find out whether the An-26 crashed."

"I'm not kidding. I'm losing maneuvering integrity by the minute. If I descend into that valley, I'm not sure I'll be able to ascend enough to get us over the ridge."

"Can you land in that valley?"

"Even if I could see the surface, I couldn't land safely."

"Can you fly over?"

Grimaldi shook his head, but said, "I'll do the best I can."

The C-130 banked slightly and for a moment seemed as if it weren't going to respond, then it slowly changed its direction, heading for the center of the valley. Bolan watched the series of small peaks pass under the aircraft and squinted into the white shifting masses of clouds, ice and snow. The vast, roughly oval tract was, at its widest, almost three miles across and fully five miles long. The cloud cover was thick near the ground, thin and wispy in the ragged fingers that stretched far enough to swirl around the wings and through the props of the C-130.

"See anything?" Grimaldi asked tersely.

"I can't see through the cover. Can't you descend at all?"

"If we do, I can't guarantee we'll get out again."

"At this height we could fly right over them and not see a thing."

"It's risky!"

"Let's give it a shot."

Grimaldi exhaled. "You're the boss."

Bolan felt the engine drone decrease. He was distinctly conscious of the pilot's struggle to keep the wounded aircraft from falling from the sky, let alone obey his directives. But he also knew there was a U.S. citizen in that Chinese-made aircraft. Bolan had witnessed the rocket attack by the Nanchangs. He'd had a clearer view of it than even the fighter pilots. The rocket had exploded against the rock, and the force of the explosion plowed into the rear underside of the An-26. There could very easily have been survivors of that hit.

The landscape of dunes and windblown ridges below was empty of detail.

"Anything?" Grimaldi asked.

"No."

"I've got to start pulling up."

"Not yet."

"I've got to!"

Bolan caught a flash of darkness in his peripheral vision.

"There."

"What? Did you spot them?"

The soldier shielded his eyes and peered through the blinding white. He saw a glimpse of a gray airplane, a blackened and broken back end and a burned body in the snow.

"Did you spot them?"

"That's them—"

"I'm pulling up!"

Grimaldi fed fuel to the engines and dragged bodily on the controls. The C-130 shook and shuddered, and Bolan barely sensed the change in angle. He quickly considered the survival possibilities of a chute jump and just as quickly discarded it as suicide.

"How can I help?"

"You can't."

"There's a depression in the ridge at two o'clock."

"Impossible!" Grimaldi exhorted. "I'd need twice as much space to make that turn. We have to go up or we're going nowhere."

Nowhere just might be where they were going, Bolan thought. The wall of the mountain ridge was looming. The C-130 was ascending with glacial slowness in the thin, high-altitude air, clawing for every inch like a cat on the trunk of a slippery tree. Bolan knew they might both be looking death in the face, but he also knew that if missing that wall was at all possible, Grimaldi was the pilot who could do it.

"It's going to be close," the pilot said.

The wall was black, rocks frosted with white sheets and veined with ice, and the C-130 hurtled at it like a slung missile. Grimaldi grunted and coaxed the controls. The aircraft ascended slightly, like a small watercraft buoyed on a swell, and the pilot gave the engines a sudden burst of fuel to take advantage of it. The top of the ridge appeared in the windshield, and the plane bounced on an updraft, descended a foot, then bounced up again and streaked across the rocky ridge with feet to spare.

LIEUTENANT LI SAT UP, realized he was alive and panicked. Screaming and pushing against the mass of broken dashboard controls that draped across his chest, he dragged himself out of the collapsed seat and stood on the tilted floor, holding the walls. His breath was coming in huge gasps he couldn't control, and a long moan was seeping out of him like perspiration.

The crash had pushed the floor up under the cockpit enough to crush the captain in his chair against the wall. His head was forced against his chest, and his bullet-wounded leg protruded from the wreckage dripping blood. He didn't move.

Li yanked at the cockpit door three times before it opened, and he was blasted with cold. The rear of the An-26 was in far worse shape than the cockpit. The small cargo area had cracked on impact and ripped during the long slide across the ice. Most of the rear end was missing. None of the seats was left. Neither was any of the passengers.

He heard someone call his name and shouted.

"Captain!" He scrambled back into the cockpit. The pilot was waving a single bloody, crippled hand in the air. Li grabbed it and pulled. Jingsheng screamed in pain as his body toppled onto the floor, lying like a twisted doll.

"Help me up," he gasped.

The lieutenant pulled him onto his feet. Jingsheng grabbed at the wall and barely managed to keep himself standing, gasping for breath.

"Go help the others," the pilot managed to say finally.

"I don't think there's any help for the others."

The captain looked at him.

"They're strewed across the ice."

"What about the American and the control unit?"

Li shrugged.

"Go see."

The copilot tried to think of an excuse, then, dreading it, did as ordered. He pushed himself through the cockpit door, shambled through the ruin of the An-26's rear end and landed in the snow. His shoes and socks were instantly freezing and wet. Trudging through the muck and the metal scraps, he came to the first body. It was one of the guards. It looked as if the upper half of his torso had caught on something, and during the crash he was nearly ripped in two. The volume of blood was immense.

There were two more nearby, both still strapped in their seats and crushed underneath them.

A moan caught his attention, and he trudged to a bright yellow mass of padding and blankets. As soon as their pursuit became apparent, the captain had ordered the American satellite operator and the THADSAC control panel to be wrapped and taped in all the padding they had in the An-26.

Li stood over the woman. She was a big, long yellow mass, like a fat cigar, with only her head exposed. The padding had saved her life. The only wound that was apparent was a scrape along her hairline, which slowly dripped blood onto the snow.

She opened her eyes and murmured through the wrinkled mass of gray tape covering her mouth.

"SURVIVORS?"

"Just her. The THADSAC looks undamaged, but I can't tell for sure."

The captain twisted his head and glared at them. Li released the American woman, and she fell against the wall of the cockpit interior, dragged down by her manacles.

Jingsheng pulled on a headset and put a red wire from the control panel in his mouth, gripping it in his teeth and dragging off the insulation. He twisted the bare copper to the back of the radio box and twisted the dial.

"Base, this is X-A."

He twisted another dial and tapped the headphone mike. "Base, this is X-A...."

The pilot's head dropped almost to his chest.

"Yes..."

Li thought for a moment that Jingsheng was going to collapse.

"Li," the pilot gasped, "you take it. Talk quick. The power is shorting out. I don't know how long it is going to last." He dragged off the headset and thrust it at the copilot.

The lieutenant grabbed it, and the pilot sank onto the remains of the panel, semiconscious.

"Li here," he said, putting on the headset.

"This is General Zheng. What's the situation?"

"All the men are dead. Captain Jingsheng is wounded and exhausted."

"What about the American?"

"She's alive. No broken bones. We padded her well, and that saved her."

"What about the THADSAC?"

"It looks intact. We padded it, too."

"How bad is the captain?"

"Barely holding on," he said quietly.

"All right, Li," Zheng said. "You're going to have to handle this situation from here on. You have to get the American out of there."

"Shouldn't we stay put? Won't it be easier for you to find us if we stay at the plane?"

"The truth is, Lieutenant, I don't know how long it will be before I can risk sending up an air search. If your battery runs low, there's no way we'll be able to track you down by the time we can get ships in the air, and you may be under more or less permanent cloud cover. Your best bet for survival is to walk out. You and the American."

"Walk out? We'll never survive. We'll freeze in hours!"

"No, you won't. You'll make it. And we'll be searching for you as soon as we can."

"Are you saying you don't even know where we are?"

Zheng sighed, exasperated. "No, Li. I don't know where you are. So it might be days before I can find you. Do you understand me? The only way you're going to survive is if you get yourself out."

Li's teeth were chattering from the cold.

"You have to get out of there now, on your own, on foot. You and the American."

"What about the captain?"

"He'll never make it. You know that."

"Neither will the American!"

"She will!" Zheng shouted over the headset. "She will survive. She must! Li, you come out of that mountain without the American and you are a dead man anyway, got it? But you rescue her, and I will be substantially in your debt."

Li looked at the captain and at the mute, wide-eyed American woman.

"She's useless without the control unit," he protested.

"The control unit will survive the cold," Zheng said, the line filling with static around his voice. "She will not. After we rescue the two of you, it will be easy to track down the crash site."

Li trembled from the cold, and the speakers in his ears rattled with static. "You don't even know where we are."

The last thing he heard before the static became silence was, "Don't fail me, Lieutenant."

"WE'RE GOING DOWN," Grimaldi announced. "Hang on."

"Do you have enough room to pull this off?" Bolan asked, looking out over the expansive field of dry grass.

"I don't have a choice."

The engines of the C-130 slowed, and Grimaldi steered the aircraft over the small village that clustered near the mountain base. Bolan glimpsed figures running out of the brick-and-wood buildings, then his view of the village was gone.

Bolan trusted his pilot friend implicitly behind the controls of any aircraft, functional or not. But assessing the length of the field and the menacing incline that stopped it, and feeling the speed of the hurtling aircraft, he was convinced the aircraft couldn't be brought down safely. Airspeed had to be maintained just to keep the C-130 from stalling and plummeting to the ground like a rock. But reaching the ground with any kind of controlled landing that didn't transform into a crash was going to take a miracle.

The C-130's landing gear locked with a thud. The speed dropped further, and the craft seemed to pause, then swoop down. The mountainside became gigantic and filled the windshield.

Grimaldi fed more fuel to the craft as one of the wings began dipping to the ground. The plane accelerated and leveled. Then the speed dropped and the plane plummeted. Grimaldi swore loudly and hit the gas, and the C-130 leveled itself as the wheels touched the dirt cart path. The sound of grinding tires filled the interior, but the airplane was still rocketing toward the mountain. The Stony Man flyboy hit the brakes and steered into the grass. The plane bounced and cracked against the uneven surface, then tilted alarmingly.

"Hold on to something!" Grimaldi shouted.

The wing touched the grass and was grabbed by it like living seaweed. The wingtip cracked against the earth and held, and the body of the aircraft tilted forward on its nose. Bolan felt it become perpendicular to the earth in a manner utterly at odds with its design. He saw the grass of Tibet out the front window as they hung there, poised for a long second, as if the plane simply couldn't decide in which direction to fall.

The speed was just shy of enough, however, to send it over on its back. The plane toppled again onto its belly with the slow, steadily increasing momentum of a great tree finally being felled. It hit the ground, crushing the landing gear, then collapsed on its stomach with a splintering of metal and crashing of glass.

"GET TO YOUR FEET."

Elise Lim rolled painfully onto her stomach and pushed against the floor with her handcuffed hands. The floor wasn't right, and she couldn't quite understand why. She tried to stand, but when she did her balance didn't work and she toppled into the wall. Halting at an odd angle, she tried to breathe through her nose. She wished fervently that someone would remove the tape over her mouth so she could breathe normally.

Her wish was granted when she felt icy fingers against her cheek, and she opened her eyes to see the copilot standing over her. He ripped at the tape savagely. It felt as if the flesh were being sliced off her body with a knife, but she could breathe again, really breathe, and she took in the cold, moist air in great, clean gasps.

The grip of the frigid air in her lungs cleared her head, and all at once she remembered everything: the hijacking, the helicopter trip, the plane journey that seemed to go on forever, the pursuit of fighter planes, the explosions, the crash.

Lim was wrapped up in blankets and padding and had suffered extreme claustrophobia, but was thankful for the padding when the plane crashed. She slammed into the roof and wall and was only shaken, and when the rear end of the plane ripped off, she was flung into the outside with the others.

But she was alive; the others weren't. She realized that now. The only people left alive were herself and the two who were in the cockpit.

Her hands were being unlocked. The copilot—his name, she recalled, was Li—held a small handgun on her with one hand as he removed one of the cuffs, then stepped back.

"Wrap yourself in blankets as best you can."

"What's going on?" she asked.

"We're getting out of here."

"Where are we going?"

"Down the mountain."

"What do you mean?" Jingsheng demanded.

Li didn't look over his shoulder, keeping his gun on Lim. The pilot was behind him in one of the cockpit seats, slumped like a boneless fish and barely conscious. "I have orders to take the American down the mountain."

"Why not stay here and wait for rescue?" the pilot asked.

"Our position is unknown."

"They aren't coming for us?" Jingsheng asked, his voice filled with terror.

"They will be coming," Li replied through gritted teeth. "But it will not be safe for them to put up an air search for some time. And we're under cloud cover. It may take them days to locate the plane. You—start putting on blankets if you don't want to freeze to death!"

Lim took the tape and the blankets used to cushion her during the crash and began wrapping them around her as best she could.

"Li," the pilot said, "I can't walk."

"I know."

Lim stopped what she was doing. "You mean you are going to leave him here?"

"Don't leave me here, Li."

The copilot waved the gun. "You shut up!" he said to the American woman.

"Please, Li. Don't leave me."

"I'll leave you plenty of blankets."

"Blankets! I'll need more than blankets! I'll need fire to survive! If you leave me here, you condemn me to freezing to death."

"No, you'll be all right."

Lim bent and used a shard of ripped metal from the

wall to tear holes in the middle of three of the blankets, then she passed them one by one over her head like ponchos. She took others and wrapped them around her shoulders. It was a stroke of luck that she had worn her black jeans the day of the hijacking—they were tough and reasonably warm. Against the cold of the high-altitude Himalayas, though...

The pilot was sobbing now.

"Don't leave me, Li. Please don't leave me."

"I have my orders. Are you done?"

"I need something to tie around me to hold these closed," she said, holding out her arms to show how her makeshift coat left gaping openings under her arms.

Li considered the problem, then ordered her to clasp her hands. He recuffed her, then used long strands of the used tape as rope, tying them around her body and knotting them to hold the blankets in place.

He got to work himself. Taking a cue from Lim, he cut holes in blankets as she had done and made himself poncho layers, tying the gaping openings with strands of the used tape. The captain was sobbing quietly against the ruined dash of the aircraft.

"Let's take him with us," Lim suggested.

"Shut up."

"I've been thinking. We can cut up blankets and twist them to make rope and use it to drag him, like a sledge."

The pilot looked up, silent now, his eyes pleading for mercy.

Li didn't even look at him. "No."

"We can't just leave him here!" Lim cried.

"We can and we will. Our chances of getting out alive are slim enough as it is."

"It's unthinkable to leave him here to die!"

"There is no choice."

"Li, it's a good plan," the pilot said. "I'm not a big man. You can just drag me over the snow. It won't be so bad."

"Shut up!"

"You," he said to Lim, "one more word out of you and I'll put that gag back on."

Li looked around the small, chaotic interior of the wrecked cockpit, as if making sure there was nothing he had forgotten, but without meeting the captain's eyes.

"Let's go."

"Li," the captain begged, "please!"

Lim looked at him. "Where is your humanity, Li?"

The lieutenant shoved her and she fell against the rear cockpit door, which gave way. She tumbled through it and half slid, half rolled, landing on her face in the snow. The cold was so sharp against her skin it was like burning flame. As she maneuvered herself awkwardly to her feet, the snow clung to her skin and melted, seeping into her makeshift coat at the neckline. The breeze whistled over her, and the chill knifed through her body. She looked into the expanse of cloud, barely able to see the dark shape of a distant mountain looming over the field.

Li emerged and slammed the cockpit door behind him, then stood beside her in the snow.

"Let's go."

"I can't walk in these." Lim held up her hands, still in their manacles. Her legs were bound with steel chains.

"I'll take them off." He bent and used his keys on the chain cuffs, then unlocked the manacles and stepped away quickly.

"Come on."

He walked into the snow.

Lim dragged off the manacles, dropping them, then balled up the chain and, impulsively, as fast as she could, stuffed it into the front of her shirt. She gasped at the horrible icy cold of the steel against her bare flesh, but stifled it when Li turned in her direction, and walked after him.

"We're going to die in this," she said matter-of-factly.

"Shut up. Shut up or I'll just shoot you dead right now and you won't have to worry about it."

"You'd be doing me a kindness."

Behind them she heard the faint sobbing of the pilot. But the wind whistled in her ears, and before long the sound faded.

"HOW MANY ACTIVE-DUTY men are aware of my sideline activities?" General Zheng asked.

"About sixty, sir," said Dai Jian, his assistant and second-in-command.

That didn't sound like enough.

"All right. What are your plans?"

The group of nervous-looking men approached the table with rolled maps and began to spread them out before Zheng. The topography charts were shades of gray, white and blue and were more or less meaningless to him.

One of the men took a red grease pencil and drew a large oval on one of the maps.

"Our search area," Jian said. He wasn't in a uniform, as he was no longer in the PRC military, unlike the others in the upper echelons of Zheng's organization. The general had recruited him when he was an army major and, after working together for two years, he arranged for Jian's "accident." China now considered Jian dead.

Zheng liked the idea of his second-in-command having no true life outside of his own organization.

"Based on what?" the general asked.

"Based on what we know of the approximate position of the An-26 when it went down. Our plan is to start by deploying ground-based search parties. We can start at villages in the search area and procure local guides."

"Do we need guides?"

"Yes. The mountains are dangerous, and the ways in and out are unpredictable. Having someone with expertise can only increase our chances of getting our men in and out of the wilderness areas quickly and with minimal danger. They will save us a lot of time."

"Agreed."

"Once the ground-based searches are under way, and once we feel it's safe to put up air searches, we use our helicopters to go hunting under the cloud cover. We start here, then here." He drew a small oval in the center of the map and another outside it. "If we have not yet located it, we search this entire perimeter."

"That could take weeks," Zheng commented.

"Yes. Without more air support…"

"No. We can't afford to use any of the legitimate aircraft. I've been specifically ordered not to engage in a search for the downed plane. I can't afford to arouse suspicion that I am doing so. We use only unofficial equipment in this search, is that clear? No marked matériel."

Jian and the other assistants nodded.

"This is not an efficient plan," Zheng said, obviously

irritated. "We need a strategy for finding the survivors in twenty-four hours. I do not believe they will survive longer than that."

His assistants looked at one another in dismay. "But it is the best we can come up with without more resources," one ventured.

Zheng stared at the huge red oval. "Proceed with the search. But I want a more efficient strategy worked up soon."

NEARLY EVERY NONGLASS surface of the two massive, Soviet-built Hind gunships was painted a light gray color, so when they approached in the hazy, overcast sky, it was as if they were invisible except for the great dark circle made by the rotors, like some dark halo.

Slowly, almost with a sense of resignation, the villagers emerged from their stone-and-grass houses and watched the massive attack helicopters hover outside their village, then descend quickly, with a purpose. Five soldiers in heavy coats and carrying heavy packs, in addition to their Kalashnikov rifles, emerged from each of the choppers, joined into a single group and marched to the village.

Sampen Zhu, sitting on an old wooden chair in front of his house, looked up when the ten Chinese soldiers approached the village center and stood in the street. The helicopters behind them took to the air and flew back the direction they had come. That was an ominous sign.

Sampen Zhu said nothing. He didn't doubt that the Chinese would make their purpose known soon enough.

"We need a guide," one of the Chinese said to the small throng of onlookers standing about a rickety wooden gate. "Who is the best guide in this village?"

The villagers seemed perplexed and discussed his words among themselves.

"Come on! I don't have time to stand around! Who is the best guide in this village?"

"Guide to where?" one of the people asked.

"Into the mountains," he said, pointing vaguely with his rifle into the mass of black stone and white ice that forever looked down on the village.

If the villagers were perplexed before, now they were mystified, but they apparently knew better than to ask why the crazy Chinese wanted to go into the frozen mountain.

"Sampen Zhu is the only one who knows his way on that mountain," one of them said.

Unlike others in the village who had his number of decades behind them, Sampen Zhu's hearing had not yet faded. He listened to the entire exchange, so he knew what the Chinese wanted when they swarmed like a street gang around the front of his house.

"Sampen Zhu?"

"Yes?"

"We need you to guide us into the mountain. It is a grave matter of the utmost urgency."

"I think you're wrong. There is nothing up that mountain but rock and ice," Sampen Zhu said, trying to keep the concern out of his voice.

"There's been a plane crash," the Chinese soldier explained. "We are the rescue party. We need your help to get us to the top."

Sampen Zhu nodded then. That was a different story. If it was true. He had no reason to trust the Chinese.

On the other hand, there was no way the Chinese could have learned about the small, old temple remains that existed far up the mountainside. And the Chinese had reversed their policy of cowing the Tibetan people through the destruction of their temples. These days the Chinese were trying instead to control the Tibetan people by controlling their religion.

So maybe there really was a crash on the mountain. Sampen Zhu could certainly think of no other reasons the Chinese—or anyone—would be motivated to go up the mountain.

"I can't help you. You see, I'm old now. I haven't been up the mountain in four years, and the last trip nearly killed me. I don't have the strength."

"You don't have a choice. National security is at risk."

"Tibetan national security? Or Chinese national security?"

"Father!"

The soldiers leveled their weapons when the figure came running through the village. The old man waved his hands to them. "It is my son—he is harmless. Put your weapons away."

The autorifles stayed where they were. The young man came to his father's side and faced them fearlessly. "What is my father accused of?"

"Nothing. We are not arresting him," the captain said. "We need him to lead us up the mountainside. There has been a plane crash, and there are survivors. We need his help to get up there."

"Why don't you just go in your helicopters?" the young man demanded.

"The helicopter search is under way. This is the ground segment of the search, and we are taking your father."

"You can't. He's an old man and he hasn't been well."

"We're taking him. We need a guide and he's elected."

"Take me instead," the young man said. "I'm fit to climb the mountain, and I know it well enough. I've been up there time and time again with my father."

"That's not true," the old man said. "He has only been up the mountain with me on a few occasions. He doesn't know the paths."

"Father!" the young man protested.

"That's enough," the Chinese captain growled. "I don't want to hear more of this. I'm taking the old man, and that's the end of the matter."

"You will not. I won't allow it," the young man said.

"Quiet now," the old man ordered. "I am going and you are not. That is *my* decision, and you will abide by it." His voice was low and steady, but obviously potent with authority. The young man bowed his head.

"I will gather the things I will need for the trip," the old man said, and took his son into the tiny building.

CHAPTER SEVEN

Sampen Sonam alternated between watching the mountain pass where his father and the Chinese had disappeared and eyeing the two guards remaining in the village. They were setting up camp in an abandoned house whose owners were killed two years earlier in a scuffle with the Chinese.

Sonam was feeling a familiar sensation—the emotion that came of helplessness. His father might be as good as dead. He was too old and weak for climbing into the cold, rugged mountains. But what could Sonam do?

The answer, as always, was nothing. He couldn't fight. To fight, his father had always said simply, was to spit into the face of Buddha.

Besides, look what had happened to the man who had lived in the abandoned house. He had tried to use violence to protect his wife from Chinese soldiers. They shot him dead. Now that family was shattered and the woman lived in shame and sadness in her sister's house.

He wondered if he didn't defend himself because he was afraid, or because he respected his father's words. Or was it because Buddha taught him not to fight?

He couldn't truly answer those questions, which made him more miserable than ever.

Then he spotted a wagon, pulled by a single cow,

approaching through the low pass. The pass cut through the mountain almost due west, so that at that time of day, when the sun was going down, it sent a shaft of light up the pass after it no longer illuminated the rest of the mountain. The pass held the one trail from the only nearby village, and when he shielded his eyes from the blazing dusk, Sonam recognized the man driving the cart as a resident of the village, a good man named Doma Thubten.

Sonam heard a shout as one of the Chinese soldiers spotted the wagon and raised his AK-47. His partner emerged from the house with his own weapon, and they strode purposefully down to intercept the new arrival. Sonam pictured Thubten being shot down in cold blood, just like the villager who was protecting his wife, and he jumped to his feet and strode after them without a clue as to what he intended to do.

"Stop. What are you doing here?"

Thubten appraised the soldiers without alarm. "I've come to visit my friends in Ghaze village."

"Why?"

"Why not?"

"What is in the cart?"

"Straw, mostly," Thubten replied.

"Leave him alone!" Sonam said. "It is no crime for him to come and visit us in this village?"

The soldiers hadn't realized he was there and they turned on him with their weapons. For a fraction of a second Sonam thought he was looking death in the face, and his heart seemed to stop in his chest.

"What are you doing here?"

"I came to see my friend Thubten, what else?"

"Get out of here!"

"What has Thubten done?"

The soldiers didn't answer, and one of them backed up off the cart path so that he could keep Sonam, as well as the cart, in his field of vision. "Go check out the cart," he told his companion.

Sonam noticed that the village was full of people, standing outside their homes, watching the altercation, maybe wondering if Sonam had lost his mind. He was wondering that himself.

The soldier strode to the rear of the cart and jumped up, poking at the straw with the AK-47.

Sonam suddenly found himself watching the most amazing scene he had ever witnessed.

A hand reached up out of the straw and snatched the AK-47 out of the hands of the shocked soldier, who gave a shout of alarm. Two feet emerged and tangled themselves in the ankles of the soldier, who flew backward out of the cart as if catapulted. A second figure was already standing up in the rear of the cart, straw flowing off him like water, a dark, massive man, faceless with the sun setting behind him. He held a massive handgun, and he swung it into firing position, but Sonam couldn't tell it he was going to shoot himself or Thubten or the second Chinese soldier. The soldier was bringing his AK-47 into target acquisition, as well, and the path of the bullets might cut across Thubten or the dark giant.

The black handgun thundered in the grip of the dark giant, then thundered again. The AK-47 remained silent. The soldier's chest exploded, and he slammed into the ground, dead before he hit the earth.

The dark figure pivoted to where the fallen soldier was snatching for his own handgun, which was strapped at his hip. He pulled it out and aimed it at the cart, and Sonam thought that the dark man was as good as dead.

He surely didn't have time to react. The two handguns fired simultaneously, and the prone soldier's biceps turned to pulp. He tried to scream, but before the sound left his throat the cart gunner fired again, and the soldier's face caved in. The scream came out in bubbles of blood.

The village of Ghaze had never been so silent as it was in the moments that followed.

The dark figure held the black handgun ready in his hands, as if he couldn't wait to find more targets.

"How many Chinese in this village?"

Sonam struggled to find words. "None now."

"Whew," said the second man, who was sitting up with the AK-47 still in his hands. "You speak English?"

"I speak English. I'm the only one still left in Ghaze village who speaks English," Sonam said. "Are you Americans?"

"Yes," the dark killer replied.

The two men extracted themselves from the cart. The one who spoke was very tall, built like a mass of hard rock, with dark hair and cold blue eyes. The other man was thin, with a weathered expression that seemed much more prone to a smile or a laugh than his big, somber companion's.

"We need a place to spend the night. And we're hoping to hire someone who might be able to guide us into the mountain tomorrow morning," the big man said, his voice quiet but commanding.

The man came across as a soldier in his own right. Both the strangers were wearing automatic rifles across their backs, and the big one had at least one more handgun holstered under his open jacket.

Sonam came right to the point. "I assumed you are

enemies of the Chinese soldiers who went up the mountain earlier today to search for the plane-crash survivors."

The Americans exchanged glances. The big one said in a voice that belied no deception or hesitancy, "Yes, we are their enemies."

Sonam nodded. "Then you are welcome in my house."

"I HAVE TO STOP." Elise Lim rested her body against the boulder jutting out from the mountainside and closed her eyes briefly. The sun was colored in dusk and turned the clouds of the high snow valley pinkish yellow.

"Keep moving," Li commanded.

"I'm exhausted. I need to rest."

She peered into the bright clouds. The wreckage of the An-26 aircraft couldn't be more than a couple of miles away, and yet it was completely hidden. She wondered if the wounded pilot had frozen to death yet.

She tried not to feel sorry for him. He was just as ruthless as the copilot, Li, just unlucky enough to be the one wounded. Had their roles been reversed, he probably would have been no less eager to leave Li to die in the cold mountaintop valley.

Still, the mercilessness of the act shocked and outraged her, and her rage was aggravated by her helplessness.

"Come on."

"Look, you know we're not going to make it, Li," she said.

"I know no such thing."

"We have no food, no fuel for heat, no containers to carry water. We're wearing a bunch of ripped-up blankets that are nowhere near good enough to protect us from the cold—''

"I know our situation," Li reminded her.

"Now it's nighttime, and we have no protection from the cold or the wind. How are we supposed to sleep?"

"Who said anything about sleep? We're going to keep moving. If we keep moving, we'll keep our body temperature up. We can rest when we get down to a warmer altitude."

"I'm already freezing and tired. I can't possibly keep going for even one more hour, let alone all night! You're insane if you think I can keep going and going until you say it's time to rest. I need food. I need to be warm."

"Well, you aren't going to be, so you might as well get used to the idea. If you try to sleep in the snow, you will freeze to death. You have to keep moving. You have no choice."

He gave her a shove. She glared at him, but with a sinking sensation in the pit of her stomach she realized he was right.

She had to keep moving despite the cold, the already gnawing hunger and the dry-mouthed thirst. Her only other option was death.

SAMPEN SONAM WAS in his early twenties, a strong, solid young man with a smoldering fire in his eyes. He also had a good memory, and mapped out the nearby mountains with confidence, although he had done little exploration of the surrounding Himalayas with his father since his father entered his fifties.

Sonam had a pot of soup and a loaf of bread he was intending to eat this night with his father. Instead he shared it with the strangers as they looked over his map.

The young man pointed out the valley and the village they had just come from. From there the slim American was able to easily track their path by air.

"This is the approximate direction we came," Jack Grimaldi said, drawing a line with Sonam's pencil. "This is another peak, right? We flew to the north of it and headed southwesterly over this series of peaks until we came to the valley where we landed. That means here is the valley where the An-26 crashed."

Bolan nodded. "You know this valley?" he asked the young Tibetan.

"Yes. I've even been there with my father, ten years ago."

"What's the likely way out if you were marooned there?"

"The only way out is a pass right here." He marked a spot on the eastern edge of the valley. "Once they take the pass, they will follow the mountain down for a long way—the way is narrow. But then here—" he ticked another point on the map "—the way becomes ambiguous. They could go any of four or five directions from there."

"If I was trying to get to that point from this village, what way would I go?"

"Like this." Sonam showed their current position in Ghaze and indicated a path leading away from the village into the mountainside.

"Doesn't look too far," Grimaldi said.

"Far, no. Hard, yes," Sonam told him. "This village is at the edge. From this point on, the way gets very hard. There are no trails after a little way. You have to get around cliffs and chasms and avoid the false ways that lead to dead ends. You need me to lead you."

"I was hoping you would volunteer," Bolan said.

Sonam had related to them the earlier arrival of the Chinese and their abduction of his father. "But there is danger involved."

"I know that. I grew up in Chinese-occupied Tibet, remember? I know what the Chinese soldiers are capable of doing."

"Good. Think you can remember the best ways through the mountain?"

"Yes. Though not as good as my father," Sonam declared. "And the Chinese have a head start."

"But we have a better advantage," Bolan reminded him. "We know where the wreck is. They don't. They only know they're in the vicinity, so they're working on the basis of broad-based search. We're operating with a specific destination in mind."

Sonam nodded. "Going on that assumption, we can hazard to guess where the Chinese might have directed my father to lead them. If we know that, we can probably get around them without them even knowing we are there, and get to the survivors first."

"Hopefully," Bolan said. "I don't think they're going to just stay put and wait for rescue. Too great a chance the rescuers will be the Chinese government. They'll run. Once we get into the upper levels, we'll be searching as blindly as the Chinese."

"But you'll be way ahead of the Chinese at that stage," Grimaldi commented.

Bolan nodded. "If everything goes as planned."

"You're not coming?" the Tibetan asked.

Grimaldi shook his head. "Your friend with the cart, Doma Thubten, has agreed to take me into the nearest city where I might be able to arrange a new set of wings. We'll need some way of getting the American survivor out of here if we find her."

"If she's alive, we'll find her," Bolan stated.

THE DARKNESS CLOSED IN, but the moon came out behind the high haze and turned the expanse of snow and the low nighttime clouds into a glowing silvery mass. Under any other circumstances, Lim thought, she would have looked on the scene and been awestruck by its natural yet ethereal beauty. Instead she looked on it and saw her own death.

She had never been so miserably cold, and she felt as if her bones and teeth were rattling in her body. Her feet felt soaking wet and as if the skin on her feet were starting to freeze into a crust of ice. Her cheeks and hands were frigid. But the worst cold was in her torso, a chill that had wormed in through her makeshift parka and finally entered her chest and stomach and made her body quake.

She heard Li trudging through the snow behind her. She realized now that the man was right when he maintained that there would be no stopping to sleep. Stopping was an impossibility. If she was to lie down and slow the circulation of blood in her body, she would freeze within hours.

But she also knew that she was already growing weak. The lack of rest and the nonstop tension of the past eighteen hours were taking their toll. Sooner or later she was going to lie down and sleep whether it killed her or not.

She wondered how long it would take to reach that level of misery.

MIDNIGHT. THE GRASS of the Tibetan valley was short, coarse and low to the ground, unlike the grasslands they had left in Russia. The moon shone on it, and the grass

became a sort of pale gold. It was easy to see the wagon
carrying Grimaldi and their new friend, Doma Thubten.
He was a middle-aged, almost monosyllabic Tibetan
who asked no questions— but something he read in the
manner of the two Americans had to have rubbed him
the right way. He was willing to take Grimaldi to the
nearest city. Bolan watched the wagon mount the top
of the hill and disappear behind it.

He dragged the heavy fur coat over his blacksuit and
shrugged into his new black pack, which had come in
Grimaldi's plane along with a multitude of fresh supplies.

"Ready?" Sonam emerged from the house with a
massive coil of rope on his shoulder and a sack of supplies.

"Yeah. Let's go," Bolan said.

Sonam left his house behind without a backward
glance, and the Executioner let him lead the way
through the village. He would have thought the collection of stone-and-wooden buildings ended at the mass
of rock and earth that protruded like a gigantic wart on
a massive thumb from the mountainside. Sonam crossed
to the side of the wart and started up a set of rocky
steps that looked half natural, half formed by human
hands. Walking up the steps took them to the top of the
outgrowth. From there Sonam turned to the mountainside and strode up a barely visible trail that led up a
slight ledge.

The wind grew colder.

GENERAL SHANSAN STRODE directly across the airfield
into the secure room. The two guards outside the room
saluted and demanded his identification nervously, as

per the instructions he had delivered over the phone to their commanding officer.

The two pilots stood at attention when he entered. He saluted and sat at the desk, allowing them to remain at attention while he made himself comfortable. Then he said, "I ordered that you be placed in a secure room without any contact with any other officer until I arrived. Were my orders carried out?"

"They were, General," the first pilot stated.

"Good. After this interview, everything about your mission tonight will be considered top secret and highly classified. You may discuss it with no one of less than general's rank in the military of the People's Republic of China. Is that understood?"

"Yes, General."

"Yes, General," the second pilot added.

"We will discuss every step of your mission today, including the behavior of the unidentified C-130 and the behavior of Tibetan forces who assisted. You will ask no questions."

"Yes, General," both pilots stated.

"Good. Let us start at the beginning."

SONAM HALTED AT THE BASE of a sheer, smooth cliff face that jutted out of the mountain. He put his finger to his lips.

Bolan froze and listened, hearing nothing. But he withdrew the silenced Beretta 93-R and scanned the rocky landscape.

The way behind them and ahead was composed of vast bare stretches of sheet rock and occasional patches of cracked and shattered gravel. He stepped into the open and swept the field for any sign of movement and spotted nothing.

The big American turned back to Sonam, who carefully pointed directly above him. Bolan craned his neck to the top of the cliff.

The sheer face stretched up about a hundred feet, then seemed to stop. There might very well be a flat shelf up there where gunners could hide. The Executioner watched, hearing and sight tuned to a high level of sensitivity, and detected nothing.

"They may not have even reached that point yet. It's hard to say how fast a team like that will be moving," Sonam said. "But I know my father. He is not a user of ropes like I am. He would direct the search party to take the path all the way out to a point a kilometer to the north of here and then back—it is the long way."

"The shortcut is straight up?" Bolan asked.

"If you can handle it."

"I can handle it."

Sonam walked along the wall with his hand brushing against it at shoulder level. He stopped at a pair of steel pegs, as wide and crude as tent stakes, hammered into the rock with a notch cut into the exposed end like a fishhook barb. Not far above that was another steel peg, and Sonam reached up and snagged the rope in the notch.

He dragged himself off the ground with the rope and stood on the lower of the two pegs, then reached for another peg high above him.

Bolan took the end of the rope and pulled himself up, past Sonam, the single peg at his shoulder level, disengaged the rope from it, then pulled himself up to stand on it. From that point he was able to find the next level of steel peg, and he pulled himself up again, then paused to allow Sonam to come up behind him.

They leapfrogged, each taking the lead for two or

three levels at a time, the other resting below. It was a crude method of climbing, but it was working.

When they were at approximately seventy feet, Bolan reached up and notched the rope in the next spike. He gave the rope a test yank, and the spike was uprooted, flying out of the cliff face with a shower of cracked granite and flinging into the open space. It tumbled through the sky and hit the rocky floor with a clang that Bolan knew might be audible for miles.

The mountain answered with silence.

Bolan searched for the next-highest spike and found it, a full five feet out of his reach. He grabbed the loose end of the rope and flung it at the spike. The rope tumbled against it and fell off. The big American looped the rope and flung it again and dragged on it, snaring the notch with the rope and setting it firmly. He gave it a tug, then leaned on it. Finally he trusted his two-hundred-plus pounds to the flimsy piece of steel and scrambled up the sheer cliff face.

The added impetus of possible detection took them up the remaining distance in minutes. Bolan allowed Sonam to climb ahead for the final stretch, but with a tug on his cuff signaled him to wait before scaling the top.

Bolan dragged himself up the last few feet and withdrew the Beretta 93-R with one hand while hanging by a rope-wrapped wrist from the final spike, set just inches below the top of the cliff. He pulled himself up to eye level with the cliff top and hung poised there for the three or four seconds it took for him to fully reconnoiter the landing. The mountain overhung it, making dark moon shadows and even darker alcoves. But they were all cold and empty.

The Executioner grabbed at the cliff edge and hauled

himself onto it, stuffing the Beretta in his holster. Then he groped for Sonam's wrist and hauled the young Tibetan up beside him.

Sonam glared into the darkness, then allowed himself the luxury of panting. "What an ordeal!"

"But well worth the effort if we saved time."

The Tibetan grinned. "We did, my friend."

Four hours later they reached the snow line. By then the moon was lost behind a mountain, but the footsteps in the snow were as visible as if it were daylight.

ELISE LIM AWOKE in the daylight.

She was standing up, leaning against the rock and solid ice wall in a slight depression where Li had directed her to get them out of the stiff breeze that had begun to blow. They had yet to become immune to the cold. If anything, every hour of exposure made them all the more sensitive to it, and even a breeze increased their torture. She had huddled into her blankets and rested against the wall, closing her eyes for a moment's escape. It was dark then. But when she awoke—surely it was just a few minutes later—the world was growing gray and soft with dawn. She had actually slept standing on her feet.

Li was watching her.

"Too bad it's too cold to get naked," he offered with a stiff leer.

"You're not serious?" she said, disgusted to the core. She marched out of the depression and into the open stretch of snow-covered rock that served as their pathway down the mountain.

For the first time since her forced march began, they were at a point where she could see for a great distance. Before her stretched the rising and falling landscape of mountains, and although she was at the highest point for miles and miles and looked down on the valleys, she could see nothing that hinted at civilization: not a dot of a building or a wisp of smoke, not even the smallest speck of wildlife roaming or swooping through the mountaintops. They were alone in desolation.

The sleep, whether it was for a few minutes or an hour, had refreshed her, and she was determined not to think about the unfathomable distances that might lie ahead. She scooped a handful of snow and sucked on it, trudging on her way.

She was determined not to give up until she was dead.

"Where're you going?" Li shouted.

"Down. I thought that was the idea."

"You go when I say."

"Shoot me if you want to stop me, Li."

He huffed and marched behind her.

GENERAL ZHENG INSPECTED the wreckage of the C-130, which was spotted by one of the Hind crews during a wide sweep that had never intended to uncover it.

"We've combed the wreckage. There's nothing of value inside. The registry is to a British individual, but it looks like that is going to turn out to be a nonperson," his assistant said.

"What did the villagers have to say for themselves?" Zheng asked, gazing about the smashed interior of the craft, which appeared to have nonfunctional hydraulics. The pilot had landed without flaps. He was very good or very lucky or both—the crash had obviously not been fatal to the occupants.

"Nothing, really. And what they say is probably lies."

"We have no one in this village?" Zheng said.

"No. Who'd have thought we would ever have need of one?"

Zheng stared down the grassy, rocky valley, cut in two by a cart track. It extended north into the village, then cut through a small path beyond it. Southward it snaked through the mountains to a paved road ten miles away.

"They said the crash survivors went south?"

"Yes."

"Then we can almost be assured they went north."

"Yes. Which, incidentally, General, takes them to a village called Ghaze. One of our ground-search parties went to Ghaze to recruit a guide into the mountains."

Zheng nodded. "Bring me some of the villagers—teenage males. It is time we did some recruiting in this village."

ZHENG HIT PAY DIRT on his second interview.

In every Tibetan village he was able to find at least one young man who could be purchased. These people made so little in a year—in a lifetime—that it was easy to flabbergast them with what had to seem to be incredible riches.

But Zheng considered his information cheaply obtained.

"We're looking for two men. Probably Americans," Zheng reported over the radio from the rear of the first Hind as they took off from the valley. "If they're CIA, they won't admit it and they won't have any ID to that effect. They traveled to Ghaze in a cart with a local named Doma Thubten. I want two jeeps to go after them. I want those two Americans in custody by the time I sit down to lunch. Understood?"

"You don't want us to go after the Americans?" the Hind copilot asked.

"No. They're on a farmer's cart. They're going nowhere. I want you to find my airplane."

Something else occurred to Zheng, and he pulled the mike back to his face. "This is Zheng again. I want this entire area isolated. All communications cut off. Got it?"

"Understood."

THREE HOURS LATER Thubten and Grimaldi reached their destination. The town clung to a steep hillside along the dirt trail, which became twice as wide and well packed in town. At the west end of the village, highest on the hill, was a small brick octagon.

"Public building," Thubten said shortly, pulling his cart to a stop in the grass along the trail side.

"Good enough for me," Grimaldi replied. What he cared most about was the black telephone cable that extended from the roof to a series of poles disappearing down the hillside.

What they hadn't been able to salvage from the wreckage of the C-130 was any useful communication equipment. But one phone call would link him again with the world as he knew it.

Stepping from the cart, the thin pilot peered up and down the road. A few locals were out and about. No one looked interested in him. He entered the public building with his quiet farmer friend.

Thubten spoke a few succinct words to an old man who had been sleeping in a weathered leather chair behind an ancient desk. Grimaldi pulled out a twenty-dollar bill and placed it on the desk. The sleepy man grinned. Grimaldi was again thankful that U.S. currency could be spent in almost every nation in the world. Even in Tibet the black market preferred American dollars.

Grimaldi picked up the ancient black phone and heard silence.

He rattled the buttons in the cradle. Nothing.

"It doesn't work," he said.

The man behind the desk took the receiver from him and put it to his ear, then frowned and spoke in Tibetan.

Thubten translated. "He says it was working last month."

CHAPTER EIGHT

Bolan heard the crack of a 9 mm handgun at the same instant a rock shattered within arm's reach. He thrust himself into Sonam, bearing him into the rock wall along their path.

"Stay put," Bolan ordered.

He dragged the .44 Desert Eagle from inside his coat and stepped into the open with it raised above his head, firing without hesitation when he spotted a hand emerging from a protective rock barrier sixty feet up the trail. The rock shattered and the hand disappeared, its owner shouting. Bolan knew that was no fatal hit and bounded up the trail. A man in a Chinese army uniform emerged from behind the rock with his right hand bloodied, but he had the gun in his left hand and directed it at the Executioner with an expression of pain and rage.

Bolan triggered the Desert Eagle on the run. The massive Magnum round drilled into the soldier's chest and punched him backward into the rock. He didn't feel it; he was already dead.

There were cries up the trail, and Bolan spotted the familiar profile of a Type 56, the Chinese knockoff of the AK-47. He crouched beside his first victim as the rattle of the Kalashnikov filled the mountainside, cracking against the stones under the thin snow layer on the trail. He targeted the wall at the emergence point of the AK-47, spotted movement and fired again. The rock shattered, and the assault rifle disappeared. Bolan rose to his feet with a curse, knowing he'd failed to score. Bolting in the direction of the gunner, he was gambling he would surprise the soldier with his openly aggressive attack. He was also cognizant of being utterly exposed.

The figure appeared around the corner and spotted the big American rampaging up the slope. He aimed the AK-47 as Bolan slid into a crouch and leveled the Desert Eagle with two hands. The AK-47 rattled out its death message, and the .44 Magnum handgun boomed twice, cutting the autofire short. The soldier dropped the rifle and staggered two steps before collapsing.

The Executioner ran to the corner of rock the gunner had used for cover and peered around it, spotting more gunmen, and he drew back just as they opened fire. The rock face began to shatter under a barrage of automatic-rifle fire.

Bolan let them waste ammunition.

After a moment the shooting stopped, and he heard voices retreating up the mountain. He waved back to Sonam, who picked his way forward around the two fresh corpses.

"It'd be ideal if we could get ahead of them somehow. Will we have an opportunity in the near future?"

Sonam shook his head. "No, but as we climb, the way is less level, much more rough. We'll have some chances, maybe, but the way will be very open, too. It will be hard to maneuver without being seen."

"That's what I'm afraid of. I'd like to leapfrog them before we get to that stage. We have to get to the survivors first."

"They might not even go up the way we do," Sonam

said. "Soon they'll have many choices. If they have a less accurate idea where the crash is, they will probably choose the wrong way."

"I would rather remove them from the equation altogether."

"You would rather kill than allow them to live?"

"If it will protect us and the innocent person I'm trying to save."

"That is very cold-blooded."

Bolan didn't bother answering. He chanced another look around the corner and saw the way clear.

GRIMALDI AND THUBTEN followed the man from the public building down the dirt road, passing a dozen houses before stopping at a home built with a small protective roof next to it. Under the roof was an ancient motorbike. Grimaldi looked it over and decided that it might still be operable.

The owner appeared at the door a moment later, blinking sleep out of his eyes as he spoke, and soon he and Thubten were engaged in low-key negotiations.

"He says he'll take two hundred U.S. dollars for the bike."

"Does this thing even start?"

The owner grew excited and brought out a key, which he inserted into the ignition. The bike coughed and began to putter.

"Tell him I will give him three hundred if he throws in that can of gas and forgets he ever even owned this motorbike or ever saw me."

The owner became even more excited and forced the key into Grimaldi's hand. They used a hide strip to tie the faded red plastic two-gallon gas can to the rear of the bike, and the pilot handed over the cash.

Thubten laid a deceptively flat-looking road map out on the dry, cool earth.

"This is Nyima, the nearest city of any size," he stated. "They have many phones there. Its elevation is much lower than here."

"Good. How far are we talking?"

"One hundred kilometers. Maybe one hundred twenty. I've never been there."

"May I take this?"

"Please."

"You've put yourself in a lot of danger for me," Grimaldi said, shaking the Tibetan's hand.

Thubten grinned. "My danger doesn't compare to yours. Be careful, my friend. The Chinese are always buying eyes."

Grimaldi stepped onto the scooter and headed onto the dirt roadway, starting down the mountain.

At least, he thought, it would be downhill to Nyima from here.

BOLAN CHECKED HIS WATCH. It was ten o'clock precisely. He extracted a small walkie-talkie from his pack, tuning it to the frequency he and Grimaldi had agreed on. "Jack?"

He was answered by static.

It was unrealistic to expect his friend would have managed to get back to the mountain by this time anyway, even if he'd had phenomenal luck in finding a phone and contacting the Farm. Bolan had a limited battery in the radio, and they had agreed he would check for Grimaldi every hour on the hour. On an unused frequency it would be unlikely anyone would be listening for them.

"Slow," Sonam said, and Bolan saw the path cut

through a break in the rock. Farther ahead the soldier saw the inclined path came to an abrupt end at a pile of rocks, the result of an old collapse.

"We go over those rocks?"

"Yes. But beyond are good hiding places."

Bolan surveyed the walls that hemmed them in. To the right, where the jumble of rocks had separated from the mountain, were ragged scars and ridges.

"I'm going up that way. They might not expect it."

"I'll go with you."

"Keep your head down."

Bolan led the way on to the rock wall, cautiously finding footholds amid the crumbling stone. He was tempted to bring out the autorifle strapped to his back—that very capable piece of hardware, found among the C-130's arms stash, would be ideal against a band of hardmen tucked among the rocks. Instead he pulled out the Desert Eagle, which was operable accurately with one hand while holding on to a rocky perch.

As he reached a point where he could see over the tumble of boulders that cut off the mountain pathway, he looked for signs of the Chinese.

Beyond the pile of rocks that blocked the way, there was rubble, rising and falling piles of broken boulders. Next to one of them leaned a single Chinese soldier. His autorifle was placed in firing position on the rock that partially protected his torso. He'd chosen the spot well. If they had approached over the pile of rock, they might not have seen him, but he would have been able to fire at them with virtual impunity. He was watching for them, obviously expecting them to come over the rock rise at any moment, his concentration so intense he failed to see the brief appearance of Bolan's face on the mountainside.

The big American ducked back out of sight. He replaced the Desert Eagle in the hip holster under his fur coat and withdrew the Beretta 93-R. The handgun was custom suppressed and fired subsonic 9 mm parabellum rounds. It was equipped with a 20-round magazine and, with the flick of a switch, could be reconfigured from single shot to 3-round-burst capability. Its unique appearance was augmented by a second grip placed under the muzzle, giving it the look of a shrunken machine gun. Indeed, its capability could be compared to that of a small machine gun, with added precision and the advantage of suppression.

Still, Bolan knew the shot he was going to attempt was a tricky one. The subsonic nature of the rounds, further compromised by the suppression, made long-distance sniperlike aim a challenge.

He lay on the irregular rocky face with the Beretta 93-R in front of him and crept slowly over the gravel, his immediate goal to get into firing position without advertising his presence.

The Chinese gunman waited patiently in his position, his attention unwavering.

Bolan gripped the 93-R in two hands and aimed it, taking advantage of the luxury of time, feeling out the occasional stiff, cold breeze.

Then time ran out. As if alerted by a sixth sense, the Chinese gunman looked to his left and spotted the dark figure lying partially exposed on the mountainside. Bolan saw the man's mouth drop open as he raised his autorifle. The coughing retorts of 93-R came so fast they almost blended into one sound. Rock shards shattered from the boulder protecting the gunman, but Bolan allowed the recoil of the rounds to carry the handgun up, and the travel directed the second round into the gunner's chest and the third into his throat. The gunner released the AK-47, which clattered on the rocks, then slumped on his protective boulder, covering it with his pulsing blood.

"Let's move," Bolan ordered, and crawled quickly down the mountainside on the far side of the tumbled boulders. He leaped from boulder to boulder until he came to the soldier. The rock on which he slumped was coated red. A quick check assured Bolan the gunman was no longer a consideration. He shoved the body into the shadowing hole in which he had been standing, then crept on top of the rock and peered beyond it.

The Chinese were eating their rations in a depression among the boulders, with another guard posted on a rise in the boulder beyond them. There were five total, as expected.

Bolan chose his weapon now for effectiveness and power, not stealth. He extracted the Desert Eagle, checked the magazine and rose to a crouch on the boulder, leveling the big gun at the guard standing in the open beyond the companions he was supposed to be guarding. He registered the appearance of the Executioner with a look of shock, but without the reflexes that might have enabled him to jump behind cover. The Desert Eagle roared, and the .44 Magnum round crashed into the guard's rib cage with the subtlety of a sledgehammer.

Bolan didn't watch the guard fall, instead turning his weapon on the soldiers crouched in the rocky depression. He targeted the first Chinese his sights fell on, and the side of the man's face exploded. He fired again, and the lower half of the skull seemed to disintegrate.

That was all the time he had. An autorifle cut loose with a burst, and Bolan dropped, allowing the torrent of 7.62 mm rounds to drill into the boulders, then ricochet away. He glimpsed Sonam, several yards behind and below him, sinking into a crouch like a hermit crab withdrawing into a shell.

The big American listened as the gunfire paused, started up and paused again. His enemies were waiting for further reaction from him, and he wasn't going to give it to them—not until he heard them moving. The sound of boots scraping against rock reached him, and he rose into firing position. This time he spotted an old Tibetan man getting pulled over the rocks, followed by a Chinese gunner. The man was leaping out of the depression, which was now a trap. Bolan fired and the .44 round hit the Chinese gunner midjump, crashing through his hip and flipping him into the rocks. His skull impacted with a tremendous crack against the unforgiving stone, and his companions disappeared behind the boulders.

"IT'S ONE OF THE MEN with the ground-search party out of Ghaze village," the radio operator said urgently. "They're under attack."

"Give me that!" General Zheng snatched the mike from the operator. "What's your situation?"

"This is Wan Zhi—"

"Where's your captain?"

"Dead. We're getting massacred up here!"

"What do you mean massacred?"

"I mean there's just three of us left out of the eight we started with. We've got a whole squad on our tail."

Zheng digested that unpleasant information. Five of his men dead in one morning?

"Are they Americans?"

"I think they're locals. They sure know the terrain.

We've only seen one of them, and he's dressed like a Tibetan. We need some backup up here, fast!"

"You've got it," Zheng said. He signed off and considered his options for all of a second.

"Raise our men in that village."

"I was just trying, sir. They are not responding."

That didn't bode well, either. "Try again."

Zheng was growing angrier with every passing hour of this fiasco. One calamity after another was plaguing him.

"No luck," his radioman said.

"All right. First dispatch the nearest Hind to the position of the ground search. The gunship is ordered to break off its search and offer support to the ground team for now. They are instructed to take out anyone on that mountain not recognizable as under my command."

"Yes, sir."

"Then get eight more men into that village. Once this squadron on the mountain is taken out, we'll replace the men they've lost."

The door opened abruptly, and Jian entered, looking concerned. "What's going on?"

Zheng glared at him. "More disaster."

GRIMALDI FOUND that the scooter, a decades-old, Chinese-built unit, warmed up like an old television, after about forty-five minutes of continuous travel. But it was designed for the streets of flat cities like Shanghai or Canton. The ups and downs of Tibet tested its muscle. Grimaldi found himself leaving the machine out of gear during the long declines and accelerating to the highest speeds the tiny engine was capable of to get up the periodic inclines.

He estimated he had traveled eleven miles out of the

town after leaving Doma Thubten when he spotted another long incline coming up. He brought the scooter to top speed as he reached the bottom of the hill and managed to coax it three-quarters of the way to the top before it slowed and threatened to stall. He stepped off and put the machine in neutral, not daring to turn it off for fear it might not start again, then walked it the remaining distance up the incline. At the top of the hill the road started down again, and by the lay of the land he was optimistic it would continue down for some time, but the road itself curved behind a house-sized boulder that had tumbled from the mountain.

There was dust in the air.

It was slight enough that he didn't even notice, but it bothered him, at first almost subconsciously. Someone had to have traveled on this road in the past several minutes. But Grimaldi had seen no one traveling on the road all morning. It suddenly occurred to him that if he was to put a watch on this road, behind that boulder would be the perfect place.

He kicked down the stand on the bike and left it running. If the noise was reaching whoever was behind that boulder, they'd be suspicious if it stopped. They might already be wondering why it was staying at the top of the hill and not continuing down the road.

Grimaldi pulled the suppressed Uzi machine pistol from the holster under his coat. He stalked through the brown, shaggy grass along the roadside, slowing as he reached the rock, where he stopped and listened.

He heard nothing: no whispers, no movement, just the steady, cool breeze of Tibet whistling in his ears.

He stepped onto the rock and grabbed at a ragged shard protruding from it, hoisting himself up and clambering to the top. Then he stepped to the far side quickly, finding himself looking down on two Chinese soldiers, huddled with their own motorcycles, AK-47s held ready.

"Hands up," the pilot said.

The Chinese were startled, and one of them turned on him, bringing his AK-47 around in a tight arc in the confined space he'd given himself, but he never leveled it at Grimaldi. The Stony Man pilot triggered the Uzi before he came into the sights of the autorifle, and the weapon stuttered in his hands, stitching the chest of the soldier with 9 mm rounds that flung him back into the motorcycles, which collapsed underneath him.

The other soldier was yelling in Chinese, but his hands were in the air, holding the AK-47 by the stock.

Grimaldi motioned with the Uzi, and the soldier tossed the weapon into the grass. He waved in the other direction, and the soldier walked into the middle of the road, where he waited while the pilot clambered to the ground and bent to assure himself the man lying among the cycles was permanently out of the picture. He was.

Grimaldi pulled out a pair of plastic handcuffs and tossed them to the soldier, who grimly put them on.

"We're going up to my bike," the pilot said with a wave.

The soldier understood and began to walk uphill, Grimaldi following at ten paces.

What was he going to do with this guy?

The question was quickly answered. The soldier ran, pumping hard against the slope.

"Stop," Grimaldi called out.

Then he saw the soldier heading for the scooter. Visible on the frame was the Browning Hi-Power, which the pilot had situated for emergency use.

"Don't do it!"

The soldier didn't hear him, or didn't understand him. He had to know he was committing suicide.

He grabbed for the Hi-Power with his cuffed hands and yanked it free.

"Stop right there," Grimaldi shouted.

The soldier turned, his finger on the trigger.

Grimaldi fired the Uzi at the last possible moment, and the Hi-Power flew out of the soldier's hands. He curled over, lost his balance and pitched onto the road. Gravity took him and he rolled over and over, legs flopping limply, until he came to stop against the pilot's feet, looking up at him. The Uzi was aimed squarely at his forehead.

But firing again would have been a waste of ammunition. The soldier was dead.

Grimaldi dragged the corpses behind the rock and tucked them away. They weren't exactly hidden, but they wouldn't be spotted accidentally. A quick examination told him both the motorcycles were undamaged from their collapse, and he chose the newer looking of the two to replace the scooter. Still not a full-sized motorcycle like one that might be found on North American highways, it was a definite upgrade in terms of speed and power from the scooter. Strapping the gas can to the back of the bike, the pilot sent the riderless scooter down the incline to the north of the dirt road. It rumbled out of sight and was gone with the sound of collapsing metal. The other motorcycle followed it.

The scene was clean. It was less than fifteen minutes since he'd first arrived, and Grimaldi considered his situation improved as a result of the encounter. The motorcycle thrummed to life, and he sped down the hill, leveled out and accelerated up the next incline, luxuriating in the feel of power.

The Stony Man pilot thought of Bolan on the mountain, facing an unknown number of enemies with the added burden of the debilitating cold. He had extreme confidence in the warrior, but under those conditions anyone could be taken off guard.

He pictured Bolan struggling through the cold, searching for the plane-crash survivors, fighting for their lives, as well as his own—and calling Grimaldi every hour on the hour. Only the pilot wasn't there to answer the radio signal.

He gunned the engine. He'd get back to that mountain if he had to steal air transport from under the noses of the Chinese army. He wasn't going to disappoint his closest friend in the world.

They'd have to kill him first.

THE THUNDER of the Soviet-built gunships echoed across the vast fields of ice, pounding them as if from every direction. Sampen Sonam clutched his fur mittens to his skull and squeezed his eyes shut. Bolan crouched beside him in the natural rock lean-to until the sound receded, then he crawled out and stood, searching for the helicopter.

"Come on," he said, giving Sonam a nudge with his foot.

Bolan led the way quickly, scrambling over ice-coated boulders and sheets of crusty snow until he spotted the Hind making a descent. He stopped and watched it land in a small valley that stretched out before them, and he made out the shapes of the members of the search party crouched against the rock, shielding their eyes from the flurry of ice crystals being raised by the tremendous rotor blast. When the helicopter was resting on the valley floor, the rotor wash decreased suddenly and the side door opened. The search party emerged to greet the newcomers.

"Who are they?"

"Probably reinforcements," Bolan muttered, withdrawing field glasses from his pack and watching the activity. The odds against him were going up again. The number of men had increased to seven, not counting the old man.

"Can you see my father?" Sonam asked urgently.

"Yes."

"How is he?"

"Hard to tell," Bolan said. He didn't want to worry the young Tibetan. The truth was that Sampen Zhu was crouched wearily away from the group, haggard and pale. But nothing could be done for him. Not yet.

The newcomers had arrived with supplies. New backpacks, it looked like. They took out maps and pored over them briefly, pointing and speaking rapidly, while Bolan considered his options. There were seven men down there now, and he was just one man. A sound strategy was required.

The Executioner's inner alarm clock went off, and he checked his watch to confirm it was the top of the hour. Pulling out the radio, he flipped it to the agreed-upon frequency and listened—just long enough to confirm that no one in the vicinity was using the frequency. There was only a low crackle of periodic static.

"Wings?" he asked into the radio finally.

There was no answer.

"They're moving out," Sonam announced.

"So are we."

THE MOUNTAINSIDE GREW dark early when the sun sank behind it, although to both the north and the south was evidence that the day still existed in some parts of the Himalayas.

The search party decided to make camp. They weren't going to see or accomplish much in the dusky shadow. Dawn would come early enough.

The tents were army mountain tents, self-contained units with floors and frames that allowed them to be set up anywhere. They weren't state-of-the-art, looking heavy without being warm, but the search party crawled into them eagerly after heating a dinner of soup over a small propane burner.

The tents were tucked into flat spaces between boulders, and one man set up watch sitting on a sleeping bag with his back to a boulder on the west side of the camp, as if he wanted to have the entire huge mountain to protect him. And protect him it did; Bolan saw no way to get close.

His companion was another matter. The second watchman sat at the southeast, tucked between boulders, wrapped in his own sleeping bag and shivering. The man seemed to be far more interested in keeping warm than in protecting the camp. He put his automatic rifle on his lap and snuggled into the sleeping bag with his hands wrapped up inside. If an attack came, he would need several precious seconds to get himself extracted from his cocoon.

Bolan crept through the rocks and ice on all fours like some improbable winter spider, making his approach with an emphasis on stealth, and found himself in position on the boulders ten feet above the shivering guard. He retreated momentarily when he saw the guard on the opposite side of the camp stir and adjust his blankets around him. He, at least, was keeping his automatic rifle in his blankets with him, at hand. He still wasn't so alert he was going to save his own life. In fact being the more alert of the two meant he was going to have to be the first to die.

Again the Executioner was forced to utilize the 93-R as a sniper's weapon, a task for which it wasn't intended. The range was long, and the dusk made targeting difficult. But it was the only suppressed weapon for the job.

If Sonam's father hadn't been present in one of the tents, Bolan would have probably just rolled in some of the explosives, picked off the guards, then gunned down any and all survivors. Sampen Zhu served as a de facto hostage. Bolan wouldn't risk the old man.

So he was forced to wage a war of attrition.

He found a comfortable position on a boulder and, leaning forward on the rocks above the wrapped-up guard, and focused on the more distant guard. He laid the 93-R across his forearm, which was braced flat on the frigid stone, and sighted on his target.

The guard may have been careful, but he didn't have the sixth sense many warriors possessed—the intangible ability to detect imminent danger. He never felt the Executioner's eyes on him, never heard the round that killed him. The 93-R coughed one time, and the guard was pushed back with a thump that had to have been the sound of his skull hitting the rock. Bolan adjusted the shot minutely and fired again, and the guard leaned forward, limp and still.

Only one man was near enough to hear the suppressed gunfire, and now it was time to address that problem. Bolan rose from his crouch and aimed the gun at the guard just a yard beneath him, who was scrambled awkwardly to get free of the sleeping bag.

The 93-R chugged twice and the guard collapsed to the ground.

CHAPTER NINE

Another village lay along the dirt road, the last stop before the paved road that would take Grimaldi to Nyima. The village was placed inside a narrow pass, flanked on either side by steep gorges. It was the only way through. The Stony Man pilot was nagged by the assurance that if another watch was posted it would have been located here, and he pulled the motorcycle off the road before entering the town. This time he didn't have the advantage of an overlook, but he quickly discovered he didn't need one. The pair of PRC soldiers strolling the single street was very apparent.

Grimaldi weighed his options.

He couldn't just ride into town. He'd be arrested or shot on the spot. But he had to get through and he had to take the motorcycle with him. Nyima was still twenty-five miles to the east.

He decided to leave the bike outside of town and come back for it later, when the way was safe. That was about as far ahead as he could plan. Missing from that plan, of course, was strategy for actually neutralizing the threat in the town.

Tucking the bike in a hidden spot off the dirt road, he studied the leisurely circuit of the guards. They were walking back and forth across the bare street between the two buildings that marked the entrance to the village. The villagers were few and far between, giving the soldiers all the space they could ask for.

Occasionally the soldiers would turn and stroll a little way into the village, bored, but their vigilance was obviously centered on the road coming into town. It was almost as if they were expecting him.

The last buildup of rock suitable for hiding a man was a few hundred yards from the village, and Grimaldi was already there. Between it and the village was nothing but the scrub grass of the lower Himalayas.

One of the soldiers headed for a building, while the other turned away and began an unhurried stroll in the opposite direction.

Grimaldi didn't weigh the possibilities. This might be the only decent opportunity in hours, and he took it, breaking into a sudden run across the low grass, which whipped at his feet. Only when he was well into the open did he consider that the man patrolling the street might turn at any moment. Or the second soldier might have entered the building to use the bathroom and return in a minute. Or there could easily be more soldiers inside the two buildings fronting the end of the village, who were even now watching him and bringing him into their gun sights....

The wiry pilot closed to within a hundred yards before the second soldier emerged. He spoke loudly enough to get the attention of his companion.

Grimaldi had no choice but to drop. He sprawled in the grass, feeling foolish—he was highly visible. If they looked in his direction, they couldn't help but see him.

The second soldier approached the first, holding something in his hands. They joined in the street and stared at whatever it was—a girlie magazine maybe—

and Grimaldi began a frantic crawl on his elbows, heading for the rear of the nearest building.

The soldiers laughed and turned in the other direction, walking aimlessly. Grimaldi stood in a crouch and bolted, trying to keep one eye on the soldiers and another on the terrain. He drew his Beretta Model 92-F on the run.

One of the guards turned, and a fraction of a second later the line of sight between him and the pilot was cut off as Grimaldi sped behind the building. Then he stood with his back against it, thinking fast. Had the guard spotted him?

He rounded the corner, heading to the back of the building. It was a large stone structure, and behind it the ground was patchy, sloping at a steep angle for a dozen feet before reaching the edge of the gorge and plummeting out of sight. A careless slip, and Grimaldi would find himself sliding into that gorge. Striker and the Farm would never know what happened to him.

He trained the gun on the corner ahead of him, came to a skidding halt on the dry earth and stepped around it. Then he twisted back to the corner behind him, in case a soldier was coming after him that way. Both ways were empty. He slipped around the corner and approached the street, then stopped to peer around the front corner, where the guards had been.

They were gone.

They could only have gone to the first two buildings, unless they had bolted into the middle of the village the moment they spotted him, which was unlikely behavior, he decided.

There was a window along the rear wall of the building he was using for cover, and he backtracked to it, standing high on his toes to peer inside. The double glass panes stood open. Grimaldi thought the weather was brisk, but maybe this was balmy weather to a Tibetan. He leaped for it, the 92-F still clenched in his hand, and clung to the windowsill with his arms, pulling himself up with a surge of adrenaline and making a lightning-quick survey of the room before hauling himself into a sitting position on the sill.

The room was a bedroom to several people. A rusty steel bed frame with bare springs and a bedroll stood at one end, and more bedrolls were propped against a wall, along with a beautiful hand-carved wooden desk, scattered with papers and dominated by a smiling Buddha.

The door was crude and wooden, cracked open six inches. Nothing could be seen in the hallway beyond. Nothing could be heard, either. Grimaldi stepped into the room and headed into the hallway.

He stopped, staring at a little boy in the large room at the end of the hall. The boy was sitting on the floor, staring toward the front of the house.

Grimaldi took another step forward and spotted a second boy, also sitting on the floor. Maybe they were having class.

So why was no one talking? Were they meditating?

Then he saw noticed the expressions, and there was nothing contemplative or relaxed about their faces. Those little boys were scared to death.

And then somehow, despite his silence, he was noticed. The first little boy turned his head and looked directly at him.

A shout erupted from the front of the room, and Grimaldi knew one or both of the guards were there. There was a sudden volley of automatic-rifle fire, and the children screamed. The wall less than two feet in front of

Grimaldi exploded under a torrent of rounds, and he bolted back the way he'd come.

He swore silently as he burst into the bedroom. There was no way he was going to return fire into a room full of kids. He slammed the door behind him and jumped through the window, grabbing on to the sill to control his leap. He landed on the dirt directly under the window and crouched there. Above him he heard the slam of the door along with what sounded like orders shouted in Chinese. A single head protruded from the window— enough for Grimaldi to make out the soldier's uniform—and he triggered the 92-F twice. Both rounds counted, slamming into the soldier in the rib cage at a sharp angle, cutting up through his chest and slicing through heart and lungs. The soldier stiffened and dropped.

Grimaldi headed out in a bent-over run that took him around the corner of the building on the west side while behind him he heard a barrage of autofire. He was counting on the second soldier's reluctance to make a quick approach, but if he happened to make a reckless run for the window, he'd spot Grimaldi and have a clear shot at his back for a full second.

It didn't happen, and the Stony Man pilot dived around the corner, then edged his way quickly to the front of the building, where there were sudden screams. He had an irrational fear that the second soldier was hurting the children for whatever reason. But no, the kids were just terrified and running from the building, scattering to their homes, crying, and Grimaldi spotted mothers and fathers racing into the streets to grab their children and haul them to safety.

The Stony Man pilot stepped to the front of the building and moved to a single four-paned window, glancing inside. The front room was indeed scattered with the paraphernalia of a grammar school: paper, pencils and books. There was another Buddha sitting on a wooden shelf in the far corner. It had to have been in his line of sight from the hallway, but he didn't remember seeing it. It smiled at him through the dusty window, and then the gleam of light on it shifted slightly. Grimaldi stepped across the window quickly and waited at the front door. The shifting light could only have been the second soldier—unless, for some reason, one of the children was still inside, or the instructor. Had Grimaldi seen an older person fleeing the building?

He'd have to be sharp about this one, and patient. He couldn't and he wouldn't risk shooting an innocent person. If it meant he had to stand there exposed to the enemy in order to identify him, in fact, as an enemy, then so be it. If he got himself shot dead in the process, well, then he would be dead. Death was preferable to living with the blood of a child on his hands, or even the blood of a harmless village teacher.

He heard a faint scuffle come through the door. Was it made by a careful soldier or by a lightweight human being?

He felt the sweat beading his forehead. He inhaled deeply, calming his nerves.

Then there was another sound, another slight noise like the shush of feet on the floor, just inside, just inches away.

Grimaldi moved fast, stepped into the room and dropped low, grabbed the little girl with his left arm and dragged her to his chest and extended his right arm, firing once, twice at the surprised-looking soldier. The 9 mm rounds slammed into the man's shoulder, and he twisted, collapsing into the wall.

But the soldier recovered quickly and raised his AK-47.

It didn't even occur to Grimaldi that he might be about to die. The little girl was screaming. He didn't have time to push her away as the soldier whipped the automatic rifle into firing position.

The Stony Man pilot fired the 92-F again, and the round drilled into the soldier's gut, a second shot ripping into the crook of his firing arm. The man dropped the AK-47, staring into the distance, and slid against the wall to the ground.

Grimaldi stood, releasing the little girl, who was now sobbing silently.

"It's all right now," he soothed.

She probably didn't understand, but looked up at him, realizing he wasn't going to hurt her.

Grimaldi changed the 92-F's magazine and pushed through the door to examine the stone building across the street. He doubted there were more soldiers inside, or they would have fired at him when he'd come around the front of the building.

A stooped, white-haired local was moving toward him cautiously.

"How many Chinese soldiers are stationed in this town?"

"Two only. They hurt my granddaughter?"

The little girl rushed into the old man's arms.

"There are more coming soon," the old man stated. "They said so. They said we could expect to have the company of the Chinese army for a few days."

"Which direction did these two come from?"

The old man looked up, pointing a single crooked finger into the empty blue sky.

"Right. Well, I'd keep everybody at home. The Chinese aren't going to be happy when they get here and find the mess I left for them.''

"Who are you?"

Grimaldi shrugged. "The less you know, the better off you'll be, I think.''

The old man nodded.

Grimaldi ran down the dirt road and grabbed his motorcycle, quickly thrumming it to life and riding into the settlement, where he found the old man standing in front of a house, the only villager in sight.

"Can you tell me the route to Nyima?''

"Yes. You'll take the right fork in three miles, then continue east when you hit the paved road,'' the old man said, then grinned with a mouth full of broken and missing teeth. "I'll tell the Chinese you took the left fork and went west.''

The Stony Man pilot raised one hand and accelerated out of the village.

SAMPEN SONAM HUDDLED in his furs and wondered if his companion would survive to return to him.

This man was unlike any he had ever known. The Chinese soldiers could be wantonly cruel, yes. But this American was merciless. He had no compunction about killing evil men, as if killing were something he had done many times before, as if violence were a familiar and everyday element in his world.

Violence wasn't a part of Sonam's world. He was raised by a father who firmly believed in Buddhist teachings. Violence in all cases was wrong. All life was sacred, and it was better to allow another man to kill you than to defend oneself with like violence.

When he was a boy Sonam hadn't questioned these

beliefs. Deep in his heart he still saw them as correct and ideal.

But the world wasn't ideal. Tibet's situation was far from ideal. Tibetans were dominated by the Chinese, who had stormed into their mountainous nation and seized it as their own. They had ripped down many of Tibet's holy places and replaced its government officials with its own. Tibet and the world cried out in protest, but the Chinese ignored them.

Ironically, Sonam understood at some level, it was the passivity of the Tibetans that had allowed this invasion to occur. If the Tibetans had aggressively defended themselves, the Chinese would probably not have been able to justify the efforts and resources needed to subjugate the Himalayan nation.

That fact hadn't gone unnoticed by the new generation of Tibetans. Young men, especially, saw a need for violent opposition to the Chinese invaders, because no nonviolent efforts were making any progress toward expelling them.

Sonam, in his tiny village, far from the centers of fomenting discontent, was long in coming to the point where he agreed with the philosophy of the rebels. But finally one day he had told his father that he thought the violent opposition was justified.

Sampen Zhu was horrified and outraged.

Violence was never justified, he declared, seething in his own quiet manner. Those who enacted violence in the name of Buddha were worse than the Chinese, who at least claimed only secular motivation for their atrocities.

Sonam had never seen his father so bitterly disappointed in him, and at last he acquiesced and allowed his father to think he was convinced.

But secretly he wasn't, and he wouldn't speak out against the brave men who he heard were taking up arms against the Chinese occupiers.

And now this man had arrived, a foreigner, a warrior who took lives from men as if he were collecting eggs from chickens, a fighter, an executioner. On the one hand this killer was the antithesis of every wise word Sonam's father had ever spoken. On the other hand, Sonam realized, this man operated under a strict moral code. And as repelled as he was by the American's methods, he also had learned a deep admiration for him in just a few short hours.

A corpse fell out of the sky and landed within arm's reach of Sonam. It was a Chinese soldier, his chest exploded and covered in dripping blood, eyes wide open and staring, retaining an expression of horror with which he had died. Sonam stifled a scream.

The American landed next to the corpse.

"I'm going to need your help, friend," he said.

"WE SPOTTED A BODY, General, but can't tell who it is."

What did that mean? General Zheng grabbed the mike from the radio operator. He had sent up the Hind first thing in the morning to offer assistance to the search party out of Ghaze, which had lost two more men in the night. Both men had been on guard duty. One was shot dead, taken by surprise to judge by the fact that he was still in a sitting position. He was killed by someone using a suppressed weapon, judging by the fact that the kill shots weren't heard by those in the tents.

The other guard was simply gone.

"What do you mean you can't tell who it is?" he radioed the Hind copilot.

"He's facedown in the snow. He's got a fur coat on. Could be anybody."

"Could be a trap," Dai Jian muttered, standing nearby.

Zheng was thinking that himself. "Could there be anybody in hiding in the vicinity?"

"Negative. We've already searched. He's lying in an ice field. He's a hundred meters from any boulders, and even those aren't hiding anybody. We checked."

"What do you think?" Zheng asked Jian.

"I don't like it, but I guess if they've found the area clear, it ought to be safe enough going in," Jian said. "Unless our adversaries have carried sniper rifles up the mountain with them."

"Or a rocket launcher of some kind."

"I wouldn't put that past them, either, but if they've got heavy hardware like that, they would have tried to take the chopper out during one of its fly-overs. If they weren't close enough for a tag then, they aren't going to be close enough to use it now."

Zheng nodded. "Agreed." He brought the mike to his mouth. "Go ahead and check it out," he instructed the Hind.

"You want us to recover the body?"

"Only if it is alive."

"Got it."

BOLAN WAS SUFFERING from perhaps the most intense cold he had ever known. It was seeping into his body from all directions, and it seemed as if he were being frozen alive.

Which was more or less the case.

The worst part of the sensation was that he couldn't move a muscle. His plan depended on remaining unseen, and that meant staying perfectly still under the snow.

He had planted the body in the ice field in the darkness. Sonam had helped him find the ideal spot to enact his plan, which involved flinging the dead guard spread-eagle on his face in the snow and then burrowing under it to wait for a Hind gunship to come in.

He knew it would come, especially after the search patrol radioed in their latest losses. Bolan stayed as warm as possible by standing next to the body in the open field of well-crusted snow, only getting into position when he heard the approaching thrum of the gunship. He sank down into an impression he had dug for himself several feet from the body, directly under where he expected the Hind to land, and quickly scooped the snow back over him. The cold was shocking, and he only overcame the intensity of it by concentrating on the task at hand. Unfortunately the task at hand had so far consisted entirely of waiting and watching through the tiny openings in the snow left for his eyes.

Eventually the chopper circled, and the belly of the Hind swung over him, hovering and circling in the vicinity. They had spotted the body but were searching for an ambush force hiding in the rocks before landing. If they descended too low, the rotor wash would whisk the snow off him and make him a clear target for the 7.62 mm machine guns mounted under the nose of the attack helicopter.

The Hind appeared again, directly over Bolan, and began a swift descent. The Executioner watched it come down, feeling patches of the snow get blown off by the rotor wash, although the heavy, icy nature of the old snow and the fact that the Hind was indeed descending almost directly over him minimized the blowing. He watched the wheels, trying to judge their path. If the massive weight of the chopper was to descend on Bolan, it would crush him in two like an insect sliced by a scalpel.

At the last minute the pilot adjusted his landing, and Bolan saw the aircraft move almost directly over his legs. He rolled quickly to the left and began to dig into the snow again when the helicopter came to a rest over him. He flung snow over his chest and legs as the side door slid open, then covered his head and burrowed his hands into the snow.

He could hear nothing over the racket of the giant engines and turned his head slightly, slowly, until he saw the occupants tramping around in the snow near the body of the dead Chinese soldier.

They hadn't seen him yet.

Two more Chinese soldiers stepped out of the gunship and paced nearby. Doubtless they had AK-47s or other capable weaponry and were watching for signs of ambush.

They didn't realize that the ambush was already under way.

Bolan made his move, slowly, keeping his hands under the snow. He felt for the rigging he had already constructed and attached to his belt. He pulled it off his belt but didn't yet lift it out of the snow.

He scanned the belly of the Hind, just a foot above his face. He had intended to make use of one of the wheels if he couldn't find anything more convenient. All he needed was a secure mounting spot on the Hind. Anywhere would do.

He found what he wanted, just inches from his chest.

Two steel panels were joined together by a series of what should have been six bolts. But at some point one of the bolts was removed and not replaced. When the gunship was given its gray paint job, the threads for the bolt were painted over, but the hole where the two panels joined was still open.

It was ideal.

The dead soldier was flipped over. The Chinese had apparently seen all they needed to see and returned to the Hind. Bolan watched their footsteps, hoping his head wasn't too exposed. The guards were the last to head for the chopper, and as soon as they turned to the door, Bolan went into action. He withdrew the rigging from the snow and brushed it off. It was composed of a metal hook improvised from a steel stay from his backpack frame, no thicker than a wire hanger. It was used to hook on and transport a single high explosive grenade, also from Bolan's backpack. The big American slid the wire through the screw hole and twisted the stiff wires together to ensure it wouldn't tumble off.

The door to the Hind slid shut, and he scooted out of his position, getting onto his knees, fighting the frozen stiffness of his limbs. The rotor speed on the chopper increased rapidly, and it began a sudden ascent. Bolan snatched the pin from the HE as the chopper started to rise, then took off over the snow as fast as his numb legs would move, fighting the blast of wind from the rotor and dodging to the left to avoid the swinging fuselage of the gunship while attempting to keep behind the tail of the Hind so that he would remain unspotted as long as possible.

THE MASSIVE HELICOPTER rose swiftly above the mountainside, and four seconds later it was engulfed in an orange ball. A half second later the fuel caught, and the explosion blasted the chopper from the inside out, sending great belches of fire and smoke in all directions, then dropping the Hind to the ground in a flaming mass of twisted, screeching metal.

Bolan didn't bother to watch, throwing himself behind the protection of a boulder until all the debris fell from the sky.

"WHAT WAS THAT?" The new squad captain nearly lost his balance on the slippery slope the team was carefully traversing behind the old man.

"Look!" one of his men shouted.

The squad captain saw it, too. A column of black smoke rose from the other side of the mountain, so thick and oily it was exhibiting a kind of adhesiveness that wouldn't allow it to easily dissipate into the clean air of the mountains.

"What do you think that was?" he heard one of his men say.

"The helicopter. What else could it be? There's nothing else up here."

The captain slowly took the radio from his belt and raised it, unable to tear his eyes from the sight of the smoke column.

"Base, this is Search Party One, come in."

"We read you."

"Base, are you still in touch with Helo One?"

"As a matter of fact we just lost radio contact."

"Oh, damn."

CHAPTER TEN

General Wei Zheng stared at the radio operator across the room, then stalked to his side. The operator had already put the incoming message on the speaker.

"There's a column of smoke. Something exploded. I don't know what else it could have been except our helicopter," the search-party commander reported.

"Can you get to the wreckage?" the radio operator asked, anticipating the general's instruction.

"Yes, but it will take a while, an hour or so. It's hard to pinpoint the location based on the smoke."

The operator looked up at the general, who shook his head.

"Negative. Proceed with the search."

"Roger."

"Try to raise the helicopter again."

The operator knew it was fruitless, but he didn't argue. "Z One. Z One. Do you read?"

The speaker answered with a faint static.

"Z One. Come in, Z One."

Nothing.

"What was your last report from Z One?" the general asked.

"They radioed that they had landed and identified the body as one of our missing search-party members. He was dead, as expected. They were going to get airborne and continue searching for the person who's been attacking the search parties. That was the last I heard from them."

"They didn't report any weapons fire?"

"No, General."

"They searched the area prior to landing?"

"Yes. They were confident there was nobody in the area."

"They were obviously mistaken."

"Yes, General. Unless it was a land mine."

"They would have set it off when they landed."

"Maybe they missed it with the helicopter. Maybe it didn't go off until one of the men stepped on it as they were heading back to the helicopter."

Zheng considered this. "Maybe," he said doubtfully. "Tell me Z Two is on its way to check it out."

The operator was quick to reassure him. "They weren't far away. They ought to be arriving on the scene any second."

"HERE THEY COME!" Sonam cried, spotting the familiar outline of the other gunship as it swung like a pendulum from behind the thousand-foot rise dominating their view.

"Get under cover," Bolan growled.

Sonam jumped behind a boulder, and the Executioner followed him as the gray gunship matched the steep angle of the rise and rocketed at them with a sudden whine of rotors. The 7.62 mm machine guns erupted at once, cutting lines in the snow and ricocheting off the boulder that was hiding them. It was wasted ammunition. The rock was a solid wall of protection that would stop any standard rounds they might fire at them. The gunship roar peaked as it swept over the rock. Bolan triggered the Desert Eagle, loosing a pair of powerful .44 Magnum hollowpoints into the belly of the beast before it was out of range. He jammed the handgun into the holster inside his coat, then grabbed for the automatic rifle in the nylon sling on his back.

The M-16 A-1 was mounted with an M-203 grenade launcher under the barrel, and under his coat Bolan had a selection of projectiles secured to his combat webbing. He selected an HE round and thumbed it into the breech of the M-203 on the run. Behind him he heard the whine of the Hind as it swept into a tight turn.

"We need cover," he ordered.

"This way," Sonam said. Bolan glanced back, placed the Hind and ran after the Tibetan, who was heading for another rocky rise. Sonam disappeared behind it, and Bolan leaped after him as he heard the Hind machine guns come to life. The helicopter slowed this time, the pilot not intending to overshoot them again. He brought the gunship to a virtual halt before beginning a slow, wide sweep of the rock, and Bolan leveled the M-16 A-1 over the rock, aiming for the spot he expected the Hind to appear, and triggered the M-203.

The 40 mm round flew at the helicopter, but the Hind pilot reacted instantly, tipping the Hind virtually on its side and swooping away from the deadly egg. The grenade passed through the empty air, then lost momentum and arced to the ground. It hit and rocked the early morning with its blast.

"We need better cover," Bolan stated. "I've probably just talked them into using their rockets."

They bounded through deepening snow and reached a sharp decline. Sonam headed into it with Bolan on his heels as the Hind recovered from its evasive maneuver and went after them. It swung into the open space above the decline and hovered there for a moment, getting a fix on them. But the gunship wasn't made for firing at targets directly underneath it. It moved out into open space to make a turn and come directly at them.

The decline was nearly a cliff, and without the layer of crystallized snow to give them traction, Bolan knew they wouldn't have been able to make the descent on foot. As it was, the snow was collapsing under his feet as he made large leaps through it, and he landed at the bottom of the decline with a heavy impact, a half second behind Sonam. The Hind came at them, gaining speed. Bolan beat them to the punch, firing another HE round from the M-203. The pilot used the speed of the helicopter to drag it into a sharp incline that carried it above the grenade.

Bolan watched his second round swoop into the snow-covered ground and explode, throwing up a sudden minisnowstorm. He didn't consider either of the grenades wasted. Each had staved off a killing attack by the Hind. But he would have much rather seen them explode against the hull of the Soviet-built craft.

"Our situation hasn't improved much," he reminded Sonam urgently.

Sonam watched the Hind perform an angled arc, and now it was heading back to the base of the sharp decline. This time Bolan was sure it would level off at a distance—out of range of his M-203 wouldn't mean out of range for the antitank rockets mounted under its stubby wings.

"Here!" Sonam made a leap onto a tumble of icy rock, and Bolan followed, watching his footing as carefully as possible. A twisted ankle wasn't conducive to flight from antitank weaponry. Then, before he expected it, Sonam made a ninety degree twist and disappeared into a mass of rock. Bolan jumped in after him.

It wasn't a cave so much as a hollow that formed when a wide, flat slab of rock had collapsed on top of a partial circle of other boulders. Now there was room enough inside to shield several men, at least from a distance. A pair of nearby eyes would have been able to easily see between the gaps in the rock through which the wind whistled.

Bolan observed the Hind through one of those gaps. The chopper had planted itself at a elevation of one hundred fifty yards, pivoting slowly, searching for them.

"I led us onto these rocks at an angle," Sonam explained. "If they think we kept going straight after our footprints stop at the rocks, then they'll think we headed there." He indicated a veritable garden of boulders and ice that extended in a broad field at the semilevel base of the decline. Bolan imagined the spot collecting boulders and rocks that came loose from the mountain above it, century after century, slowly forming into what it was today.

"Good plan."

"If they believe it."

That remained to be seen. The Hind was crawling through the air, its gray body panels almost disappearing against the sky, its great rotor disk an evil shadow. It tipped like a nodding head and swung from one side to another, like a monster's face looking down at them. Bolan knew they couldn't see him. He also knew that didn't matter if they decided to bombard the area with antitank rockets.

The great head turned to the field of rocks and descended twenty yards, backing off at the same time, maintaining a safe distance should the elusive grenade launcher erupt from within the field of rocks.

The Executioner looked up at the gunship broadside now. The pilot was carefully attempting to keep the helicopter out of range of where he thought Bolan was, but he had inadvertently put himself in range.

Firing the M-203 would instantly alert the helicopter crew to his true location. Unless the first HE round scored a killing blow, Bolan and Sonam were as good as dead. They wouldn't be able to outrun the antitank missiles once they started coming in their direction.

His natural inclination was to step into the open with the M-203 blazing, but his warrior's wisdom told him to bide his time.

He would get his chance eventually.

The Hind opened fire, the first missile trailing gray smoke and slamming into the boulders with a blast that rocked the mountain underneath them. Sonam crouched against the rear of the hollow, and Bolan swung his arm over his face, feeling meteoric dust blow against him. Out in the rocky field a cracked mass of stone the size of a semitrailer lurched onto its side.

The helicopter turned five degrees and fired again. The second missile hit the middle of the field and created a sudden crater, ice, earth and stone flinging outward in all directions. It was almost immediately followed by the third rocket. The gunner on the helicopter had effectively created havoc over most of the rocky field.

Bolan had little doubt that if he or his Tibetan companion had been ensconced anywhere among those rocks, they would be dead now.

The crew of the Hind seemed to agree with that assessment. The gunship passed slowly over the rubble, no longer intent on staying out of grenade range. Finally it sank to just two feet above the rocky surface and, unable to land, hovered as two of its men jumped to the ground.

Then the Hind gained altitude and roared away over the mountain.

"They've gone to check out the wreckage while these two look for our bodies. They'll want to ID us," Bolan said.

"What'll we do?"

"You'll wait here."

"Are you going to kill them?" Sonam asked.

"Yes."

Sonam watched the two men as they picked gingerly among the rubble. He nodded slightly, as if to himself. "Be careful, friend."

Bolan unsheathed his Randall fighting knife. The blade, anodized black before the start of the mission, now showed scrapings of shining steel through the blade. It hadn't been whetted in days, but held its edge.

In the other hand he gripped the Desert Eagle. He would have to use caution before firing it. The soldiers would doubtless be equipped with a radio to stay in contact with the Hind. He couldn't allow them to give warning to the gunship, or it would come back and cut him down.

But he wasn't willing to neglect an opportunity to further compromise his enemy's strength.

He crept over the rocky surface, glancing back and forth between the uneven, broken surface and the soldiers. He moved from shelter to shelter, spending more time crouched behind black or gray boulders than actually in motion. But his patience was rewarded when he reached the edge of the rocky field.

One of the men was just eight or nine paces away from the Executioner, probing in the broken rock for signs of bodies. His companion was another fifteen yards distant, digging in a pile of small black stone as if he thought he might be on to something.

Bolan climbed to them with precision and grace, like some sort of lethal ballet dancer on a chaotic stage, soundless as a ghost, unseen by the soldiers. He stepped up to the nearer searcher undetected and reached around his neck, placing the cold steel against his throat and the Desert Eagle into his back simultaneously.

Then the other soldier sensed something and leveled his AK-47 from the hip.

"Freeze!"

Bolan did freeze, feeling a trickle of blood flowing over the blade of his knife and wetting his fingers. Another inch, and the man would have dropped—and the second soldier would have had no reason not to open fire.

"Let him go," the soldier said.

"Drop the gun," Bolan answered.

The Executioner's victim pleaded with them both in Chinese.

"No way, American!" The soldier with the AK-47 grabbed a walkie-talkie from his belt with his free hand and brought it to his face.

Bolan slashed through the throat of his hostage and fired the Desert Eagle, the Magnum round tearing past the collapsing man and striking his companion in the thigh. He fired again, creating a red crater in the chest of the second soldier and sending him flopping on the rocks. The walkie-talkie hit the rock with a crunch but remained intact.

Bolan grabbed the walkie-talkie, finding it silent, and

cracked it against the rock. Then he returned to the soldier with the cut throat. The blade had done its work.

"Sonam," he called.

The Tibetan emerged from the shelter and waved.

"We need to get out of the vicinity quick," Bolan shouted.

"We backtrack. This way."

The Executioner rejoined him, and they marched through their own footsteps along the base of the steep decline, deviating when they reached the point where they had arrived at the bottom. They needed only to trek twenty paces through the snow before emerging onto stone and start up the glacierlike expanse of rock, ice and snow.

"This will take us back up to the top," Sonam said. "But it's not going to be easy or quick."

"Then let's get started."

They had made little progress when they heard the Hind's rotors. The men tucked themselves behind the biggest stretch of nearby boulders and watched the helicopter descend to the two soldiers.

The Hind paused at two hundred yards, its occupants looking down at the bodies. Then the gunship began to fire again and again. The antitank missiles cracked against the mountainside, exploding the entire field of rock, blasting the bodies of the Chinese soldiers to oblivion, crumbling the boulders and rocks along the vast field to pebbles and sand.

Sonam gasped when one of the rocks scored a hit within a few feet of the small shelter they had been using just minutes before and transformed it into a small, empty pit. He hid himself behind the rock and leaned against it, catching his breath.

Bolan continued to watch the gunship. When its supply of missiles was used up, the mountainside was pockmarked, the jagged aspect of the huge boulders smoothed out, but none the worse for it. Even missiles couldn't kill rocks.

Then the Hind climbed high above the mountain and stormed away.

Bolan checked his watch and pulled out his own radio, flipping it on and checking the frequency he and Grimaldi had agreed upon.

"Wings, come in."

He received no answer.

It was far too early to start worrying about Grimaldi.

NYIMA WOULDN'T have been more than an overgrown small town back in the United States. In a nation as geographically sprawling as Tibet yet containing only six million people, a small metropolis like Nyima still qualified as one of the country's population centers.

The people on the streets were mostly Tibetan, Grimaldi observed. Nyima was far enough west that it didn't suffer from the cultural ravages of a huge Chinese population influx. In the eastern cities Tibetans were so outnumbered by Chinese that the religious and cultural identity of the native people was diluted to nonexistence. Qamdo, for instance, was a Chinese city now, never mind that it was inside Tibetan borders.

Grimaldi had entered Nyima under the cover of darkness and stayed out of sight as morning brought people into the streets. He observed nothing like a modern skyscraper in the city. It was composed primarily of squatting, five-to six-story brown buildings, plain except for some vague decorative treatment above the doors and top-floor gables. The streets were narrow, most of them paved decades earlier but now cracked, broken and universally covered in dirt that wouldn't be washed away until the next rainy season.

Grimaldi would forgive all its failings if Nyima could provide him with a communication link to the outside world.

There was no way the common folk were going to have phones in their homes. His need to keep a low profile meant he couldn't just walk into one of the few affluent-looking businesses and ask to use the phone. Those businesses would probably be Chinese controlled, anyway, making them even riskier.

What he needed was a hotel, one that catered to Westerners, if there was such a thing. Did the tour groups even come through Nyima?

A few poverty-stricken street merchants who spoke smatterings of English directed him to the city's small hotel district, and Grimaldi picked the most opulent-looking establishment, one that displayed its name in English. The Nyima JC was a building that might have known some grace and grandeur fifty years earlier, before the Chinese stormed in.

Inside, the feeling of deteriorating elegance remained. The carpet was burgundy but so worn that the white base of it actually showed through in high-traffic areas, and the silk draperies hanging over the front picture window of the lobby were separated into individual threads in spots.

The man behind the counter, incongruously, was dapper in a crisp wool suit. He was Chinese and gave Grimaldi a stiff, well-practiced smile.

"Your name, sir?"

"Oh, I won't have a reservation," he said. "I was with a tour group until this morning. They're all starting back to Lhasa, but I wanted to stay and see more. It's a fascinating city."

"Yes." His smile was pasted on.

"Do you have any rooms?"

"Yes, of course." The clerk filled in a check-in form hastily.

"Do you have phones in the rooms? I haven't talked to my wife in days. She couldn't make the trip."

"Yes, of course."

Grimaldi's identification, supplied by Stony Man Farm, gave his name as Elliot Paige. The pilot presented his passport when it was requested and waited as the clerk jotted down the passport number and compared the photo to the real man. The photo matched, but if the clerk began to turn pages looking for the special Tibet travel visa issued by the Chinese government, he was in trouble. When the Farm prepared the documents for him they hadn't anticipated a trip to Tibet from Siberia.

But the passport number was all the clerk seemed to need. He took an imprint of Elliot Paige's credit card.

"No bags?"

"Oh, the representative for the tour group said he'll send them within the hour. Can you have them brought to my room?"

"Yes, of course."

Grimaldi ascended the stairs to the second floor and found his room. He gave it a cursory glance—he planned on being there only minutes—and headed for the phone. He was pleased to find that he didn't have to go through a switchboard, and made a direct call to a cutout number that would eventually connect him to Stony Man Farm. As the connection went through, he pulled the tiny scrambler from his pack and connected it to the handset. About the size of a cassette-tape box, the unit would scramble his voice and descramble the incoming signal. A similar unit on the Farm's phone would perform the same function. Anyone who tried to tap into the line would hear gibberish. Unless they had a similar device and could tune it identically.

The phone operator at the Farm picked up before the first ring was completed, and Grimaldi said only, "Scrambling."

He heard no response, but that didn't worry him. When he spoke again, he knew the scrambling on the telecommunications system in the complex in the Blue Ridge Mountains would be operable.

"Grimaldi. Give me Price."

"Yes, sir," a stranger answered. That didn't bother him, either. There were a number of men and women working with Stony Man Farm, too many for Grimaldi to know them all personally. And like any agency, they came and went as their tours changed. But there was never a government agency whose staff was more thoroughly evaluated than the staff at the Farm.

"Jack?" Barbara Price said.

"Yeah."

"Where are you? Are you okay?" Her response was oddly delayed by the telecommunications lag that existed when one phoned from one side of the planet to the other.

"I'm at the Nyima JC Hotel, in Nyima, Tibet."

"Striker?"

"He's okay, too. At least he was the last time I saw him." He gave Price, Stony Man Farm's mission controller, a quick rundown of the events since they had last communicated during their flight into Tibet.

"I need transportation to get back up there. Striker's

trying to get to the crashed An-26 survivors before the Chinese do, but he'll need help."

"Do you think he can do it?"

"He knows where the crash is. I don't think the Chinese do. At least not yet. But they've got a couple of Hind attack helicopters, and they can do some pretty rapid searches of large areas with them, no matter what kind of cloud cover they're contending with. That's why I need to get back up there right away."

"That's not going to be easy, Jack. It's Chinese airspace, for one."

"I know that, but whatever the hell these guys are up to, they don't have the blessings of the Chinese government. It was a PRC plane that shot down the An-26."

"Hold the line while I see what I can arrange."

"Okay. You should know I'm not feeling too secure where I am at the moment."

"I'll hurry."

Grimaldi waited, pacing next to the bed in the dingy hotel room, listening to silence. He had the urge to get moving. Who knew if he was spotted upon entering the city, or if the clerk below had notified someone of his presence? By now the entire district might be watching for a tall, lean American man on his own. There might be Chinese soldiers marching up the hotel stairs even now.

He listened to the building around him and heard nothing, just sparse traffic from the street.

"Jack!" It was Hal Brognola.

"I'm here."

"Barb, you there?"

"I'm here, too."

"I understand you're pressed for time. A rendezvous

is being arranged now,'' Brognola said. ''We've got a chopper flying in from Tadzhikistan, from the same base you and Striker refueled at on your way in. I can't guarantee what we'll be able to send you in terms of equipment.''

''Give me anything with a rotor, and I'll be able to get to the wreck,'' Grimaldi said. ''When and where will the meet take place?''

''You tell us where,'' Price said. ''We've got damn little on Nyima.''

Grimaldi had anticipated this need and already had a plan. ''There's a paved road that goes west out of the city into the mountains. About three miles outside city limits is a small dirt road that veers off to the north for about a mile to a village named Zheqin.'' He spelled it rapidly. ''I'll plan on meeting up with the helicopter just outside the south end of that village. What time frame are we talking about?''

''Five, six hours, at least. You're going to have to hang out for a while. If you can get in touch with us again later…''

''I don't see that happening,'' Grimaldi said, feeling increasingly agitated. Maybe he was paranoid. Maybe he had learned a little warrior's sixth sense from Mack Bolan. Whatever was triggering it, an alarm was ringing in his skull, too loud to ignore.

''I've gotta go,'' he said suddenly.

''Good luck!'' he heard Barbara Price call out to him, then he put down the phone and unsnapped the scrambling device. He withdrew his Beretta 92-F and stepped silently to the door of his hotel room, peering through the peephole and seeing nothing. He opened the door cautiously and looked for signs of life.

The hall was empty in both directions. He took two

steps toward the stairs and saw the shadows of the lurkers.

He fell back at once. The sunlight shining in through the big lobby picture window tossed shadows of two people on the wall as they came up the stairs, and Grimaldi knew no ordinary guest or hotel employee would have reason to be sneaking up the stairs the way this pair did.

Grimaldi backtracked to his room, then crossed the hall to another door and knocked sharply. He twisted the knob and found the door locked. It was an old solid knob, probably original hotel equipment from the thirties, and wouldn't budge. He gave up on that idea and bolted down the hall to a small alcove where the housekeeping cart was stored behind swing doors. He dragged the cart into the hall and stepped into the alcove himself.

The two creepers each brandished a large handgun. If Grimaldi had any doubts as to their intention, they vanished when the armed men stopped before his hotel-room door, their handguns up and ready.

They spoke a single word to each other, then the nearer man fired into the doorknob and kicked open the door. They went in together, one aiming high, one low, and Grimaldi took the opportunity to leave the alcove. He scooted the old wooden cart toward the door to his room and parked it several feet away, then crouched behind it and aimed through the lower shelf.

Seconds later the gunmen reappeared, and Grimaldi fired before they had a chance to realize the cart had changed positions. He aimed at what he could see, sending two rounds crashing into the knees of the nearer man and scoring a hit in the back of the second man's thigh as he turned to run. Both gunmen fell to the floor, moaning and clutching their wounds as they writhed on the dingy carpeting.

Grimaldi stood and saw the thigh-shot man, the less seriously wounded of the two, bringing his handgun into firing position in a shaky grip. The Stony Man pilot triggered two more rounds from the 92-F, taking the man in the stomach and chest, and he went limp. The second man screeched in rage and pain and snatched a long dagger from an ankle sheath, the move so swift Grimaldi almost didn't notice it. As he came around the cart, the pilot leveled the 92-F at his skull from a proximity of under two feet and fired one time. The knife and the man collapsed on the carpet and didn't move again.

Grimaldi stepped over the bodies and reentered his room, heading directly for the window, which he dragged open against the protestation of old, humidity-swollen wood. There was no fire escape, and he lowered himself from the window without a clear idea how he was going to get to the ground. If he had to drop, it was only fifteen feet or so....

There was a crash from inside the hotel and shouts of alarm. Reinforcements, the pilot thought grimly, and that was when he found an old rubber pipe braced to the wall, assuming it was a gutter. He grabbed it with one hand and transferred his body weight from the windowsill as a gunshot filled the room. As he slid down the rubber pipe, the braces gave way, and he allowed himself to descend at what was just less than a fall, but the pipe continued collapsing under the strain and he hit the ground hard, barely managing to stay on his feet.

The open window of his room was still empty, and he kept his gun trained on it until he ran around to the back of the hotel.

He searched for more attackers and didn't find them. They'd be there soon, fanning out through the city as soon as his escape was discovered.

Grimaldi ran.

CHAPTER ELEVEN

Elise Lim put her arm over her eyes and instantly regretted it, because doing so opened the gaps along the sides of her makeshift coat and the frigid breeze slithered like icy eels into her clothing. She dropped her arm and tried to snuggle up again inside the ragged blankets, and shut her eyes against the painful whiteness. Her foot landed on something crooked, and she felt herself toppling.

She was so exhausted and drained of energy she didn't make any attempt to catch herself. Hitting the ground wasn't painful. Once her body broke through the icy crust, the snow cushioned her, caught her in gentle arms. Where the snow surrounded her, it acted as a windbreak. She was actually warmer where she was covered by the snow. If she just wriggled and cuddled down into the snow completely, let it cover her from head to toe, then she would be toasty warm, surrounded in softness. She could sleep.

"Get up."

She opened her eyes, and whiteness stabbed into her head. The dark, blurry blotch crouching over her was the familiar profile of her tormentor, Li.

For the thousandth time the sight of him made her think of the chain in her coat. It had lain there, icy steel that somehow never got warm even though it was nestled like a papoose against the bare flesh of her stomach. It was her secret security, although she hadn't yet determined what security it could offer her. She would use it eventually, if she didn't freeze to death first. And when she did use it, she would use it on Li. Would she strangle him with it? Beat him with it? She'd do something. That chain was the man's doom. She knew it in her heart. It was the only incentive to keep her going.

Struggling onto her stomach, she pushed against the warm embrace of the snow, rising onto her knees, then, with tremendous effort, pushing herself onto her feet again.

Hanging her head like a beaten dog, she glared at Li.

"Go on," he said.

"I want to rest."

"If you rest, you'll freeze."

"Then let me freeze."

"My order is to bring you down the mountain, and I'm going to bring you down the mountain."

"Fuck you."

Li, exhibiting no urgency, pulled the AK-47 from where it dangled on his back and leveled it at her.

"It is your choice," he said. "You want to stay, fine, but I won't leave you alive."

She looked at him for a long moment, trying to make her thoughts work, trying to determine if he was bluffing.

Then she turned away from him and trudged down the mountain.

The shadows were lengthening.

TRACKING MEN in the snow wasn't like tracking them in a forest. Once you found the tracks of your prey in the snow, you found your prey. There was no skill involved.

But for hours Bolan and Sampen Sonam hadn't been able to locate those tracks.

"My father is not taking them up the mountain," Sonam said. "There are two ways they could go from this altitude to get to the peak. We've surveyed both of them, and there's been no sign of them."

"So where's he taking them?" Bolan asked.

Sonam shrugged. "That's the problem. He could be going anywhere. He knows this area intimately. Better than anyone since the death of his father. If he's decided to lead them astray, then he could have them circling for days."

The problem, Bolan knew, was that the mountain wasn't a single simple rise in the land with a flat cone of territory along its sides for the search party to ascend. It was a true landscape, with fields and valleys of ice, gorges and caverns, bridges of ice that lasted for a hundred years before collapsing and disappearing overnight, and hundreds of peaks ranging from man-size bumps to plateaus and pinnacles so tall and imposing they were really secondary mountains in their own right.

"Your father could take them up a false mountain," Bolan suggested, "make them think they're going up the true peak. They'd waste days getting to the top."

"He could. That may very well be what he is doing."

"If it was, where would he go?"

Sonam considered that, then bent at the waist and began to etch a crude map with the tip of his mittens. The map was a full four feet in diameter, and at the far south end of it he put a dot.

"Here's where we started, in Ghaze," he said quietly. "Here's the true peak. Here, right next to that peak, is the level valley where you spotted the wreckage of the plane. That's only about five hundred feet lower than the peak itself.''

He added contours and lines. ''Here's where we are now. Here's where you destroyed the helicopter today.''

Bolan tried not to allow himself to feel disillusioned by the short distance Sonam was showing they had traveled so far.

How in the world was anyone going to survive up there? He was freezing, feeling his strength being sapped by the cold, and he was wearing a warm Tibetan parka. And he was thousands of feet below the altitude of the survivors.

But he had to concentrate on what Sonam was saying. He bent, resting with his hands on his knees.

''There are two other huge peaks, but I think this is where my father would take the search party if he really wanted to keep them off the track for days.'' He drew the lines of another peak almost due south of the main peak.

''It's smaller than the primary mountain, but it is still very high and massive. My father might lead them up this side—'' he traced a path along the south side of the mountain ''—and they would never get a glimpse of the main mountain until they reached very close to the top. If they reached the top at all. Only then would they realize that they were not on the main mountain.''

''We're not taking into account that they have the support of the other chopper,'' Bolan said.

''The helicopter is concentrating on searching elsewhere, you said.''

''I'm sure it is.''

''If the helicopter is searching elsewhere, then it

might not be coming back to the search party today. And it won't come in the dark, I don't think.''

"So..."

"I think my father is taking that chance. I think he's leading them up this peak. Just to delay them, cause them trouble in his own fashion.''

Bolan stood. Bending over like that for just a couple of minutes had allowed the cold to stiffen his back. "He's your father. If that's your best guess, I'll go along with it.''

"It's not a guarantee,'' Sonam added. "I'm not saying I understand him completely. Sometimes my father behaves in ways I can't begin to comprehend.''

"I understand that,'' Bolan said. Old memories dredged themselves up involuntarily, and he knew what Sonam was talking about.

THE HIKE ACROSS A BROAD expanse of crusted snow was an ordeal that took several long hours that afternoon. Roped together about the waist, they took turns leading the way, poking at the path in front of them with each step.

Bolan could feel his eyes straining against the brightness of the sun on the snow, which was blinding even through his dark sunglasses. When they were well into the field of snow, and well out of range of any firearm the search party was likely to have, he finally donned one of the strips of woven wool cloth Sonam offered him. Wrapping it around his face and eyes, he left only the thinnest slit to peer through. He found it was all he needed.

But every hour, when he paused to check the radio for the return of Grimaldi, he also took off the blinders to scan the landscape for signs of any other life.

He didn't find it.

The sun was preparing to duck behind the Himalayas, even though it was at least two hours before flatland dusk. Shortly after that, as he trailed ten paces behind Sonam, he heard the crack. It seemed to come from the air, from the snow, from the very mountain itself, and a fraction of a second later he realized what was happening. He threw himself backward and twisted, and as he was doing so he witnessed the snowy earth disappear under Sonam's feet. The Tibetan cried out briefly, and his hands flew into the air, although Bolan knew there was going to be nothing for the man to grab on to. In his hand Bolan had the old, battered mountain-climbing pick Sonam had given him, and he hacked at the earth with it, feeling it sink through the snowy crust for several inches before digging into ice and earth. Then the rope around his waist tightened and yanked at his body. The big American spread his legs as far apart as he could, digging into the snow with his boots. Sonam's weight pulled him over the snow, which plowed up under his boots, and he felt a solid chunk of earth come free under the hammer. Bolan yanked it above him, as high as he was able, and slammed it into the earth again, feeling it bite, and he held it with an iron grip. His slide across the snow came to a sudden halt.

Pain screamed in his shoulders, and his fingers became stiff with strain and cold. He could feel the changes in tension on the rope around his waist as Sonam swung over empty space in the newly created gorge. Bolan didn't hear a word from the Tibetan, not a sound, and he pictured the young man dangling from the rope with a freshly bloodied head from an impact with the rocky wall of the gorge.

Bolan released his hold on the pick with one hand,

snatched at the Randall fighting knife in its belt sheath and stabbed into the snow with it. The act had taken under two seconds, but it was enough time for his other hand to practically slide off the handle of the pick.

The blade penetrated the surface. Bolan used it to hoist himself forward a few inches, then grab a better grip on the pick. He dragged at the pick until it was under his chest, grasping it by the head, forcing it down into the surface and away from the gorge at the same time. The leverage was solid.

He began to kick with his feet and legs to clear the snow from where he lay. It was awkward, almost futile work, but he cleared it away until it was just a few inches of packed snow.

Putting all his weight on the pick head, Bolan used his other hand to grab the rope and haul up on it by just a few inches, and used the slack to maneuver his body sideways before releasing the rope again. His body was now removed from the cleared space, and he used the big knife to chop, finding solid ice beneath it. He hacked at the ice furiously, finding it deep and strong, breaking off in tiny chunks. His forehead was covered in moisture, and he could feel his body perspiring from the combined efforts. The job took only minutes, but to Bolan it seemed to have taken hours.

When he was done he had created a cutout in the ice that was almost a foot deep.

He shuffled his body and allowed Sonam's weight to drag him into position, then turned on his back and wedged his heels into the ice cutout.

Now he had some real leverage. He grabbed the rope that extended from his waist, crouched into the cutout and hauled on the rope.

The rope was cutting into the snow and ice at the

edge of the gorge, and there was no way of knowing if it was being dragged against a jagged piece of ice or rock that might sever it at any second.

Bolan hauled, feeling the swings of the body at the end of the rope grow smaller as the body reached the top of the gorge. Then he felt movement on the line. There was a clink, the distinctive sound of a pick being inserted into the ice, and Bolan raised his head up to see Sonam's arm over the top of the gorge.

He braced himself and hauled again, and Sonam emerged sideways over the lip of the gorge. His body was dragged a few feet farther away from the gorge, then his arms and legs went out instinctively into a spread-eagle position to hold him in place, and he lay there, unmoving, like a half-dead rabbit in a snare.

Bolan lay on his back with his eyes closed, letting the tension run out of him, unable to recall when he had been through a single more physically exhausting experience. It was a great effort to force himself to his feet.

Sonam raised his head out of the snow and said weakly, "How about we take a breather?"

Moments later the sun went down behind the mountain.

THE SUN WAS GOING DOWN, but the tiny village of Zheqin was miles from the nearest peak. It wouldn't fall into the shadows of the upper Himalayas for another hour, at least, Jack Grimaldi judged.

He wasn't going to be making it out of there this night, he guessed. Even if his rescue chopper showed up, he couldn't go flying around in the mountains in the dark. He wouldn't be able to locate anything—Bolan or the An-26 wreckage. It would be a waste of fuel.

Grimaldi was using his time to catch a few winks. It had been a long time since he'd had any decent sleep. He'd been moving nonstop for more hours than he cared to count.

In Nyima he'd come closer to being taken out than he cared to think about. He'd avoided the Chinese soldiers by jumping out a hotel window and running through the city to the spot blocks away where he had parked his stolen motorcycle. The stealthy backtracking to the village of Zheqin had taken almost an hour.

He'd spotted the sign for Zheqin on the way in, and was glad to find it was no bigger a metropolis that he'd pictured it to be—a hundred brick-and-stone buildings, maybe. The road from the highway became paved when it reached the town, but it was the only paved road.

Grimaldi parked his bike on the side of the road when Zheqin appeared ahead, laying it in a ditch where it couldn't be spotted from the road, then searched for a place where he could keep watch on this end of the town. Somewhere around here the air transport from Stony Man would be arriving. How they'd get it here from the Russian AF base in Tadzhikistan were logistics he didn't even want to consider. If the Russians became uncooperative, he and Bolan might be stranded here and not even know it until their expected assistance failed to materialize.

He'd sighted the ruins of a small, old farm building of some kind. It was falling in on itself and sat in a field south of the town limits. Grimaldi approached it from the south, keeping the structure between himself and the town, and crawled inside, positioning himself so he could keep an eye on the stretch of grassland between himself and the town. Ideal, he thought.

He was thankful this excursion into Tibet was occurring during what essentially passed for summer in this part of the world. The late afternoon was cooling off, but Grimaldi wasn't uncomfortable.

The shadow of Himalayas touched the abandoned brick building, and a stiff wind passed through it, sending a chill through him and forcing him to huddle down in his coat.

"YOU SURE YOU WON'T take this?" Bolan asked, extracting the Browning Hi-Power from his pack.

This time Sampen Sonam looked at the gun for a long moment, considering it.

"I don't want to pressure you to do something that's against your basic principles, but you might need protection."

Sonam shook his head after several seconds. "No. Please do not ask me again."

"Fine. How you feeling?"

"Okay. Much better."

Sonam had been groggy for a full hour after the battering fall he'd sustained, but he was complaining of no specific pain outside of a few sore ribs and a collection of bruises about his waist, where the rope had almost cut him in two, and along the side of his body where he had slammed into the wall of rock. Somehow he had avoided hitting his head.

They were trudging along again as soon as the Tibetan felt ready, and before true dusk they spotted the trail of the Chinese search party.

Now they were on more-solid ground, without the deadly deception of snow cover, and Bolan led them stealthily after the search party until they spotted the white glow of a flashlight.

There was a collection of tents being assembled

against the base of a short cliff, and one of the Chinese was cooking on a small burner attached to a fuel bottle. The smell of rehydrated soup drifted to them as they planted themselves behind an outcropping and observed the camp activity.

"What will we do?" Sonam asked after watching the warrior's intense scrutiny of the layout.

"No matter how we play it, it's going to be a tricky situation," Bolan said. "There's a lot more of them than there are of us."

Sonam looked at him sharply. "I won't apologize for being unwilling to fight with a gun."

"I'm not asking you to. But it is a strategic disadvantage that I need to consider. Think you can get to the rear of the camp by climbing over that cliff top and descending on the other side?"

Sonam examined the cliff that towered over the camp. "The incline here isn't insurmountable. Whether I can get down on the other side is another question. I won't know until I cross to it."

They watched the camp huddle around cups of the soup and chunks of hard bread, taking advantage of the time by making a meal of their own from the supplies in their packs. Shortly thereafter the members of the search party crawled into their tents, leaving two men on watch. Sonam's father, Sampen Zhu, was put in a tent in the middle of the camp, where both the guards could see it at all times.

"I'm going. I'll signal when I am in position," Sonam said, and marched off to the base of the incline.

He stopped when he was twenty paces from Bolan, stood there for a long minute, then returned.

"Give me the gun."

Bolan said nothing, but extracted the Browning Hi-Power from his pack and put it in the Tibetan's hand.

Sonam stared at the heavy black handgun for a moment, then hoisted it in his hand, getting the feel for it. Bolan gave him a quick rundown on the firing of the weapon.

He wondered at the wisdom of giving the gun to a man who had never used a firearm in his life. How could he be expected to walk into a lethal battle with one and defend himself?

Still, Bolan considered, it was probably better then letting him go in unarmed.

Sonam put the weapon in the big pocket of his insulated hide trousers and tied the pocket shut. Then he walked away from Bolan and began his climb up the side of the cliff.

IT TOOK SONAM an hour to get into position. The Executioner watched the guards closely through his binoculars, keeping an eye on the landscape beyond them during the rare moments when they were both turned away from it. Finally, as the two guards were talking and facing Bolan's position, he spotted the brief wave of a hand in the rocks far behind the camp.

Time to move in.

Bolan had used the time to fully prepare himself for the hard probe of the camp. He would be going in with the suppressed Beretta 93-R as his lead weapon for the initial stage of the penetration, trading it for the M-16 A-1/M-203 combo when the need for silence was gone. The Desert Eagle was prepped, just in case, and he would go in with his coat open for access to the 40 mm grenades secured in the combat webbing over his chest.

The moon was out, big, clear and bright, but partially

behind the cliff, so that a deep black shadow lurked at the bottom of it.

Bolan stepped into the open, timing his approach as the nearer guard turned and paced toward the center of the camp, and synchronizing his steps with the guard's to disguise the noise his feet made in the crystalline snow. The other guard, a good hundred yards distant on the opposite side of the camp, was standing with his back to the cliff edge, half in its shadow. No one was going to be sneaking up on him from behind. But he wasn't exactly well situated to watch the egress ways to the camp. In fact, he looked as if he was daydreaming.

Bolan's strides were long and carried him to within ten paces of the closer guard before the soldier turned back in the big American's direction, arms folded tightly on his chest as he vainly attempted to keep warm.

He gave a small cry when he saw the intruder and grabbed for the gun slung over his shoulder, which perfectly exposed his chest to the Executioner's triburst. The three subsonic rounds made a coughing sound as they exited the 93-R and crashed into the guard's sternum and face with bone-shattering power, toppling him in the snow.

Bolan had flattened himself in the shadows against the cliff side before the body stopped moving.

The guard on the other side of the camp heard something, turned toward his companion and stalked in his direction, reaching the middle of the camp before noticing that the other guard was now flat on his back.

He called out the dead guard's name, not too loudly, slow to grow alarmed.

Bolan took advantage of the darkness to aim carefully, taking the 93-R in two hands and firing it with a marksman's precision.

But the guard saw the black ruin that was his companion's face and panicked in that moment, stepping toward the camp and shouting. The triburst winged to where he had been standing and took him in the arm and shoulder instead of the abdomen and chest. He twisted and collapsed, screaming, and a second triburst finished him off.

But the jig was up, and Bolan pushed the 93-R into its holster, unslinging the M-16 A-1/M-203. He aimed over the center of the camp and triggered an incendiary grenade, which slammed into the most distant nylon tent and transformed it instantly into a ball of fire.

A soldier raced out of the nearest of the four remaining tents, jumping to his feet as he dragged off a sleeping bag to reveal a mini-Uzi. But he couldn't get it ready to fire fast enough to save himself. Bolan triggered the M-16 in full-auto mode and cut across the Chinese hardman's waist, bending him double and dropping him in the snow. Another man was scrambling behind the collapsing corpse and pushed it in the buttocks, sending it flopping to one side, while Bolan thumbed a buckshot round into the breech of the M-203. The grenade launcher was essentially transformed into a shotgun. He triggered the buckshot round, the blast ripping the nylon tent to shreds, along with the occupant, transforming them together into a ragged, bloody mess.

Another gunner was crawling frantically out of the third tent, coatless and fisting a large revolver. Bolan triggered the M-16 and created dark holes in his shoulders and across his back. He screamed and fell on his face, the impact shutting him up. Another incendiary went into the breech, and Bolan triggered it into the tent, assuring himself there would be no more trouble from its occupants.

A stutter of automatic fire cut through the arctic air inches from Bolan's skull. He hit the ground and rolled to his left, landing on his chest in the snow with the M-16 already in firing position before him, then stopped before he could fire it, finding the central tent blocking him from the other remaining tent. He wasn't going to risk Sonam's father.

He rolled again and launched himself to his feet, bounding for the shadows and collapsing on his knees in the snow as another stutter of automatic fire cut through the night. He stayed low, feeling rock shards bite into him as they were chipped from the cliff side. He pushed himself into a bent-over run and leaped again as he was somehow spotted and more rounds chopped through the air. The warrior stayed flat on his face, sure he was out of sight of the tent as long as he stayed down.

He crawled along the ground and pushed himself to his feet when he had put some distance between himself and the camp, heading for the outcropping that had been his starting point. More automatic fire forced him to hit the ground again before he reached his goal and slithered around it like a cold-weather serpent.

Finally in a protected position, he stopped to get his bearings. In camp he saw nothing except the burning, melting tents. At about three hundred yards, the second tent was theoretically within the range of the M-203....

He simply couldn't chance a miss that might incinerate Sampen Zhu. A grenade launcher wasn't made for long-range precision firing.

There were shouts coming from the two tents, then

Bolan saw the middle tent's flaps open. The old man was shoved out and was followed close behind by the leader of the party, a burly, middle-aged Chinese captain. In the moonlight Bolan made out the black handgun in the captain's grip, which was shoved into Sampen Zhu's back as the officer dragged the old man upright by the back of his collar. The captain was looking around furiously, unable to spot Bolan in the dark rocks, but he knew the general direction and was determined to keep the old man between himself and the attacker.

He backed the old man to the other tent, and two more soldiers climbed out. They stood there for a moment, confused, before they started grabbing their packs. Once the two soldiers were loaded down, they started back away from the Executioner. The captain moved his handgun from the old man's back to his skull, making it more visible, sending a clear message to Bolan.

Any aggressive moves on his part would result in the death of Sampen Zhu.

The probe couldn't be considered a total failure, he decided. He'd reduced by better than half the number of players in the Chinese search party.

But it was by no means a success, either—not until Sampen Zhu was safe and the rest of the search party was removed from the equation.

As soon as they crossed over a rise in the rocks that took them into the dark recesses of the rising mountain trail, Bolan emerged from his own shelter and crossed the smoking ruins of the camp, becoming cautious as he searched for the Chinese, as well as Sonam. They hadn't anticipated this turn of events. Would Sonam hide while the Chinese passed him, then rejoin the warrior? Bolan found a shadowed incline covered in snow and protruding low rocks that reminded him of a lunar landscape, and he moved from boulder to boulder, following the disturbance in the snow that clearly showed the direction the search party had taken.

There was no sign of Sonam.

Minutes later he caught up to the Chinese and from the shadows watched them contend with a new dilemma. The path was gone. They'd come to the end of the road. The small level area was surrounded by high, impassable walls on all sides. The nearly circular enclosure was maybe sixty feet in diameter, and filled with boulders that had fallen from above.

Even during most daylight hours the walled-in room had to have been deep in shadow. But in the dark of night, with the moon hidden behind tons of rock, it was nearly pitch-black.

Bolan rustled in his pack and donned thermal imaging glasses. Instantly the warm figures of the human beings materialized, highly contrasted against the cold rock and snow.

The Executioner stepped into the open with the certainty that he wasn't going to be seen approaching the search party. As he did, he spotted more hot movement, behind the search party, rustling among the rocks. Sonam.

Bolan slowed and circled the Chinese. Even if he couldn't be seen, he might still be heard. He withdrew the battered and bent Randall fighting knife and stalked his prey like a cat on the trail of a family of rats.

The captain hissed in Chinese, and Bolan used the opportunity to move in. The rearmost guard doubtless thought he was the least vulnerable. He was facing the entrance to the enclosed area, gun at his hip, ready to fire. He never saw the Executioner creeping up behind him. He never knew he was under attack until the razorlike blade of the combat knife bit into the flesh of his neck.

Severing the trachea turned off the soldier's voice, and his death was silent. Bolan grabbed his shoulders and lowered him to the ground.

The other gunman, just a few paces away, never even knew his companion was dead. He was speaking with the captain. The words were unintelligible to Bolan, but not the tone. They were arguing about something.

The other gunman was clinging to the captain, close enough to touch him, and Sampen Zhu was being held in position without complaint. In fact he was silent, as if the lethal danger of the situation was of no consequence.

The second gunman hissed in Bolan's direction, then spoke again, a little louder. The Executioner was close enough now that he knew he had to be visible as a lump of shadow in the darkness, so he answered with a noncommittal grunt.

The second gunman spoke sharply, suspicion potent in his voice.

Bolan didn't bother answering again, stepping into the gunman, the fighting knife in his left fist. He struck hard, sinking the blade through the gunman's heavy coat and into the fleshy muscle just under his sternum while he snatched the automatic rifle from his hands and flung it away. He hoisted the gunman off his feet, thrusting the blade deep into his heart, sending a flood of blood into his coat. He lowered the body, using the knife as a handle, which he removed when the corpse was down.

But the captain was facing him now, and Bolan's

glasses washed out completely when a flashlight blazed to life. He threw himself away from the beam and dragged off the glasses, dropping the knife and gripping for the 93-R, which he aimed at the light as he rose to his feet.

"Stop!" the captain shouted. "Lower that weapon or the old man dies."

He stood where he was, the 93-R pointed at the earth, covered in snow.

The beam of the flashlight illuminated him like a performer on a stage.

It flickered away momentarily, flashing almost playfully over the bodies of the knifed gunmen, then back to Bolan. The Executioner stood where he was, unable to move.

He was trapped.

He could see the outline of the old Tibetan. The captain's arm snaked around Sampen Zhu's body, who was terrified to show himself to the Executioner.

"Who are you?" the captain asked.

Bolan considered the question rhetorical and was silent.

"Are you American?"

"Yeah."

"You are vicious. I've known CIA before, but I have never met an American who was so brutal."

"I'm not CIA."

"Who are you, then?"

"Let the old man go."

The captain laughed, a short bark. "No way."

Another voice came out of the night.

"Let him go."

It was Sonam, and in the confusion he had made his way behind the captain.

The officer started to turn.

"Do not move or I will shoot you in the head!"

"Sonam?" It was the old man speaking now. He turned in the captain's grip and peered into the darkness behind him. "Sonam, throw that gun away!"

"I will when you are safe."

"I will not allow you to use that weapon! I would rather die than see you kill a man!"

"Step away from him," Sonam shouted.

"You heard him," the captain growled over his shoulder. "Put the gun away."

"That is not going to happen," Sonam said confidently.

"Please do not do this," Zhu pleaded to his son. "You are breaking my heart. If you have any respect for what my life means, you will put that gun away!"

"I will not do it, Father. I will not allow my dignity to be trampled by Chinese filth any longer. I will not be passive."

"You think they trample your dignity—you are wrong," Zhu said sharply. "You nullify your dignity yourself by taking that weapon in your hand! I am telling you, commanding you as your father, to throw that weapon away."

"You do not have the right to make that choice for me," Sonam replied.

"I am making the choices here," the captain said.

Bolan's body was as tense as taut string.

"Put down that gun," the captain said, terse with finality.

Sonam didn't move.

The captain turned suddenly, pulling the old man between himself and Sonam, resting the gun on the old man's shoulder.

Zhu cried out.

Sonam took a step away, putting his hands in the air.

Bolan raised the 93-R and fired a round at the captain's head, keeping to the outside, risking a miss, knowing he might be shooting the old man—or, if he missed, he was condemning Sonam.

An instant after his Beretta coughed, Bolan heard the retort of the captain's automatic.

Blood and tissue flew from the captain's scalp, and he sank to his knees, dropping the flashlight onto the crusty surface of the snow, clinging to the back of the old man's coat. Then he made a sound like a laugh, full of bitterness, and he put the automatic into the small of Sampen Zhu's back and fired one time.

Zhu pitched onto his face in the snow.

Sonam shouted wordlessly, then jumped over the body of his father and fired a gun for the first time in his life, directly into the grimacing face of the Chinese captain. The face was obliterated, and the captain went limp.

The young man went to his father's body and held the old man's head in his lap.

Bolan found the flashlight in the snow and turned it off, then sat on a rock in the icy darkness, listening to Sonam sob.

CHAPTER TWELVE

"Get in," Li ordered.

The shelter he had found was a tiny cave, set deep in the rock.

"You think I'm going to spend the night in there with you?" Lim asked incredulously.

"Yes, if you want to live."

"You're going to kill me if I don't sleep with you in that cave?"

"No, you stupid bitch. I will not have to. You will be dead by morning anyway. Haven't you noticed how cold it is up here?"

Lim had gone through stages of cold throughout the ordeal, but with the onset of darkness, and the blowing of a fresh, brisk wind, she was shivering uncontrollably again. The cold was seeping into her clothing from all directions and soaking into her bones.

She realized Li was correct and hated him for it. She couldn't possibly survive out here. Even protected from the wind and sharing body heat with Li, she might not survive.

Once the decision was made, she couldn't wait to get into the frigid-looking hole in the wall to try to get warm.

"All right. You convinced me," she said. "Let's go."

Down on their knees, they eagerly began stripping off the blankets they had tied around them. Several were laid out on the floor of the small cavern. They crawled inside the hole, making quick work of arranging the remaining blankets over them.

Lim turned away from Li long enough to grab the steel chain from inside her shirt and fling it behind her at her feet.

Li didn't notice, and then they were wrapping their arms around each other with the desperation of dying people. Lim felt repulsed and disgusted by the contact. She hated this man, despised him utterly. But the potency of that disgust and hatred was buried deep below her instinct to survive by any means.

And soon she was getting warmer. Her feet were still frozen, but the trembling in her torso became less intense.

She began to feel as if she might live through another night.

SONAM LAID HIS FATHER against a wall, behind some rocks, away from the dead Chinese, as if he were protecting him from having to associate with the Chinese even in death. He folded his hands on his chest and arranged his clothing neatly. He didn't ask for Bolan's help, and the big American didn't offer it. He moved out of the shielded area into the cavern and made camp out of sight of the dead men.

Sonam came to the camp an hour later and took some hot tea.

"Is it possible," he asked, "for a man to not fight,

even under the most serious provocation, and still retain his dignity?''

Bolan nodded. ''One of the most dignified men in the history of my country once said, 'I will fight no more forever.'''

Sonam nodded. ''A man must decide which way is the best for him, then live up to that decision.''

''But the dignified man of whom I spoke was a warrior. Later he became a man dedicated to peace. And during both those times of his life, he was a great chief, deserving of the respect of his people,'' Bolan explained. ''One can deem a time right for fighting and a time right for peace.''

''You will never find a time when peace is an option,'' Sonam said.

''That does not mean you can't.''

Sonam considered this. ''Perhaps I will find a time for peace. A time when I can live by my father's ways.'' He looked out into the mountains, cold, hard and oppressive. ''But that time isn't now. Right now I'm filled with a mountain of rage. I can't bury it in inaction. Now is the time to try to be a warrior.''

Bolan pictured Sonam shooting the search-party captain. ''I think you already are,'' he said.

GENERAL ZHENG COULDN'T sleep. At three o'clock in the morning, he finally rolled out of bed and got dressed. He made some tea, which didn't help. He poured a cup and took it with him outside.

This night Zheng was in his secret Himalayan compound. It was compact, nestled in a spot in the mountains that seemed inaccessible. In fact it nearly was. Building it had been a logistical nightmare and had taken a full year. But now it was complete, and he was proud of the complex, composed of several buildings placed in a narrow gorge, invisible to the outside world, a secret even to the inhabitants of the nearby village. There was a tiny opening in the hill that barely allowed access by ground transportation, but no one knew of the road leading to the compound. No fixed-wing aircraft had room to land anywhere nearby. Virtually everything and everyone came in via jeep or helicopter.

Zheng had procured the Hinds from his Russian contacts shortly after embarking on his current project. They were as vital as this compound—his way of patrolling and monitoring activity in his precinct of Tibet. With these unregistered, unknown aircraft, he could watch activity that he should officially have had no interest in.

Like the activity of other military operations in his district of Tibet.

He didn't like other Chinese generals to become too powerful here. Tibet was his. He claimed it. Or he would one day.

China had flexed her muscle when she took Tibet, but she had weakened her hold since the 1960s, allowing the ridiculous pacifist locals to use their very weakness as a weapon. Eliciting sympathy from the world community with their pathetic pleas, even tugging on the heartstrings of upper-level Chinese officials, they had convinced the Chinese to compromise their grasp on this nation. There had even been intensifying pressure on China, internally and externally, to enter serious negotiations with the Dalai Lama on the official adoption of the religious leader's five-point peace plan—a plan that would eventually grant Tibet a form of independence again.

As if the Tibetans could run their own nation. They

didn't have what it took to operate in the world community. They lacked strength. They lacked aggression. They couldn't seriously hope to run a nation based on pacifist principles. Who would take them seriously?

General Zheng didn't take them seriously; that was for certain.

He was beginning to not take the Chinese leadership's policies in Tibet seriously, either.

He saw the weakening of the Chinese hold in the Himalayan district as an opportunity. Zheng had no doubts that someone strong would move in and seize control when the Chinese reticence became apparent. It might be an isolated group of Tibetans, but Zheng had to think that any group of locals with the guts to engage in real battle would be damn small. It more likely would be a group of Indian terrorists. India had never been happy with the close proximity of the Chinese in Tibet.

Or it might be an enterprising group of well-organized Chinese, led by someone like General Wei Zheng.

He'd been strategizing the takeover for years. He'd developed an understanding of the Tibetans' mind-set. His years of command in the region were marked with demonstrable successes in terms of mollifying the Tibetan population to Chinese control. This was accomplished through an open willingness to cooperate with the locals, to the extent he could within the limitations of the Chinese controls. He rebuilt monasteries toppled by the Chinese in the 1950s and 1960s. He allocated funds for the destitute Tibetans, giving them opportunities within his own military organizations where he could.

Simultaneously he waged a secret war against them, silencing the voices of the locals who saw him not as a benefactor, but as a despot attempting to lull his victims into a state of contentment so he could keep them more firmly in his power. He hired locals to keep lists of malcontents, then saw to it that the malcontents and the squealers were silenced together.

There were a few slipups during the years. Some Tibetans had expressed their dismay at the disappearances. But most of the towns were small and well separated, and the sheer number of missing people was never guessed. So the Tibetans never knew how carefully they were being manipulated by the Chinese general.

They would figure it out. Sooner or later Zheng would be ready to make his move.

Getting his hands on the THADSAC would move him that much closer to his goal, ensure unprecedented security of his territory. He could watch everything that went on inside Tibet and throughout most of the surrounding regions of China, Nepal and India. He would know who was trying to move in and he could retaliate—with the air power he also intended to take control of.

But he didn't anticipate forceful resistance. Part of the genius of his plan was that he would take over cities on the east end of Tibet, heavily populated now by citizens of the People's Republic of China.

It was like having a few million hostages.

Beijing would never risk the public outcry that would result if they tried to forcefully expel Zheng's forces and ended up killing a substantial number of Chinese in the process. And any aggressive move by Beijing would most definitely result in the deaths of many Chinese. Zheng's strategy called for it. Beijing would know that very soon after Zheng put himself in power.

There was a chance he would go down. Beijing might call his bluff, might bomb him out of existence, and no matter how well his eye in the sky functioned and no matter how well his perimeters were guarded, he couldn't hope to match the military power of China. But if Zheng went down, thousands of Chinese would die with him, and that would inevitably result in an outcry and rebellion that would bring down the ruling regime of the People's Republic.

So Zheng would offer the government of China a choice—suicide or acceptance. They either took him down and themselves with him, or they acknowledged his rule of Tibet.

Zheng's battle wouldn't be fought just with weapons. He had a massive worldwide public-relations campaign planned. He was already seen as some sort of friend of Tibet. When he took control of the country, it would be seen as a move in the right direction by the Tibetans. And Zheng would foster that image. For a while. Let the religious leaders return. Give the Tibetan people what they wanted, on the surface. But eventually they would pay the price for his rule. They would be forced to send their young men to his army.

Tibet was just the first prize in Zheng's campaign.

He sipped his tea, standing in the middle of his compound, which was silent. Most of his personnel were sleeping. The few guards along the walls and at the gate had seen him and recognized him and let him move about unchallenged. There was only a chill wind blowing, a slight whistle in his ears. Quiet now, he thought. But the storm he was destined to create had begun brewing in earnest on the horizon.

A door opened and slammed shut. He heard boots on metal stairs, then a figure walked quickly across the compound from the command center to Zheng's quarters. The figure noticed him standing there and stopped short.

"General." It was one of his aides, a young man with a lot of energy and intelligence. "We've lost contact with one of the search parties."

TWO MINUTES LATER Zheng was staring at the map, where his aide was pointing out the last known position. "We were scheduled to get a report from them at 1:00 a.m. It never materialized. We've been trying to raise them on the radio ever since."

A sleepy-looking man entered the command center, still buttoning his shirt. "Yes, General?"

"We've searched this mountain?" Zheng demanded.

The pilot focused on the map and nodded. "Yes, General. We've performed two searches of this entire quadrant."

"There has been someone on that mountain besides us. They've killed more men than I care to count, and they've destroyed one very expensive helicopter. Now it appears they have wiped out another search party. You want to tell me why?"

The pilot stuttered wordlessly.

"That's where the wreckage is. That's what our enemies think. I think so, too. They have gone to great lengths to get rid of people on this mountain. They know something. We don't seem to know anything."

The pilot looked at the map intently, as if it would offer him an excuse. "General, I did both those searches myself. I saw no wreckage." He waved his open hand over the map to indicate a great swath of square kilometers.

"Give me weather reports for this area for the last forty-eight hours," Zheng said suddenly.

His aide knew right where to find the information. He grabbed a computer printout and handed it to the general, pointing to a section of the page. "This is specific to the areas you're looking at."

"Snow." Zheng nodded. "That's why we found nothing. That mountain was a part of a snow belt that passed over the night after the crash. The debris was covered. Did you take that into account when you searched this area?"

"I was never told there was snowfall in this area," the pilot said with sudden conviction, seeing an out. "Otherwise I would have made the search with that in mind."

Zheng nodded, expressionless, thinking. The pilot wished he could take a step backward. The general had the look of a very large firecracker lying on the pavement seconds before it exploded.

"At first light you'll go to the search-party campsite, which was here. You will find few or no survivors among our men. I hope you'll find some of our enemies among the dead, but I am not counting on it. From that point you will make an in-depth search of this entire region. I want a detailed search. I don't want a square meter missed. Understand?"

"Yes, General."

"How long will such a search take?"

"Depending on cloud cover, most of the day," the pilot said. "That is a massive area."

Zheng nodded again. "Take a full contingent. I think you are going to find the wreckage tomorrow."

The pilot nodded, hearing the *And if you do not…*

implied in the statement as clearly as if it had been spoken aloud.

ONE BATTERED, tiny automobile and two carts pulled by cattle had come down the road from the main highway into the small town of Zheqin in the hours since Grimaldi planted himself in the abandoned building. He could barely make out the town, and it was so quiet that, if not for the glow of the lights that winked on as the dark settled in, he might have thought it was deserted.

He slept on and off throughout the night, and at about 5:00 a.m. began to worry.

There might be any reason the air transport he requested wasn't reaching him. Whoever was watching this region might have air support sufficient to watch for intruders, even those flying under radar. The Farm might have hit some bureaucratic snag before they even managed to procure a vehicle. If they failed to show, he'd have to get back into the city and attempt to call in again. He wasn't looking forward to that.

The moon cast a silver gleam across the broad stretches of land, and he kept an eye out for trouble, although he didn't see how he could have been followed from Nyima. The silence, the emptiness, helped to sustain the level of tension.

When he heard the distant rumble of a helicopter, the tension elevated suddenly as if a volume knob were twisted.

Grimaldi grabbed the radio in his pack, already tuned to the frequency he had agreed upon with Stony Man, but as the chopper approached and created a silhouette against the moonlit sky he froze.

It was a Hind gunship, traveling at a tremendous rate.

It was streaking along the irregular ground, coming out of the mountains at an altitude of fifteen feet, creating a speedboatlike wake in the grass. Grimaldi stepped away from the window as it went by the ruined building. Then he spotted the horizontal stripes of white, blue and red painted against the side panel—the Russian flag that had replaced the hammer and sickle.

He thumbed on the radio. "G-Force to Russian helicopter."

"G-Force, we don't see you!" someone said in heavily accented English as the Hind rotated forty-five degrees and slid sideways over the empty field just on the border of the town. Grimaldi spotted lights coming on in the houses.

"I'm eight or nine hundred yards south of your position. See the building in the field?"

"G-Force, be alert! Unfriendlies arriving!"

Even as the faceless Russian was speaking, Grimaldi spotted headlights on the road, and a topless jeep tore over the rise. He didn't have time to guess if the Chinese had their frequency. If they did, he had just told them where to aim the machine gun mounted in the rear of the vehicle. He moved to the back of the building and crawled out through the gaping hole that had once been a door, then sank to the ground and huddled against the bricks as the headlights swept the field and passed, heading for the Hind.

Grimaldi spotted the shape of a large, thick tube being readied in the jeep. The launcher was swung into position on the shoulder of one of the jeep's occupants as the vehicle braked with a flurry of dust.

"This is G-Force—get out of here!" he said into the walkie-talkie. "They've got some sort of a grenade launcher!"

The Hind pilot didn't wait around to discuss it. The gunship abruptly spiraled directly up from where it was sitting in the sky. Grimaldi's instant evaluation told him the gunner in the jeep had the advantage.

He already had the mini-Uzi in his hands, and he fired wildly as he bolted toward the jeep. The burst of gunfire got the intended result. The three Chinese paused long enough to allow the gunship to get clear of the grenade launcher's range. Grimaldi slowed to get a decent shot and triggered the mini-Uzi. The gunners hit the deck, and the man with the grenade launcher didn't get up again.

The driver fired a 9 mm automatic over his shoulder, and Grimaldi dived for the ground, feeling the shots pass close overhead. The jeep surged ahead, and the corpse flopped out the back end. The Stony Man pilot reached out in the grass and fired the mini-Uzi, cutting into the vehicle's tires, then pushed to his feet. The jeep veered off the dirt into the grass, bouncing crazily, forcing the driver and his passenger to hold on. Grimaldi bolted after them, then fired again when he saw the brake lights go on. The passenger was cut down before he could react, but the driver jumped out of the vehicle, hitting the grass with the jeep between them. His judgment was fatally poor—the jeep was still moving, and a second later it rolled away, revealing the man to Grimaldi. The pilot didn't allow him the chance to roll over and make use of the automatic, emptying the mini-Uzi into him as he struggled to get his bearings. Seven rounds stitched his body up and down and left him limp on the grass.

"Russian pilot," he said into the radio, but didn't have a chance to complete the thought. Two more jeeps appeared over the rise and raced along the dirt road. It didn't take them long to notice the disaster that had befallen their comrades.

Grimaldi was already back at the jeep, where he made a grab for the grenade launcher that had tumbled behind the seats. It was firing 37 mm explosives, and he didn't bother to investigate what it was already loaded with as he took aim at the first of the jeeps and triggered.

The grenade was a high explosive, and it struck the hood of the jeep as the driver made a frantic bid for survival, spinning the wheel to the left and narrowly failing to avoid the projectile. The jeep became engulfed in a ball of orange and white, with body parts and scrap metal flying in all directions.

The second jeep veered off the road as the explosion erupted, slowing slightly with squealing brakes, then moving out again. Grimaldi spotted sudden activity in the rear of the vehicle, as the machine gunner maneuvered the mounted weapon to get off an accurate burst.

Grimaldi didn't wait around for it, making a leap that took him behind the stalled jeep, which became a sounding board for 7.62 mm rounds that clanged against its bodywork. The pilot reached above him and opened the driver's-side door and groped inside as best he could, expecting to feel a stream of rounds cut off his left hand at the wrist at any second.

He felt an open metal box on the floor behind the seat and, praying for luck, grabbed inside it. A cylindrical metal object fell into his hand. He snatched it, loaded the launcher and waited for a pause in the machine-gun fire.

The fire was changing, and Grimaldi knew the jeep was trying to get a clean shot at him. He could either let it keep chasing him around the vehicle or hope to get in the first good shot.

He stayed where he was, aimed the grenade launcher at the open area where the jeep would appear and tried to make out the sound of its engine, but couldn't over the battering of rounds into his vehicle. The nose of the other jeep came into view, and Grimaldi fired, dropped the launcher and lay flat.

The grenade landed on the front-seat floorboards and exploded at the feet of the passenger, who was obliterated. The body of the driver was flung into the grass eight or nine yards away, and the machine gunner flipped head over heels before crashing to the ground at the moment the fuel tank exploded, transforming the vehicle into a ball of fire.

Grimaldi got up on his knees and assured himself there were no other vehicles coming. At the moment.

He grabbed the launcher and the box of grenades, loading one just in case, and moved away from the flaming wreckage.

"Russian pilot, this is G-Force," he said into the walkie-talkie.

Small figures were on the streets of the village five hundred yards away, watching in silent amazement.

Thank God the battle was fought at this distance, he thought. There would have been little he could have done to save any villager who strayed into the machine-gun fire.

"G-Force, what is your situation?"

"Three vehicles and their occupants are out of commission. I've lit a landing flare for you. Come on in, pilot."

"Good work, G-Force. I'm coming in."

Thirty seconds later the Hind appeared out of the

mountains at top speed, coming to a halt over the burning vehicles. Grimaldi gave it a brief wave, and the Hind descended in a rush of wind.

CHAPTER THIRTEEN

Dawn arrived in the Himalayas without warmth. Elise Lim staggered out of the tiny cave and held the two thin blankets in her hand, staring at them, not even feeling the cold. Her head was pounding where Li had hit her. Her mind was as numbed as her feet, although deep inside, in an almost hidden place, she was screaming.

She glared at Li as he tied his own blankets in place.

"You have some of my blankets," she said quietly.

"I'm freezing cold. What I had wasn't keeping me warm enough."

"So I'm supposed to just freeze to death?"

"Those will do."

"If you were just going to let me die anyway, I wish you would have done it before you did what you did to me."

Li grimaced like a lecherous coyote. "I enjoyed our night together. And I think you did, too."

A stiff, cold breeze blew over Lim and knotted her stomach. She felt light-headed and staggered to the rock wall, holding on to it and crouching as her stomach heaved, but there was nothing in it to come up.

"You can't fool me," Li said. "I was there, remember. I heard you moaning in ecstasy."

"I was in pain!" she managed to choke out.

"You were in heaven."

She sobbed and lost her balance, falling onto her hands, and her guts heaved again. When she opened her eyes, she saw the manacles that she had carried with her since leaving the wrecked airplane. She had used her leg to scoot them out from under her when Li forced himself on her, conscious of it even under those conditions.

He had never known the chain was there. He didn't know she had it now.

She heard him turn away and walk to the wall. There was a zip, and she grabbed the chain with both hands, careful not to let it rattle.

Standing up as quickly and as quietly as she was capable, she saw Li standing facing a boulder, relieving himself. He wasn't looking in her direction.

There would never be a better opportunity than this moment, and then, for a fraction of a second, some part of her recoiled from the thought.

Another part of her chimed in with a recollection of Li's hand, holding a chunk of rock and rapping it against the side of her head in the dark, in the cave, in the night. The smell of his breath, the feel of his hands when he—

The act was already begun, and she hadn't even made the conscious decision to carry it out. She observed her own actions as if from a distance. Coming behind him, she looped the chain around his neck and yanked. He fell backward and she twisted the chain, twisted his body so that he landed on his stomach. Crying out, he tried to reach behind him, but the huge bulk of the blankets he was wearing gave him no room to move. Lim crushed him into the ground by landing on his back on her knees, using her full weight. The rush of air out of his lungs made a whooshing noise, and she twisted the chain tighter, causing it to distort the flesh of his neck. His feet were kicking, and his arms were flapping like the tentacles of a beached squid.

Holding the chain with one hand, she grabbed the assault rifle off Li's shoulder and dragged it off his arm, then released the chain and snatched the handgun from his holster. She stood and quickly put a distance of several yards between them.

Choking and coughing, he pushed himself to his hands and knees, then looked at her like an angry dog.

"Get up," she said, her teeth chattering, but she was feeling no physical discomfort at the moment.

"You made a very big mistake not killing me when you had the chance," Li said, his voice low and rumbling.

"I can still kill you any time I want," she said, gesturing with the rifle.

"Like you know how to use that piece of equipment."

Lim didn't reply in words. She flipped off the safety and fired a single bullet. The 7.62 mm round slammed into the ice and splattered Li with frozen particles.

"Get up," she repeated.

Li stood, rubbing his neck and dragging off the manacle chain, which clinked on the ground.

"Now start taking off the blankets."

He nodded and untied the piece of rope that was keeping the blankets on, then dragged off several of them.

"All of them."

"I'll freeze!"

"All of them."

He dragged the rest of the blankets over his head and

stood in his shirtsleeves, trembling violently. Lim knew she should be feeling cold, as well. She was as unprotected as he was. But the sweet taste of revenge was keeping her warm like swallows of powerful, syrupy liqueur.

"Now the shirt, shoes and trousers."

"You must be joking!"

She didn't answer.

"You can't make me do it!" Li pleaded, but began to unbutton his shirt. He took it off and laid it next to the blankets, then dragged off his shoes and stepped out of his trousers, standing in the cold wind in just his shorts.

"All right?" he said. "All right? Do you think I've learned my lesson?"

"Put the manacles on your wrists," Lim said emotionlessly. "Then get into the cave, headfirst, and stay there until I tell you to come out."

"I'm freezing! I won't last long!"

"Then you had better hurry," Lim said. "Time is being wasted."

Li sobbed in misery and grabbed the manacles, clicking them onto his wrists, then slithered into the tiny cave.

Lim walked to the pile of blankets without taking her eyes off his feet, which were sticking out of the cave in thin black socks. She laid the rifle next to her, where she could grab it in a second if she needed it. She put on all the blankets she was wearing the day before, one at a time, and then several of Li's blankets. Then she tied them in position, becoming aware of the tremendous cold she was experiencing. But the blankets would ease it soon enough. With all the layers she was wearing, she would warm up, no matter how cold it got.

"All right, come out."

Li scooted out of the cave. His face was deathly white and his lips were blue. He tried vainly to keep parts of his torso warm by rubbing his hands over his chest and hips rapidly. He looked longingly at the clothes and the few remaining blankets at Lim's feet. A few minutes of intense suffering had transformed him into a pathetic, scrawny creature.

But Lim wasn't done yet. Still all too clear in her mind was the memory of those same hands rubbing against her in the night, feeling her, hurting her....

A plan was there in her head, though when it had materialized she couldn't recall. She pointed at the rock Li had urinated on. It was about eight feet high, pointed, with the rubble of several smaller rocks littered around it.

"Go. Loop your hands over the top."

"What?"

"Do it."

"You're not going to leave me there?" he demanded.

"What I am not going to do is discuss it."

"I'll die. I do not want to die! Not like this!"

"Then you'd better do what I say or I'll shoot you dead right now."

Li was biting his lower lip as he walked to the rock and stood on the biggest of the surrounding boulders, unsteady and threatening to slip off. With a giant stretch he managed to get his manacled wrists over the top of the pointed boulder. Pressed against the ice-cold rock, which acted like a heat sink to draw his body warmth out of him, he began to sob with the intensity of the cold.

Lim grabbed the rest of the clothes and the remaining blankets and rolled them quickly into a ball, which she took with her as she headed down the mountain. Behind her she heard agonized screaming.

There was no one for miles around to hear him. Lim knew that well. Last night, when she was screaming, no one had come to help her, either.

THE HELICOPTER HUNG over the camp for a solid two minutes before finally landing, channeling away billowing clouds of ground-level fog. The pilot finally felt confident there was no danger in the immediate vicinity and took the Hind down.

"Everybody out and secure this camp fast," he ordered. "I want the entire area searched. I don't want any surprises."

The leader of the ground troops understood the danger. Whoever was on this mountain had caused unbelievable havoc among their ground troops and had eluded their traps repeatedly. Unless he was very much mistaken, they were about to find another entire search party wiped out.

He stepped onto the snowy ground as the Hind was coming to rest on the snowy surface within fifty paces of the camp. A single tent in the center of the camp remained standing.

"You," he ordered to one of his best shooters, "keep that tent covered. But don't get close. The rest of us, let's cover the vicinity."

The ground-force leader and his other two men spread out, searching the small nearby gorge and behind the rocks at the base of the cliff wall, finding nothing. They had assured themselves from the air that the cliff, which looked directly down on the camp from about fifty feet, was empty now, although it showed footprints.

They moved into the camp itself and found it filled with frozen corpses. One tent looked as if it had been obliterated with a gigantic shotgun that shredded the material of the tent and the flesh of the occupants into a single unidentifiable mess. Other soldiers were cut down throughout the camp, and some of the tents had been exploded, using some kind of incendiary device—with the occupants still inside, as was obvious by the charred skeletons partially coated in melted plastic.

They stood around the one remaining tent, with their weapons trained on it as the ground-force leader sliced open one of the flaps and ripped it aside.

Inside was only a jumble of two empty sleeping bags.

Tracks led to the walls of the mountain, which rose up in towering cliffs on either side of the small level area. The snow made it easy to follow the direction many men had taken.

The ground-force leader noticed one of his men watching the tracks carefully as they followed them.

"What's the matter?" he demanded.

"These tracks are the matter. They show five or six men heading into this area. But two of the men came out again." He pointed to a distinct set of tracks heading in the opposite direction, back to the camp.

"What does that mean, do you think?"

The tracker shrugged. "I think we'll know soon enough."

Each harbored his own guess. The path curved just enough for them to see the solid wall that blocked the way. They entered a wide, round area in the rock. It was clear there was only one way in or out, and it was the way they had just come—unless a person had the skill and equipment required to scale a sheer rock face.

The mystery of the footsteps came to what the

ground-force leader saw as its logical conclusion. The rest of the members of the search party were here, all dead. One had his throat cut and was lying in a frozen lake of his own blood. The leader of the party had been shot in the face.

Even the local Tibetan they had grabbed as a guide was dead. But he was laid out against the rock wall, hands on his chest, as if someone actually respected or cared for the old man. Somehow the sight of the old man, peaceful in death, eyes closed as if meditating, was more unnerving than the slaughter of their Chinese soldiers.

The leader of the team felt a cold shiver pass through him. "Let's get out of here," he said.

"WINGS, TELL ME you're hearing this."

There was no reply from the radio.

"Any luck?" Sonam asked.

"No."

Bolan put away the radio and took his glasses from Sonam, who had been watching the activity in the camp. Bolan glanced down long enough to see the new arrivals emerge from the corridor to the final slaughter. They were in a hurry to get back inside the Hind.

"If they disturbed my father..." Sonam said.

"They didn't have time to do more than take a quick look around back there," Bolan assured him.

"You about ready to head out?"

"Let's wait for them," Bolan said with a nod to the Hind. "I don't want to take any chances of being spotted."

"Right."

The soldiers entered the helicopter like frightened chicks collecting under the mother hen, then the gunship roared to life and lifted into the air, heading up the mountain and passing almost directly over their heads.

Bolan and Sonam ducked under the outcropping that had shielded them from the wind throughout the night.

"I don't like the looks of this," the big American commented.

Sonam nodded. "It sure seems like they know where they are going this time."

"They were bound to find it eventually. I'd just hoped it would have taken them longer."

"When's your friend going to be joining us again?"

"I wish I knew," Bolan said.

The Hind disappeared above them, though the sound of it still echoed over the mountain.

"Come on," Sonam said. "That's the direction we're heading."

LIM CLIMBED six or seven feet up a rocky ledge, then wiggled into a wedge-shaped hollow in the mountainside. She aimed the AK-47 at the way she had come, and she didn't have to wait long.

Li ran into her field of vision, sobbing and crying like a drunkard. He staggered and tripped, falling into the snow, emerging again covered with it. Lim could see it melting against his skin, and an icy sheet clung to his back. He brushed at the snow as if it were a swarm of bugs, then ran away, continuing down the mountain. He was searching for her and didn't realize he had just passed her by.

She gave him a couple of minutes. He didn't reappear.

Now she would need to be careful. He was dying of

cold, but he was panicking, and that panic was dangerous.

He had nothing to lose.

THE HIND DESCENDED into the vast valley near the peak of the mountain and began a slow zigzagging search pattern, stirring up billows of cloud cover.

The pilot was telling himself the general was a monstrous idiot—he'd already covered this valley two times!—when the man in the copilot's seat spoke up.

"Look at that."

The pilot slowed the helicopter and brought it down to an altitude of fifteen feet. He saw a black piece of metal protruding from the snow, which could be anything.

But in the typically pristine upper Himalayas, it was highly unusual.

"Let's keep looking. If we don't see anything more, we'll come back and check that out," the pilot said.

It wasn't another forty seconds before he spotted the next piece of wreckage himself. And that was all it took to convince him that was what it was. They had found the remains of the An-26.

He turned the helicopter and rose out of the clouds, quickly evaluating the valley from a pilot's point of view. He saw the narrow entrance that might have been used by a daring pilot, and the gap between the peak and a lesser peak that might have been a way out. Then he guessed the direction the An-26 would have been traveling if it crashed somewhere in between. He maneuvered the Hind down again, into the ground-level fog, heading for the side of the valley where a short peak jutted up and walled it in.

Then all at once there it was, swimming up out of

the mist like a ghost plane, at first, then solidifying into reality.

The other men were shouting. The pilot grabbed for the radio.

"Give me the general," he said.

THE CAPTAIN of the wrecked An-26 was waiting for them in the cockpit, and he was laughing.

He'd been wounded in the legs, and although he had still been able to fly the plane skillfully, there was no way he could have marched and climbed through the Himalayas.

How long he lasted after the departure of his copilot and his captive was unknown. He had been busy. Somehow he had even managed to build a fire, but it hadn't lasted long, and the captain eventually froze to death. He was laughing when he finally died. His expression was locked in a twisted, openmouthed smile as if his last minutes of life were filled with insane hilarity.

The pilot of the helicopter shut the door to the cockpit with a shiver.

"Found it," someone shouted. The pilot stepped through the open hole in the An-26 fuselage and approached the others as they gathered around a large object sitting in the snow, not far from one of the other rock-solid corpses.

"It looks pretty intact, from what I can tell," one of them said.

The THADSAC was still in its protective wrapping, and a drift of snow had half covered it since it landed there. The soldiers began to scoop the snow away and they lifted the unit together, struggling with it over the snow, awkwardly loading it into the transport bay of the Hind.

"There's not much room for us," one of the soldiers complained.

"You're not going far," the captain said.

HIS BAREFOOT FOOTPRINTS meandered along the level areas, and at the bottom of several short drops was the disturbed snow that showed he had essentially fallen over them. Lim went more carefully, watching for his return, which might come any second, and moving with extreme caution born out of the knowledge that if she hurt herself she was as good as dead.

She found his body in midmorning. He had to have been practically crawling on all fours when he reached a six-foot drop and tumbled over it, landing on a crusty layer of snow less than six inches deep. There he struggled, but the cold had sucked the strength out of him. He could no longer push himself to his feet. Lying on his back, he stared at the sky, the snow melting around his body, refreezing, encasing him in a thin cocoon of ice. He died, eyes open, staring at the solid blue sky.

Lim didn't feel sorry for him. He'd deserved no less misery.

Still, she hoped she didn't die like that.

THE SOUND of the massive helicopter roared against the mountainside and reflected back at them, almost physically shaking the soldier on the long nylon line as it ascended back up to the hovering gunship.

"There are still tracks," he shouted when he reached the cabin and slammed the door shut behind him.

The Hind descended slowly, avoiding the narrow spaces in the mountain, but try as they might they couldn't spot the footprints from the air. Nor could they spot the copilot and the woman themselves. It was as if the mountain had swallowed them up.

The level area that they assumed the two would be following came and went abruptly, making it impossible to follow the logical path from the air.

The soldier was sent down again on the nylon cord. He reached the ground and made a quick survey of the land. He didn't notice the nylon cord ascending without him until it was almost back inside the Hind, which hovered at ten yards.

Another soldier came down after him a moment later, but the look on his face said he wasn't pleased about it.

"We're supposed to continue on foot," he shouted to his companion. "The general radioed he wants the control unit taken back to the compound without delay."

A third soldier appeared, dangled over them and descended quickly. Then the Hind nodded forward and raced away, leaving them in the lifeless, frozen wilderness.

"Well, let's go," the tracker said. "You'll stay warmer if you keep moving. Luckily there are still tracks to follow. We must be close behind them at this stage. I don't see them getting much farther than this. The sooner we get to them, the sooner the general will get us down."

THE TRACKER WALKED slowly in a wide circle, staring at the snow, while the soldiers stood silently behind him, shivering and cursing.

"Well? What's going on?"

"They were here, I think just this morning. Something very strange is going on."

"Like what?"

"Look at this." The tracker pointed at the ground heading away from the landing and the tiny cave. There in the snow was an almost perfect footprint showing the clear shape of a foot, without showing individual toes. "See these tiny lines—that's from material that wrinkled when the step was taken. This person was walking around without shoes."

"Why would one of them be walking around without shoes?"

"No good reason," the tracker said.

ELISE LIM FELT almost cheerful. Li would never bother her again, and she was warmer than she had been in as long as she could remember—the temperature was definitely higher as she moved down the mountain.

But she was still ravenously hungry, and her feet still felt frozen. There were times when the vista opened up before her, and she saw nothing but sheets of ice-blanketed mountain for miles.

Plus she was lost. Aside from generally trying to go down, she hadn't a clue where to head. She might wander for days or weeks without seeing any sign of civilization. What if she was fifty or even a hundred miles from the nearest town?

This was no time to feel euphoric. There was still a very good chance she would die up here, frozen to death like Li, or starved to death, even more slowly and miserably.

She came to a halt as the gradual descent of the ground transformed into a steep drop that went out of sight beneath her. Falling into that gorge would be certain death. If the fall didn't kill her—and depending on the incline and the depth of the snow layer, she might actually survive the impact—she would be trapped at the bottom without hope of rescue.

To her right the rock wall showed a narrow ledge covered with a thin snowdrift. The land widened again beyond it, or so it appeared. The heavy snow covering might be disguising nothing but an intraversable ice bridge.

She had no other way to go.

Lim stooped and brushed at the snow with her hands as she walked onto the ledge, which was hard and crusty. She used the butt of Li's gun to chop at the snow, methodically clearing a safe path.

The going was slow on her hands and knees, and it was a full twenty minutes before she managed to cross the ledge to its most dangerous point, where a protrusion in the rock created an actual break in the ledge.

Standing, Lim explored the rock face above her and found the best available crevices to place her hands, then she swung her leg over the outcropping and straddled it while she kicked at the snow and ice at the ledge on the opposite side. Once she had created a reasonable place to stand, she transferred her weight to it and groped for another handhold.

Vertigo swept through her out of nowhere, and against her own will she glanced over her shoulder. She could see nothing but the chasm, and she had the impression she was hanging suspended in the sky by an enigmatic force that would surely fail at any moment.

She closed her eyes, and her hand fell into a crevice in the rock, which she grabbed hard, and she swung her other leg over the outcropping.

From that point she looked only at the face of the mountain, inches away, with the occasional furtive glance at the ledge. Moments later the ledge widened, and she was able to walk normally. She leaned against

the rock wall, a few paces from the drop, and caught
her breath.

She was safe again, for the moment.

HIS CLOTHES WERE rolled up and tossed to the ground
just a few feet from where he lay dead in the snow, as
if in mockery of him.

"You think he went crazy?" one of them asked.

"I think she did it to him," the tracker said. "She
went on without him. See?" He indicated the shoe
prints that left the scene calmly. "We're not far behind
her."

"How can you be sure?"

The tracker shrugged. "I can't. The cold keeps the
footprints fresh longer. But we can't chance losing her.
Let's go."

SHE WAS GETTING COLD, anyway, standing in the shade,
and there was no way of avoiding the white expanse
waiting for her. She might as well get started.

Lim approached the snow and waded into it, feeling
it get deeper with every step, until she was lifting her
legs as if yanking them out of mud for every step. Without the benefit of a stick or pole, she began to bang
through the snow with the Chinese-made Kalashnikov.
But the snow was deep, and thrusting the rifle into it
was awkward work. She didn't want to risk abandoning
the exercise. What if the solid-rock surface turned to a
flimsy layer of snow and she stepped off into it?

The sun on the exposed skin at her nape almost felt
warm. That made the snow even more dangerous. If she
ventured out onto snow that was weakened by
warmth...

Lim heard voices.

Alone for only a couple of hours, and she was already starting to hallucinate.

Then the voices became clearer, hollow sounding over the snow, but real, speaking Chinese. She looked around wildly, at first expecting to see Li's ghost standing nearby, then spotting three Chinese soldiers standing at the edge of the drop-off next to the ledge.

Lim knew instantly how they had got there. They had to have been dropped off at the An-26 or somewhere along the way. They had been following her and Li, maybe since the very evening of the crash. They finally caught up with her. Now she had spent almost an hour traversing the ledge and the snowy bridge; that's what finally enabled them to catch up.

They spotted her at almost the same moment she saw them, and shouted.

"Stay there!"

But Lim had no intention of being taken by the Chinese again. Not alive. She would rather freeze to death or die of a fall through the deceptive snow cover. She trudged through it as fast as she could, ignoring the need to check for weak spots, while she banged and shook the AK-47 with her hands to dislodge the snow from the barrel.

There was a brief release under her feet and she gasped, but her stance was solid. She checked back on her pursuers. They had started along the ledge.

She trudged on a few more minutes until the Chinese came to the protrusion of rock. They were taking their time getting around it. The leader pounded a steel stake into the wall beyond with a small hammer, attached a rope to the stake, then reached over the protrusion with his hammer to pound in another stake. The rope went through a harness at his waist somehow. Lim stopped and faced them as the leader started climbing carefully over the protrusion.

Now was as good a time as any. She raised the AK-47, flipped off the safety with a quick prayer and triggered the weapon. Four rounds hammered along the rocky face above the soldiers, and Lim realized that she had somehow configured the weapon for autofire. Before she could release the trigger, the weapon went dry.

The soldiers were starting to panic, and they raised their own weapons. Lim dived to the ground, landing flat in the snow, and heard the sound of autofire echoing in the mountains. She expected to feel bullets boring into her flesh like metal worms, but the pain never came, and she used the time to grope for the automatic handgun she had also appropriated from Li. Raising her head out of the snow, she saw that the Chinese were concentrating on getting themselves past their exposed position.

She couldn't let that happen. She had to somehow put time between herself and the soldiers. Crawling through the snow, she aimed carefully at the lead soldier. He had made it over the protrusion and was passing the line to the next soldier. Lim aimed the handgun. The distance was too great; she couldn't possibly make the shot. She squeezed the trigger and felt the gun buck in her hand, spotting an explosion of rock erupt within eight inches of the leader, whose eyes went wide. Lim breathed deeply, set up the shot again, adjusted it down and to the left as the leader groped wildly for a perch that would carry him along the ledge, then she triggered another round.

The shot was off the target, which was the small of the leader's back. Instead it hit him in the back of the right leg two inches above the knee. The leg ceased to function, collapsing, and the soldier screamed in pain while his right hand flailed for a hold on the protruding rock as his other hand grabbed for the cliff face for any kind of handhold. His fingers slipped away on either side, and he fell backward, almost in slow motion, like a tall tree falling, and the rope, secure only on one end, whipped out of its harness. His scream filled the mountainside, transcending his pain and transforming into raw terror that dwindled into the gorge below. The scream hiccuped when the soldier hit the steep, snowy decline, then stopped abruptly as he reached the bottom.

Lim stood to watch the other two soldiers retreat in a panic, filled in equal parts with fear of a fall and fear of Lim's gun. She had killed two men in one long morning. She wondered if she ought to be experiencing guilt. But all she knew was the satisfaction of once again protecting herself.

The two Chinese gunmen went into hiding after reaching the wider level area on the far side of the ledge. She saw them peeking out at her.

She had two choices: run from them and deal with them later—and they would most certainly follow—or stay and face them if and when they finally tried to traverse the ledge.

No choice at all, really. Their helicopter would be coming back eventually. They probably had radios. She was standing out in the open, a dark target in a plain of white. She had to get out of there quickly.

She marched across the snow swiftly, not caring if it opened up and swallowed her. But solid rock materialized under her feet, and she found herself half walking, half sliding down a steep incline. The Chinese were gone from sight.

They would be on her tail again before long.

CHAPTER FOURTEEN

A distant rumble filled the mountain. Lim had been dreading the sound, knowing it would come. But she had hoped to have more time. She made a run for a tumble of boulders and crawled between them.

The helicopter approached and came to a halt not far behind her, and she knew it was hovering over the ground patrol. After less than a minute it was coming toward her again, getting louder.

Suddenly Lim realized she had to have been making tracks in the snow, and she craned her neck to see through the rocks. Sure enough, there was a clear trail of footprints that led to her hiding place. Scrambling to her feet, she bounded away, looking for bare rock or ice that would hide her trail, but not finding it. The pitch of the aircraft's roar changed when the helicopter came into the open.

One glance told her it was some kind of warship. Rockets were mounted under stubby wings, and antennalike machine guns protruded from the nose.

It seemed to stall, then dive at her like a kite that lost its wind. Lim turned and ran, terrified, heading for the nearest rock she could find. She hurtled over a low boulder, landing on both feet in the soft snow behind it, and cowered there as the helicopter's sound grew unbelievably loud. Then it swept over her position, creating a cloud of icy snow particles. The expected machine-gun fire never came.

Of course they didn't kill her. They wanted her alive.

The helicopter came to sudden halt a few hundred yards in front of her position and descended onto the snow in seconds. The side doors were opened, and men started jumping out.

Lim ran.

BOLAN CHECKED the radio. It wasn't time yet, but he heard a helicopter nearby on the mountain.

"Wings. Come in, G-Force."

Sonam looked at him expectantly. But there was no response.

Above them they heard machine-gun fire.

"Come on," Bolan growled.

The two men headed for the tumble of rocks that signaled the last stage of their climb, then heard the gunfire again, along with the roar of the Hind. Bolan had the M-16 A-1/M-203 combo in hand as they took cover in the rocks to assess the situation through his field glasses.

There was an oddly clad figure running and tumbling over the snow, coming down the hill at a breakneck pace, while farther up the hill was a collection of Chinese gunmen running after her, snow flying around them. The Hind sped into view from the rocks beyond them and leveled out at seventy-five yards, then dived again at the fleeing figure. Bolan saw the figure look around wildly, see the attacking gunship and tumble into the snow. There was a flash of long dark hair and a feminine face that was red with exertion and fear, drawn with exhaustion and starvation.

"It's the satellite operator," he said. "She's making a break for it."

The Executioner stepped into the open and targeted the Hind as it sailed over Lim. The pilot spotted him as he brought the craft to a halt and instead threw the gunship forward with a burst of speed. Bolan fired the HE grenade too late. It sailed under the tail rotor of the helicopter and hit the ground with a burst of yellow fire, white snow and slate gray rock.

LIM ROSE to her hands and knees, then felt the explosion shake the ground beneath her and she screamed and fell flat again. They were bombing her from the helicopter! She jumped to her feet again, relieved to see the aircraft veering away, although she knew it would be back soon, and ran for the protection of the nearest pile of rocks. Only then did she see a dark figure standing in the snow waiting for her, facing her.

He had dark hair and a grim face, and there was no mercy in his expression. He held a complex-looking weapon of some kind, aiming it from his hip.

Lim knew she would get no quarter from this man. He would cut her in two with that evil-looking weapon and probably forget about her an hour later.

She had lost the battle.

Then his voice rumbled across the snow.

"Get down!"

Lim flung herself forward without knowing why. His command was simply not to be disobeyed. Something flew from his weapon, and a moment later there was a flash and a concussion that rocked the hill behind her. He grabbed something from inside his coat, pushed it into the weapon and fired again. There was another blast far up the hill behind her, and it was slowly dawning on her that he had spoken English with an American accent. And he was gunning down the Chinese. For the first time in hours, a small measure of hope reappeared in her heart.

"Come on," he growled, stepping to her and reaching out a hand.

She raised her hand and felt a powerful grip hoist her out of the snow. A quick glance behind her showed her two huge craters and the lower torso of one of the Chinese flopped in the snow.

"They took cover, but they'll be back for more."

THE WOMAN SEEMED overwhelmed and dazed, but energetic enough. She couldn't collapse now. She wasn't safe and she had to be made to realize that.

"I'm Elise Lim," she said suddenly.

"Mike Belasko," Bolan said. "This is Sampen Sonam, a local who's helping me. Glad to find you alive."

"I'm glad to be alive. Were you coming in after me?"

"Yeah. You and the THADSAC."

"How in the world did you find me?"

"That's a long story, and there's no time to tell it. I hope you don't think your odds have greatly improved."

"Here comes the bird," Sonam said, hopping down from a perch on a rock.

"Take cover," Bolan ordered, wedging himself into a narrow spot between two rocks and aiming the M-16 A-1/M-203 into the blue sky. The Hind hovered into view, and he triggered the grenade launcher, deliberately skewing his aim. The grenade missed the gunship by two yards, but Bolan followed it up with a magazine-draining full-auto spew from the assault rifle. The rounds clunked against the belly of the Hind, which was already spinning into the sky. The grenade arced through the air and hit the snow with a muffed explosion and a cloud of smoke.

"That'll keep him thinking for a few more minutes. All I've got left are smoke grenades, and only a few of those. If the pilot thinks I've still got some real explosives, he'll keep his distance," Bolan explained, then glanced up the hill. "You two make a run for the next shelter at the bottom of this hill while I try to deplete the competition's ranks." He saw Sonam about to protest. "Go!"

He brooked no argument, and Sonam grabbed Lim by the arm and steered her into the set of tracks he and Bolan had made on the ascent.

Bolan changed magazines on the M-16 and checked his grenade supply, already well aware of his current stock. There were no more HE or incendiaries, but he still had a single CS grenade, more or less useless in these wide-open spaces, and a few buckshot rounds.

He thumbed the buckshot into the M-203 and waited for the Chinese to move in closer. There were four left. The first two came barreling down the hill and circled the rocks, spotting the fleeing forms of Sonam and Lim. They waved back up the hill and shouted in Chinese. The others couldn't be far behind. Bolan stood stone still, sandwiched between boulders. The first two loped down the hill after Sonam and Lim, then two more figures, breathing hard and looking haggard, followed after them, letting gravity do most of the work.

The Executioner extracted himself from the rocks, checked up the hill for stragglers, then turned on the final two soldiers. They heard his movement and whirled, surprised, but their reactions were dulled by long, hard exertion. Bolan triggered the M-203, which the buckshot round had essentially converted into a shotgun. The round slammed into the nearer soldier and transformed his chest and head to hamburger. He collapsed abruptly onto the hillside. His companion had absorbed only a fraction of the blast, and he began to scream, grabbing at the ruined side of his face. Bolan triggered the M-16 briefly and cut him down, ending his agony.

He crouched in the rocks again as the other two soldiers turned on him, firing uphill with their AK-47s. The 7.62 mm rounds bounced among the rocks, and the big American waited for the firing to slow before rising up enough to bring the gunners into view. Sonam and Lim had disappeared behind them, and he triggered high with a long burst, steering the stream of bullets across the gunmen at chest level and sending them tumbling down the incline.

There was a sudden roar, and the Hind dived down on him from behind at a tremendous speed, its belly-mounted machine guns firing at a monstrous rate. Bolan heard the approach far enough in advance to get to cover. Pushing himself against the rocks, he inserted himself again into his twin protective boulders, scrunching deep in a hollow at the base so that his body was shielded from attack.

The torrent of fire chopped into the rocks and sent dust and shards of stone flying in the air. Bolan covered his eyes until the fire stopped, then thumbed the last CS grenade into the M-203 and watched his small, limited view of the sky for the Hind to reappear. It had obviously halted a few hundred yards away and was coming back to the rocks with caution, hoping to see his body.

It finally peeked over the rocks like a shy bride, stuck in the sky about four hundred yards above Bolan. It was most likely out of range of the M-203, but he jumped to his feet and fired up at the gunship, skewing his aim just enough to assure a miss. The CS grenade flew almost directly at it, missing the belly as the pilot spotted it and fed the rotors fuel, carrying him up and away. The CS grenade tumbled out of the sky and smacked into the hillside with a disappointingly feeble pop and puff of smoke. But by then the Hind was accelerating away from the hillside. If the occupants saw that explosion, they would probably know he was firing nonlethal grenades.

Bolan was sure he knew what was coming next, and it was time he made his break. He vaulted the rocks and hit the snow running, bypassing the bodies of the first two dead soldiers, one eye locked on the Hind as it made a high-altitude one-eighty. He sprinted down the hillside and hit the ground flat when he reached the second pair of dead men. The Hind was facing toward him now but was a half mile off, staying well out of range as it positioned itself for the next attack.

Bolan's survival depended on their not being able to see what was happening on the mountainside. From a prone position he grabbed one of the corpses and half dragged it on top of him, half slid himself underneath it.

The Hind accelerated at the rocks, and the two rockets left their mounts under the stubby wings with twin flashes of fire. They homed in on the hillside in under a second and exploded, debris flying through the air for hundreds of yards. Bolan felt the rocks pummeling the corpse that covered his torso and head, and something smashed into one of his legs, which was partially exposed.

The sound of the Hind retreated over the mountain. Bolan got to his feet and watched it disappear.

"The chopper is going back for reinforcements, and that won't take long," Bolan said when he caught up to Lim and Sonam. "Are you wounded?"

"My feet may be frozen, but I'm still able to get around," Lim answered.

"Good."

Bolan snatched the radio and flipped it on, speaking into it briefly and in vain.

"Let's move out," the Executioner said, tucking the radio away.

Where was Grimaldi?

JACK GRIMALDI WAS FUMING, and he had to consciously restrain himself from accelerating the gunship to fuselage-rattling speeds.

The Russians were willing to allow him use of the Hind, but only on the condition that no Russians actually be on board. On the one hand they were embarrassed about losing the Americans' satellite controls—not to mention the satellite controller. On the other hand they weren't about to risk allowing Russian military personnel to get killed or captured in Chinese-controlled Tibet. They could always report the Hind was stolen if it was caught or downed.

So on top of the infuriating wait at the village, the Hind flight crew had insisted on being flown to a rendezvous point 125 miles to the southwest. Grimaldi had no choice but to accommodate them, leaving them in an empty lowland area near a small Tibetan town. They had to have arranged for transportation from there. Grimaldi didn't see any, but he didn't care. His one thought was getting into the mountains and finding out if Mack Bolan was still alive.

The sun was getting higher. Grimaldi checked his charts, then his watch. Almost there!

"ALREADY?" SONAM DEMANDED when the sound of the gunship came back over the mountain.

"They know where we are," Bolan growled. "They may have set up a command post in Ghaze."

Sonam paled at the thought of his village inhabited by Chinese military forces.

Bolan grabbed the arm of the Chinese-American woman and propelled her across a nearly level stretch of land that disappeared a couple of hundred yards ahead. Sonam said the drop there was steep but negotiable.

Lim stumbled and would have fallen without the firm support the Executioner was giving her. They had given her handfuls of food that she devoured greedily. Bolan hoped that would revive her somewhat. Her weakened state wasn't doing much for their speed.

The Hind appeared directly in front of them, rising from below the drop-off like a movie monster emerging from the earth, and roared at them over the snow. A single rocket sped from under its wing and passed well over their heads, bursting on the ground behind them. The machine guns fired next, peppering the snow to their right.

"Keep moving. They want you alive, remember," Bolan said, then stepped in front of his companions and leveled the M-16 at chest level, firing a handful of rounds at the gunship, which steered clear and maneuvered into the distance, traveling in a huge circle and descending at the base of the drop-off.

"He's going to plant troops down there," Bolan stated.

"That's our only way out of here!" Sonam answered.

Time was up.

Bolan grabbed the radio and thumbed it on.

"G-Force!"

"I'm here, Sarge!"

"We've got a gunship about to drop off a squadron of soldiers. We're low on ammo, and we won't get past them. Anything you can do for us?"

Bolan heard it now—another helicopter rocketing over the landscape at a tremendous speed. Grimaldi had the pedal to the metal.

"One distraction coming up!" the Stony Man pilot announced, and a flash materialized under the distant helicopter, searing into the mountains and erupting with a boom. The Chinese Hind stopped at ten yards and turned.

"I see him, Sarge," Grimaldi said.

"He's coming after you. Be careful."

"I'm as well armed as he is, buddy."

The Chinese helicopter leveled off at one hundred yards and accelerated to meet the intruder, and Bolan saw Grimaldi was approaching in an identical gunship, with a big Russian flag visible on its fuselage. The Stony Man pilot curved away from the mountains and shot almost directly into the sky, the Chinese Hind struggling to follow him.

"Stay out of his sights," Bolan said into the radio.

"I'll stay out of his. Let's see if he can stay out of mine!" Grimaldi shouted. Bolan saw the Russian Hind make a sharp twist and dive out of the sky. The Chinese aircraft overshot it by a wide margin and turned late, accelerating in an attempt to catch up. First Grimaldi, then the Chinese helicopter sped behind the mountain at a tremendous rate and disappeared.

The morning became deathly quiet.

JACK GRIMALDI EMBRACED a level snowbank and twisted and turned like a motorcycle driver to avoid the rocks, then pulled back hard and shot up along the hillside. The Chinese chopper stayed high, avoiding the rocks, and struggled to chase him. Grimaldi laughed grimly, in his element, and aimed the aircraft at a looming outcropping that would have stopped a freight train. He slowed slightly and followed the curve of the massive rock, crawling over the top of it like a bug defying gravity, then twisted to the left and ascended again, hugging the incline of the mountain.

The Chinese Hind was on his tail but falling behind, acting sluggish. It was loaded down with Chinese soldiers and couldn't possibly react with the precision Grimaldi was exercising.

He reached a peak and felt the cold seeping in as the clouds blasted against the windshield of the Russian helicopter, then found himself in the open again, above the mountaintop clouds, feeling as if he were on the top of the world. He leveled off, spotted the Chinese Hind break into the open altitude a quarter mile behind him, and dived again at the first open area he came to. It took him into a forest of rocky peaks and he slowed the craft only as much as he had to for navigating the rocks and crags.

He was flying under a ceiling of clouds and became concerned when the Chinese Hind didn't follow him in. Maybe the pilot knew these peaks and was waiting to get the drop on him. Maybe Grimaldi had made a mistake.

The path he was meandering through came to an abrupt end against a new mountain wall and he climbed, spotted a hump in the mountain and swerved to avoid it, slowing even more. The cloud cover absorbed the aircraft for less than five seconds, and Grimaldi broke into the open, only to find himself face-to-face with the Chinese aircraft.

Grimaldi almost threw himself bodily to the left and fed fuel unreservedly into the Hind, tearing across the peak, sensing the enemy aircraft sitting and rotating calmly where it sat, its aiming system targeting him.

He dropped abruptly, knowing it might be suicide, and clenched his teeth as the Hind fell into the cloud cover like a rock falling from the sky. If there was another peak or a tall formation of boulders, he was going to crack like an egg hitting a sidewalk. He fed fuel to the rotors only when he was inside the cover, craning his head to see if he had killed himself. The snowy ground appeared in an instant, about to crash into his underside.

Grimaldi flooded the rotor turbines with fuel, and the gunship almost bounced as the rotors caught the air and leveled the craft at an altitude of a few feet, maybe less. The Stony Man pilot didn't give himself time for relief. He punched the controls that sent a rocket hurtling into the ground a few hundred yards in front of him, where it shocked the mountain with its impact. The force of the explosion billowed up through the clouds.

He sat where he was, buried in cloud cover, wheels almost marking the surface of the snow, waiting. The rocket blast just might fool the other Hind into thinking he had crashed. But the deception couldn't last long.

Grimaldi lifted himself through the cover and peered out. There was no sign of the other Hind.

He grabbed the radio. "Sarge, he's on his way back."

"I copy that. We could really use some hardware, Wings. Our ammo supply is low, and we've got nothing useful in terms of explosives."

"I have what you need. Our friends in Tadzhikistan supplied us well. But why don't I just come pick you up?"

"Negative. We're on the way down. There's no place you could make a safe pickup. If you sit still anywhere, the enemy is going to be all over you."

"Roger. I'll try to send you down a care package anyway."

"Don't take any foolish risks, Jack," Bolan said.

"Never," Grimaldi said. "See you in a few."

BOLAN AND SONAM HAD SCALED the cliff wall just hours earlier, and the spikes they had placed in the wall would be useful now. The Executioner attached the rope to the topmost spike and flung the rope down the tall, sheer rock face.

They listened to the growing pitch of a nearby helicopter with a mixture of apprehension and hope. Bolan scaled a pile of boulders with his field glasses and spotted the new arrival, easily identifying the Russian flag.

"I see you, Wings," Bolan announced into the radio. "We're sitting on a cliff face at your one o'clock."

"I see the place. Here I come."

The Hind redirected at them and swept into open space, facing the cliff wall. Bolan hopped down and gave a brief wave, as did Sonam and Lim.

"Your friend looks very nice, Sarge. But she could use a new wardrobe," the pilot said as he hovered over their perch. "I can get you guys up here in minutes. This beast does have a winch."

"No time," Bolan replied. "Send down the pack."

Grimaldi opened the side door and with his foot tipped out the canvas pack, which he had stuffed full of the hardware and incendiaries supplied by the Russians. It dangled a few yards under the Hind and quickly descended into Bolan's hands.

"The other chopper's coming!" Lim shouted.

The big American unhooked the sack and said into the walkie-talkie, "I've got it, and our friend is on his way back. Get out of here!"

"You told me so," Grimaldi said, and steered the Hind up and away. "But I hate abandoning you guys!"

"You're no good to us blown to bits. Did you check out that chasm we're heading into? Think you can put it down in there?"

"Yeah. It'll be tight but not impossible. I wouldn't want to have to do it in a hurry."

"I copy. Get safe. I'll keep you up-to-date on our situation."

Grimaldi reached a plateau of sorts and hopped over the top. He had seen a field of cloud cover there, and he descended into it carefully. He put the aircraft down on the snow underneath, then put the rotors in idle. The stewy cloud cover began to reform overhead despite the rotor wash.

He sat staring at the misty ceiling, immensely frustrated. There was nothing he hated worse than twiddling his thumbs.

BOLAN HURRIED his companions into the rocks before the Chinese Hind closed in. It swooped over the chasm, and he could see the Chinese staring into it. Maybe they saw the rope dangling from the cliff side.

Then they rushed up and over in pursuit of Grimaldi. Bolan hoped his friend had put down somewhere out of sight or made a quick run for it.

"Come on," he said, dragging Lim and Sonam to the cliff edge.

"I've never done this before!" Lim said as Bolan looped the rope around her waist.

"You'll figure it out. Sonam's going first. If you descend too fast, you'll run into him and he'll slow you down."

"Not too slow," Sonam added.

"Right. That chopper could be back in minutes. You know what to do when you get to the bottom."

"That doesn't sound terribly safe, either," Lim complained.

"We have no safe options at the moment," Bolan declared. "Get going."

Sonam kicked himself over the cliff edge and started making big jumps down the cliff side, pausing twenty feet below them and looking expectantly at Lim.

"I don't know about this!"

"No time to discuss it," Bolan said. He gave her a shove, sending her out into the open space with a scream. She snatched at the rope and hit the wall, bounced and descended again.

"Good!" Sonam called, and pushed off his feet, descending in a big leap.

"Wait for me!" Lim shouted.

"Keep coming!"

Bolan heard the return roar of the Hind, which was good news for Grimaldi, bad news for them.

"The helicopter's back," he shouted. "You've got about one minute."

Sonam descended at breakneck speed, and Lim swore at him loudly, then screamed shortly and plummeted out of control. She twisted and hit the rock wall off balance, missing with her feet and slamming against her hip and shoulder. Sonam stopped and allowed her to slide into him, then descended again, shouting at her, shocking her into action.

Bolan had no time to watch the end of their descent. Sonam seemed to have it under control. The Executioner couldn't be in the open when the Chinese Hind reappeared. He bolted for his cover in the rocks as the chopper swung into view overhead.

The Hind wandered over the rocks and the mountainside, searching for them, all at once veering off and heading for the chasm. Lim and Sonam were spotted. It hovered directly over the chasm opening, and Bolan, peering out of the rocks, looked almost directly into the cockpit, seeing the pilot and one of the gunners staring almost straight down. The rumble of the aircraft became more directional as it passed into the cavern and descended from his field of vision, then he ran to the cliff edge with the canvas sack of hardware Grimaldi had supplied.

Below, Lim and Sonam were in the open but running for cover at the rear end of the chasm. They had nowhere else to go. There was a way out of the chasm at the opposite end, but they would never make it past the spot where the Hind was about to land.

Bolan pulled open the canvas sack and groped at the contents, watching his companions. They were making their way as best they could, but the snow at the end of the chasm had built up to very deep levels. Lim took a step, and her entire leg sank into the snow. Bolan saw her shout to Sonam, but the sound was lost in the roar of the Hind. The aircraft was at fifty feet and had slowed its descent as the walls of the chasm closed in. Clearance was tight, and the pilot was being careful. Their victims were trapped at the far end of the chasm, and they weren't going anywhere.

The Executioner stood on the cliff edge feeling impotent, a series of incendiaries arranged on the ground at his feet. He could do nothing at the moment. Sonam swam back through the snow and grabbed Lim's hand and dragged her out of the hole she had sunk into. They half crawled across the deep drift.

The Hind descended to forty feet and slowed even more.

Sonam pushed Lim behind the boulders at the end of the chasm. She sank out of sight, and he leaped on top of her.

They were as protected as they were going to get.

Bolan yanked the pin on the Russian grenade and pitched it into the open air of the chasm as the pilot of the Hind adjusted his descent, moving to a better position in the center of the chasm. The grenade missed the rotors by a yard, plummeted to the ground beneath and exploded. The Executioner had already snatched up the second grenade and pulled the pin, and he lobbed the bomb into the open space, adjusting his aim to accommodate the change in the Hind's position.

But as the grenade took to the open air, the pilot reacted to the first grenade blast by veering away from it, dangerously close to the wall of the chasm. The second grenade sailed past the rotors again and hit the ground. The explosion this time was even closer under the belly of the gunship, and the pilot's sharp wits were all that kept him from steering the helicopter right into the canyon wall. Instead he fed fuel to the turbines and ascended rapidly.

But Bolan was faster. The third grenade was already being launched, and now he could aim almost directly down at the gunship. The grenade slammed into the translucent circle of the rotor and exploded. At least one of the blades sheered off, and the Hind lurched in the air as if it were drunk. The next grenade hit less than a second later and blasted into the top of the turbine rotor drive. The helicopter plummeted thirty-five feet and slammed into the ground like a dropped tank. The fuel caught fire, and a yellow explosion seemed to fill the chasm. Bolan recoiled from the edge to avoid flying debris, covering his eyes, then looked back over the edge hoping to see if the blast had reached the shelter Sonam and Lim had sought.

He heard the rush of another helicopter and looked up in time to see the Russian Hind spin into view over the top of the nearest peak and descend over the chasm.

Grimaldi sat in the sky almost exactly at Bolan's eye level, and both of them watched the chasm depths. The snow seemed to have melted instantly in great puddles in proximity to the blast, but long black marks on the snow showed that tongues of fire had reached out to superheat the chasm from virtually end to end.

Then there was movement. Lim struggled to her feet from behind the rock, then Sonam, and both waved.

Grimaldi drew a big grin and gave Bolan a thumbs-up.

The big American took out his radio.

"How about we get everybody together and get off this damn big cold rock," Grimaldi said.

Bolan thought that sounded like a good idea.

Doma Thubten smiled and poured her more tea.

CHAPTER FIFTEEN

"Why can't I stay with you?" Lim asked.

Doma Thubten spooned up more *tzampa*. The gruel was pasty and flavorless, but Lim couldn't seem to get enough. She stared at the bowl greedily and almost snatched it from his hands. He smiled and poured more tea for her, as well. The sweet aroma filled the interior of his small hut.

"Because staying with me is not going to be safe," Bolan said. "The job here is less than half-done. I'm going to find this General Zheng you told me about and put him out of commission."

"What about the THADSAC?" Lim asked.

"What about it?"

"Are you going to try to rescue it?"

"I doubt that," Bolan said. "The U.S. can always build another one. If I happen to run across it, I'll be sure to put it out of commission. My understanding is it can't be operated without training."

"Oh, they could figure it out eventually. What they really need is access codes, which I've got." She tapped her forehead with one finger.

"All the more reason to get you out of this country. If Zheng figures out you're still in the neighborhood, he'll make recapturing you his number-one priority."

Lim nodded, swallowing a mouthful of her lunch and washing it down with steaming tea. "I would love to get back to the United States and have some American food. Maybe a big juicy cheeseburger." She looked at her Tibetan host. "No offense."

Doma Thubten smiled and poured her more tea.

"Right," Bolan said. "Jack will take you back to Tadzhikistan. The Russians will provide you with military transportation to Moscow along with military escort as far as Paris. There you'll be put on a flight directly back to Washington, D.C."

Lim nodded. "All right. But what's your plan here?"

Bolan shrugged. "Take down Zheng's organization. Cause some trouble."

Grimaldi appeared in the door of the small hut.

"We about ready, folks?"

"Yes," Lim said.

"Yeah." Bolan stood, grabbing the freshly stocked pack he would be carrying into this new campaign. Inside were sufficient tools of the trade to keep him in business for a substantial period of time.

He thanked Doma Thubten. The Tibetan nodded and smiled, telling them to come back any time.

The Russian Hind was parked on the outskirts of the village. They had stopped in the village just long enough to drop off Sampen Sonam and get proper clothing for Lim. It was unlikely Zheng's troops would track them there. They were going to be slow to recover from the loss of their only remaining versatile transport craft. Their airplanes weren't terribly useful among the mountains.

Sonam had begged to accompany Bolan during the next phase of his campaign against the general, but the

Executioner didn't need an amateur at his side, no matter how sincere he was.

The young Tibetan understood, and waved as the Hind lifted off. He still had the Browning Hi-Power inside his coat, along with a supply of ammunition. The gun's power was as much symbolic to him as it was real.

But as the aircraft took to the sky and roared off into the mountain peaks, he wondered if he would ever really use it again. He thought of his father, dead in the great mountain that towered over his own village, and thought of what Sampen Zhu would have said about the gun.

"'To use such a weapon is to spit into the eye of Buddha.'"

He thought of the Chinese who dominated his land. At best they were despots. The People's Republic sanctioned destruction of their Tibetan culture, symbols, identity and faith. They even foisted upon the Tibetans their own choices for leaders of the Buddhist faith.

Still, what was the best way to deal with the Chinese? Was it through methods of violence such as *he* had used, the warrior who went even now probing deeper into the tiger's den? Or through passive acceptance, such as Sampen Zhu had preached?

Sonam didn't have a clear answer. He had killed a man in the mountain, and he had experienced some sort of satisfaction in the act.

Now he was feeling shame. But just a little. He would have to meditate on the events of the past few days.

Meanwhile he wasn't giving up the handgun.

THE VILLAGERS of Zheqin came into the streets when the helicopter appeared over the grassy farmland just south of their town limits for the second time in a day. This time its arrival was quick and peaceful.

Bolan watched the land looming up as Grimaldi brought the gunship down fast. The pilot was keeping an eye on the village. The general might have stationed troops here, although it was doubtful he would have foreseen his faceless enemies returning here for any reason.

The general didn't know about the motorbike stashed in the ditch in the field.

"Same frequency," Bolan said. "I'll be in touch hourly, as before."

"Understood," Grimaldi replied. "Good luck."

The helicopter touched the soil, and Bolan turned away, pulling open the door. He jumped out, with the pack hanging over one shoulder, the M-16 A-1/M-203 on the other and a five-gallon fuel canister in his hands, and raced across the open ground to the ditch.

The Hind was taking off, but Grimaldi kept it at a hover a hundred yards above the field, watching the surrounding territory and waiting for Bolan's okay. The Executioner filled the tank on the motorcycle and strapped the canister with a couple of remaining gallons to its rear end. The bike started on the first try, and with a twist he accelerated away from the village.

"Everything's in working order," he radioed to the Hind.

"Roger," Grimaldi radioed back.

The Hind swerved to the west, heading into the mountains for the long, arduous flight out of Tibetan airspace. Grimaldi would need to keep low to stay out of Zheng's radar. Bolan wasn't worried about him.

Behind him the village of Zheqin was gone from sight. He imagined the villagers were very glad to see the Hind and himself leave.

In a few hours General Zheng was going to be wishing the same thing.

BOLAN WRAPPED the M-16 in a canvas sack before entering Nyima city limits. He wanted to make his presence known, but he wanted to be at least somewhat subtle.

He found Grimaldi's hotel, the Nyima JC, without difficulty. Chances were that every hotel in the city had an informant for General Zheng, but Bolan didn't want to waste any time.

The faded elegance of the lobby wasn't lost on Bolan. The few important visitors to this rather isolated Tibetan city had to have stayed at this hotel back in the 1930s, when it was new. Who knew how many decades had passed since the carpet was replaced or the walls painted?

The clerk at the counter matched Grimaldi's description of him: a well-groomed young Chinese man in a crisp suit.

"I'd like a room for a couple of nights, but I don't have a reservation," Bolan said. "Any chance you've got rooms available?"

It was a stupid question. The establishment was as quiet as a church. There might not be any other guests in residence at all.

"Yes, of course."

"Good." Bolan presented his ID. He'd been tempted to make use of Grimaldi's Elliot Paige identification, then decided there was no point in being too blatant. He gave the clerk his well-used Belasko ID. It didn't matter, really. The clerk had already exhibited frank suspicion, especially when Bolan placed his canvas carryall on the ground with a heavy metallic clank.

"Second-floor room if you've got one," he said.

"Yes, of course."

The clerk presented him with a key, then stepped from behind the counter. "Our bellboy is off today. I'll help you with your bag, Mr. Belasko."

"No!" Bolan said forcefully. "I'll take it myself."

The clerk raised an eyebrow. "Yes, of course."

If there was any lack if suspicion in the clerk's mind, Bolan had just cleared it up. He started for the stairs and took the first flight, turned and walked just far enough up the second flight to take him out of line of sight of the desk clerk, then looked back around the corner. The clerk snatched at the phone and began speaking in rapid-fire Mandarin Chinese.

Bolan went to his room. He didn't think he would have long to wait.

He entered the room, switched on the old transistor radio beside the bed and drew back the curtains, allowing in the bright afternoon sun. He cranked on the shower in the bathroom, then shut the bathroom door and left the room, crossing to another guest room. Using the picks he always carried, he opened the lock in under twenty seconds and slipped inside.

Bolan closed the door all but a crack and watched the stairs, pulling the door gently shut when he saw the new arrivals.

It was a group of at least four armed men, one of whom toted a shotgun. The others carried drawn handguns. They were prepared to go in blazing. They strode down the hall without making any attempt to hide their footsteps, which shook the old structure. They stopped at the door across the hall.

Bolan waited with the Desert Eagle in his fist. He saw no need for the quiet-fire capability of the Beretta, and he wanted the instant stopping power the big .44 Magnum pistol offered. It was four men against one, despite the Executioner's skill and experience, and he couldn't afford to allow any errant shots in his direction.

He waited for them to make their move and heard a kick. When they forced the door open, the bright light from the wide-open curtains cast their shadows in the hall, which Bolan saw clearly under the door he was hiding behind. He watched the shadows shrink as the men entered the room, then judged it was time to engage the enemy.

He stepped into the hall just as he heard the sound of a gun blast that sent the bathroom door flying open in his assigned room. More shots followed as the gunner stormed into the bathroom, filling the room with fire before realizing it was empty.

There was a shout of confusion. The rear man turned toward the hall and saw Bolan. He had the shotgun aimed from the hip, but the Desert Eagle thundered first. The .44 Magnum round blasted through the gunner's chest and sent him sprawling into his companions.

Bolan didn't wait for the others to get their bearings or allow them time to defend themselves. He aimed at a stumbling man, whose mouth made an O of surprise, and triggered a second round. The damage inflicted by the Desert Eagle from the proximity of just a few paces was substantial. It crashed through the rib cage and filled the lungs and heart with bone fragments and jagged metal pieces that destroyed everything in their path. The figure collapsed.

The man who had fallen beneath the first victim was curled in a ball. Bolan stepped into him and kicked him in the ribs while he reached into the bathroom and fired at the gunman who was scrambling for cover. The bathroom figure managed to forestall his death by seconds. The Magnum round ripped through his blazer sleeve and arm, and he howled, bending over the hurt arm but reaching for the door with a revolver in his good arm.

Bolan retreated and allowed the heavy-caliber rounds to crash into the bathroom doorjamb and continue into the room beyond. Then he reached inside, aimed by instinct and triggered a round, adjusted his aim slightly and fired again. There was a crash, and he stepped back into the door, finding that his second round had drilled the gunman in the pelvis and driven him to the floor where he sprawled unmoving.

Bolan grabbed the sole survivor with the cracked ribs and dragged him to his feet, sweeping the automatic handgun out of this grip. The man croaked in pain. The Executioner stood him at the base of the bed and put the Desert Eagle to his forehead.

"I'd like to know about General Zheng."

"I know nothing about General Zheng," the would-be assassin protested.

Bolan withdrew the Desert Eagle and slammed his fist into the victim's good ribs. There was a distinct crack, and the figure toppled on the bed, bouncing for a moment and screaming in pain.

"Now, about General Zheng."

"What do you want to know?"

"Where are his bases?"

"Tenzing."

Bolan put one knee on the bed and slammed his fist into the wounded assassin's stomach. The Chinese expelled a rush of air, then was curiously silent, doubled over, face crimson as he tried to get his breath back.

The Executioner gave him a moment as he walked to the window and peered down. There were three gunmen in sight, one directly under the window, the other two across the street keeping an eye on it. They'd be getting worried about their comrades' activity, or lack thereof, about now.

"I'm asking you one last time," Bolan said. "Then I'm pulling your plug. Got it?" He placed the muzzle of the Desert Eagle against the assassin's heart.

"Okay, I'll tell you what you want to know!"

"Make it quick."

The man started to talk.

BOLAN HEARD something from the hallway, maybe a step on carpet or a whisper.

He was jotting down names in his black warbook, a notebook of his targets. Slipping it into his jacket's inner pocket, he dragged the dead shotgunner off the floor, relieved him of his weapon and hoisted his body out the open door into the hallway. The corpse hit the opposite wall and hung there for a part of a second, as if his legs were struggling to work, as if he were on the verge of coming back to life. In that moment the hallway filled with automatic gunfire and the rounds slammed into the body, which gave it up, collapsing, and the gunfire abruptly halted. There was a swift cry, and Bolan stepped into the open and fired the 12-gauge shotgun before he had a target sighted.

A single Chinese gunner stood in the hall, and the desk clerk was five paces behind him. The gunner's face wore an expression of shock when Bolan appeared, but he didn't have reaction skill sufficient to save himself. The cloud of buckshot filled the hall and crashed into him, flaying the skin from his body and sending him to the floor in a sudden surge of flowing blood. The clerk caught buckshot in the face and shoulder and screamed, grabbing at his eyes with the heels of his palms. Blood poured from under his hands, and he stumbled sideways, slamming into the wall, then tottering to the stairs.

As Bolan turned back to the bedroom, he saw his bedridden victim making a move for freedom, dragging himself off the bed and groping for one of the fallen handguns. The Executioner targeted the back of the man's skull as his fingers closed on a .38. The .44 Magnum round drilled through the gunner's skull and exploded out his face, cutting off brain functions instantly. The corpse collapsed, fingers going loose on the .38.

Bolan had what he came for, spelled out in the pages of his warbook. It was all the information he needed to start a one-man campaign against General Zheng.

As he made his way downstairs, he saw that the front of the lobby was dominated by a huge picture window. Several gunmen were waiting there, and Bolan decided the entire hotel had to be surrounded.

Getting out could be a problem.

He had things to do and places to go, and time was being wasted.

It occurred to him that the building might be encircled at street level, but it would be unguarded at the top.

The hotel was surrounded by five-story residential buildings that were prevalent throughout the People's Republic of China, and were nearly identical to any inexpensive housing that might be found in any major city in the world.

He ran up ten flights of stairs to the fifth level and kicked open the first locked door he came to. The room was empty, and Bolan was engulfed with stale, musty air. He dragged open the curtains, and the room filled with afternoon sun.

An apartment building was across the street. The shutters were closed on the window directly opposite him, but the one next to it was uncovered. There was no sign of movement behind the glass.

The street below was a flurry of activity. The guards were running toward the front of the building, two of them disappearing around the front. The third stopped short as someone shouted to him.

They'd discovered the massacre on the second floor and would be combing the building soon.

Bolan withdrew the hook and rope Sampen Sonam had provided him in case he had the need for further mountain climbing before leaving Tibet. This wasn't quite the purpose the equipment was intended for, but it would do the trick. The Executioner wrenched open the hotel window and straddled the ledge. Twirling the heavy steel hook over his head, he flung it suddenly. It sailed over the narrow street and crashed through the apartment window. Bolan pulled carefully on the rope until he felt the hook set in something, then yanked it hard, burying it. He tied the rope to the iron radiator in the corner of the room.

The guard on the street seemed oblivious as Bolan grabbed the rope and began swinging fist over fist, fifty feet above the cobblestoned street. He had reached the halfway point when something gave. The rope went slack, and Bolan fell five feet, grabbing with his free hand, and the rope went taut again. He felt his fingers loosen but managed to retain his grip, then the rope went slack again. It was the radiator in the hotel that gave up the ghost. Bolan felt himself swinging toward the apartment building, then come to a halt as the radiator crashed into the wall base below the window. He found himself facing a steep upward climb on the rope to get to the open window.

His two-hundred-plus pounds proved too much for the precarious balance of the iron radiator, and it was dragged out the window. Bolan felt it happening and looked back—it was, in fact, just a section of the iron radiator that had been wrenched from the rest of the ancient assembly. It flopped out the window and swung into open space. The big American locked his hands on the nylon rope, feeling himself sliding down it as the rope became perpendicular to the earth. The section of radiator swung across the open street and slammed into the building with a crash that broke windows on either side of it.

Riding out the impact, Bolan knew there was no way the gunman on the street was going to miss that little display. He began to haul himself up the rope and came to a window two stories below the window he was aiming for, but now wasn't the time to be picky. There was a shout from the street and a rattle of gunfire. The rounds crunched against the brick below his feet, and Bolan drew them up to his chest and kicked at the brick, sending himself flying away from the side of the building as the bullets crawled up the wall to his former position. He swung back at the window, momentum controlling him, but the gunman with the autorifle was unable to follow his erratic actions. Bolan never felt the impact of the 7.62 mm rounds he expected to pepper his body. He slammed into the glass and the wooden frame, which collapsed into splinters and shards, and found himself crashing to the floor inside a small, dingy kitchen.

The warrior felt the familiar sting of small cuts, and

he was sure a daggerlike shard of glass was protruding from his back. He would deal with it later. He got up from the floor and raced through the door into a front bedroom, where an elderly man and woman were sitting, frightened and bewildered. Bolan rushed out their front door and into the hallway.

Zheng's goons knew where he was. They'd be storming into the lower level of the apartment building in seconds. Bolan could only go up or out again. He rushed around the circular hallway to the other side of the building and found a woman coming out of her apartment. She took one look at him and gave a small cry, flattening herself against the wall and dropping a brown paper parcel she was carrying. Bolan stomped into her apartment, finding it configured like the one he had just left, and made for the tiny balcony where an old woman was pinning clothes to a thin rope that dangled across a dark alley.

Bolan ignored the screaming woman. A quick check confirmed that the clothesline was secured into the brick building with a nail. It was made to hold a lot of wet clothing in strong winds. Whether it would hold a man of his weight was another matter—and one the Executioner didn't have time to think over. He grabbed the line and swung into open space.

Bolan reached hand over hand and crossed the alley in seconds, swinging up his legs to loop them over the railing on another balcony, and that was the moment the clothesline gave it up. Bolan felt himself plummeting. His knees hooked over the railing, and he clenched his muscles, feeling his body weight trying to yank his legs free from the rail and feeling the railing loosen simultaneously. He grabbed at the pack that tried to slip off his shoulders and swung it up and over onto the railing, then grabbed at the wobbling railing himself and slowly dragged himself over it.

The old woman across the alley was wailing continuously. She stopped when she saw he was safe and stood looking at him with frank bewilderment. Bolan gave her a quick wave and disappeared into the new apartment.

The dwelling was empty at the moment, and Bolan burst out of it and stormed down the five stories of stairs in huge leaps, waiting for the Chinese gunmen who might appear any minute. They hadn't yet determined the direction in which he had fled, and when he looked out one of the ground-level doors, the street was inhabited by only a few vegetable merchants.

Bolan stepped onto the street and headed for the throngs of shoppers in the market section nearby. He stepped into the crowds and instantly felt safer.

Flowing with the throngs, he made his way to his motorcycle, which was tucked in the back of a stall where an old merchant was selling blankets and furs.

Bolan had already paid the man well for the use of the hiding place. He took out another wad of bills and passed them to the merchant, whose smile went ear to ear.

"You never saw me," the big American said.

"But I hope to again some day," the man replied in broken English.

CHAPTER SIXTEEN

By late afternoon Bolan was on the road to the tiny village of Kalon, the first test of the reliability of the Intel he had extracted from the Chinese assassin in the hotel. The assassin had sworn that this tiny village was converted into a storage center for General Zheng's hardware for extended ground-based warfare.

Bolan had carefully examined the roads leading into the mountains where Kalon perched, one thousand feet higher than the city of Nyima and, while only a dozen miles away as the crow flew, twenty to twenty-five miles away via ground transportation.

Two roads led into Kalon. The traditional road was an old cart path that made a slow, twisting and turning climb up the mountainside. The new road, built within the past two years, had required the blasting of great expanses of rock and earth but had resulted in a relatively direct highway without sharp turns. Navigable, Bolan realized, by tank transport rigs, whereas the old road couldn't have been.

So Bolan took the old road, knowing it would be less carefully guarded, pushing his motorcycle to its limit. He found himself navigating hairpin curves and hugging steep cliff ledges.

It was here that he came across three men in ragged,

dirty clothing heading in the opposite direction. They were all in their late forties, but had lined faces and eyes set deep in masses of wrinkles that made them look much older, as if worn by great care. All three wore pads on their knees.

They didn't look at Bolan. They were concentrating on their praying.

As each men took a step, he would lower himself onto his knees, then flat on his stomach, and would make a silent prayer. He would then rise, take another step, lower himself and pray again.

Bolan knew these were considered devout men who made pilgrimages praying every step of the way, sometimes spending years on their painstaking journeys.

Different men, he was reminded again, were driven by many different but equally potent motivations.

By late afternoon the map told him he was coming to the end of the line. He parked the bike off the road and went for a hike.

THE EXECUTIONER crested a ledge with sun at his back and crept down the other side, hiding in a tuft of the sparse grass and peering into the village of Kalon with his field glasses. Perhaps his Intel had been a pack of lies after all.

Unlike the village of Ghaze, or its neighboring village, Kalon wasn't built on the edge of a valley. Instead it was perched in a series of small flat areas on the mountainside, with no more than a few terraced steppes on the mountains nearby.

This village was larger than Ghaze, and had more money, with a cobblestoned road and numerous brick buildings that seemed to have been built within the past few decades.

But there was certainly no evidence of storage of weapons of war.

He watched the town go about its business, people walking among their houses, a few merchants selling food. This was a small Tibetan town of no consequence. Bolan was convinced he'd been sent on a wild-goose chase.

Then the truck appeared.

It was a semi rig pulling a long, very low flatbed that was empty. The curious thing was that it emerged from behind a house on the hillside where Bolan would have been sure no truck could have hidden.

His interest piqued, he went back down to the old road and followed it on foot, ready to run for cover when he saw other traffic, which didn't materialize. Everyone was using the new road.

Bolan reached a small hill and examined the town from close proximity through his glasses. Only the new highway lay between himself and the town now, but there was still no evidence of anything out of the ordinary. The produce merchants were calling it a day and packing their stalls. Two young women carried plastic jugs of water up a steep walkway, which occasionally changed to steps, to a few high-perched houses.

No more trucks emerged, and Bolan still couldn't make out how the truck had managed to stay hidden behind the small house, which he could see clearly.

The sun dipped behind the mountain, and dusk arrived. Lights started going on in the lower houses, while at the top of the town the high-perched buildings might have light for another half hour.

Bolan climbed down the hillock and bolted across the empty highway, running for cover behind the nearest brick building of the town. From there he moved quickly, from building to building, until he came to the tiny house that had hidden the truck.

Behind the house was a solid outcropping—or so it appeared. Now as he closed in on it, Bolan could see a gap between the mass of rock behind the tiny house and the mass of the mountain. In the light of day it was detectable from about fifty feet, and as the sun sank in the west and it entered into darkness, Bolan couldn't tell it was there from a dozen paces.

The darkness let him move a little more freely. Still in the coat Sonam provided him, giving him the appearance of a local, Bolan walked in front of the house, strolling without urgency, and glanced to his right.

What seemed like a tiny driveway as it passed behind the house widened to five yards and sloped downward, crossing between the mass of stone behind the house and the rest of a mountain. The fresh-looking scars in the rock attested that the passageway was created or widened through blasting. The passage opened into more darkness beyond the rock, darkness into which Bolan couldn't see—until a pair of headlights lit the way, coming in his direction.

The big American bolted for the steep trail up to the collection of houses perched at the high-altitude end of the town of Kalon. Reaching it where it opened onto a flat, bare area of earth, he found himself out in the sun again, which he didn't like. He wouldn't pass muster as a Tibetan or a Chinese in the light of day. Heading for the last house, then into the grassy, unused land to the right, he hoped to look down into whatever lay beyond the village.

He hiked carefully down the incline and sank into a crouch in the grass, hidden from the houses. He raised his field glasses and peered down into a wide, flat valley, as he had expected to find.

But there was nothing in it.

What the assassin had said was at least partially true. This was a perfectly hidden spot in the mountains for hiding hundreds of tanks or portable missiles or whatever was required. And maybe that was what Zheng intended to do. But right now it was a field of small rolling hills.

Very regularly sized rolling hills, in fact.

The more Bolan looked at them, the more they bothered him.

TWENTY-THREE MINUTES later the shadows finally reached the upper area of the town, and Bolan started a descent into the valley, made arduous by his lack of rope.

He had to rely on his hands and feet, but the way down was at least dry and devoid of ice, and the temperature wasn't extreme enough to cause his hands to stiffen. He'd done more-strenuous climbing in recent days.

By the time he reached the ground level, dusk had turned to night. Warmed by the exertion of the descent, he slipped out of the jacket and stashed it in the rocks. He moved forward in his blacksuit with an assortment of grenades attached to his combat webbing—40 mm grenades for the M-203, as well as Russian hand grenades. He had the Beretta 93-R, suppressed, holstered in shoulder leather, and the Israeli-made Desert Eagle .44 Magnum handgun on his hip.

He was all dressed up, but did he have anywhere to go?

After touchdown he stood in the darkness listening

for the sound of a guard and heard nothing. So maybe there was nothing to guard.

He went to ground and crabbed through the grass toward the oddly symmetrical hillocks sprouting from the center of the valley floor, pausing time and again to listen. He heard nothing but the stiff Himalayan breeze.

As he approached the first "hill," his suspicion was confirmed. It was a canvas tarp, covered with glued-on clumps of grass, staked over something big. Crawling on his stomach, he reached under the canvas and felt a steel tread.

It was what he had expected to find.

The "hill" was a camouflaged tank.

He crawled to the front of the vehicle, where the canvas draped over the front cannon and created open space enough for him to stand. Inside the camouflage he pulled out his flashlight, adjusting it to a narrow focus. Crawling onto the body of the tank, he quickly found the identification he was looking for. It was a Russian T-64, a 38,000-kilogram powerhouse that had proved itself in Soviet battles over the thirty years it had existed in one form or another.

Bolan wormed from beneath the camouflage and crawled to the next tank, which turned out to be a Merkava, an Israeli-designed tank. The evidence of whatever military force it had once belonged to was now long-gone.

Examining two more camouflaged tanks, the Executioner located the outline of the stars and stripes still visible under slapped-on splotches of dark green paint. The first was a "battle taxi"— an M-113 A-1 Armored Personnel Carrier. Finally, most alarmingly, was an M-1 A-1 Abrams Main Battle Tank. Although its sleek profile might give the impression the vehicle was designed for looks, the M-1 A-1 was in fact a serious piece of battlefield weaponry. This was a newer unit, fitted with depleted-uranium-alloy armor that rendered it especially battlefield tough. It was powered by the AGT-1500, a 1500-horsepower turbine from Avco-Lycoming, turning an X-11-3B transmission built by Detroit Diesel. Its 120 mm main gun was augmented with two 7.62 mm machine guns and an M-2 .50-caliber machine gun.

Bolan suspected the U.S. Army or Marines were unaware a renegade Chinese general had his hands on some of their equipment.

General Zheng did indeed have access to some seriously capable, not to mention illegal, hardware.

The big American climbed out from under the canvas and crawled onto the camouflaged top of the M-1 A-1, trying to decide what to do next. He hadn't carried in firepower necessary to render this collection of heavy equipment useless. His quick count showed him forty-six pieces of camouflaged machinery, which was enough to fight a small war.

It all had to go.

His gaze traveled to the narrow entrance to the mountain from the village. There was no other way in. Every single piece of this equipment had to leave the valley from the tiny entrance next to the small house in the village. If that door was permanently shut...

That line of thought was cut off by the appearance of figures on the gravel road from the village. Bolan sank flat on top of the camouflaged U.S. tank and watched them stroll to the valley floor. They walked past his hiding place minutes later, moving casually, chatting in Chinese.

Where were they going? Bolan was wondering if he had missed something else in the darkness, something well camouflaged. He hadn't thought there was anything out on that side of the valley but patches of bare grass and cracked, dry earth.

Realization dawned when he heard the aircraft. It was the sound of large, droning engines, and a moment later the night sky was filled with the black outline of an Antonov An-12 Russian transport plane, a four-engined turboprop carrier with payload capacity approaching twenty thousand kilograms. The general had more than one way to bring his weapons of war into and out of the Kalon valley.

The An-12 came in low over the mountain ridge and as it did, a string of lights flared up in the valley.

The An-12 had to go, too. The question was how to permanently disable the Russian aircraft, close the front door on the general's valley storage area and make sure nobody else was going to come in or get out in the near future.

The transport plane settled on the earthen runway and rumbled toward the far end of the valley, slowing.

Bolan came to a decision. Now was the time to act. It was dark, he was inside undetected and he had other targets to hit. He didn't have time to wait for a better opportunity.

As the An-12 circled and rolled to a stop, the Chinese guards approached. The side door opened and a figure waved, shouting in Chinese.

Bolan cut the ropes and dragged the camouflage from the Abrams M-1 A-1. He pulled at the hatch and slid inside.

General Zheng was reasonably trusting of his guards, it seemed. There were no security locks in place on the tank. Bolan started up the vehicle from the driver's seat.

There was no reaction from the gunmen gathered

around the An-12. The plane's huge Ivchenko engines were slowing, but their decibel level was still considerable and more than masked the noise of the tank.

Bolan knew getting their attention wasn't going to be difficult.

He was pleased to see the general kept his hardware in battle-ready condition. The Abrams was fully fueled. He spun it and moved toward the An-12.

He didn't hear the yell from the aircraft, but he spotted the figure in the entrance to the aircraft waving his hands. The gunmen faced the tank. Bolan brought the vehicle to a halt, jumping to the controls of the commander's M-2 machine gun.

Two of the gunmen were making a run for cover, the other three diving for the open door into the transport plane. Bolan triggered the M-2, following the fleeing gunmen and chopping through them at hip level with .50-caliber rounds. They fell screaming on the hard earth.

Bolan moved to the controls of the M-256, the Abrams's 120 mm main gun. He aimed and fired, disappointed to see the round cut through the night air and buzz the top of the fuselage of the aircraft. It was a miss measurable in inches.

But the transport plane began to move, and Bolan knew there was a pilot with quick reflexes inside the aircraft. He'd started the engines at the first sign of trouble.

The An-12's huge props increased their rotation, and the aircraft moved forward. Bolan jumped back to the tank controls and maneuvered the Abrams to a better position, then fired again, sending a second 120 mm projectile over the front end of the transport plane. The round hit the earth in the path of the plane, and the aircraft immediately jeeped into the crater, its tires bouncing and the entire fuselage rattling. The pilot responded by feeding the aircraft more fuel, pulling the plane along faster, away from the Abrams.

Bolan maneuvered the tank into a tight right-hand turn that brought him onto the runway on the tail of the An-12, and for a full ten seconds he hung on to the rear end of the transport plane, maintaining a distance of mere yards. Then the transport craft gained momentum and speed as the tank reached maximum speed of just over forty miles per hour. Bolan triggered the M-256 without time to aim, hoping for a hit based solely on the proximity of the target. A hit at this distance, no matter where on the transport plane, would doubtless cripple it. But the round snaked over the rear of the fuselage and passed between the front and rear wings, slamming into the ground and raising a cloud of high-velocity dirt and rocks that slammed into the fuselage and were ground up by the props. The An-12 continued increasing speed, unharmed, as if protected by providence.

Bolan coaxed a single extra mile per hour out of the AGT-1500 turbines and jumped to the main-gun controls again, sighting the plane as it increased the distance between itself and its pursuer. He triggered another heat round from the gun and felt good about it.

The 120 mm projectile slammed into the rear of the An-12 as the front end started leaving the ground, and the rear stabilizers disintegrated in fire. The force of the blast blew the rear end away from the earth, and Bolan couldn't hear the sudden whining tone taken on by the props as they fought with unusual air streams. The explosive clouds billowed through the hollow body of the plane and flamed from the windows.

For a bizarre moment the An-12 was traveling almost horizontally over the earth, but pointed at a steep angle at the ground, until the force of the air on the main wings and the pull of the props took over and carried the nose into the ground, crushing it like an accordion. The transport plane continued to skid across the earth on its wings with its burning back end protruding into the air. The fuel exploded, and Bolan watched the aircraft became a sudden skeleton of its former self, filled with yellow-white fire. Then the skeleton disintegrated, and the aircraft collapsed upon itself.

Bolan steered the Abrams away from the burning wreckage and off the airstrip. He stopped at a distance of several hundred yards and redirected the tank's main guns at the landing strip, aiming carefully. He fired the round and watched it detonate precisely where he had wanted it to.

He aimed again, ten yards farther down the strip, and fired again, repeating the process three more times. When he was done, the airfield looked like an especially bad section of the moon's surface, cratered and cracked. There wouldn't be any other transport planes landing there any time soon.

Next he steered the Abrams toward the entrance to the valley, where he saw, in the flickering yellow light of the dying flames from the transport plane, figures standing at the top of the road watching him. He ignored them. Some might be more of Zheng's guards, but he couldn't be sure that all of them were. Some might be innocent villagers, and he wouldn't risk hurting any of them.

They departed as soon as it became clear he was heading their way. He barreled up the incline, reached the top and drove into the village square, then turned and moved forward into the pass again. He targeted the wall of rock to the right of the entrance path and fired.

The 120 mm round slammed into the rock from less than five yards and cracked it. The wall hung for a moment, then fell in on itself. Bolan targeted the opposite wall and fired again. Tons of massive rocks and boulders tumbled into the entranceway.

The big American backed the tank to the top of the pass and fired into the wall directly to the rear of the small house that blocked the view of the passage. The entire section fell to pieces and crashed into the road.

Somebody was going to spend days or weeks, using a lot of heavy equipment, to make that valley accessible again.

The general's equipment was locked inside. For now.

Bolan backed into the square again and spun the Abrams, driving it down the incline of the village to the main highway. He crossed over and took the old road, following it until he was almost out of sight of Kalon. Then he turned the tank back toward it, searching for any sign of pursuit.

He had expected none, but he wanted his departure to be as mysterious as possible. Because Zheng would hear about it soon. Bringing the U.S. Army tank to a halt, he opened the hatch and withdrew a single fragmentation grenade. He dropped it inside, slammed the hatch and jumped down, ducking behind the tread. The Abrams seemed to belch and the hatch slammed open, issuing smoke and a tongue of flame.

That piece of equipment would be useless to the general, as well.

But Bolan's work was just beginning. He wanted more than just the general's apparatus dismantled.

He wanted the general himself.

He headed to his hidden motorcycle.

CHAPTER SEVENTEEN

The town was called Lhamu, and the barracks was composed of two huge buildings backed against the mountainside. One was a large brick structure that had the look of a holy building, although didn't seem to be configured like the Buddhist temples Bolan knew. Another three hundred yards above on the hillside was a squat wooden building that looked more like army barracks. Both buildings towered over the village, looking down on it, dominating it.

The Executioner had again tucked away the motorcycle. After leaving it and starting to hike into the town, he was passed by a troop-transport truck, forcing him into hiding in a ditch along the roadside. He made out enough to see the truck was full of armed soldiers heading to Lhamu.

As the truck disappeared, he broke into an easy run that took him to a hill near the village ten minutes later, where he was in time to see the last of the men jumping out of the rear of the troop-transport vehicle. They were piling heavy coats, tents and other gear next to the vehicle and staggered up the tower of stairs to the brick building, looking exhausted.

Bolan realized these were members of the search parties that were positioned by Zheng in the mountains to find the broken An-26, its occupants and its cargo. They hadn't had the advantage of being ferried off the mountain by helicopter, by the looks of them. Which meant they had suffered a long, arduous climb down after a long climb up.

That was fine with Bolan. When the shooting started, they would be burdened with slow reflexes and drained energy levels.

First Bolan wanted to get a better handle on the situation.

He climbed down the hill and crept into the lowest levels of the town, then back up the other incline, which led in steps to the barracks buildings. The homes he passed on the lower level were mostly hovels. They looked unheated—there was no smoke issuing from their chimneys tonight, and it was cool enough. Their windows were dark.

One of the huts ahead was lit, showing signs of activity, and as he homed in on it he heard the distinctive crack of flesh against flesh. There was a cry and the sound of a body hitting a wooden floor, followed by shouting.

He moved in closer, peering through a window imperfectly covered by a goatskin.

A Tibetan man stood over a younger Tibetan woman, who nursed a bright red cheek as she glared at him, full of bitterness. He yelled at her and pointed to a large iron pot that bubbled on a coal stove. Bolan smelled stew.

The woman backed to the wall and stood slowly, never taking her eyes off the big man. She rushed to the pot and grabbed it, lifting it in her hands as if she knew that with the pot she would be safe from further beating.

Under the weight of the pot she walked to the door and backed into it, pushing it open, watching the man with flashing eyes until the door slapped shut behind her.

Bolan had an idea what she was up to and maneuvered around the hut and started up the narrow flight of stairs ahead of her. The young woman trudged up the narrow flight to the second landing. With her eyes looking at her feet, as if terrified of spilling her load, she was oblivious to the presence of the warrior until he took her arm.

Bolan grabbed the pot when she cried out and lowered it to the landing.

The woman backed to the landing rail.

"Speak English?"

She nodded slightly, and her fear became amazement. "What are you doing here?"

"It would be better if you didn't know. But I need your help."

She was silent.

"I need to know if there are any non-Chinese in the barracks."

"I don't know the word 'barracks,'" she answered.

"The temple," Bolan said, pointing up the mountainside where the great brick building could be seen through the rising stairway

She looked up, still confused, then understood. "It is no temple. It was a monastery. This town was once proud to have that monastery here. Then the Chinese came years ago, and all the monks were killed or taken away and never seen again. Then the new Chinese came. The secret Chinese. They built the wood building for all their extra men. They don't wear uniforms. Some of my people support them and give them assistance. It is a shame on this town that we help these men.''

"Like your father?" Bolan asked.

Her eyes grew bitter again. "He is my uncle, not my father. My father is dead at Chinese hands seventeen years ago, before I was even born.''

"But he helps these 'secret' Chinese?" Bolan asked. "Does he know they are murderers of Tibetan people?"

"He knows," she said almost in a whisper. "Have you come to kill the Chinese?"

Bolan didn't want her to know any more than was absolutely necessary. Knowledge might prove very dangerous for her. "They are my enemies."

Her eyes traveled over him. He was in his blacksuit, covered in combat webbing, glistening with grenades, and the two big handguns were plainly visible. The menacing handle of the big battle blade hung from his hip, and the deadly M-16 A-1/M203 protruded over his shoulder. The woman took in his warrior's aspect with a gleam of satisfaction. "I will help you," she said simply.

"You're going to serve dinner to the new arrivals, I assume?"

She nodded.

"Do it. Act normally. Don't let on that there is anything unusual going on. But find out if there are any other Tibetans inside the monastery or the wooden barracks. I don't want any innocent bystanders hurt. I'll meet you right here when you leave, and you can fill me in."

The woman seemed to curl up suddenly. Her head

sank to her chest and her hands crossed over her body, gripping her shoulders.

"I will not be allowed to leave after I have served the meal."

Bolan understood. She was forced to act as more than waitress, and she was nearly overwhelmed with shame.

The Executioner remembered a similar situation many years earlier and vowed he wouldn't allow her to be touched again by the men in the monastery.

NAMKHA DORJEE NUDGED OPEN the door with her foot and entered the room with her head bowed but her eyes looking furiously from side to side.

Seven men had returned in the truck, and they were all in the large front room of the monastery living quarters, which served as a dining and social area. A table fully twelve feet long took up most of the room. At one end a large fire burned in a fireplace; the other held a cast-iron stove burning coal. The men had been in the cold, climbing a mountain on a search mission, or at least that was what her uncle had said. She didn't understand why Chinese soldiers would want to climb a mountain. But now they were back, and they wanted to be warm and they wanted hot food.

They began to gather at the table when she appeared, and she noticed at once that they were a very tired bunch of men. There was no laughing and joking as there usually was.

She used a broken cup to scoop cold cooked rice into each bowl, then used a tin ladle to spoon the stew on top of it. She didn't look at the men, holding out each filled bowl with her eyes downcast and letting whoever wanted food to take it from her.

Then she poured them goat's milk or water in cups or fetched them bottles of Chinese beer. By the time they had the beverages they wanted, there were clamors for second helpings of food.

The meal was over in fifteen minutes, and she piled up the dirty dishes and wrapped the dirty spoon in a cloth. She stacked them all in the now-empty iron pot and lifted it.

"Wait, you. You can stay with me awhile tonight."

She looked at him. It was one of the captains, one of the three high-ranking men who stayed in the monastery.

"Come on!" he said gruffly.

She lowered her burden and stood where she was.

"I will not go with you."

"You will come with me if you don't want to get beaten."

"Do your worst. A beating is less disgraceful."

The Chinese captain said no more. He strode to her in two long steps and grabbed her by the arm. She cried out and felt herself get thrown to the floor for the second time in as many hours. But the captain was a stronger man than her uncle, and the impact shook her to the bone.

He grabbed her again in the same spot on her arm. She was pulled onto her feet, where she hung dangling like a broken marionette until his hand hit her face and her head flopped to the side.

"Anything more to say about it?" the captain asked.

Namkha was too dazed at the moment to speak, and she felt herself being half-carried through a doorway into a cool, dark room, and she was flung away again, this time to land on a lumpy, rag-stuffed mattress, and she knew she was in the captain's private bedroom.

She seemed to recall a man who said he would protect her from all this, but at the moment, with her mind ringing with the beating, she wondered if it were a fantasy.

The captain grabbed at the throat of her linen frock and pulled hard. She felt her breasts become exposed to his gaze and covered her eyes with her hand, feeling how wet they were, and she wished for oblivion.

BOLAN WAITED in the darkness until he spotted the guard he knew would be there. The man wasn't taking his job seriously, and shortly after making a round of the front of the building he sat on a bench in the shadows and reclined, his AK-47 clutched at his chest.

Bolan thought about the monks who would have walked here and rested on that bench, who were now dead. They deserved more respect than the careless ignorance of a Chinese soldier. The big American walked silently through the darkness, keeping to the bare dirt, withdrawing the Beretta 93-R and standing over the dozing man.

The soldier sensed the cold hand of death on his shoulder, and his eyes popped open. He tried to bring his rifle into target acquisition but was too slow.

Bolan triggered the 93-R, and three 9 mm parabellum rounds took the guard in the stomach and lower chest. The air in the man's lungs, intended for a scream, instead bubbled out through the blood, and the guard went limp. The Executioner leaned him back in his sleeping position.

The warrior made his way to the front entrance and

through the crack in the door watched as the men shuffled out of the dining area and Namkha began to gather up the dishes.

He saw one of the men reappear and speak. Namkha froze.

There was a glow to his left, and another guard came around the corner, lighting a cigarette. He glanced at Bolan and his brow wrinkled, the cigarette drooping in his lips. The Executioner was already leveling the 93-R, and a triburst took the guard down with a grunt.

Bolan glanced inside, certain the sound of the gunfire had been heard. But the noise was covered by the activity inside. Namkha was knocked to the floor by the soldier. He picked her up again and slapped her. Bolan opened the door, quickly but quietly, and stepped behind him, but by then the soldier was dragging the woman into one of the rear rooms. The warrior crossed the empty dining area and paused at the door. A thump told him she was thrown down again.

Adjusting the 93-R to single-shot mode, he pushed at the door and swept the room. He spotted Namkha. She was on her back, her frock stripped off and her body pale and pure in the dim moonlight that came through a dirty window. The soldier was taking his shirt off.

Without a word Bolan fired the 93-R, the round cutting a massive bloody wound across the soldier's throat that destroyed his trachea and severed his carotid artery. Blood pumped down his chest in spurts. Silently, as if he were already a ghost, he turned to Bolan, open-mouthed, too shocked to be in pain but terrified beyond belief. He sank to his knees, then flopped on his side and spasmed as the blood pumped out of him and he died.

The Executioner grabbed the shirt the soldier had dropped on the bed and brought Namkha into sitting position. The blows had muddled her, and she seemed to recognize Bolan like an unreal but familiar character. She allowed him to drag the shirt over her arms like a lifeless child.

"Come on," he said gruffly. "You've got to do better than that."

Her eyes fell on the dead captain, and she inhaled sharply, coming to awareness. "He's dead!"

"Very. Are there other Tibetans in the monastery or the wooden barracks?"

"No. I am the only one from the village in the monastery. Only cleaning women go to the wooden building and only during the day."

"Good. Now you've got to get out of here in a hurry."

"Why?"

"Because the rest of them are going to be joining him very shortly, and I'm certain they won't feel inclined to. Get down the steps and don't come back here. Understand?"

"Yes."

He stepped over the corpse and opened the door enough to find the way clear and ushered her out. He walked with her through the dining room.

"My dishes!" she cried.

"Leave them."

He opened the door and found the night peaceful enough, the two dead guards disinclined to cause Namkha trouble.

"I'll cover you until you're out of sight."

"I want to stay with you!" she whispered, and embraced him around the chest with unexpected fervor.

He peeled her off. "No, you don't. Get out of here."

"My uncle will kill me if I leave the dishes."

"Tell him I stole them from you. Tell him to come and get them himself if he wants them."

He didn't allow her to protest further, shoving her out the door. She crossed the open space quickly, looking furtively to the sides, then started down the steps. She was looking into his eyes when she finally stepped out of sight.

Bolan wheeled, alerted by his warrior's sixth sense, and stopped cold. A figure stood in the hall area between the dining room door and the door to the dead captain's room. The Executioner leveled the 93-R, but the man may have been blessed with the same sixth sense; he twisted as if caught in a sudden dust devil and was gone from the doorway. The 9 mm round from the Beretta drilled into the empty wall where the man had been standing.

He jumped into the hall and found no target, withdrawing as double barrels protruded from one of the dark doors at the end of the hall. It cut loose, filling the hall and the dining area with buckshot that ripped sand out of the stone ceiling. The sound filled the monastery, and the jig was up. Bolan tucked the 93-R in its holster and secured it with snaps while unslinging the M-16/M-203.

Time to fight fire with fire.

He grabbed a buckshot round from his web belt and thumbed it into the breech of the M-203, then sidestepped in front of the door, triggering the grenade launcher. There was a scream, and the door flew open. Bolan triggered the M-16 A-1 and sent 5.56 mm tumblers streaming into the room. The scream was cut off, and the black figure dropped.

Another man raced around the corner at the end of the hall, spotted Bolan and his deadly M-16/M-203, and retreated again. The warrior triggered a burst of 5.56 mm rounds that caught the runner in the leg. The Executioner rushed forward and found the runner on his face on the floor, shouting in Mandarin. He craned his neck, spotted Bolan and tried to unlimber a sidearm with a cry that was half fury, half pain. Bolan cut into him with three precision-fired rounds that left him limp.

The big American leaped the man and found himself on a landing at the top of a single flight of stairs. He kicked at one of the doors, spotted a Chinese soldier launching himself from a bunk and grappling for the AK-47 hanging from the wall, and burst him open with rapid-fire rounds from the M-16. The other bunk was empty, but there was a shift in the shadow underneath it, and a handgun blasted from the close confines. Bolan felt the heat from the round pass near his leg, and he triggered another rapid burst. A limp hand fell out of the shadow, and a Makarov clattered on the stone floor.

The Executioner left the room and kicked at the next door, falling back from a torrent of autofire. Before the door could swing shut, Bolan thumbed in an incendiary grenade and fired. The 40 mm bomb cracked against stone almost immediately, and he turned and ran, falling to the ground in a ball. The door flew off its hinges, engulfed in a blast of heat.

The occupants of the room never made a peep, but the fire cracked through the wall into the adjoining room. Two figures rushed out screaming, already burned bald, trying to slap out unquenchable fires in their flesh. Bolan rose onto one knee and triggered the M-16. The rounds punched through their groins and stomachs and drove them to the floor, where they continued to burn without complaint.

He moved to the top of the stairs and pulled out a flash-concussion grenade. He lobbed it down the stairs and stepped back to avoid the blinding burst of light and disorienting shock of noise that erupted from it, then leaped down the stairs as the light was still dying. Two gunmen writhed on the floor in the room below—they'd taken the blast from just feet away. One still managed to hold on to his Makarov, and both were struggling to squint through momentary blindness.

Bolan triggered a full-auto burst into the armed man, who grunted and collapsed. The unarmed man became terrified and ran toward the doorway, but fell victim to another burst from the M-16 and collapsed to the floor.

Changing the magazine and thumbing in another grenade, Bolan flattened against the wall and kept an eye on both the dark passageways that entered the landing. He sensed movement in both of directions and unleathered the Desert Eagle. He crisscrossed the weapons, aiming the Desert Eagle, in his left hand, at the right passage, while aiming the M-16 at the left passage.

He waited.

There was a shout from one of the passages, then a quick answer from the other.

They knew he was waiting for them.

Something small and metal sailed out of the right corridor and hit the wall, falling to the stone floor, but by that time Bolan had identified the grenade and was on the move. He bolted to the right, from which the grenade had come, hoping the move would come as a surprise. He triggered the M-203 buckshot round into the darkness ahead of him as he stormed into it, leaping when he spotted at least one figure collapsing in front of him. He hit the ground and pivoted into what seemed to be a dark extension of the room to the right, slamming into a warm body as the grenade detonated, filling the corridor behind him with light and fury.

Bolan's battle-honed reflexes took over, automatically transforming the thrust of the blast, which sent him stumbling forward off balance, into a judo fall-and-roll. He swung his legs as he came out of the somersault and scissored them around the Chinese soldier crouched before him, flinging him into the brick wall with a skull-crushing blow.

Lying on his back, Bolan swept the room with the Desert Eagle and found it otherwise deserted. He grabbed the M-16, which he was forced to release during the somersault, and gave it a cursory inspection, deciding it looked undamaged.

He jumped to his feet and made his way back to the corridor, crouching in the shadow at its entrance. The landing was a wreck of broken stone. One of the bodies there was blown almost in two by the force of the grenade, and the other was burning brightly.

The hardmen in the other corridor were conversing rapidly, and Bolan made out only two distinct voices. He held his position until one of the men edged up to take a look at the carnage.

A quick burst from the M-16 cut into him, and he flopped forward into the room, wriggling slowly. Bolan snapped off another three rounds that slammed into his skull, ending his suffering. The surviving gunman responded with a torrent of 9 mm lead. Bolan didn't have to move a muscle to avoid it but leaped to his feet as it concluded, driving himself into the far wall and bringing him face-to-face with the last gunman. He was fisting a fresh magazine for his mini-Uzi. As his mouth made an exaggerated grimace, he slapped the fresh mag into the SMG. Bolan triggered the Desert Eagle, drilling a single .44 Magnum round into his forehead.

The freshly prepped mini-Uzi tumbled to the floor, unused.

The monastery became utterly silent.

Bolan headed up the steps and through the building, searching for survivors, but he found none. Then he stopped at the front door and looked outside in time to see a tall, fat Tibetan man walk to the top of the stairs. He paused to examine the fallen guards, then started around the building. It was Namkha's uncle. Bolan didn't think he was up to any good and became the Tibetan's shadow.

A grassy area along the back of the monastery was surrounded by the ruins of a wooden fence. Beyond it was the newer set of steps leading up another thousand feet to the wooden barracks.

The uncle reached the steps and started up, huffing, and Bolan followed at a distance, on the watch for Chinese who might have been alerted by the din from the battle. How much of the noise would have reached up the mountain to the wooden barracks he couldn't guess.

As he started up the steps, he was grudgingly impressed by the lengths the general had gone to to hide his troops. Who would have thought to look for a secret stash of highly trained soldiers in this little village, miles from any civilization center? But the compound had access to a full support staff in the village below.

He increased his speed on the steps, finding them solid, masking the noise of his movement, and came to the top fifty paces behind the Tibetan, who was wheezing and had slowed to a walk. The warrior crept across the wide-open ground—he glimpsed a field outfitted for training, with an obstacle course and a shooting range—and he was within ten paces of the uncle before the big man happened to glance back.

The Tibetan spun and cried out, raising a cleaver in his fist. Bolan saw movement at the front of the wooden building, and a voice cried out in Chinese.

The fat man shouted and ran toward the building, and Bolan dived to the ground to avoid a burst of fire. On his elbows he targeted the guard and took him out with a swift burst from the M-16, then spotted another guard run out the front door of the building. The uncle screamed, and Bolan cut the guard down before he could react. The Tibetan grabbed the door from the corpse and disappeared inside.

He would raise the alarm, which gave Bolan seconds to act. He primed the building with a couple of HE grenades, which he launched from the M-203 into both ends of the structure. As they exploded, they crushed in the front corners, and when the explosions ended he heard shouting inside.

Taking advantage of the confusion and smoke, he rushed to the building, grabbed a thermite can from his webbing, primed it and rolled it inside the front door. There was a shout of alarm and Bolan retreated in a hurry, the mental countdown proceeding in his brain. He heard sudden voices as men exited the building behind him. They might start shooting at him at any time, but he couldn't bother to stop to defend himself. The count reached one, and Bolan dived into the grass, down a slight rise in the land, the best protection available at the moment. Then the thermite detonated, spreading white phosphorus within the already burning building. The shrapnel was like antimatter, burning through anything in its path—steel, concrete, wood and especially flesh, burrowing at incinerator temperatures into skin and bone, unstoppable until the phosphorus was consumed. The barracks filled with screams and fire.

Bolan lay where he was, silently evaluating his body for the sudden sensation of unbearable heat, but he'd been spared. He turned and peered over the rise in the land to the conflagration he had created.

Men were running from the building, shrieking and flailing at themselves. Some looked unharmed, the tiny black holes that were boring through them invisible in the night, and others were smoking or flaming and flapping at themselves to put out the fire. If they caught even a pinprick of phosphorus, there wasn't going to be any putting it out.

A big figure slammed through the burning timbers and staggered into the lawn, his mouth open, bellowing in pain, zigzagging in quest of relief from the agony that was consuming him. Namkha's uncle roamed in Bolan's direction, and the warrior prepared to shoot him, but the figure was moving blind and he tripped, slamming into the grass, silent and still. Tiny whiffs of smoke puffed from a collection of black holes in his face and skull.

Namkha wouldn't be beaten by him again.

Two more figures moved in his direction, dying

quickly, and he triggered a single round into the skull of each, turning off their suffering and hurrying the inevitable end.

The warrior started a slow retreat.

As he reached the stairs, he saw men who had been in the rear of the structure when it was attacked start to emerge from the conflagration, blackened and burned but spared the phosphorus. Bolan wondered how many were dead and how many alive. It didn't matter, really. This compound was destroyed.

The Executioner had made his point.

CHAPTER EIGHTEEN

Bolan checked his watch and gauged he had just one hour before the pink light of dawn began filtering into the Tibetan sky.

He was perched on a rocky ledge that never would have held him if he wasn't holding a staked length of rope. Below, the heavy guard of the Tenzing Chinese army compound circled and paced with wasplike nervousness.

General Zheng was very aware of the damage inflicted on his organization in the past several hours.

Bolan wondered what he had told the soldiers at the Tenzing compound.

Most of them wouldn't even know that the barracks at Lhamu or tanks and troop-transport machinery at Kalon existed, let alone that they had both been attacked and severely compromised since dusk. Maybe Zheng told them this was a drill situation. Maybe he had invented some imaginary threat from Tibetan rebels. Perhaps he had offered no explanation whatsoever. Whatever his expressed motivation, he had the military compound in a state of high alert. There were at least thirty men on guard about the perimeter, plus two in each of a forward and rear watchtower. Bolan also spotted a video surveillance system, with cameras on the guard towers.

After driving for an hour and a half, it had taken Bolan most of the night to climb up the steep precipice of rock that served as a wall of protection behind the compound. The Chinese military had never anticipated infiltration by a single man a likelihood.

Now he had to figure out how to get down, undetected, inside the compound. He had to get to the general, past the man's unusual and elite personal guard.

The biggest challenge would be getting past the soldiers. He reminded himself again that most of the men in the camp were just typical Chinese grunts. They weren't power-hungry. Just men who happened to be under the command of a would-be despot whose clandestine operations were located at secret bases elsewhere.

Some Tibetans would have argued that any Chinese who in any way contributed to the continuing occupation of Tibet was essentially a part of a murdering force that was raping the Tibetan land, stealing its culture, killing its people.

Bolan wasn't a big one for political agendas. He killed killers. But he wouldn't take down some innocent Chinese kid just because he happened to be stationed in Tibet as a member of the regular Chinese army.

So this probe could only be selectively hard, which could prove difficult.

That was the most difficult probe to perpetrate.

What made it worse was his uncertainty that the general was even in residence. He might be at one of his other secret bases. Bolan knew he had received only some of the facts from his unwilling informant in Nyima. Among the missing Intel was the location of the general's primary base of operations for his revolutionary war.

He had to come away this morning with that Intel, if nothing else.

Testing the thin nylon rope again, Bolan edged himself off the ledge into open space and dangled at a little under twenty-five yards above the camp. In his hand was another length of rope, which he had appropriated from the Lhamu barracks.

He lowered himself three yards, assessed his position and lowered himself another two feet, then gripped the cliff face with his feet and kicked away.

He swung away from the cliff, then swung back, catching himself on his feet and kicked away again. Grains of sand rubbed away from the rock tumbled down the cliff face.

Bolan caught himself on the wall and kicked again, putting all his muscle into it, and let the second rope sail. It drifted through the open air, the lasso floating down toward the small steel piece protruding from the roof of the rear guard tower. He saw at the final second that his throw wasn't accurate, that he was going to miss the piece of steel. But the rope was still going to hit the top of the guard tower and maybe swing past it. He yanked on the end hard, and the rope sailed back to him.

The Executioner rushed to the cliff face again and he caught himself with his feet, cushioning what would otherwise have been a bone-shaking impact. He hung there, perspiring under the blacksuit, but his face and hands were cool from the damp, early-morning chill.

A minute later he pushed away from the cliff once, then on the second swing was ready. He released the lasso, which sailed out and down and headed directly to the protruding steel spike. Bolan yanked it at the last possible moment, tightening the lasso just as it closed on the steel shaft. It tightened, and the big American allowed the rope to burn through his hands as he swung back to the cliff. He managed to keep it taut without creating a sudden yank that the guards, on watch just a few feet underneath, would have detected. Bolan was too preoccupied with this to catch himself perfectly, and he slammed into the side of the cliff with tremendous force.

He rested again for a full minute, then began to pull on the new rope. As it tightened, it drew him slowly away from the cliff side.

Bolan hung suspended between the two ropes at a steep angle when he released a few feet of slack in the rope to the cliff edge above. Then he pulled on the rope to the tower roof again, moving in a little closer. His arm muscles were screaming, and his body felt as if it were being ripped apart.

He repeated the process, each time moving just a couple more feet across the gap between the cliff edge and the tower top. Occasionally he would glimpse movement of the guards under the tower-roof overhang, but they were still unaware of his approach.

As he came to within toe-touching distance of the tower roof, he felt the rope to the cliff top give. But it stopped.

There was no way to know if it had wedged in a new, good position or if it was ready to pop out of the rock.

A secondary spike had been driven into the cliff, so Bolan wouldn't fall to his death. But he would most likely go crashing into the guard tower on the sudden excess slack. Then his stealthy approach would have been blown. He could easily be gunned down before he even had a chance to recover from the fall.

He had to get to the tower top quickly. He pulled on the rope to the spike, creating tension greater than any he had created so far during the descent, but it seemed to hold. He tied it in place on his belt and released some of the tension of the cliff rope.

When the tension released, the tower moved slightly, imperceptibly, but enough to send a creak of stressed metal through the structure.

There was no way the guards didn't hear it. Bolan hung frozen in the night, resisting his subconscious urge to grab at the 93-R.

But there was no reaction from the tower. Maybe the guards heard such creaks from time to time, when the wind blew.

Bolan drew himself in and slowly allowed his body weight to rest on the tower roof. His first move was to the monitoring camera, which was on the opposite side of the roof and pointed down at the compound floor. Bolan took one cautious step at a time until he reached the wiring for the camera and snipped it with the wire cutters in his multipurpose tool. Then he reached for the power wire that fed into the tower and severed it.

He could hear the guards speaking, undoubtedly discussing the power loss.

The door opened, and one of them started down the ladder. Bolan waited until he had reached the earth and disappeared into a small, illuminated building before making his move.

The warrior used the rope attached to the roof of the

tower to support him as he stepped into the open air and swung to the small landing outside the door of the watchtower. He ripped open the door and stepped inside, driving a powerful fist into the face of the Chinese soldier. The man collapsed and looked up, stunned by the attack, to find himself staring into the muzzles of the large, deadly looking M-16 A-1/M-203. He started to speak, but Bolan slashed his hand across his throat. The soldier shut up.

The tower began to shake lightly, and Bolan glanced out to see the second guard returning.

The door opened, and the man spotted his companion sitting against the wall with his wrists tied behind his back and his knees and ankles bound together. A strip of cloth gagged his mouth.

Bolan placed the M-16 against the guard's kidney.

The guard whirled on him, using a skilled block to move the muzzle of the combo unit away from him, but Bolan stepped back and leveled the Beretta 93-R directly at his head, just out of reach.

"Don't do it."

"Who are you?"

"Shut up and get on the floor, on your face."

Bolan had the second guard bound and gagged in minutes. So far so good. The guards would be angry and sore for a few days but no worse, long-term, for their treatment.

Now to get to ground and see what he could find.

DAI JIAN PLACED a cup of tea on the general's desk, but Zheng didn't see it.

All men had dreams, but sometimes they turned into obsessions that drowned compassion and humanity.

Zheng, in the inner reaches of his mind, was watching his dream. At this moment, when it should have been closer than ever, it was in fact further away than it had been in years.

"They said it was just one man," the general muttered.

"That's a lie if you ask me, General," Jian retorted. "One man simply cannot inflict that much damage."

"One man in a tank," Zheng reminded him.

"Granted. But what about the monastery?"

"What about my satellite expert?" the general said. "She was stolen from me by one man."

"There were two men on the mountain."

"That other one was just a local guide. It was one man who destroyed my gunships and killed off my search parties, one after another."

"That's hard to swallow," his assistant stated.

Yes, hard to swallow, but Zheng had no doubts. He had received the same description time and again. Big, dark-haired Caucasian with fire in his eyes. He'd been spotted on the mountain, in the village, in Nyima. He had taken Zheng's satellite expert, and Zheng wanted her back. He had taken down more of Zheng's men than the general wanted to try to calculate. He'd rendered temporarily unusable Zheng's massive assemblage of hard-gotten weaponry, including destroying one of his most expensive and vital pieces of equipment, the Russian-made transport plane. How in the world was he going to replace the An-12?

Zheng stood at the window watching the Tenzing compound. There was no point in trying to sleep. His nemesis was dominating his every thought.

Just how good was this man?

Zheng watched one of his elite guards bend over as if to pick up a dropped coin, then turn, stagger and collapse, losing his weapon.

At that moment the general realized the man was pretty damn good.

BOLAN FOLLOWED the glow of yellow light to a large, official-looking building. It was two stories tall, maybe eight or ten rooms on a floor that looked like offices. A PRC flag flew from a pole in front of it, and there was a designation in Chinese on a brass plaque on the front entrance. He couldn't read the words, but the building looked pretty official.

He imagined the general would be awake tonight. The damage Bolan had inflicted to his clandestine organization would have the general too preoccupied to sleep. So he homed in on a second-floor suite of offices with its lights on.

The warrior moved silently across the asphalt, under the cold light of flood lamps, searching for a shadow to hide in. The best he could find was against the side of a jeep, low to the ground.

From there he was able to watch the window and watch the guard who was on duty at the front entrance.

The lighted office held at least one man, pacing, agitated, talking fast. His pinched features didn't convey the authority of a Chinese general, but that didn't mean he wasn't Zheng.

It was five minutes before he spotted the second occupant in the room, a man with a heavy jowl and thin hair. That fit Bolan's image of Zheng. Of course, he couldn't be sure.

He'd just have to get inside and find out.

A guard crossed the asphalt and stood by the jeep, a step away from the Executioner. Bolan studied him carefully; this was no ordinary Chinese soldier. He wore an army uniform, but on each upper arm he had added a white silk armband embroidered with a bright red Chinese character. He was armed with a Walther P-38 on one hip and a walkie-talkie on the other, and in his hands, as if he were ready to shoot at any second, was a Heckler & Koch MP-5 SD-3 submachine gun. The unit came from the factory with a sound suppressor installed. It wasn't the kind of weapon Bolan would expect to see being carried by a Chinese soldier.

The answer, of course, was that he wasn't a typical soldier.

Bolan scanned the other guard and found him armed with the same hardware and wearing the same armband.

The presence of the armbands said something to Bolan; the general was worried. He had to be worried to take the risk of bringing his personal soldiers into his official army base. He probably told the regular soldiers they were some sort of official army division. But if word of their presence got back to the PRC's higher command, they would know immediately that the armbands were in no way official, and they'd have some serious questions for Zheng about them.

But this night Zheng's fear outweighed his need for caution.

Bolan had no compunction about taking down the killers and renegades Zheng had signed onto his personal cause, and when the opportunity came—when the guards at the front of the building strolled to the corner for a moment and faced away—he struck. He rose from the shadow and reached around the guard, slashing across his neck with the Randall combat knife, silencing him. The gunman's reflexes were superior, and he retaliated with a well-placed elbow delivered to Bolan with blasting force. The Executioner rode out the blow and fell to the asphalt, twisting onto his hands and rebounding to his feet like a dancer. The gunner's life force was draining away, and he staggered at Bolan as he grasped his neck and tried to hold in the blood, then collapsed at the big American's feet.

The Executioner couldn't have asked him to die more conveniently, in the shadow.

He crossed the stretch of asphalt and bare dirt, drawing the 93-R, where the guard was turning back to pace toward the front doors. Bolan stopped in a firing stance, leveled the machine pistol and fired. A 9 mm triburst stabbed into the guard before he even knew he was under attack.

He fell in the open. Bolan decided the time would be better used trying to locate the general than hiding the body, and he entered the building, bounding up the stairs and finding himself on a darkened landing looking through a wooden door with a single narrow window. The hallway beyond it was dark, too.

He put his hand on the door, then stopped.

He used his foot to push the door open, and the hallway filled with an explosion of gunshot that splintered the door. At least a couple of buckshot rounds made it through the wood, narrowly missing Bolan's ankle.

The door hung open, barely attached to its hinges. Bolan popped a CS grenade from his combat webbing and sent it flying through wrecked door, then ran down four or five stairs and crouched. There was a loud pop, and a surge of gray smoke filled the hallway, some of it seeping into the stairwell. Bolan waited with the M-16 configured for automatic fire. A figure wearing an armband crashed into the door, coughing and tearing at his eyes, and Bolan triggered a short burst that took him down. He waited another eight seconds, then jumped onto the landing and burst through the door. He did an instantaneous assessment of the smoke-free section hallway that was behind him, finding it empty, then stalked into the dissipating smoke before him.

Another fleeing figure raced toward him, his arm over his eyes, making it easy to see his armband. Bolan stepped out of his way and tripped him neatly. The soldier cried out and hit the floor, reaching for the handgun on his hip. The warrior triggered a burst that cut him down where he lay.

A large-caliber handgun fired from up ahead in the smoke, and Bolan fell to the floor, catching sight of a figure well ahead of him, nearly obscured. A man stepped forward, wiping his eyes with one hand, coughing, and holding the gun in the other. Bolan rolled to the wall and let the gunner walk past him. The man never saw him, although the Executioner easily made out the pinched features of one of the men he had seen in the window of the office.

The man came to a stop with his feet touching the dead gunner. Bolan stood behind the man and grabbed him by the shoulder, whirling him and slamming his handgun out of his grip, then grabbing his collar. He propelled the man down the hall, where he stumbled and nearly fell. The big American grabbed him again before he got his wits about him and plowed him into the wall, the hand on his collar all that kept the figure from collapsing. Bolan found they were at the door to the office, and he shoved the figure inside and unslung the M-16 A-1/M-203. He found no targets.

"Are you Zheng?" he demanded, but he already suspected the answer—Zheng was the other man he had seen in the window. And that man had successfully made an escape.

"No, I'm Dai Jian, his second-in-command," the man croaked.

The man didn't appear to have military rank, which meant he was the second-in-command of the general's extracurricular activities. The Executioner heard the wail of a siren and knew he had to get out.

But he needed one tiny piece of Intel if he was going to sustain the momentum of this battle.

"Where's Zheng's base of operations?" he demanded.

"You are standing in it, you fool."

Bolan raised the M-16 to Jian's forehead, placing the bore directly against the man's skin. "I've already taken out several of your comrades. Killing you would just add one more to the list. Where's the base?"

Jian licked his dry lips, then looked up at Bolan with fear bordering on shock. "I will tell you."

"You have less than five seconds."

"Xuntian! That's the base, three kilometers north up the mountain outside a village with that name."

Bolan pulled back, and Jian collapsed to the floor, shaking in fear.

"Thanks for the information. I'll tell the general you were very helpful."

Jian glared up at him, even more terrified. "He'll kill you the moment he sees you!" The Chinese made a move toward his hideaway gun, holstered at his left

ankle, but Bolan caught the move and fired a triburst
that drilled the man in the upper chest.

Jian staggered to the door to the office and veered to
the left. Bolan followed. If the second-in-command had
an escape route, he wanted to know about it. There was
a door at the end of the hallway, which Jian grabbed
and pulled open with great effort. He staggered inside
and grabbed the rail on a steep set of dark stairs.

Bolan heard movement in the hall behind him and
grabbed another CS grenade from his webbing, lobbing
it at the approaching shadows, then entered the new
stairwell. That smoke grenade might not slow pursuit
by much, but he couldn't be sure there wouldn't be
regular soldiers in the new arrivals. Otherwise a high-
explosive egg would have provided more stopping
power.

He heard the CS pop, and in front of him Jian missed
a step as the loss of blood weakened him. He collapsed
on the steps. Bolan didn't bother to check his vitals,
although he seriously doubted the man had long to live.

At the bottom of the stairs was a single door, which
he crashed through to find himself at the far end of the
building. There were two armband guards stationed
there, watching the activity in the compound, and they
turned in surprise at Bolan's appearance. Bringing the
M-16 into firing position, he saw one of the guards
make the identical move with his MP-5 SD-3. It was a
race just milliseconds long. Bolan felt the hot 9 mm fire
scorching the air next to his shoulder. But his own initial blast was on target, and the gunner took the rounds
in his arm, pectoral and throat, leaning far back and
sending the SMG fire into the sky before falling onto
his back. He swept the fire into the second gunner, who

never had the chance to fire his weapon before he was cut down.

Running around the rear of the building, the Executioner spotted a single jeep starting up and he fired a short burst from the M-16 just as the vehicle tore away. The rifle stopped cold on an empty magazine, and Bolan thumbed a high-explosive round into the breech of the M-203 and triggered it. But the jeep driver turned at the sound of the brief gunfire and witnessed the launching of the grenade, swerving to avoid it. He bounced into the rocky dirt, and the 40 mm projectile hit the earth where his vehicle would have been, exploding with a crack.

Bolan had seen the driver's face long enough to recognize the man from the office. Zheng.

He pursued the general over the bare patch of earth and saw the jeep roll to a halt without brake lights. Bolan's awareness flared, and he slapped a fresh magazine in the M-16, sweeping the darkness as he came up on the rear of the jeep. It appeared empty, and the warrior grabbed at his thermal imaging glasses and scanned the immediate area.

The general had jumped from the jeep at some point, using the dark as cover, but where had he gone? It was as if he had vanished.

Bolan glimpsed a flare of moving warmth that he targeted and fired on before his brain processed the fact that it had moved behind a parked dump truck and was shielded.

There was a rattle of machine-gun fire, and Bolan glimpsed troops moving in from the building. More troops were closing in on him from the left, where Zheng had vanished.

Anger cascaded through Bolan. Zheng had slipped through his fingers. If he continued pursuit of him, he'd have to start wiping out all innocent Chinese soldiers in his path. And as they deployed in large numbers, he would probably get taken down himself.

The Executioner had no choice but to break off the hunt.

Removing the thermal imaging glasses, he used the open land between himself and the Chinese troops as a firing ground, sending incendiary grenades whistling through the air in rapid succession. As they exploded in white-hot fires, he leaped into the jeep and headed toward the explosions, driving through their wakes to the fence of steel posts and wire that enclosed the front half circle of the compound not protected by mountainside. At least five or six guards were stationed at the fence, spaced every ten feet apart, and they bunched to face down the enemy vehicle as it sped toward them.

Bolan stood up in his seat and fired the M-203 over the front window, sending a CS grenade flying at them. The soldiers spotted the bomb and bolted, but none of them took more than a few steps before it hit and blew. If it was any deadly type of explosive, most of them would have been killed instantly. They didn't take the time to evaluate the explosion and cleared out fast.

Bolan held the wheel with his legs as he thumbed in an HE, aimed at the fence and fired, collapsing in the driver's seat as the fence blew, sending metal shards and fragments clanking onto the hood of the vehicle and cracking against the glass. He stomped on the gas pedal, and the jeep accelerated into the new entrance to the compound, bounced furiously into the fresh crater, then bounced out again. The engine's roar became a smooth purr when the vehicle hit the pavement and sped away.

CHAPTER NINETEEN

General Zheng hadn't taken the same chances with his central compound at Xuntian that had been taken with the barracks at the monastery at Lhamu. The people of the village of Xuntian weren't involved in the upkeep of the compound.

In fact few of them realized the base existed just a mile and a half from their little mountain town. At least, if they knew they weren't telling.

Bolan had recruited Sampen Sonam again for the intelligence-gathering mission. The Executioner believed the location he was told by the general's assistant was good, but that didn't mean it would be easy to find.

They reached the village of Xuntian in early morning and spent a lot of time speaking to the various locals and learning nothing. Sonam protested more than once that Bolan's presence made it less likely the locals would open up to him.

The big American wasn't willing to let Sonam wander around alone and unarmed in a village that might be patrolled by the general's assassins.

"But I am armed," Sonam protested. He pulled on his coat to display the Browning Hi-Power. The young

Tibetan had carefully worked a leather holster for it much like the holster Bolan used for the Beretta 93-R.

The Executioner wasn't convinced, but he did keep his distance when Sonam approached an old man who was tending a tiny herd of goats grazing on a steep grassy area along the village outskirts. Though Xuntian was at a high altitude, even compared to most Tibetan villages, it was situated on a wide, relatively flat plain, surrounded by peaks. The snow line started a few thousand feet above it, and the chill in the air stunted the grass. The old man treated his few goats like prized possessions.

Sonam seemed to be getting somewhere when Bolan saw two Chinese soldiers approaching, each with a handgun buckled on his right hip. The warrior stepped behind the old man's tiny house before the soldiers spotted him and observed their approach.

Sonam didn't appear perturbed by their arrival, and the old man merely gave them a brief look until the soldiers made it clear they weren't on an idle stroll. They began to make harsh demands of the pair. The old man shook his head vigorously. Sonam was less cordial, and without understanding the conversation, Bolan knew clearly that tempers were heating up. He withdrew the Beretta 93-R and prepared to step in and end the altercation if need be. But he—and Sonam, he knew—was prepared to go along with the soldiers if it would ultimately provide them the information they needed.

The handcuffs came out. Sonam was clearly demanding to know why he was being arrested. It was all for show. Bolan, Sonam and the soldiers all understood he was being arrested for asking too many questions.

They clicked the cuffs in place behind his back and

marched him away from the old man, who watched them go, then looked pointedly at Bolan. The warrior hadn't even realized the old man was aware of his presence, but now he was clearly wondering what he was going to do about the latest development.

Bolan couldn't reassure the old man, but the truth was he could and would do plenty. He set off after the soldiers.

They marched Sonam into the middle of the town to what appeared to be a typical Tibetan house, large enough for an extended family. They opened the door without knocking and pushed Sonam inside. Bolan watched for guards from a distance and saw none. What he did spot was a jeep parked against the wall of the house. As he reached the vehicle, he could hear the conversation inside, and knew he couldn't blow the tires without the noise being overheard. He needed a silent method of disabling the vehicle—a nonpermanent method, in case he wanted to make use of it himself later, would be ideal.

He leaned inside and groped under the steering column, pulling out a small braid of variously colored wires. A few quick snips with wire cutters guaranteed the jeep would fail to start.

Then he heard the first crack of a fist. Sonam was being persuaded to reveal the intentions of his questions in the town. It was time for intervention.

Already determining that all the windows were shaded, Bolan made his entrance through the front door.

With a quick push of his foot, the door swung open and banged into the wall, giving the warrior a full view of the interior. A third soldier was present, and Sonam was on the floor rubbing his jaw.

The third soldier stood guard during the questioning procedure with a Browning Hi-Power, probably the one taken from Sonam, and he turned it on Bolan the instant he spotted the figure in the doorway holding the 93-R. Bolan targeted him and triggered a triburst that knocked him flat into the wall and sent the Hi-Power tumbling. The warrior turned swiftly on the other armed soldier, who unsnapped the handgun from his holster and grabbed it, but the Executioner loosed another swift, precision 3-round burst that ripped through inner organs and shut them down.

Then there was just the questioner, who had forgotten to lower the fist he made with his right hand.

Sonam got to his feet. "I knew it wouldn't take you long."

"What did you learn?"

"The old man started talking about a pass called Lodi—three kilometers outside the village, leading high up into the mountain. There has never been a need for any man to go there, and yet in the past three years there have been sightings of people there and even a dirt road being made for easier access."

"Sounds like what we're looking for," Bolan replied. "Mind filling us in on the details?" he asked of the would-be questioner.

The soldier just glared, and Sonam translated. The soldier spoke in broken Tibetan.

"He says he doesn't know what we're talking about," Sonam interpreted.

"Fine," Bolan said with a shrug. He carefully switched the 93-R to single-shot mode and aimed it squarely at the soldier's skull from just out of arm's reach. The soldier backed against the wall and followed the gun barrel with his eyes until it aimed without hesitation at his forehead and he shouted.

"He says he'll talk," Sonam stated.

Bolan didn't alter his firing position. "Tell him I'll believe it when I hear some good information."

CHEN QING COULDN'T LOOK into the eyes of the American. He saw a dark fire there, a will to kill. Qing was thankful he hadn't been holding a weapon when the man burst in, or he knew he would be on the floor with his two former companions.

He was just a Chinese soldier, recruited to join Zheng's special campaign after he left the army of the PRC. His family was a part of the massive Chinese immigration to Tibet, settling in the Tibetan city of Qamdo. Yes, he believed in the Chinese right to control the people and lands of Tibet. General Zheng had described to his group as they were being recruited how the Chinese needed to purge the Tibetan culture and make it a new culture. And he, Qing, could be a man of influence and position in the new Tibet once Zheng consolidated his power.

Everyone who was a minor soldier in the battle to take control of Tibet would be a governor in the new regime Zheng would install.

Qing had swallowed Zheng's obsession whole.

He was raised in Chengdu. He was a street bully, rolling the other kids for their money and food, while at home he was beaten and humiliated by his father. When he became a young man, he couldn't seem to make his old techniques work for him. Instead of earning respect for his antagonistic street attitudes, he found himself victimized by his victims. Finally a group of street vendors he was trying to eke a living from had hired a group of Qing's former schoolmates to teach him a lesson. They thrashed him nearly to death.

Qing was unable to understand this turn of events. Why wouldn't people give him what he wanted? When he didn't have what someone else had, why wasn't he able to take it away from them? It was what his father had always instructed him to do.

When he recovered his strength and entered the army, he had thought he would recover that personal power he thought he had once possessed, only to find himself manipulated by his superiors and outsmarted by his fellow soldiers, who tricked him out of his money, humiliated him and ganged up on him when he tried to steal back what they had taken.

He had left the army only to find his military service bought him no respect or admiration on the streets of Qamdo, where his family now lived.

That was when Zheng's men appeared. They took him to one of the nicest restaurants in the city, a place where he could never afford to eat. They told him of their plans for him. They had been watching him, and they saw in him a certain spark they appreciated.

That night they bought him a hotel room and provided a young prostitute who let him slap her around before pleasuring him all night long.

His decision was made.

Now it was three years later. He had enjoyed his time with the general's forces. He lived well and ate well, and occasionally he was given the responsibility of questioning certain local people, which was what he truly enjoyed.

But this American with the big gun—Qing saw in

him the same spirit that was in the group of local boys in Chengdu when they gathered together, under the collective will of the community, and beat him nearly dead in an alley, and left him there bewildered.

Life wasn't fair.

"General Zheng came in before dawn," he told the Tibetan man who just two minutes earlier was under his control. "He went into the compound."

The Tibetan asked him why they had come and arrested him.

"We have people in this town who watch out for us for suspicious activity. They get paid to report to us if and when anybody comes nosing around. This is the first time it has happened since the compound was constructed. They radioed to us at the compound, and we came to find you."

The Tibetan asked for the exact location of the compound. Qing bristled at first. It wasn't right that they should ask that question. In fact it wasn't right that they should try to shut down the general's operation. The success of the general was the only chance Qing had for getting into a position where he could control people as he needed to. That was the only way he felt right. These two men were a threat to that turn of events. It wasn't fair.

The American spoke, his voice a gruff rumble.

"He is asking me if he should shoot you now," the Tibetan said. "Are you going to answer the question?"

"I cannot tell you where the compound is," Qing said, and he knew his voice was whining like a sick dog's.

"Then I will tell him to go ahead," the Tibetan said, and began to speak in English.

"No! I will tell."

Qing felt overpowered. That was the worst feeling he knew. But he related everything he could about the locale and geography of the compound the general made in the mountain.

Meanwhile he was thinking of a plan, a way to turn the tables. Yes, turn the tables on these two the way they had turned the tables on him. Because being the one who overpowers others was the most satisfying feeling, just as being overpowered was the least satisfying.

And if this American was the one who was causing all the trouble for General Zheng in recent days, and if Qing caught him or killed him, the rewards from the general would be substantial.

"You need the key to the handcuffs," Qing said. He was standing over his former companion, Tieying, whose hand still gripped his Makarov handgun lightly in death.

"Yes," the Tibetan said.

"I have them in my pocket."

"Reach for them carefully."

Qing moved his hand to his back pocket and dug into it. The American didn't appear to be alarmed. Qing pulled his hand out of his pocket and slid the knife out of its sheath, the knife that would have been used on the Tibetan if he was given the chance.

He whipped the knife at the American and fell to his knees, snatching at the Makarov from Tieying's hand.

But the American had somehow avoided the knife, and his suppressed handgun tracked Qing's movements. There was the sound again, the coughing sound of a single bullet. Qing felt himself get pushed into the wall and he sat down next to the corpse of Tieying. He didn't understand. He was overpowered again. It wasn't fair. His thought processes shut down.

Bolan felt his neck briefly, then announced, "He's dead." A quick check revealed that the torturer did in fact have the keys, but they were in his front pocket. Seconds later he uncuffed Sonam.

"Now what?" the Tibetan asked.

"Now I go to the compound."

Sonam shook his head. "*We* go, friend."

CHAPTER TWENTY

One of Zheng's contacts had been in touch with one of the general's counterparts in a neighboring district, alerting him of the infiltration and attack. Before Zheng could issue convincing assurances, an investigative team was on its way to Tenzing. The survivors of his personal bodyguard had immediately taken their dead and left the compound.

But they didn't think to account for Jian, and he was taken to the infirmary and somehow kept alive throughout the night.

General Zheng was gone by the time the army investigative team had arrived at Tenzing. It would have looked very strange for him to have attempted to curtail their investigation anyway. But one of his miserable lieutenants at Tenzing had told the investigative team about the stranger they discovered half-dead in the compound.

Zheng's army second-in-command met with him at a halfway point between Tenzing and Xuntian. Li Peng was calm about the meeting, although he knew what it might entail. The general was waiting for him in the rear of his car, a simple army transport jeep that was restyled with luxurious trappings. Zheng gave him a stiff smile and a drink when he sat inside.

Peng informed the general he was cooperating with the team, which wanted to ask him about the stranger found wounded in Tenzing after the attack. It seemed some of the men at the base were admitting to seeing this stranger around at times, in the presence of the general, but never in uniform. The investigators were also hearing rumors of a special force of soldiers armed with nontraditional weaponry sometimes seen in the general's vicinity, like a personal guard. These soldiers, the investigators were being told, were on hand during the attack.

Zheng instructed his second-in-command to tell the investigators he would return to Tenzing in a few days, but right now was protecting himself from the threat of another such attack. He certainly didn't know the wounded man in the base infirmary. He was undoubtedly one of the attackers.

"You're my number two now," Zheng said, "if you want the responsibility. Jian is out of the picture. I need somebody to stand by me when I make my move, and I will be accelerating my schedule substantially."

"How substantially?" Li Peng asked.

"I'll be beginning my attacks within the next twenty-four hours."

Li Peng's mouth went hard in a sort of smirk. "Do you have the resources to pull it off, General?"

Zheng nodded. "I lost a lot of men yesterday in Lhamu, and most of those that lived through the fires are wounded or ran off. But that wasn't even half my ranks. I still have men at Xuntian, and you know the scope of my recruitment efforts in Tenzing. I anticipate that once we make our first aggressive moves and the others at Tenzing see which way the wind is blowing, they'll jump to join us.''

"You may be right, General," Li Peng said, "but what about hardware?''

"I still have Tenzing, and one of the first moves I make will be to take some of the equipment I liberate at Tenzing to Kalon, where we can free up what I have stored there. I examined the destruction at Kalon personally. There's been very little damage to the tanks. All we have to do is get them free. I anticipate we can clear the way in twenty-four hours once I have the equipment. Then I have enough ground-based artillery to fight a small war.

"Initially I'll be able to take control of a smaller district of Tibet than I had originally planned. But I foresee this operation growing almost exponentially. Think about it, Peng. The Tibetans will join us because they think we're on their side. If this becomes a war for Tibetan independence, we'll get support from all over the world! We'll bring in CNN and show them how the brave Tibetans and a few of their Chinese friends are standing up to the last great totalitarian government in the world. China will be too red faced to try and thwart us.''

"But if they do?''

"If they do, they will fail, Peng, because I almost have the THADSAC on-line. My men have managed to get it operational, and they are learning its control functions more thoroughly every hour. At this very moment I have a broker purchasing the access codes I need to get it on-line. I anticipate that by the time I start my attacks tomorrow morning, it will be seventy-five percent functional. The People's Republic will not be able to make a move without us knowing about it. We'll be able to counter every aggressive tact they take. We can spot their attack fighters in the air well before they reach Tibetan airspace. We'll see ground-based forces hours or days before they reach our targets. We can even feed THADS images to the media—it will embarrass the People's Republic if the world knows about their ruthless attacks against the helpless Tibetan people at the very moment they are occurring."

After a moment's consideration Li Peng said, "You can count on me, General. I'm at your command and no one else's."

"That's what I wanted to hear."

Zheng began to list his commands.

MAJOR LI PENG WAS a ruthless man, a man Zheng knew should have been entrusted with more responsibility months ago. But part of the general's strategy was to keep his chosen recruits at arm's length until their official tour with the army was ended, then bring them firmly into his confidence or have them killed to prevent them spreading what he had already revealed to them.

But now the clock was ticking so much faster.

Li Peng reached the Tenzing compound again in late afternoon and was immediately approached by one of the four majors involved in the team investigating the strange attack of the night before.

"You should have informed us that you would not be on-site this morning!" he blustered. "We have been stalled waiting for you."

"I had more-important matters to take care of."

"More important?" the major asked. "Major, we are

finding some very disturbing information in this investigation, information that may very well bring General Zheng to court-martial proceedings. And unless we get better cooperation from you, I think you will be going down with the general.''

"I don't think so," Peng said. "I have just been to see the general. He's given me new orders. Once I carry out those orders, I feel you will have a better understanding of the situation, and this investigation will cease."

"Oh, really?" The major sounded amused.

"Come with me, please."

Peng strode to the infirmary bed of the comatose Jian.

"Well?" the major asked.

Peng pulled the side arm from his hip holster and aimed it at the major's chest.

"What are you doing? Are you insane?"

"Take out your gun, Major," Peng ordered.

"What?"

"Take it out now!"

The major slowly, carefully unsnapped his handgun and began to pull it gingerly from its holster with two fingers. As he held it in front of him like a dead fish, Peng snatched it and at the same time shot the major through the heart. He pressed the major's handgun against the mass of bandages over Jian's chest and fired twice. He strode out of the room.

"What happened?" It was one of the medics, looking alarmed.

"Too late, Doctor," Peng said. "They killed each other."

Leaving the medic to clean up the mess, he walked out from the hospital across the compound to the offices of the general, where the previous night's infiltration had occurred. He found two of the guards he was looking for and ordered them to accompany him.

They took the first set of stairs, and Li Peng halted abruptly at the landing.

"The time has come," Peng said simply. "If you are having any second thoughts, you had better come out with them now. We have a dirty job ahead of us."

The two soldiers looked at each other and nodded. "We're in," one of them said.

"Good."

Peng outlined quickly what they needed to do.

They flipped off the safeties on their AK-47s and marched up the next flight of stairs. In the hall they ignored the black stains from the previous night's smoke grenades and strode without hesitation into the interview rooms set up by the investigative team. The team had been listening to different versions of the infiltration from different members of the Tenzing staff and its members were currently comparing notes.

Peng stood between the two guards, who aimed their autorifles at the three majors. The officers appeared dumbfounded, and one of them started to speak.

"Shut up," Peng said. "Fire."

The guards opened fire, and four seconds later the din stopped.

"The investigation is over," Peng stated.

"JUST ABOUT READY," Bolan announced.

They were standing at the top of another icy peak. It had taken them four hours to scale it, moving slowly with the load of weaponry Bolan had insisted they bring. Now they were standing on a precarious summit that disappeared in front of them into a free fall of three hundred feet. Bolan was preparing to climb down the edge.

He pulled on his headset and adjusted the tiny mike briefly. "Testing."

Sonam was wearing a set himself. "Roger that."

Bolan walked backward over the edge of the cliff, boots slipping a little on the ice, then reached the rock wall that continued more or less straight down. He rappeled down the mountainside for about a hundred feet before reaching the camouflage.

To camouflage the compound, General Zheng had constructed a massive aluminum frame that was mounted into the walls of the cliffs that nearly surrounded the secret site. The frame was covered with lightweight white translucent nylon. The material allowed the sun to shine through and illuminate the compound during the day. But from above, from any sort of aircraft, it would appear to be just another expanse of ice and snow among the cliffs, which was what it was before Zheng moved in.

"I'm at the framework," Bolan said.

"Roger," Sonam answered.

He and Sonam had spotted the framework when they reached the top of the peak, and Bolan had immediately planned for its destruction. He tested the strength of the frame, finding it more than strong enough to support him, and began to crawl along it.

A quick evaluation showed that there were actually two separate frames mounted on each side of the cliff. Three aluminum arms protruded to make up each frame, with more than sufficient strength to support the lightweight nylon, which had the same thin, tough feel of material used for parachutes. The frame supported the nylon sheets at a thirty-degree angle, probably so that snowfall would slide right off without adding to the weight burden. They were designed to stand up to any storm.

They wouldn't last against the Executioner. He extracted a lump of plastique and worked it in his hands, forming it around the base of one of the frame pieces and rigging it with a detonator, which he left off for the time being.

Crawling along the eight-inch-wide aluminum base girder, he reached the second and then the third of the frame protrusions, rigging each with a tiny, radio-controlled detonator. He activated the last one, then activated the second and first detonators as he made his way back to his descending path.

"Sonam."

"I'm here."

"The detonators are live. Be ready to blow them."

"I'll be waiting for your signal."

"I'm about to start putting some eyes out."

As soon as Bolan crawled around the edge of the camouflage frame, he was exposed to the compound below, but as the day grew long the sun grew dim. Dusk came prematurely to Zheng's base of operations under its artificial sky. The warrior knew that in his blacksuit, against the dark rock, still almost two hundred feet above the ground, chances of his being spotted were small.

Now he made his way sideways along the wall, using only his hands and feet to keep him from falling. The metallic clang that came from pounding in steel stakes would easily have been heard below.

But he couldn't be underneath the frame when it blew.

He decided his position was good. He readied the M-16 A-1/M-203 unit. An incendiary was already in the breech, and he had several more.

The compound below was composed primarily of wooden buildings, as best he could tell in the encroaching dusk. He had a feeling they would all burn well.

"I'm in position," he said to his companion over the radio.

"I'm ready when you are."

Bolan grimaced. All hell was about to break loose for General Zheng. "Go."

There were triple flashes and cracks from the frame, and the huge tubes of aluminum tumbled from the wall along with massive amounts of rock.

Bolan ignored it, targeting the main buildings. The far end of the long building, at the opening in the rock enclosure, was probably just out of the 375-yard range of the M-203 grenade launcher, but he was willing to give it a try. He fired high for a little extra distance and watched the deadly canister tumble against the building roof at its end and erupt.

The face and roof of the building were instantly blanketed in fire, and Bolan heard screams from within as the phosphorus bits incinerated their way through the wood like hot coals burning through tissue paper and finding victims inside. Then he began sending one incendiary after another into the main building until it was composed of five separate and distinct fires that were rapidly chewing their way toward one another. Men raced out of the buildings, some landing in the snow wreathed in steam and smoke.

Next Bolan thumbed in an explosive round and targeted the vehicles. Two troop-transport trucks at the front of the compound were out of his range, but behind them were more transport trucks and five or six jeeps. There was also an M-577 command vehicle staged in front of four personnel carriers as if they were ready to speed into battle. Bolan began a thirty-second campaign of destruction against the vehicle pool, blasting them with explosive rounds. The M-577 took one of the grenades in the side and rocked violently. When the smoke cleared, it was clearly inoperable. Most of the other vehicles fared no better.

Then he noticed a group of soldiers at the front of the compound, but as yet they hadn't spotted him. He needed to get to ground quickly. If he was made on the wall, he was a paper duck in a shooting gallery.

He harnessed the M-16 A-1/M-203 and grabbed his hammer, pounding in a fresh stake, confident the noise would be ignored now, and hooked in his rope.

A shout erupted from below, and he turned to see a figure pointing at him and shouting at the group of mercenaries. He was obviously a man in charge. Was it Zheng?

No time to try to figure it out. The mercenaries started gunning for him on the wall. Bolan dragged on his gloves and made a descent that was less rappeling than plummeting. He hit the ground so hard his knees buckled, but he caught the ground in one hand and pushed himself onto his feet again, losing the gloves and unslinging the assault rifle combo. He spotted two men closing in, and they went for their guns. The warrior triggered the M-16, cutting them down, then made his way left, crashing into the inferno of the burning building. At that end, where the grenade hit, the wood was almost entirely consumed, and Bolan leaped among the remaining flames until he had put the building between himself and the closing group of mercenaries. There was a narrow alley between the back of the building and the cliff wall, and the warrior was surprised to see a steel flight of stairs disappearing directly into the rock. He ran toward it and spotted a flat steel panel inset in the cliff. A single door stood open, and a figure was running up the steel stairs.

"Zheng!" Bolan shouted.

The general turned and looked at him without slowing, and as he reached the top of the stairs, he jumped behind the door while Bolan triggered the M-16. The round bounced against the steel, which swung shut with a clang.

The door was flanked with a pair of machine guns that whirred to life, going through a swift series of startup motions. Bolan didn't know if they were motion-sensing robot machine guns, or if they were being controlled from inside by human beings. He didn't care to find out. He fed an explosive round into the M-203 and sent it into the top of the stairs where it cracked, flinging the machine guns to the sides and leaving them dangling on their posts, bent and broken.

The door was still intact, and Bolan raced up the warped stairs. He had retained a good chunk of the plastique and swiftly wedged it into the tempered-steel door latch, inserting an electronic detonator.

Some of Zheng's Chinese mercenaries appeared through the burning building, and Bolan fell into a crouch and laid a sweep of 5.56 mm rounds at their feet, sending them back into the fire long enough for him to take flight. He slammed down the steel stairs in three leaps and veered to the left, into a wall of billowing smoke. The fumes were noxious, and Bolan fought his way through them trying not to breathe, finding cleaner air beyond it. Then he moved through the burning building toward the center of the compound again, raising his hand to protect his bare face from the searing heat. He stopped behind a wall of ash and flickering flame, and saw the group of mercenaries getting into attack formation for another try at the steel door. They charged through the burning ruin again.

The Executioner was hot on their tail, coming up behind them and keeping himself hidden in the flames and blackened wood. He saw that the mercenaries had found the steel steps deserted and were searching the open ground for him. Some started up the steps while others deployed beneath them.

Bolan grabbed the detonator radio transmitter from his pocket and flipped it on. A tiny red light glowed, and he depressed it.

The steel door blasted white and yellow, transforming the steel stairs to shrapnel that ripped through the mercenaries like so many flying scythes and butcher knives. Bolan chose the horrifying seconds following the explosion to make his entrance.

He stepped out of the wreckage of the burning building, searching for survivors. There was a man nearby who was moaning and grabbing at a mangled foot-long tube that protruded from his abdomen. Bolan administered a mercy round without hesitation.

Far to the left another mercenary was on all fours, dazed but functioning. He rose to his feet and clawed at the holster on his hip, drawing a large revolver. Bolan drilled three rounds into his midriff before he had a chance to use the handgun.

The big American found himself alone and he headed for the steel door. The stairs were gone, but he managed to find handholds in the broken metal and rock to bring him to the disintegrated door. The black maw that stretched into the mountainside looked as if it went clear to the center of the earth.

Bolan withdrew the Beretta 93-R as he crawled to his feet and stepped into Zheng's command center.

He stepped through a vestibule, which was more or less destroyed, and entered a room beyond, where a large bank of computer and communication equipment stood dead and silent. Bolan spotted a piece of equipment in a small alcove among the electronics with an official-looking decal reading, in English, *Tibet High-orbit Aggression Defensive Satellite.*

The device looked intact.

Bolan was about to examine it when he heard sounds from the room beyond. A pair of guards rushed out of the next door, and the warrior dived to the floor, dropping the M-16 combo and firing up at the mercenaries with the 93-R. Holding the big handgun sideways meant that the recoil moved the quick burst of bullets across the mercs. At least one round punched into each, and Bolan fired again twice in quick succession, taking the wounded men down to the ground.

Another figure stepped out of the darkness of the last doorway, holding a Heckler & Koch MP-5 SD-3 sub-machine gun on Bolan. The warrior rose to his feet, holding the 93-R on the man.

''You've caused me more trouble than I ever knew

possible. Who are you?" the figure with the SMG demanded.

"It doesn't matter, Zheng. I'm here to take you down."

The general laughed. "You think you can shoot me before I cut you in two with this toy?"

"Yeah," Bolan said. He triggered the 93-R and heard the suppressed fire of the MP-5 SD-3. He expected to feel the numbing impact of a series of 9 mm rounds from the SMG, but he felt nothing. The weapon was still firing as Zheng's legs bowed and he collapsed on to his back.

Bolan saw a smoking hole in the tile floor a centimeter from his foot. The general hadn't missed by much.

He walked to the fallen body and saw that the general's eyes were still open, glazed in death.

The world was free of another potential despot, but there were plenty more where he came from.

The warrior walked to the rear room of the compound, where he discovered a telecommunications center. He found a functioning telephone inside and was in touch with Stony Man Farm in minutes. It was time for an extraction. Time to head home.

Don't miss out on the action in these titles!

Deathlands

#62527	GROUND ZERO	$4.99 U.S.	☐
		$5.50 CAN.	☐
#62530	CROSSWAYS	$4.99 U.S.	☐
		$5.50 CAN.	☐
#62533	ECLIPSE AT NOON	$5.50 U.S.	☐
		$6.50 CAN.	☐
#62534	STONEFACE	$5.50 U.S.	☐
		$6.50 CAN.	☐

The Destroyer

#63210	HIGH PRIESTESS	$4.99	☐
#63218	ENGINES OF DESTRUCTION	$5.50 U.S.	☐
		$6.50 CAN.	☐
#63219	ANGRY WHITE MAILMEN	$5.50 U.S.	☐
		$6.50 CAN.	☐
#63220	SCORCHED EARTH	$5.50 U.S.	☐
		$6.50 CAN.	☐

(limited quantities available on certain titles)

TOTAL AMOUNT	$	
POSTAGE & HANDLING	$	
($1.00 for one book, 50¢ for each additional)		
APPLICABLE TAXES*	$ _____	
TOTAL PAYABLE	$ _____	
(check or money order—please do not send cash)		

To order, complete this form and send it, along with a check or money order for the total above, payable to Gold Eagle Books, to: **In the U.S.:** 3010 Walden Avenue, P.O. Box 9077, Buffalo, NY 14269-9077; **In Canada:** P.O. Box 636, Fort Erie, Ontario, L2A 5X3.

Name:_____

Address:_____ City:_____

State/Prov.:_____ Zip/Postal Code: _____

*New York residents remit applicable sales taxes.
 Canadian residents remit applicable GST and provincial taxes.

Don't miss out on the action in these titles featuring
THE EXECUTIONER®, STONY MAN™ and SUPERBOLAN®!

The Red Dragon Trilogy

#64210	FIRE LASH	$3.75 U.S.	☐
		$4.25 CAN.	☐
#64211	STEEL CLAWS	$3.75 U.S.	☐
		$4.25 CAN.	☐
#64212	RIDE THE BEAST	$3.75 U.S.	☐
		$4.25 CAN.	☐

Stony Man™

#61907	THE PERISHING GAME	$5.50 U.S.	☐
		$6.50 CAN.	☐
#61908	BIRD OF PREY	$5.50 U.S.	☐
		$6.50 CAN.	☐
#61909	SKYLANCE	$5.50 U.S.	☐
		$6.50 CAN.	☐

SuperBolan®

#61448	DEAD CENTER	$5.50 U.S.	☐
		$6.50 CAN.	☐
#61449	TOOTH AND CLAW	$5.50 U.S.	☐
		$6.50 CAN.	☐
#61450	RED HEAT	$5.50 U.S.	☐
		$6.50 CAN.	☐

(limited quantities available on certain titles)

TOTAL AMOUNT	$
POSTAGE & HANDLING	$
($1.00 for one book, 50¢ for each additional)	
APPLICABLE TAXES*	$ _____
TOTAL PAYABLE	$ _____
(check or money order—please do not send cash)	

To order, complete this form and send it, along with a check or money order for the total above, payable to Gold Eagle Books, to: **In the U.S.:** 3010 Walden Avenue, P.O. Box 9077, Buffalo, NY 14269-9077; **In Canada:** P.O. Box 636, Fort Erie, Ontario, L2A 5X3.

Name:_____

Address:_____ City:_____

State/Prov.:_____ Zip/Postal Code:_____

*New York residents remit applicable sales taxes.
 Canadian residents remit applicable GST and provincial taxes.

GEBACK17

It's a jungle out there—and the Destroyer may
become the next endangered species

THE Destroyer

#108 Bamboo Dragon

Created by
WARREN MURPHY
and RICHARD SAPIR

Deep in the Malaysian jungle a group of scientists gets a
lethal surprise, and a lone survivor rants about a prehistoric
monster who eats men alive. The survivor dies with bizarre
symptoms—and CURE's Dr. Harold Smith wants answers.

Look for it in July wherever Gold Eagle books are sold.

From the creator of Deathlands comes...

OUTLANDERS™

An all-new series by James Axler!

Enter the future—a postholocaust world where the struggle between the classes takes on a whole new reality...where the misery of the final conflagration gives way to a promise of a new beginning...and where the inhabitants of the entire planet find themselves facing a new, all-powerful and alien enemy....

Available this June
wherever Gold Eagle books are sold.

OUT-G